I0831867

Yerrin

A Book of Underrealm

Garrett Robinson

YERRIN

Garrett Robinson

The author greatly appreciates you taking the time to read his work. Please leave a review wherever you bought the book or on Goodreads.com.

Interior Design: Legacy Books, Inc.
Publisher: Legacy Books, Inc.
Editors: Karen Conlin, Cassie Dean
Cover Artist: Sarayu Ruangvesh

1. Fantasy - Epic 2. Fantasy - Dark 3. Fantasy - New Adult

First Edition

Published by Legacy Books

To my wife
Who gave me this idea

To my children
Who just make life better

To my parents
Who are the only reason I'm able to do anything at all

To Johnny, Sean, and Dave
Who told me to write

And to my Rebels
Don't forget why you left the woods

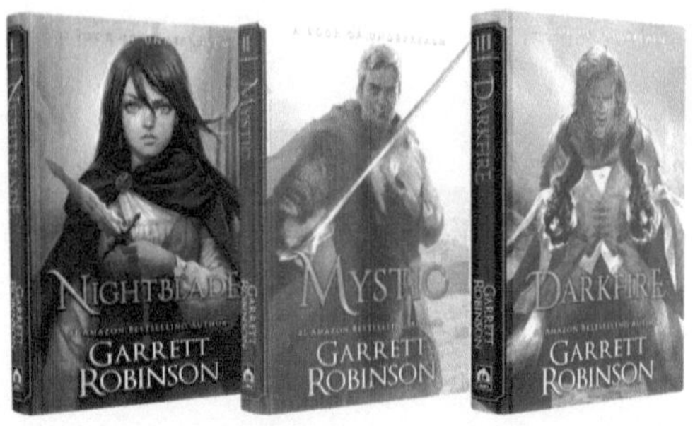

GET MORE

Legacy Books is home to the very best that fantasy has to offer.

Join our email alerts list, and we'll send word whenever we release a new book. You'll receive exclusive updates and see behind the scenes as we create them.

(You'll also learn the secrets that make great fantasy books, *great.*)

Interested? Visit this link:

Underrealm.net/Join

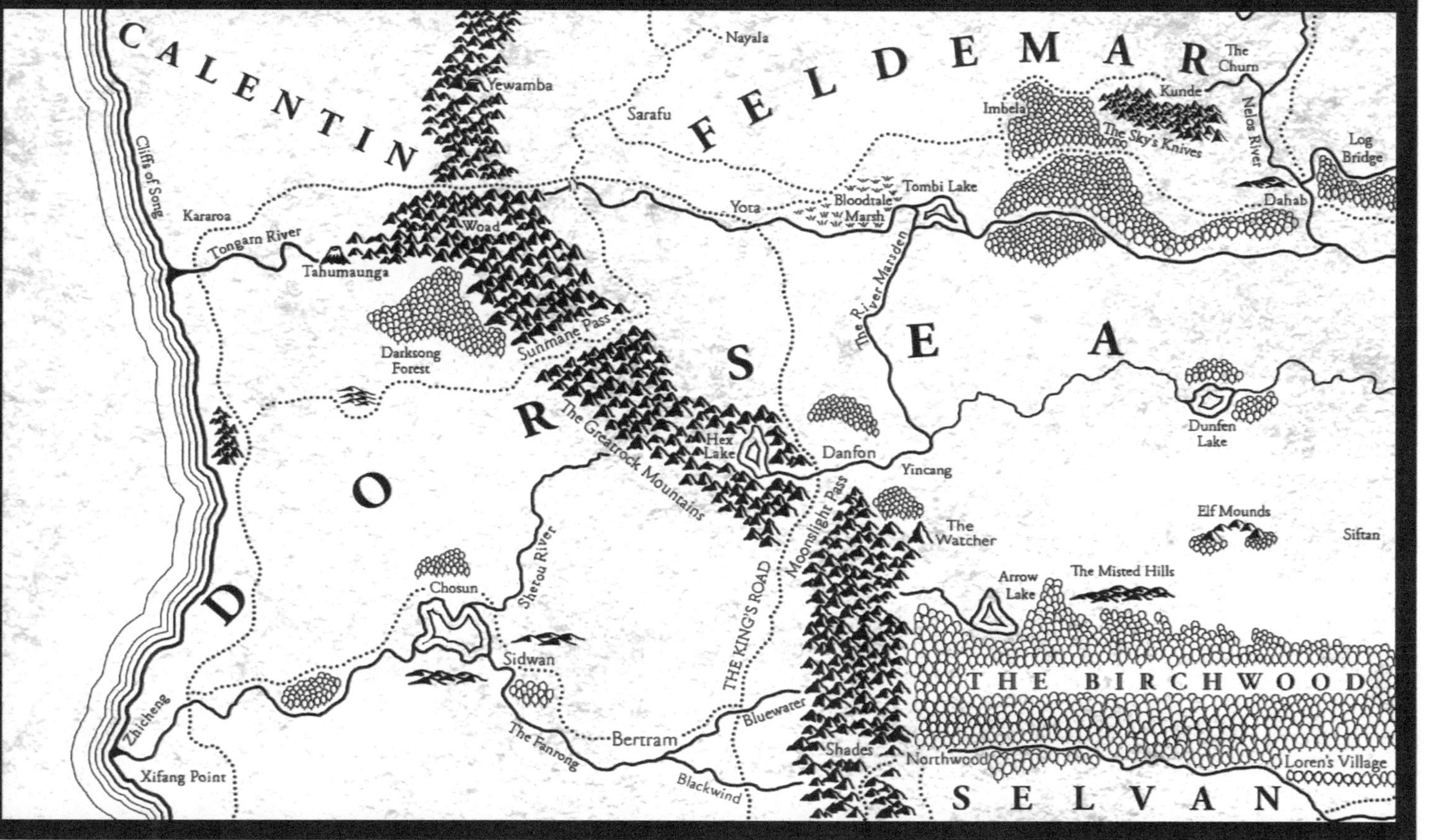
CALENTIN
FELDEMAR
DORSEA
SELVAN
THE BIRCHWOOD
Nayala
Yewamba
Sarafu
The Churn
Kunde
Imbela
The Sky's Knives
Nelos River
Log Bridge
Dahab
Cliffs of Song
Kararoa
Tongarn River
Tahumaunga
Woad
Yota
Bloodtale Marsh
Tombi Lake
Darksong Forest
Sunmane Pass
The River Marsden
The Greatrock Mountains
Hex Lake
Danfon
Yincang
Dunfen Lake
Elf Mounds
Siftan
The Watcher
Moonslight Pass
THE KING'S ROAD
Shetou River
Chosun
Sidwan
Arrow Lake
The Misted Hills
Zhicheng
Xifang Point
The Fanrong
Bertram
Bluewater
Blackwind
Shades
Northwood
Loren's Village

Yerrin

A BOOK OF UNDERREALM

Garrett Robinson

ONE

WINTER HAD ALWAYS HAD A WAY OF BEING ESPECIALLY cruel to Loren, and so she hid now with her friends from its bitter snows. Which was not to say that they had entirely avoided the rough weather; for weeks, they had pursued the merchant Damaris back and forth across the northwestern reaches of the kingdom. Through snows and storms they followed her, from tiny villages to modest cities, through woods and over fields and across rivers. Always Damaris had remained just ahead of them, taunting them, ever out of reach.

Now they had a room at an inn in the town of

Sidwan, far south of Feldemar and west of the Greatrock Mountains. They had arrived only the night before. Some might have called the dwelling modest, but Loren thought that would be far too generous. She guessed the inn's master rarely had his floors scrubbed or bedding changed, for everything reeked. Two threadbare pallets of straw lay on the floor, but Loren could almost see the fleas crawling across them. They ate rarely of the inn's food, which caused their bellies to roil and complain, but instead ate from the rations they had kept in good supply during their travels. Of all the inn's offerings, only the ale was passably good, and so of that they drank freely.

Loren's little council was even smaller than normal, for Uzo and Shiun were away at the moment. Chet sat on one of the pallets, idly rubbing his arms and staring at nothing. His oft-washed skin was red and raw, but mayhap not so bad as it had been last week. Loren hoped that was a good sign. Gem had gone to fetch himself a snack—the boy's stomach seemed to be made of iron, and he was the only one who did not turn up his nose at the common room's meager fare.

Annis, as was her custom these days, sat on the floor with a map of the nine kingdoms. With her forefinger she traced lines between towns and cities, her eyes darting back and forth, her lips slightly parted but never moving. Every so often she would wince and shake her head, then return to tracing routes that were clear only in her own mind. Loren worried about her. Annis' determination to find Damaris had neared obsession. The merchant was her mother, and that made her feel a greater burden than all the rest of them.

Other than Chet, of course.

Loren sighed, kicking her boots against the floor and toying idly with the knives at her belt. The blades were new, purchased at the first blacksmith they had found after entering the kingdom of Dorsea. They were neither so fine as the dagger on the back of her belt, nor as modest as the hunting knife in her boot. The smith had balanced them perfectly for throwing. Half of her wished to go out behind the inn and practice, but she feared to be away if Uzo and Shiun returned with news.

She thought of the one who had taught her to throw knives in the first place. Her fingers recoiled as though the blades had burned her.

It is a useful skill, she told herself. *It does not matter who taught it to you.*

She looked at Chet and wondered if she truly believed that.

He seemed to feel her gaze upon him, for he looked up at her. He tried to give her a smile, but it came out frail.

"I think I may try to sleep," said Loren.

His smile faltered. "Oh? Have you rested poorly?"

"It has been a long road, and we have ridden hard."

"Yet too much sleep can make one even wearier."

Loren spread her hands. "There is little else to do just now."

Now his smile died at last, and he stared at the floor. "Those are pretty words, but not true ones. We both know why you want to sleep. Yet that is not how the dreams work, or so you have said."

"I suppose not," said Loren. "But we know I cannot have one if I am awake."

He subsided, turning away from her. Loren's pulse had quickened, and she forced herself to take a deep breath. It was not Chet's fault that her sleep had been dreamless, but she was frustrated, and it made her irritable. A small part of her feared what the dreams might mean and where they might be leading her. But the greater part of her wanted any clue, any hint about where Damaris might be. If that knowledge came to her in a dream, she thought she could accept whatever harm her visions might bring.

She sighed and pushed herself up from the floor, going over to sit beside Chet—but not too close, not where she might accidentally brush against him.

"I want a clue that will lead us to the end of this road," said Loren. "I want to bring Damaris to justice."

Chet shook his head slowly. "I suppose I do as well. But will that truly be the end?"

Loren gritted her teeth. Damaris' capture would not entirely end the war, and they both knew it. "It will be a good first step. And the dreams will help.

When they come, we will use whatever I see to find her. I swear it."

Chet drew a breath as though he was about to speak—but then the door flew open. Loren shot upright, hand going to one of her knives. But it was only Gem, stumbling in with a tray of food and ale. He kicked the door behind him, and it closed with a loud *thud.* Annis' head jerked up, but the moment she saw Gem she flushed and turned away.

Loren scowled. "Sky above, Gem. Are you trying to wake the whole inn?"

"Wake them?" said Gem, eyes wide and innocent. "It is scarcely sundown. If anyone is abed already, let them rise so that they may know how lazy I think them."

"This from the boy who has spent more time asleep than all the rest of us combined," said Chet. He chuckled and shook his head. It warmed Loren's heart to see. Whatever chill had settled between him and Loren, he had lost none of his affection or good cheer towards the children, nor even towards Uzo and Shiun.

"But that is another matter entirely," said Gem, lifting his chin. "I am unquestionably the handsomest of our party, and retaining such beauty requires more rest. That is not laziness, but only due consideration for the beautification of your lives."

"What noble sacrifice. What a selfless gift," said Loren, clutching her hands over her heart. Then she snatched the tray with one hand and shoved him gently with the other. "Now if you truly wish to make all our lives better, still your flapping lips for a little while and let us drink in peace."

Gem rubbed his chest where she had pushed him, but his smile remained. "I suppose I can do that," he said. "After all, my lips have flapped enough for one day—in the common room, where one or two of my tales were most welcome."

Loren's heart skipped. "What tales? Gem, what have you—"

He waved a hand airily. "I did not tell them who we are, or where we are bound, or why. But I heard some patrons in the common room discussing our black-cloaked friend. I gave them a few nods and winks at the right times, and told them some small stories that I had heard and they had not."

"Stories you heard?" said Loren, arching an eyebrow. "It is more accurate to say that you lived them."

Gem spread his hands. "They are different words, but they mean much the same thing."

Loren sighed. Gem had been spreading tales everywhere—not only since they entered Feldemar, but a long time before that, ever since the two of them had escaped from the city of Cabrus. She had long ago given up trying to stop him.

Gem snatched two mugs of ale from the tray and went across the room to Annis. He stopped more than a pace away, looking at her fitfully. One foot scraped at the back of his other ankle to scratch an itch. He wore thick and warm shoes, recently bought—a necessity against the snow outside, but clearly something he was unused to.

Gradually Annis became aware of the room's quiet. At last she looked up to see Gem. Her cheeks darkened, and she quickly looked back down at the map.

"I . . . er, would you like to have a drink?" said Gem, proffering one of the mugs.

"Oh, ah. No. Thank you. Or, wait, I suppose so." Annis' hand jerked back and forth a few times, as though her mind kept changing even in the act of reaching for the mug. At last she gripped the handle and pulled it towards her—but the movement was jerky, and a bit of ale spilled over to splash on a corner of the map.

"Blast!" said Gem. He knelt and tried to scrub at the stain. "I am sorry."

"No, it was my fault," said Annis.

She took a corner of her sleeve and reached to wipe away the ale. But as her hand brushed Gem's, they both yelped. Gem leaped up as though stung and scuttled away. Then he realized he had forgotten his own mug on the floor beside her, and he darted back to get it. He retreated to the farthest pallet and sank into it, studiously inspecting his drink.

Loren winced at the exchange. Things had grown more and more awkward since Annis' disastrous confession of love in Feldemar. Gem clearly felt awful for rebuffing her, and Annis seemed determined to forget the whole thing had ever happened. But it hung between them always, and what had once been a bosom friendship was now an ever-strained and painful interaction.

It did no good to dwell on such thoughts. Loren went over to Annis and sat across from her, ignoring the girl's flushed cheeks. She studied the map, but it meant very little to her. Loren could recognize the drawings—the mountains and rivers, the lakes and oceans—but she had never learned to read, and so the names of places were a mystery. But Annis looked at the map as though it were an elaborate tapestry, with every detail plain before her and no mystery hidden. Or at least, none but the greatest mystery of all—the one that kept her hovering over the map day and night, trying to unravel the secret.

"How goes your search?" said Loren. "Have you any idea why Damaris might have come here?"

"If I had, I would have said something," grumbled Annis. She sighed and rubbed her eyes with the heels of her hands. "I am sorry. I grow ever more frustrated the longer this goes on. My mo—Damaris' course through Dorsea makes no sense. First she goes in one direction, and then another. It seems clear she is trying to throw us off her trail. But even if that is the case, I feel I should be able to guess her ultimate aim. Yet the only thing I can see is that she always goes farther south, and there is no place in the south of Dorsea that makes sense as her final destination."

"What if it is a ruse, then?" said Chet. "What if her ultimate aim lies farther north, and she plans to double back?"

Annis pursed her lips. "I have considered it, of course. But there is nothing significant west of the Greatrocks, and I do not think she would go east of them. There lies Dorsea's capital, Danfon. There is no greater concentration of officers of the High King's law in the kingdom. She would put herself at far too great a risk. That, I believe, is why she has restricted herself to smaller towns—like this one."

"I think even the word 'small' overstates the case," said Gem. "'Tiny' might be more accurate. I have seen no horses in Sidwan besides our own."

Loren sighed and shook her head. "I am less worried about where Damaris is going and more worried about what she means to do."

"Are we so sure she means to do anything?" said Chet. "I thought her goal was to take Yewamba, but we chased her from there. She may simply be trying to escape."

"Never," said Annis. "Oh, I am certain she wants to evade us. But there is something else at work here. There always is. She has not given up on . . . well, on whatever goal drove her to Yewamba in the first place."

"But what goal?" said Loren. "Something to do with the war, no doubt."

"Yes, but that is far too general," said Annis. "She will never be an ally of the High King—not after what she has done—but she may not be on the side of the Necromancer any longer, either. She seems aimless, but that is only because we do not know what larger game she is playing."

"Could she be making her way towards one of your family's holdings in Dorsea?" said Loren.

"She could—except that those are few and far between, and none are very grand." said Annis. "I think that may be why she wanted Yewamba. She could have given it to the Necromancer as a great stronghold in the war. Or she might have meant to lurk there in safety while the war raged on without her. Without knowing the machinations of all our enemies, it becomes harder to predict what any one of them is doing."

"I, for one, doubt she still stands by the Necromancer," said Chet. "The High King has declared war at last, and eight kingdoms stand behind her. Not even a great fool would join the wrong side of that fight, and your mother is not a great fool."

The room went silent, and Loren shot Chet a look. Annis dropped her gaze to the floor, and Chet's cheeks flushed. They had taken to avoiding the fact that Damaris was Annis' mother. It was not a comfortable truth for the girl to hear, and even less so now that their mission was to bring her before the King's law—a law that was always swift and always fair, but not always merciful.

"In any case," said Loren, "all our wonderment

might be for nothing. If she is indeed here in Sidwan, and we can bring her to heel, then her ultimate aim becomes of far less consequence."

As if in answer to her words, they heard footsteps in the hallway outside. The footsteps stopped outside their door, which opened to reveal Uzo. The dark young spearman wore plain clothes for travel, and had changed his red Mystic cloak for one of brown. Snow dusted his shoulders, already melting into little droplets at his feet.

"It is time," he said. "Shiun has found her."

They were on their feet in an instant. Chet snatched up his quarterstaff from where it leaned by the door, and Gem began to buckle on his little sword.

Almost too little, now, thought Loren. The boy was growing by leaps and bounds. She had already noted that he needed new clothes, and now it seemed he should have a new blade as well.

Loren turned to Annis. "Wait here for us. We will return soon."

"Be sure that you do," said Annis. "Sky above, I hope we have found her this time."

"We have never been so close," said Loren. "If the worst should happen, and she evades us again, we shall catch her in the next town."

Annis dropped her gaze to the floor. "Her escape would not be the worst that could happen. At least not to my mind."

Loren gave a little smile and stepped forwards to

wrap the girl in a quick hug. "We will be safe. See that you are the same."

She turned, cloak whirling about her, and followed Uzo from the inn.

TWO

SIDWAN WAS A TINY CLUSTER OF INNS AND CRAFTSHOPS that might not have existed at all, except that a bend in the nearby road met a bend in the nearby river, and the fertile land all around was perfect for farming. Farmers thus formed the largest portion of the town's populace, and of the patrons of its taverns and shops. Travelers would stop in the town for a drink or to repair a shoe or harness, and in the evenings the locals would gather around to hear news of the wider world. Loren and her friends had worked hard to dissuade such interest. The less notice anyone took of them, the better.

Near the center of the town was its largest inn: a stone building, and one of the few that had a second floor. That was where Shiun and Uzo had gone to search for Damaris. But Uzo turned away, leading them down a smaller side street towards the edge of town.

"She was not at the inn?" said Loren.

"No, though we wasted a fair amount of time searching there. It was only by chance that we saw two dark men passing through the town. They did not wear green cloaks, but they looked and moved like trained fighters. Mayhap they had been sent to fetch supplies for the next stretch of the journey. In any case, Shiun followed them to one of the finer houses on the edge of town. There we saw many more guards and some horses in the stables, and soon we spotted Damaris in one of the windows."

"It *is* her, then," said Loren. A thrill of excitement ran through her. Their long hunt that had now stretched across two kingdoms might finally be over.

But not yet. First they had to capture Damaris, and that would be no easy feat. The merchant traveled with several guards—hardly an army, but more than the paltry five of Loren's party. And there was always the threat that Gregor had rejoined her.

Gregor. The bodyguard had not been in the stronghold of Yewamba. But if he had heard what happened there, Loren knew he would cross the sky and the darkness to be by Damaris' side again. His devotion to her dwarfed even his massive size. He was a terrifying fighter, and Loren feared to face him even with all her friends at her back. If Gregor was here, Loren knew they might not all survive—if any of them did.

Uzo stopped them behind a cobbler's shop, and he and Loren peered around the corner. Before them was a home that would have been modest in any of Underrealm's great cities, but it looked like an opulent jewel here in Sidwan. Loren smirked to herself. Even when on the run, it seemed Damaris could not help her taste for finery. Two guards stood at the front door, and though they did not wear the family Yerrin's colors, they had the right look.

"We saw her upstairs."

Loren jumped. Shiun's voice had come from nowhere, and now she crept up behind them. The woman was a scout beyond peer, and Loren still marveled at her ability to move silently, to see even the smallest sign of her quarry's trail in the wilderness. Chet had grown up a hunter, and he had taught Loren the ways of tracking a beast in the woods, but Shiun's knowledge eclipsed even his.

Gem's face had paled. "You move more quietly than an Elf."

"I doubt it, though I have not seen one," said Shiun.

"Are you certain it was Damaris?" said Loren.

"No," said Shiun. "I have never seen her, either. But she was a Yerrin woman in fine garb, and the others certainly seemed to obey her commands."

"Very well," said Loren. "We should take the house, and quickly."

"One thing more," said Shiun. "There is a man I have not seen before. He is large, and he wears more armor than the other guards."

Loren shuddered. "Gregor."

Shiun's mouth twisted. "I thought it might be, from the description you gave."

"He is only a man," said Uzo. "Even a giant may be taken by surprise."

"You do not know him," said Loren. "We must be cautious. He is twice as vicious as he is large, and he will defend Damaris with his dying breath."

"Then I will make him take that breath." Uzo's hand tightened on the haft of his spear.

Loren's jaw clenched. "Kill only if you have no other choice. The more of them we capture, the more information we can gather about the High King's enemies."

Uzo rolled his eyes, but Shiun nodded and spoke for them both. "As you say, Nightblade."

There was a long pause. After a moment, Shiun and Uzo glanced at each other, their brows raised. At last Uzo cleared his throat. "It might be best to secure the bottom floor first. That way we can watch to make sure she does not slip away."

Of course. Loren was supposed to come up with the plan of attack and tell the rest of them what to do. In Feldemar, Niya had given orders when it came to fighting, and Loren was still unused to it. Her cheeks flamed, and she hoped they attributed it to the cold air.

"That seems wise," she said. "Do not climb to the second floor until the first is in our hands. And Gem—you must run into town and summon the constables."

"What?" said Gem. "But there are only two of them, and they hardly seemed to be trained fighters. They will be of little help."

She fixed him with a hard look. "They represent the King's law, and we will need them to restore order once the fighting is done." She extended a hand to Uzo. He gave her his Mystic badge, and Loren placed it in Gem's hand. "Give them this so that they know you are not some urchin boy."

He folded his arms and pouted at his feet. "I *am* an urchin boy," he muttered. But he turned and left them, slipping through the buildings back towards the town's center.

Loren motioned the others off, and they spread out to attack the building from both sides. Loren approached the left corner of the manor with Chet close behind her. She drew one of the throwing daggers from her belt.

One of the guards was only a pace away. Loren leaped from her hiding place and brought the hilt of her dagger crashing down hard on the back of the woman's head. The guard fell senseless to the ground. The other guard whirled, scrabbling for his sword. Before he could muster the wits to shout, Uzo pounced from behind. His arm wrapped around the guard's throat, and he squeezed. The man's eyes rolled back, and Uzo lowered him to the ground.

"Two taken care of, and easily," said Chet.

"Do not gloat until it is done," said Loren. "Fate despises the boastful."

"The back door," said Shiun. "Less chance of a heavy guard."

Loren nodded. "Uzo, stay here to prevent escape through the front."

The rest of them moved single file around the building. No guards were posted at the rear. Peeking in through a window, Loren saw a small sitting room with a fireplace. Two guards sat on chairs there, holding their hands out towards the flames.

She looked back at Shiun and Chet and held up two fingers. They nodded. Loren gripped the door's latch and looked at the crack of the doorjamb. There was no lock or bar. She lifted the latch and threw the door open.

Both guards shot up from their chairs with a cry. One was a spindly woman, the other a stout man. Chet struck first, his quarterstaff cracking down on the spindly one's shoulder. She grunted with the pain, but she managed to draw her sword before he swung again.

The stout man launched himself at Loren. She sidestepped his first swing, but it was no wild attack. These were disciplined soldiers. His reverse swing almost caught her arm, and she had to drop to her knee to avoid it.

Shiun leaped in to the fray, landing two quick punches at the man's throat. He fell back, gasping. Loren took advantage, shooting up to kick him hard in the groin. He wheezed and fell. She kicked him full in the face, and he rolled over, unconscious. The two of them leaped in to help Chet, whose opponent was forcing him back with wild swings. In a moment Shiun had disarmed her, and soon she went down to a punishing strike of Chet's quarterstaff.

They heard a commotion from the front of the house. Two guards burst into the back room, swords already drawn. They paused in shock for half a moment.

Shunk

The tip of a spear burst through one of the guards' chests. She looked down at the spearhead, eyes wide. The other guard only had a moment to be surprised before Shiun leaped forwards and planted her short sword in his gut. Both of them sank to the ground, their last breaths gurgling. Behind them stood Uzo, a grim smile on his lips as he gripped his spear.

Loren glared at him. "That was not necessary."

Uzo shrugged. "You said we needed to be fast."

Shiun said nothing, wiping her sword clean on one of the guards' cloaks. Loren shook her head and made for the stairs.

The staircase was short and open at the top, so she

crept up carefully. There was little chance that anyone upstairs had missed the noise of all the fighting, but no one had come down. She hoped that meant there were no more warriors above. Mayhap Gregor was not here after all, but that seemed too fortunate to hope for.

She reached the top of the stairs. A large foyer stretched before her, and at the other end of it was a guard. There were no lamps lit here, and the windows cast him in a large silhouette.

Loren's steps faltered, and her throat went dry with fear. But it lasted only a moment, and then her eyes adjusted to the darkness. The man before her was large, truly, and he carried a sword and shield. But it was not Gregor. He did not have the ice-grey eyes, and a thick beard covered his face. Though he still stood taller than any of Loren's party, he was nowhere near the size of Gregor.

Relief washed through her just as suddenly as the fear had. It seemed the bodyguard had not yet found Damaris.

"Leave now," said the man, "and you may live."

Loren could not help herself. She snorted. "I have heard the same promise from foes far more dangerous. I have never taken them up on their offer, yet here I stand."

He growled and stepped forwards. But there was a *hiss,* and an arrow planted itself in his thigh. He roared and fell to one knee. Glancing back, Loren saw that Shiun had taken her bow from her back and was already drawing another arrow.

Chet stepped forth. When the man tried to swing his longsword, Chet blocked it with his staff. Another strike knocked the blade from his hand, and then he cracked the butt of his staff right between the man's eyes. His head snapped back, and he fell.

Uzo snickered. "'Leave now and you may live.' Honestly."

Loren allowed herself to share a smile with him. She motioned them all forwards. "Come. It is almost over."

The final door opened easily under her hand. Loren stepped through it into the master bedroom. And there she stopped.

A woman stood before her. But it was not Damaris. She wore clothes just as fine as the merchant, and there was something similar in the haughty tilt of her head. Mayhap she was another Yerrin. But Loren had never seen her before.

Loren growled in frustration. "A ruse. Darkness take that woman. She knew we would follow her here, and she set a false trail to lead us to this impostor." She shook her head and gestured at the woman. "Capture her. She may still have information that can help."

But the woman did not recoil in fear. Instead she smiled.

And then her eyes glowed black.

"Stop."

Everyone in the room froze. Loren frowned, her eyes flicking to her friends. They stood rooted in place as though held by some unseen force. Uzo was even in mid-stride, but there he remained.

The woman spoke again. "Kill each other, but leave the Nightblade alive."

Slowly, Chet, Uzo, and Shiun turned towards each other, raising their weapons.

Loren's blood ran cold. The woman was a wizard, and she had eaten magestones—the black glow in her eyes said that much. But this was some magic Loren had never seen before, and her mentor, Jordel, had never told her of it.

But her dagger kept her safe. This wizard could not know of the weapon—an ancient tool of the Mystic mage hunters, and proof against all spells. It had saved her life from a mad wizard before, and it kept her from enchantment now.

She drew the dagger and leaped forwards. The Yerrin woman barely had an instant to look surprised before Loren brought the hilt crashing down on her temple. Her eyes rolled back, and she folded like parchment.

Loren whirled. Shiun had eschewed her bow in such close quarters and was attacking Uzo with her sword. Uzo managed to keep her at bay while also trying to strike Chet with his spear, but Chet was defending himself well with his staff—at least for now. Their movements were slow, sluggish, as though they fought to throw off the mental commands they had been given.

"Stop!" she cried. "The woman has no power over you."

They acted as if they had not heard. The command had been planted, and they would not stop until they carried it out.

Loren leaped and took Chet in a flying tackle. She winced as his head cracked on the wall. Chet cried out, groping gingerly at the back of his head. Slowly his eyes focused on Loren.

"I . . . what happened?" he said.

"I do not know," said Loren. "But stop the others!"

She leaped up and dashed at Uzo and Shiun. With Chet out of the way, they had turned their full attention on each other. Loren thrust herself in between both of them.

They both froze, weapons held high. The wizard had commanded them to leave the Nightblade alive, and now they could not attack each other without striking her.

Chet gripped Shiun from behind in a tight hold. Her sword arm dangled, useless. But her other hand came up, scrabbling for Chet's eyes. She scratched his face, and he grimaced.

"Chet!" said Loren. She lunged, trying to pull Shiun's hand away.

Uzo took advantage of her distraction to move around her, and slowly his spear came forwards, poking for Shiun's gut. Then, from outside the room, Loren heard the pounding of footsteps making their way up the stairs.

More guards, she thought. Her heart sank. She and

her friends could not fight their way out while two of them were determined to kill each other.

A voice came from outside. "Loren?"

Her pulse skipped. "Gem! In here!"

The boy burst into the bedroom. On his heels were two constables in red leather armor. Both of them huffed and wheezed mightily. It appeared they had run all the way here.

"Uzo and Shiun are enchanted!" she said. "Stop them, but do not hurt them badly!"

With the help of Gem and the constables, she and Chet managed to pry Shiun and Uzo apart. Then Loren remembered how Chet had come out of the enchantment. She went to Uzo and punched him full in the face—not as hard as she could, but hard enough. He recoiled from the blow—and then his eyes cleared. He rubbed at his jaw.

"What . . . did you *hit* me?"

Loren sighed with relief. "I did, and you will have to forgive me."

She went to Shiun, who was still trying to fight off Chet and the other constable. Balling a fist one more time, Loren struck her. Shiun blinked hard as the enchantment passed away.

"You all were gripped by some spell," said Loren. "It came from the wizard. I have never seen anything like it."

"Mindwyrd." Shiun spat on the floor. "A mentalist power, gained by eating magestones. It lets them control the will of others."

Loren shuddered. "I am glad we rid you of it in time."

Uzo gave Loren an odd look. "It did not seem to affect you."

Loren kept her face carefully neutral. Jordel had often warned her against revealing her dagger to anyone. "It must have been a weak enchantment."

"It was," said Shiun. "Else we would not have been freed from it so easily. And her magic must have been weakened further by trying to control more than one person at a time."

Uzo's curious expression lightened, much to Loren's relief, and he shook his head. "Sky save us from wizards. We should have brought a mage hunter."

Loren had nearly forgotten about the constables, but now one of them stepped forwards—a large man with a drooping mustache. As he studied the prone Yerrin woman, confusion made his lips twist and jump, and the mustache shivered like a dying squirrel's tail.

"I beg your pardon, but what exactly happened here?"

"Everyone in this house is a member of the family Yerrin," said Loren. "They are criminals under the King's law, and that one is an abomination." She pointed at the wizard.

Both constables blinked at Loren before giving each other an odd look.

"An abomination?" said Loren. "An eater of magestones?"

They jumped and took an involuntary step away from the woman.

Loren sighed. "She is harmless now. Blindfold her and bind her before she wakes. That will keep her from being able to use her magic. But do it quickly, and do not remove the blindfold for any reason. Do you have a jail here?"

"I . . . yes. Yes, my lady, and we will secure them right away." The large constable motioned to his companion. "Fetch some helping hands from the village, and be quick."

"I leave it in your capable hands," said Loren. She beckoned to her friends, leading them down the stairs.

"Capable hands?" said Gem once they were out of earshot. "I do not know that I share your assessment."

Loren frowned at him as she led them out behind the house. "We will remain here for a moment, at least until all the Yerrins are taken into custody."

Chet shuddered. "That woman . . . her magic was terrifying. It was if my body was not my own."

"Be thankful she was a weak wizard," said Shiun. "Else it would have taken more than a simple knock on the head to remove her spell."

Loren pursed her lips. "You know something of this . . . mindwyrd. Are you a mage hunter, then?"

Shiun shook her head with a wry smile. "No. But in my time in the Mystics, I have met many who are. Some of their secrets are not for others to know, but they loose some of the smaller details from time to time—if you get them drunk enough."

"I am glad to know it," said Loren. "There may be more dark wizards ahead in our future."

"There are too many in our past, if you ask me," muttered Gem.

Loren looked away from the house, over the snow-covered farmlands that ran to a forest in the south. A long breath escaped through her nose, and her hands formed fists before she managed to relax them.

Chet saw the movement, and he frowned. "Damaris was not here."

"No," said Loren. Did he think she did not know that?

"We will find her."

Loren almost snapped at him, but she restrained herself just in time. "I need a moment." She began to walk south.

Chet took a half-step forwards. "Where are you going? You should not be alone."

She glanced back at him. "I will not be long. I need to relieve myself."

He flushed, but his mouth remained a firm line. "Still, someone should go with you."

"I will do it," said Shiun. She slung her bow across her back and went to Loren's side.

They walked a road between two farms, their breath misting on the frosty air. A light fall of snowflakes danced around them, eddying in the wind of their passing. Snow lay in shallow drifts, and the people here waited for spring's warmth to welcome new plantings. That would not be long now. The season's turn was nearly upon them.

Soon they had reached the outskirts of the forest. Loren felt better the moment she stood beneath its boughs. She leaned back against a tree, folding her arms and staring into the far distance. Sidwan was reduced to the size of a candle, the lights of its homes shining in protest against the approaching evening. Loren blew another long sigh, enjoying the way it floated around her like smoke.

The impostor was troubling. How long had they been following a false trail?

Curse the visions from my dreams, she thought.

Her foresight should have come as they rode across Dorsea, giving some clue that they no longer pursued Damaris. Loren could not guess at the purpose of the visions, of course. Mayhap there was no purpose at all. But she needed every bit of help she could get, and if she must wrest that help from dreams and visions, she would. Yet she seemed to have lost even that advantage.

Shiun cleared her throat and turned away. "I will give you some privacy."

"There is no need. I do not actually have to relieve myself."

The Mystic's eyes sparkled. "That was obvious, but I thought I might help you keep up the pretense."

Loren's mood did not lighten. She only frowned harder and scuffed her boot in the snow.

"I thought we had her this time. Now she has slipped away, and who knows if we will find the trail again?"

"We could not have done anything different than we did."

Shiun's tone was less reassuring than her words. She sounded irritated. Loren glared at the ground. No doubt Shiun blamed Loren for losing the merchant. And why should she not? Loren was in charge. Yet this whole expedition seemed to have become a flight from one disaster to another. Jormund had left them some time ago—albeit at Loren's orders—and two other members of their company were dead. Worse, one of them had turned out to be an enemy in disguise. Loren should have known. Should have seen. Even without her visions.

"I will not rest until it is done. Until Damaris is in our hands and the hands of the King's law, and order is restored to the nine kingdoms."

Shiun was silent for a long moment. "That would be a great feat," she said at last.

Loren flushed. She had spoken like a silly girl. When had Underrealm ever been a place of perfect order? Border squabbles raged and bandit squadrons roamed, creating a thousand conflicts great and small, and each led to bloodshed in the end. Yet they faced a far greater threat now—a war that might lay whole kingdoms low. Loren had not started it, but she had taken a solemn vow to help finish it.

But she did not say any of this to Shiun. "I suppose we have wasted enough time for them to think I did my business," she muttered. "Let us return."

She pushed off from the tree and strode north, Shiun at her side.

THREE

THE DREAM TOOK HER.

She stood on the High King's Seat. Both moons hung full in the sky above her. The streets looked familiar, but she could not place them. Then she recognized the main road that crossed the city from east to west. She had passed this way when . . .

Again she looked up at the moons. Yes. It was the night she had followed a wizard's trail across the Seat. She had found a lock of hair and burned it on her dagger. Its magic led her east, but she had found nothing there.

Dejected, she had returned to the palace—but not before visiting a tavern. She whirled. There it was. A warm glow poured from the edges of its door, which was poorly mounted in the frame.

But now a man leaned on the door. He was tall, his shoulders broad. Many knife scars crossed his arms and face, and even his nearly-shaved head. He was clad all in black leathers, making it hard to see most of his body in the darkness. But his eyes were bright even at night. The glow was akin to magelight, yet Loren had never seen anything quite like it.

Before she could ask who he was, he laughed and pointed to her left. Loren caught a flash of movement at the edge of her vision. She turned and saw a woman in a red cloak. Her brown hair was cut short in a bob, and her sleeveless shirt and vest showed her thick, muscular arms.

Niya.

Rage filled Loren, a rage more terrible than she had ever felt while awake. She launched herself after Niya, who ducked into an alley. Loren plunged into the darkness, pulling a magestone from her cloak and eating it to gain night vision.

Auntie stood there, no longer disguised as Niya. Her clothes had changed as well. Now she wore black robes in a style that looked somehow familiar. Yet it was Auntie's thin, svelte form, her smooth brown skin and dyed blonde hair. And her eyes, which Loren knew she could never forget.

"You!" cried Loren. "You live!"

Auntie frowned at her. There was no recognition in her expression, no anger—only confusion.

"Who are you?" she said.

Loren screamed in rage. If the witch thought to escape by deception, she would find that a folly.

Loren raised her dagger and leaped. Darkness take her vow not to kill. Auntie had died already, but Loren would kill her again in her dreams. She would do it a thousand times, and relish each kiss of the dagger.

Auntie cried out in fear. She raised a hand, and her eyes glowed.

Loren froze in midair, held in place by mindmagic.

But . . . but that was impossible. Auntie was a weremage, not a mindmage. A wizard could only command one branch of magic.

Just as Loren was about to scream her frustration, Auntie vanished. The magic released her, and Loren fell hard to the ground. A hand took her shoulder, and she almost recoiled—but the hand was gentle, and it raised her up.

Before her stood a young woman of surpassing beauty, mayhap a few years older than Loren. But this woman had none of the raw, animal seduction of Auntie. Hers was a softer, gentler grace, a promise of great love and great kindness. She was clad in wispy, silky blue. Loren wondered how the winter air did not freeze her to the bone.

But it is not winter, she realized suddenly. She had visited the Seat in early autumn.

Recognition crashed in upon her. She had seen the woman before. Not in true life, but in another dream. Loren had seen her in a house of lovers, and she had wept for a man Loren did not know. But now she did not weep. She only gave Loren a sad smile.

"That was not the one you fear," said the woman. "The one you fear is dead. You must remember that when you see her."

"When I—what?" said Loren.

The woman smiled and leaned forwards to kiss Loren's cheek. Her sweet and pungent scent penetrated the air, and Loren's heart went skipping.

"You shall have such a hard time after he goes," said the woman. "But you will carry on. Because you must."

"Please," said Loren. "Please, tell me what you mean. I do not understand."

"That boy Chet," said a voice behind her—a voice she knew. "He will leave, you know."

Loren whirled as she shot to her feet. Her surroundings shifted, and now she shivered in bitingly cold wind atop a mountain. Snow covered the landscape in all directions. Loren's stomach lurched as she tried to place herself.

She was in the Greatrocks. The knowledge came crashing upon her, the way it does in dreams. Her peak overlooked a mountain pass. They had taken such a pass through the mountains only a few weeks ago, chasing Damaris into Dorsea. She studied the mountains, trying to find something familiar, but she could see nothing.

And then, there was Mag.

The woman stood in the snow, wind gusting around her. She wore a shirt of chain with thick, fur-lined leather beneath it. Fresh blood covered a mighty spear in her right hand, and a battered shield hung on her left arm. A mournful expression pulled at her cheeks, the corners of her eyes. She stooped, seemingly weary beyond reckoning—nothing like the proud barmaid Loren remembered from Northwood. Where she and Albern had sacrificed themselves so that Loren might live.

Loren fell to her knees. Tears sprang to her eyes unbidden.

"Mag," she whispered. "Mag, is it really you?"

"I cannot come with you," said Mag. Her eyes, too, glistened with tears. She sank to the ground and seized Loren's shoulders, drawing her into an embrace. "Darkness take me, Loren, I cannot come with you. And I cannot tell him."

I cannot tell him. The lover in blue had once spoken the same words. Did they speak of the same man? Who was he?

"Who, Mag?" said Loren. "Please, tell me."

Mag only tossed her head, indicating something over Loren's shoulder. Loren turned to look.

There stood the man in black, the one she had just seen outside the tavern on the Seat. Now he leaned against a different building. It looked like a smithy. The sound of ringing hammers came from within, and smoke poured from its chimney. Its door was plain wood, but above it hung a blue sign with a yellow hammer.

What was a smithy doing in the mountains?

"Your boy," said the man.

"My . . . boy?" said Loren. Then she realized he might have answered her question. "Do you mean Chet? Is that who you all keep speaking of? Mag, what do you wish to tell Chet?"

She turned. Mag was gone. Only the dark man remained.

"Your boy," said the man again. He gave a leering smile. "He is leaving—but then, you have known that for some time."

Grief coursed through her. "You are lying," she said, striding towards the man in black. "You know nothing of Chet. Or of me."

"Ask him yourself." The man pointed over her shoulder. Loren did not want to turn, to find herself somewhere else again with questions still unanswered. But the dream took hold, and her body moved without her intent.

Chet stood a pace away, in the vast entry chamber of a grand palace. Its beauty nearly rivaled that of the High King's palace itself. But no one walked the halls, and no guards stood at the doors. Red plaster formed its pillars, and the roof peaked in two great curves. Just next to them stood wide doors leading outside. Beyond those doors, Loren heard voices.

She ignored them and took a step towards Chet.

"Chet," she said. "Are you all right?"

"I am leaving you," he said. "You cannot follow me anymore."

Loren balked. "What? What do you mean?"

"You cannot follow me anymore."

"Chet, I have not followed you anywhere. *You* have followed *me,* no matter what I—"

He ignored her, stepping out the palace's front door. That door had been closed a moment ago, Loren was certain.

She followed Chet, expecting to find herself in another strange place. But the world did not shift around her. Before her, a massive staircase led to a wide courtyard. The stairs were wider than some ships she had sailed on. On the other side of the courtyard stood a white wall, and beyond that, a grand city. She could see manor houses and military strongholds, as well as countless smaller homes and shops. Nearly all of them had the same sort of curving, peaked tile roof as the palace, barely visible under snow.

But at the bottom of the steps sat Damaris and Gregor.

Loren panicked, looking for Chet. She must not let Damaris find him. But Chet had vanished, and Damaris did not look the least bit interested in finding anyone. In fact, she and Gregor did not seem to have noticed Loren. They sat at fine chairs beside a fine table, furniture that seemed more at home in a merchant's study than out here in a palace courtyard. They had a bottle of wine, and Damaris took delicate sips from a pewter goblet.

"Sidwan?" she said.

Gregor shook his head. "A failure. They overcame the wizard and captured or killed the rest."

Damaris' eyes sharpened. "But we gave Unwe magestones. How did they overcome her mindwyrd?"

The bodyguard's glower deepened. "I do not know. She was never very strong with the gift."

"Yet the magestones . . ." Damaris sighed and pinched the bridge of her nose. Loren's stomach did a turn. She had seen Annis make the same gesture countless times. "I suppose we should not have expected it to be so easy."

"No. It appears they have more wit than I gave them credit for."

"Forgive me, but that is no surprise," said Damaris. "You have always hated Loren, and it blinds you to her many admirable qualities—of which her resourcefulness is among the greatest."

Gregor's jaw clenched. "Just because she is cunning—"

Damaris chuckled and leaned over to pat his hand. "Oh, do not get so angry. We knew Sidwan might not be the end of it. This is not even a setback. It was planned for."

Loren thought she had gone unseen. But now Gregor looked up the steps at her. She quailed at the hatred she saw in his eyes. Suddenly his face changed, becoming the pale, decaying corpse she had seen in dreams before. His throat gaped from a wide wound drawn by a terrible blade. Loren shuddered to think of a warrior who could best the giant in a fight and inflict such damage upon him.

His throat rasped hideously as he spoke. "And when the plan is complete, I shall have her at last."

Damaris, too, turned to look at Loren. She smiled with teeth covered by a red stain. Loren took it for wine, until she realized it was blood.

"And you shall take your time with her."

Loren tried to run, but her legs would not answer the call of her mind. The ground began to shake beneath her feet. Through the courtyard's front gate poured soldiers in strange armor. More came marching from around the edges of the palace. They converged and made their way up the steps towards her—but they parted around the table where Damaris and Gregor sat, flowing like waves around a rock. They stared at Loren from beneath horrible, twisted masks.

A hand gripped Loren's arm, making her jump. She turned and saw Niya. Loren tried to recoil, but Niya held her firm.

"There is only one way out," she said. She was not panicked, but only solemn—even a little sad.

She pulled Loren back into the palace. They went

at a dead run through the halls. Niya led her this way and that, past tapestries on the walls and fine urns on side tables, until Loren was hopelessly lost.

Finally Niya skidded to a halt with Loren just behind her. Ahead of them stood wide double doors that opened to a great dining hall. The other end of the hall had another set of doors, beyond which was a courtyard, and beyond that, a gate leading out to the city. No one blocked their path to freedom.

Niya pulled Loren away, towards a small iron door in the wall. Loren drew back.

"That way is safe," she said, pointing through the dining hall.

"That way is for the others," said Niya. "It is not for you."

Loren looked around. There were no others. "What do you mean?"

"Come."

Niya pulled her through the iron door. Inside was a small serving room with trays and dishes. There was no other exit.

Loren froze. Niya had trapped her.

But then Niya went to the other end of the room and pulled down a shelf of dishes. Pottery smashed on the floor. Behind the shelf was a passageway, open but utterly dark inside.

"What is in there?" said Loren.

Niya did not answer. Instead she pulled Loren close and kissed her. Loren's knees went weak, and she shivered as she had when their lips met in Dahab. All the knowledge of what had come after, of Niya's betrayal and her crimes against Chet, seemed for a moment not to matter. She gripped Niya's shoulders, and they clung to each other for a few precious heartbeats.

Then Niya pushed Loren into the passage. Loren stumbled and fell. Before she could rise, Niya had lifted the shelf to cover the way out again. Loren tried to push it away, but the shelf did not budge.

Beyond the shelf, Loren heard the room's door crash open. There came the sound of many feet tramping in. The masked soldiers had found them—or rather, they had found Niya, for Loren was now hidden.

The Mystic's battle cry split the air, a berserker scream that Loren had heard in the halls of Yewamba. She shuddered as she remembered how Niya had hacked down every foe in reach. Now she pictured the Mystic tearing into the masked soldiers that must be pouring into the room.

A blade pierced flesh with a sharp *shunk*. The berserker cry faltered.

Niya laughed instead, a feral noise. Loren heard still more soldiers dying. But at last Niya began to cough blood, and then her voice failed.

There came the sound of many, many swords sinking into a body.

Bitter tears ran down Loren's cheeks. But she could do nothing for Niya now. She turned back to the passageway.

It was utterly dark, but a magestone still coursed through her veins. When she put her hand on her dagger, she could see as if by daylight. The passageway turned twice before ending at a ladder leading up. She climbed it and found herself in another passage like the one below. Again it turned, but she saw no branches to go in any other direction.

After a little while, she reached the end. Before her hung a tapestry, and below it came a gentle breeze. A room lay beyond, but Loren feared to enter it.

Her the only other choice was to return to the room full of soldiers—and Niya's corpse.

Loren set her jaw and pushed the tapestry aside.

She was in a chamber with two doors on either side leading to bedrooms. A third door led out to the rest of the palace. A small table rested in the middle of the room, with a plush couch and two chairs surrounding it. Three lamps lit the place, but they were not on the walls—they sat on side tables at the edges of the room, and they cast many shifting shadows. Everything was of the finest make, just as Loren had seen downstairs.

At the other end of the room was a fourth door, leading to a balcony that overlooked a courtyard. The same courtyard Loren had seen below, on the other side of the dining hall.

Standing in front of the door was Gregor.

The giant faced out into the world beyond. But now he noticed Loren, and he closed the door as he turned to her.

Loren turned and threw the tapestry aside, desperate to escape. But the passageway had vanished. Now she faced a wall of solid stone. She could not get out.

"This is the only way," said Niya.

She stood just beside Loren. Wounds covered her body, and her throat was cut—because, of course, Chet had cut it in Feldemar. But her voice did not rattle, her words did not rasp. She looked at Loren with tears in her eyes.

"It is the only way out," she said again. "Even the Elves told you."

Gregor stalked towards Loren in the darkness.

FOUR

THE DREAM RELEASED HER.

Loren woke in their room in Sidwan. For a moment she panicked, clutching at her thick blanket.

But she did not scream. She kept still and silent, squeezing the blanket, feeling the rough wood floor upon which she lay. In a moment the terror passed. A long sigh rushed out of her, and she closed her eyes.

She gained greater control of the fear each time, much to her relief. The terror of her dreams had been awful in the beginning, and she did not miss that in the slightest.

The others still slept, and she heard no noises from the inn downstairs. Slowly, quietly, she dressed herself and went to the common room. The innkeeper gave her barely a glance as she walked by him to the front door. Outside, the sky had just begun to grey. Dawn would come in an hour or two. Loren went to the innkeeper and bought breakfast—bread and water only, for she did not trust the meat they served here.

After eating, she went for a brief visit with Midnight in the stables. Modest though the inn was, the staff kept the horses well supplied with oats. Midnight nuzzled Loren's shoulder, as though offering comfort against the fear of her dreams. Loren fed her an old apple she had saved.

She returned to the room and waited for the others to wake. It did not take long. Shiun and Uzo stirred before dawn, and Chet and Annis rose from their pallets soon after. Only Gem remained asleep, curled in the back corner and snoring loudly.

"Shiun, Uzo," said Loren. "We will ride out today. Go into town and replenish our supplies. Get a new waterskin for Gem—his has nearly fallen apart."

"We shall need some more coin," said Shiun.

Loren's gut did a turn. "Of course," she said lightly.

She went to her saddlebag and pulled out her coin purse. A few forlorn weights fell into her palm. Loren handed two of them to Shiun.

They were near the end of their money, and she dreaded having to fetch more. Loren served the High

King; by law, she could fetch more gold from any Mystic stronghold. But Loren had feared to turn to the Mystics thus far, and she still did. The redcloaks would have to report the transaction to Kal of the family Endil, and that might cause a reunion with the grand chancellor that Loren would rather put off.

Kal had sent them chasing after Damaris in the first place. He had once mentored Jordel, and now the High King had placed Loren under his command. But Loren had been overzealous in her pursuit of Damaris, and Kal would be furious. Strictly speaking, Loren had not disobeyed any direct order. But Kal had not granted permission for her rash course, and Loren had not even captured Damaris. Now her best hope was to find the merchant before Kal found her, and hope her belated success might earn some forgiveness.

She cast her thoughts aside as Uzo and Shiun left the room. The Mystics knew nothing of her dreams, and she meant to keep it that way. Once she was sure they were out of earshot, she went to the corner and roused Gem by shaking him hard. He came awake with a start, swatting at her with his scrawny arms.

"Wha—what?" he groused. "What is it? I am resting."

"Yes, and overlong," said Loren. "Get up, for we must all take counsel. I have had a dream."

"And so have I," said Gem. "In it were many beautiful young men and an overabundance of food. I wish you had not dragged me from it."

Loren fixed him with a look. Gem glared back for a moment, but then his eyes widened.

"Oh. You mean *that* sort of dream."

Soon he had dressed himself, and then he, Chet, and Annis gathered around Loren in a little circle on the floor. For a moment she felt a rare nostalgia—she knew they must look similar to when the old storyteller, Bracken, would gather the children in her village and tell them tales.

"What brought the dream?" said Chet. "Was it something that happened yesterday?"

"I have never known what causes the dreams," said Loren. "It is nothing I can control, nor has the waking world ever had much influence upon it. It is as though some unseen force jerks on my strings, dragging me this way and that like a puppet."

"Yet whatever this force is, it seems to want to help us," said Annis.

Chet stared at his hands. "If the dreams were meant to help, they might have warned us about Niya."

They all went silent at that. Chet drew his knees up to his chest. His right hand scrubbed at his left arm, though he was already immaculately clean.

One by one, Loren held them in her gaze. "I mean to tell you everything," she said. "Everything I saw. No more half-truths. If I had told you everything from the beginning, we might have avoided much sorrow—and then again, we might not have. But I think now that avoiding the truth helps no one."

But even as she said the words, she winced inside, for there was one thing she could not say. The magestones. Gem knew she had them, and he knew something of their power. And Loren had told Annis not long ago. But she still had not told Chet. He worried too much about her as it was, and he was still too righteous. He held a greater respect for the King's law than any of the rest of them. The urchin and the smuggler's daughter took her use of magestones in stride, but she knew in her heart of hearts that Chet would not do the same.

But the magestones had not been an important part of the dream in any case, and so it was easy to avoid mentioning them. She told them all the rest, about the mysterious lover in blue, the cruel man in black, and Mag. Gem wept a bit when Loren mentioned her. Loren told them every strange place she had visited, the ones she had seen in the waking world and the ones she had not.

Then she came to Chet's part in the dream. Loren paused. She heard his words again as though he spoke them now: *I am leaving you. You cannot follow me anymore.*

Loren repeated the words exactly. She neither avoided Chet's gaze, nor looked at him too closely. Then she paused, while Gem and Annis shifted uncomfortably where they sat.

"Of course, I have seen many things in my dreams," said Loren. "It means nothing, as we all know."

"Naturally," said Annis. Gem nodded eagerly.

But Chet met her gaze for a moment. He quickly looked away. But in that moment, she saw an aching sadness within him. As she carried on with the story, he refused to look at her.

The dream spoke true, thought Loren. *Sky save me. He is going to leave.*

It made her pause, her voice faltering to nothing. In the moment's silence, Chet glanced at her by reflex. They looked at each other quietly for a long moment.

How could Loren blame him? He had never wanted to go on this mad quest in the first place. Chet had only ever wanted to return home with Loren, there to build a quiet and happy life, letting the world's troubles pass them by. But he had followed Loren out of love, and he had suffered a fate worse than Loren could imagine. Auntie had bedded him without leave. He would bear the scar of that always. It was what made him sit in the corner staring past the walls, what made him scrub at his too-clean skin.

It was why he could no longer stand to have Loren touch him.

She forced herself to go on. When she finished the tale, Gem shook his head.

"It is an absolute mess. How are we supposed to read the tale of it? Can you not make any of it a bit more clear?"

Loren frowned at him. "And how do you think I should do that? I do not control the dreams, Gem.

They come when they wish, and they show me whatever they will."

"*I* can control my dreams," said Gem, sniffing. "Most often I turn into a firemage and roast my enemies with flame. Can you imagine me as a wizard? No doubt fate kept the gift of magic from me because I had been given such a long list of exceptional qualities already."

"Who could doubt it?" said Loren evenly.

Annis had been sitting in thought after Loren finished her dream-tale. Now she tapped a finger on her chin. "The city you described . . . it sounds like one of the great cities of Dorsea. And the palace you described sounds very like the king's palace, in the capital of Danfon."

Loren frowned. "But I thought you said your mother would never go there."

"I thought not," said Annis, shrugging. "Too much power is concentrated there—and therefore too many agents of the King's law. She could be seen by any constable or Mystic, and then she would be in grave trouble. King Jun and his royal senate have been seeking a way to appease the High King. They could hardly think of a greater gift than to capture and turn over the merchant Damaris, one of the most renowned traitors in the nine kingdoms."

"Then there you have it," said Loren. "Damaris could not have gone to Danfon. It is no more true than the idea of her sitting at a fine table in a snowy courtyard."

"Yet the dream showed her in Danfon," said Annis. "Did you not say that you saw Hewal in Dahab? And that is where we found him."

"I did," said Loren. "But I saw Damaris there, too, and we know now that she never went to Dahab."

"This is still the best clue we have," said Annis. "And your example only proves the point. Even when your dreams are unclear, they bring us to Damaris in time."

Loren shook her head. "I am not sure. Fetch your map. Let us at least see where Danfon is."

Annis hurried to retrieve it. She laid it out on the floor and began to point out markings. "This is Feldemar to the north, and here is Sidwan, where we are now. To the northeast is the Moonslight Pass that leads to Danfon. If we faced no delays, we could reach the capital in less than a week."

But Loren's eye was drawn, almost against her will, to another part of the map. She saw the Greatrocks where they bent south, and little drawings of trees that marked the Birchwood. But to the west of the mountains was the name of a place. She could not read it, but she could not draw her eyes from it.

As she studied the name in silence, something appeared. A small building, almost like a model built of little sticks. At first she did not recognize it, but then she saw that it was a smithy. Its door was plain wood, but above that was a blue sign with a yellow hammer.

Loren shuddered. The building she had seen in her dream. The smithy in the mountains.

Her visions had only ever come to her in dreams, never in the waking world. Was this the same thing? Some effect of whatever magic she had? Or did her imagination play tricks on her now?

Loren put her forefinger on the map. To her eyes, her finger seemed to pass right through the little smithy. That sent another shiver of fear up her spine.

"What is this place?"

Annis frowned. "That is Bertram. A sizeable city, and very important to Dorsean trade. Why?"

Bertram.

She had heard the name before. Xain had told her of it in past days, when they had conspired to sell the stones. He had mentioned it again just before Loren left the High King's Seat. A smuggler named Wyle lived in Bertram, buying and selling goods beyond the King's law. In particular, Xain said the man trafficked in magestones.

"I think we should go there," said Loren slowly. "There is a man in Bertram named Wyle. Xain told me of him. He is a smuggler, like your family, though I am sure he is less well connected."

The others frowned at each other. Loren knew she must appear mad.

"But Loren," said Gem, "what does he have to do with Damaris?"

Loren shook her head. "I do not know. Only . . . only I . . ." She swallowed against a suddenly dry throat. "The smithy I saw in my dream. I see it again, sitting there on the map."

A long silence stretched. Gem leaned in to peer closely at the name of the town, as though he expected to see the smithy drawn there.

"That has never happened before," said Chet.

"No, it has not," said Loren. "But it is happening now. And Xain told me of Wyle. This cannot be a coincidence."

Annis shook her head. "I still do not see how it would help. Wyle may be a smuggler, but he is not the criminal we seek."

"Yet he may be a valuable man to know," said Loren. "He must have friends and contacts across Dorsea. He may know something of the family Yerrin's activities. Damaris is gone, and we do not know to where—not for certain. I do not think we will find her by relying on Shiun's skill as a tracker, considerable though that skill might be. Mayhap Wyle has information that can help."

"If what Annis says is true, your dream showed us the capital, not Bertram," said Gem.

"It *could* have been Bertram," said Annis, pursing her lips. "They are both great cities. Bertram has at least one palace that could have been the one Loren saw."

"And even if my dream showed me Danfon, the visions are not always clear," said Loren. "In Feldemar I saw you turn feral and rip out my throat with your teeth."

Gem sniffed. "I would use a dagger," he muttered.

Then his eyes widened. "Not that I would ever do such a thing at all, of course."

Loren flipped one of her throwing knives from her belt and pointed it at him. "You had best not try it." But she smiled at him.

Annis tilted her head side to side, her expression thoughtful. "In any case, Bertram is a good deal closer to where we are now than the capital is. Even if our search there reveals nothing, we will not have wasted much time."

"Then it is settled," said Loren. "We go to Bertram, and then, mayhap, to the capital."

Gem gave a long sigh. "More riding for endless leagues," he groused.

But Chet sat silently, his arms folded across his knees. His left hand still idly scrubbed at the skin of his right arm, and his gaze looked at something far away.

"Chet?" said Loren. "What is it?"

He jumped. "What? Nothing."

"Your thoughts seem to be elsewhere."

"They are," he said, shaking his head. "But they are of little consequence."

"Not to me," said Loren quietly. Almost she put a hand on his arm, but she stopped herself just in time.

"I . . ." He frowned. She could see some battle taking place behind his eyes. "I do not think this is a good idea."

Annis arched an eyebrow. "What? A journey to Bertram?"

"Yes," said Chet. "I think you are wrong about it."

Annis' voice took on an undercurrent of annoyance. "I was not aware you knew much of the great cities of Underrealm. What gives you doubt?"

Chet's cheeks flushed. "I think . . . I think we should carry on the way we are going."

"But we have run out of ideas," said Loren. "We do not know what to do, if not this."

"And do you not think that odd?" Chet spoke quickly now, his words pouring as though through a widening chink in a dam. "That we have pursued Damaris this long, and you dreamless, only to finally have a vision after she has evaded us entirely?"

"But that is a gift," said Gem. "Whatever force has granted Loren these visions, they have given us another just when we needed it most."

Chet snorted. "Forgive me if I doubt the kindness of whoever has infiltrated Loren's mind. But it seems no one else is even curious why the dreams come at all."

And would you feel the same, if the visions did not reveal that you plan to abandon me?

The thought came before Loren could stop it. She hated herself for it, biting her own tongue to keep the words from escaping.

Gem opened his mouth to speak again, but Loren stopped him. "Enough," she said, quiet but just sharp enough to halt his words. "This is the only plan we have. If we think of a better one, we shall act upon it. But in the meantime, we cannot remain in Sidwan until we rot."

Chet's gaze darted to her. For a moment she thought he would argue, but then his shoulders sagged. "Very well," he muttered. "If that is your wish."

She gave him a smile, and after a moment they began to pack their things for travel. But Loren glanced at him as they worked, and her thoughts gave her no peace.

FIVE

Once Shiun and Uzo returned, Loren told them she meant to ride for Bertram. They accepted the news with silent nods and readied their packs for travel. Loren wondered what they thought about this sudden change in tack. Thus far in their travels, the party had relied on Shiun's tracking. This new course must have seemed strange, but the Mystics neither complained nor questioned her.

In truth, she had begun to question herself. The visions in her dreams were strange enough, and she drew no closer to understanding them than she had ever been. But the vision of the smithy on the map . . . that was something new, and it disturbed her even more. What else might she see in the waking world? When something from her dreamsight appeared in true life, a great unease and disorientation came over her. Sometimes it left her almost unable to act. Now she feared that, in a moment of danger, she might see something that was not there at all. The thought discomfited her. As the day wore on, she caught Chet and the children stealing glances at her from the corners of their eyes, and she wondered if they thought the same thing.

Loren decided to spend one night more in Sidwan before setting out. Damaris' trail had grown stale, and one more day would make no difference. Since entering Dorsea, they had never spent more than one night in the same place. They needed a rest, and they more than deserved one.

A short while before going to bed, Loren caught Chet's eye. "Our quarters grow stuffy. I could use a walk in the fresh air before sleep. Would you come with me?"

He smiled too quickly, the way he always did these days, and nodded. But he donned his boots slowly, and after they left the room he walked sluggishly a half-pace behind her. He likely thought she meant to discuss her dream with him.

In fact she wanted to, but she promised herself she would not. They had not spent much time together lately—especially because they had not lain together since Yewamba. Niya's crime—or Auntie's—had left a lasting mark upon him. The mind required time to heal from such a thing, but it also needed help. Few people were better suited to help Chet than Loren. And more than that, she was partially responsible for what had happened. She owed him more attention than she had given.

The town shone in the afternoon light around them. The low sun's red glow bounded from every snowy surface to fly back into their eyes, so that Loren had to squint whenever she turned towards it. Lazy smoke drifted from smokestacks all around, floating up into a clear sky. Loren hoped the weather remained this fine on their journey.

Soon they walked through farmlands. The path south went up a hill and then turned east, bending back and forth at the corners of each farm until it joined the main road that would lead them to Bertram. Here in Dorsea, farmers used small copses of trees to mark the borders of their property. Each time Loren and Chet walked beneath the branches, it felt for a moment like they walked in the Birchwood again.

"Do you remember Northwood?" said Loren. "The way you used to take me walking each day?"

Chet's head jerked towards her as she started talking. But her words calmed him, and he gave her a genuine smile this time—warm, and not too fast. Loren thrilled to see it on his face again.

"Of course I do," he said. For a moment his eyes

clouded. "Those were dark days for you. As these days are for me."

"It was painful, then," said Loren softly. "But it was better to know the truth about my father. Indeed, I think it helped me. I had traveled for months, and I thought I rode a tall horse, staring down my nose at those below me who resorted to violence. Little did I know I had made my first kill before I even left home."

Chet shook his head. "That is not the whole truth, Loren. You did what—"

"I did what I had to," said Loren. "I know. And even after learning the consequence, I have not turned into a killer. Yet it *has* shaped me. I know now that others, too, do what they must."

"You are speaking of me and . . . and her," said Chet.

Loren shook her head quickly. "That was different."

For a moment she forgot herself. She reached out to him and took his arm. But Chet jerked away from her as if she had pressed a red-hot poker into his skin. Loren recoiled, drawing her hands to her chest.

"I am sorry," she said.

"No, it is I who should apologize," said Chet. "I . . . I have been getting better about it. But still, when I see you, still some part of my mind sees . . ."

"No, Chet," she said, trying to keep her voice kind and firm at the same time. "You must never apologize. You did nothing wrong, and you have done nothing wrong since. I am at fault. I have been ignoring you. That

is why I wanted to walk with you now—to try and bring back the memory of Northwood, when the world was a better place and we were . . . well, not happy, entirely, but happier. So much darkness has come since then."

"It has," said Chet. His hand rose to his chest, to the place just above his heart where the dagger of a Shade had pierced him. It no longer gave him pain, but he would rub at it on occasion—and ever more often since Auntie. "Darkness came, but it always passed. But not this darkness. Not now."

Loren ached. She wanted to reach out to him, wanted to hold him. She felt the desire constantly, and she knew she only meant to help him. Always she had to remind herself that it would *not* help, that it would only hurt him more.

She folded her arms and turned to walk again, keeping her pace slow so that he did not feel the need to hurry. "I thought the same thing, you know. After Jordel died, I mean. I thought the grief would never leave me. In truth, I suppose it has not. But it has become bearable. Mayhap you can hope for that."

Chet was silent for a long moment. Then he stopped walking. Loren turned and, to her shock, found him weeping.

"I do not want to leave you," he whispered.

She did not answer at first. She did not trust herself to speak. Tears did not come, but she felt the ache of them in her heart, her throat. They choked her, and she fought to master them.

"I do not want you to go," she said at last. "But I want you to be happy, and I want you to be safe. I fear that neither of those may be possible if you remain with me."

A sob burst from him, and he scrubbed at his eyes with his hand. It was all Loren could do to keep from embracing him then.

"I am not faithless," he said. "I came with you to find Damaris. That is what all this has been for, and I think . . . I *feel* that we are close. Even after learning that she has evaded us, I think I can sense her just in the next town. I want to see it through."

Loren looked down at her feet. "Do you think it will help? Help *you,* I mean?"

He sucked in another cry as his head swung back and forth. An answer? A rejection? Loren did not know.

She could not hold him. She could not take his hand. So she gestured back towards Sidwan.

"Come," she said. "Let us return to the others. We have a long ride tomorrow, and we both need our rest."

Chet nodded and walked beside her. By the time they reached the town and returned to the inn, he had mastered his emotions. Likely the others thought his flushed face came from the cold. But Loren lay awake long into the night, listening for every sound of him shifting on his pallet, wondering if he hid the motion of another silent sob.

They set out for Bertram the next day. The folk of Sidwan seemed sorry to see them go. They had likely caused a greater commotion than the town had seen in years.

Before leaving, they checked in on the constables one last time. The Yerrin wizard was bound and blindfolded. Magestone sickness had not yet set in, but Loren knew it soon would. She did not envy the constables, who would have to remain here to witness it. The other Yerrins sat in a small cell, the only sort of jail for leagues in any direction, and not built to hold five prisoners.

"We shall see to them," said the fat constable with the drooping mustache. Loren had learned he called himself Ham. The name was almost too appropriate. "A letter has been sent to the city of Chosun, and some of our brethren will arrive soon to escort them to better holdings."

"Thank you," said Loren. "Do not forget to tell them of the mindmage. She will no longer be so dangerous as she was, but no wizard should be trifled with."

Ham shuddered. "I will remember it. Thank you, Nightblade."

Loren gave him a sharp look. She had not told him that title. No doubt this was some work of Gem's. Glancing back, she saw the boy's crooked teeth flashing in a grin.

"You are welcome, constable," said Loren. "Your service will not be forgotten."

He puffed up his chest and saluted with his hand over his heart. Loren gave him a final nod and led her party out of the town.

The road to Bertram was easy enough, though somewhat slower because of the snow. The king paid local workers to clear it away from time to time, but they had not done so since the last snowfall. Sometimes Loren's party had to cut into the countryside to avoid a large drift that had piled up. They rode as long as they could while the sun was high, and each night they stopped early enough to gather firewood before dark. At first Loren had been hesitant to light fires, but Shiun had advised it.

"Bandits are more active during winter," she said. "But they are not likely to trifle with our party. At least four of us look like we can fight."

Gem glowered. "I would say five."

Shiun arched an eyebrow. "As you say. In any case, I think they will leave us alone. Our greatest foe is the cold."

One night Loren and Gem went out to fetch firewood together, taking Chet's hatchet with them. Loren cut down dead-looking branches and piled them into Gem's arms, and soon the boy had a sizeable stack. Once he might have struggled with such a burden, but now he bore it easily. Over their long journey together, he had shot up like a weed, and he had begun to grow some muscle as well.

"I have been meaning . . . er," Gem began. He

cleared his throat and tried again. "I have meant to ask if I might start taking a watch at night."

Loren looked at him in surprise. "That would be most welcome," she said carefully. "But mayhap we will pair you with someone else, at least to start. I would hate to wake in the morning and find you had fallen asleep."

Gem scowled at her. "Do you think I cannot remain awake when I wish to?"

"I would never say such a thing," said Loren, keeping her face carefully neutral. "Except that I would, for you have tried standing a watch before—with me, in the Greatrocks. I had to nudge you thrice an hour. You enjoy your rest, master urchin."

His scowl deepened. "And what wise man would not?"

Loren chuckled. The boy's insouciance and seemingly bottomless cheer had been a comfort through many dark times. She wondered how she had ever thought to leave him behind, as she had long ago. A journey without Gem seemed a foreign concept after they had ridden so many leagues together. And the same went for Annis.

At that thought, Loren turned to regard Gem carefully. "I have been meaning to speak with you, as well, but of another matter. How long do you and Annis mean to keep up this strain between you?"

Gem's cheeks and ears grew bright red, and he ducked his gaze. "I . . . it is not something either us have planned, exactly, I think."

"And I notice it has not been pleasant for either of you. That goes for the rest of us as well."

He sighed. "I know it."

"You know that what happened is not your fault. Nor is it Annis'. If either of you blames the other, or yourself . . ."

Gem shook his head quickly. "Of course not. I know that. Only . . . only, is that not the worst part? When no one is to blame? If she had done something wrong, I could take her to task for it. Or if I had done something wrong—outlandish as the notion might seem—I suppose she could do the same to me, and then there might at last be an end to . . . to the discomfort. But neither of us have done anything wrong, and so what can we do to fix it?"

His words were all too familiar to Loren. She had said something very similar to Xain back on the High King's Seat. Many whom she held dear had left her, one way or another—first Jordel, then Albern and Mag, and finally Xain. Yet they had had no choice. Jordel, Albern, and Mag had been slain, all of them in defense of Loren and her friends. Xain had been reunited with his son, and had remained on the Seat to see to the boy's safety. None of them had any choice in what they had done, and Loren had had no choice but to move on. Yet that had not diminished the pain of their parting, and in some ways had only inflamed it. It had taken her a long time before she could think of them with anything but heartache.

"Mayhap it only requires a bit more work," she said. "On both your parts, I mean. Finding a way to turn your friendship warm and easy again, the way it used to be."

Gem looked down at his boots. Then he shrugged, feigning a nonchalance Loren knew he did not feel. "In any case, I suppose it was foolish of me not to predict such an outcome. I should have known long ago that Annis would confess such feelings for me."

Loren cocked her head. "Because of the way she acted? She *has* fawned on you almost from the moment you met."

"She has?" Gem's eyes went saucer-wide. "I have not seen that, nor is it what I meant. I mean only . . . well, how could any young maiden keep herself from desiring such a man?" He held the bundle of sticks in one hand while gesturing at himself with the other.

Loren kept herself from cuffing his ear, but it was a mighty struggle. Still, she felt the need to pierce the bubble of his high opinion of himself.

"I hope she did nothing wrong by it, but Annis told me something of your conversation. And she made some mention of Uzo."

It worked. Gem deflated at once, and his cheeks flushed anew. "Yes, I . . . well, he is very . . ."

"He is," said Loren, nodding. Uzo was indeed a beautiful young man, though she had never felt the same connection towards him that she had with Chet. *Or with Niya,* whispered her mind, though she quickly banished that thought. "But unless it has happened without my noticing, I do not think that you have said anything more to Uzo than Annis said to you for a long while."

"You have not missed anything," said Gem with a sigh. "I may think very highly of myself—and with good reason—but I hold no illusions about Uzo. He scarcely seems to notice me, and when he does, he seems to regard me mostly with annoyance. And besides, how old do you think he is? What would he want from one who is scarcely more than a boy?"

"You are not much younger than I am, and Uzo is not much older," said Loren. "Yet I see what you mean. He is a soldier, after all, and from what little he has told us about himself, I do not think a great romance is something he desires."

"Well, I long for such a romance enough for the both of us," said Gem. He looked up at the sky as if searching for strength. The firewood almost fell from his hands. "But I suppose that is my lot. I think every great scholar, and artist and warrior—and sometime medica—only lives a more complete and fulfilling life if they have suffered a great unrequited love in their youth."

Again Loren's hand twitched, itching to slap the back of the boy's head. "No doubt," she said instead. "It seems almost a requirement."

Her thoughts went to her dreams again, the way they so often did these days. She saw Gem's terrible snarl, the way his face twisted in a rage she had never seen there in the waking world. Her head twitched as she felt his teeth tearing at her throat.

She cut down another branch. But after she put it atop the pile, she took the firewood from his arms and set it down on the ground. Then she took Gem by the shoulders and turned him to face her. He looked up at her—though they were getting near to a height of each other now—and they remained that way for a little while, studying each other in silence.

"You know that I care for you, do you not?" said Loren. "You are one of my dearest friends. I will never stop looking after you."

Gem's brow furrowed. "What under the sky are you talking about? It is my job to look after *you,* not the other way around."

Loren shook her head. "Your wit is one of my favorite things about you. But be serious for a moment. I do not jest."

His mouth worked. Without warning he leaped forth, wrapping his arms around her in an embrace.

"I know it," he said. "And you may be my favorite person in all the world. And that is quite a statement, as I have seen so much of it."

She patted his hair gently. "Good. I never want you to forget it."

Gem drew back and looked up at her, and she saw recognition in his eyes. "This is about your dream. About how you have seen me attack you."

Loren nodded, suddenly nervous to speak.

"Then take my vow, though I have given you one before. I vow never to do you harm. I would end my own life first." He cocked his head and pursed his lips. "Though I would rather not do that either, if it is at all possible."

Loren smirked and embraced him again. "And I command you never to do so. I only wanted you to know how high of an esteem I hold you in. As long as you know it, I am satisfied."

He bounced on his feet and stooped to gather up the firewood. "Then be satisfied! Only we should be getting back, for I am sure the others will not be happy until they have had a chance to warm their frozen limbs."

She smiled and hung the hatchet at her belt, leading him back towards the camp. But a shadow remained over her heart. She had told Gem of her dreams, yes. But she had left one thing out, something she had only realized recently. Whenever she saw Gem turn vicious with rage and attack her, he had been a grown man.

It means nothing, she told herself. *Do you trust your dreams more than the boy at your side?*

Loren glanced at him and hoped she believed her own answer.

SIX

Two days into their journey, the road began to wend through the western foothills of the Greatrocks. The skeletal trees grew fewer and farther between, giving way to an open but hilly landscape that must have been brilliant green in summer, but was now a dead, dark brown where it was not covered in snow. After four days of hard riding, they emerged through a great cleft in the earth onto a highland, and there they came to Bertram at last.

The city had been built at the confluence of two rivers that came leaping down out of the Greatrocks to the east. The waters joined to form the Fanrong, which ran west to Dorsea's coast to meet the western sea. No kingdoms contested that coastline, and Dorsea drew great wealth from its fertile lands. Eventually, that wealth spread through the rest of the kingdom by way of the river.

They paused for a midday meal of rabbit that Chet had shot that morning. While they ate, they gazed down at the city. Gem leaned forwards suddenly and pointed. "Is that the King's road running through the city?"

"It is," said Shiun, nodding. "Bertram was the capital of Dorsea for hundreds of years. When the Dark Wars ended and the last Wizard King vanished, the High King took some of Feldemar's lands and gave them to the Dorsean king—or, you might say, returned them to her. They were Dorsean lands in the beginning, or else the kingdom would not have earned its name, for it would have bordered only two of the oceans."

Gem's eyes widened as he stared at her. "The last Wizard King? What do you mean they vanished?"

Shiun paused for a moment, and she looked at the boy carefully. "It is not something that is widely known, and it might have been better for me not to mention it. But the last Wizard King ruled in Feldemar, and held her kingdom long against the other eight. When the war turned against her, she vanished. The High King Andriana searched everywhere, but never found her. Underrealm lived in fear of her return for many years, but that is now centuries past. She died long ago, though we may never know where. In any case, when the northeast lands were reclaimed, the Dorsean king moved the capital to its original home in Danfon. Therefore Dorsea has had two capitals, but they are both on the King's road, in accordance with the ancient edicts."

Loren stared at the scout. She did not think she had heard the Mystic woman speak so much in all the time they had ridden together. "I thought you were a woman of Dulmun."

"I am, but I was stationed in Bertram for a number of years," said Shiun. "In that time I learned something of its history." She bowed her head and tore another hunk of rabbit from the bone, looking slightly embarrassed.

They reached the city just after nightfall. Loren feared they might find the gates closed, but they stood open. The war with Dulmun was far away, and Bertram had no reason to fear any attack. A constable at the gatehouse asked a few questions, but when Uzo and Shiun flashed their Mystic badges, the woman quickly waved them on.

"You should have a badge," Gem told Loren as they rode through the gate.

Loren frowned. "What sort of badge?"

"A mark of office," said Gem. "You are not some simple traveler. You are the Nightblade."

She gave a quick glance around in case anyone was close enough to overhear, but the street was mostly empty. "I have a writ with the High King's seal," she said in a low voice. "That is good enough."

Gem lifted his chin. "It is not as impressive, certainly."

To Loren's surprise, Uzo snickered aloud at that. Gem beamed for the rest of their ride through the city.

They found an inn with good stables for the horses. In the common room, Loren bought dinner and a few bottles of passable wine. They had not had the opportunity to eat well since leaving the city of Dahab in Feldemar, and that seemed a lifetime ago. Loren thought a decent meal might be good for the others' mood—and mayhap hers as well. It took half the coin left in her purse, but she tried not to think of that. Once they found Wyle in Bertram, she hoped she could sell some of her magestones to replenish her reserves. And if nothing else, she could find a presence of Mystics in the city. Her identification from the High King would be as good as a bank note to them, and they would fill her purse to bursting. They would send word to Kal, but Loren could leave Bertram far behind before he found her.

In the middle of their meal, she turned to Annis. "How might we go about finding Wyle?"

Annis thought hard, and then gave a quick glance at Uzo and Shiun. "The only thing we know about him for certain is that he traffics in certain goods beyond the King's law. But we cannot simply walk into a jeweler and ask for such a man."

"A jeweler? Why a jeweler?" said Gem.

Annis arched an eyebrow. "They are familiar with the transport and safekeeping of small but very valuable objects. It makes them particularly suited to smuggle similar goods."

"Can we not simply ask for Wyle by name?" said Chet. "He does not need to know what we wish to speak to him about."

Gem and Annis rolled their eyes in unison—then they each saw the other doing it, and there was a moment of uncomfortable silence.

"That is not quite how it works," said Annis, a flush in her cheeks. "Smugglers do not like strangers who ask about them. Too often, such people are the King's law in disguise."

"How does one meet a smuggler, then?" said Loren.

"By personal introduction," said Annis. "A friend who knows the smuggler brings in a new contact. If Xain were here, he might be able to help us, but he is not."

"So we must find someone with whom we can establish trust quickly enough to get such an introduction," said Loren. "That seems a tall order."

Annis sighed. "It is. These circles are carefully guarded even in the meanest of towns, and Bertram is a grand city. Still, if we promise—or at least hint—that there may be a considerable amount of gold available to our contact as a reward . . ."

"Very well," said Loren. "We will rest well tonight and start tomorrow."

They went to bed soon after their meal, and rose before dawn. In the morning, Loren faced a dilemma. She had to leave someone in the room to guard their possessions. During their travels so far, that person had been Annis, but now she needed Annis for the negotiations. Gem was streetwise beyond compare, and could be of great use in the city. Shiun knew something of Bertram already, and Loren wanted Uzo in case things came to a fight. That left Chet, and she did not think he would enjoy being left behind. But when she proposed it to him, he accepted quite easily.

"I am the best choice," he told her, giving a small smile. "Besides, how could I complain about being allowed to rest? We are all road-weary. If anything, I feel guilty that the rest of you must remain on your feet while I sleep the day away."

With the matter settled, the party moved out into the city. Loren had not been able to see much of Bertram during the night, but now its splendor was laid before her in the dawn. It was nowhere near as grand as the High King's Seat, but it rivaled Dahab for both its size and its proud history. The buildings were crafted with exquisite care, with solid white walls and glistening red tile roofs. Contrary to many cities she had seen in her travels, this one seemed to have been laid out with careful consideration. Streets did not twist and turn with the land, but had been laid out in a careful grid that made navigation easier. The roofs peaked the same as many in Dorsea, and very similar to the ones she had seen in Danfon in her dream.

Shiun led them towards the part of town where the jewelers lay. All the crafters' shops clustered near to the river, where the workers could easily dispose of the refuse and rubbish of their daily work. Annis carefully considered the jewelers one by one, and stepped into only the ones that seemed exceptionally fine.

"Would it not be better to try the poorer ones?" said Loren. "Surely the less reputable shops would be the ones to associate with someone like a smuggler."

Annis arched an eyebrow. "Do you think so? There is a great deal of coin to be made in dealings beyond the King's law, at least until you find the noose around your neck. Those who walk such dark roads know it, and they like to spend their coin while they have the chance."

Loren smirked and deferred to Annis' judgement. But though they entered many shops, and while Annis dropped many broad hints that they had "very valuable gems" to sell, they did not seem to have any luck. The shop owners did not seem to take the hint, except for one or two who vigorously denied dealing in cargo they called "too valuable." When Annis pressed the point, they asked Loren's party to leave, no matter how much coin was offered.

After their fifth such attempt, Loren was beginning to grow nervous. "Some of these jewelers almost certainly understand what we are talking about," she told Annis. "But they are nervous to speak to us for some reason. Do you not think they might send word to Wyle that we are searching for him?"

"There is little we can do about that," said Annis. "We must hope that we find someone more amenable before Wyle catches wind of us."

Loren sighed and nodded—but then she came to a sudden stop in the street. The others paused, looking at her curiously.

"Loren?" said Annis. "What is it?"

Only a few paces away was a building. It had a plain wood door and a blue sign with a yellow hammer. It was the smithy she had seen in her dream, and in miniature on the map—and now it stood before her in Bertram. Loren felt a sensation that had become too familiar, a wild churning in her stomach and a disorientation that made her dizzy.

"I think we should look here," she said, pointing to the smithy.

Annis looked at it and frowned. "This place? It is a smithy. If I read its sign right, a steelsmith, though they may deal in silver as well. But they do not traffic in gems, and that is where our interest lies."

"Yet I think we should investigate," said Loren. She gave Annis a look. "Something about the place looks familiar."

Annis' eyes widened slightly, and she glanced at Gem. He looked from her to Loren, and the three of them nodded at each other.

"If you are finished passing messages back and forth with your eyes, mayhap we should go inside?" said Uzo. His tone was carefully neutral, but Loren thought she heard an air of exasperation behind his words.

"Very well," said Loren. "Annis, lead the way."

They went in. The smithy was larger than it looked from the outside, for the room stretched far back, mayhap twice as large as most of the other buildings. On the other end of the wide workroom, Loren saw another door leading to the street on the other side. With such an impressive presence, she guessed this place had a great deal of business.

Near the room's center was the smith. She leaned over a bench in conversation with a young man—one of her apprentices, Loren assumed. But when she looked up and noticed Loren's party, she came to them at once. Her arms and chest were bare beneath a leather apron that covered her front, and every bit of her bristled with muscle. Her black hair was long but bound up in a folded ponytail—no doubt to keep it free from the heat of the forge while she worked. She spent a moment sizing the party up, considerable arms folded over her chest. Loren was reminded of Niya for an uncomfortable moment.

"Good morn," said the smith. "Or near enough to

afternoon, I suppose. I am Kanja, and master of this place. Are you here with business? I hope you do not wish to apprentice with me, for I have help enough, as you can see."

"Not at all," said Loren. "We are travelers who have come far on the road. Some of our possessions require repair. Bits and bridles, and things of that sort."

Kanja nodded, her eyes roving over the group. They seemed to linger for a moment on Uzo, and her cheeks reddened. "I can be of help there. But you should know that my shop's craftsmanship is famous. My apprentices and I do good work, and my prices reflect our quality."

"We would expect no less," said Annis smoothly. "Indeed, an artisan who takes pride in their work is a treasure beyond the value of mere gold. If that is how you feel about quality, could we beg a recommendation?"

The smith dropped her gaze from Uzo to Annis. Her eyes sharpened as though she was surprised to hear such careful words from such a young girl. "I am not fond of begging. But what sort of recommendation do you seek?"

"While we are in Bertram, we have certain goods we wish to sell," said Annis. "We have been searching among jewelers all morning, but none of them seemed quite right for the sale, you might say. It is as you just said—our goods are very valuable, and we price them in equal measure to their quality."

Kanja's nostrils flared. "I may know someone who could give a fair price for such valuable jewels."

Loren leaned forwards and dropped her voice. "I have heard of a man in Bertram who is just such a friend to many people. Mayhap you know the name?"

The steelsmith looked over her shoulder to ensure none of her apprentices were close enough to hear. "What name would that be?"

"I was told it was Wyle."

Kanja gave a very slight nod. "I know him. And if you seek to trade in certain very fine goods, there is no one better. I would know." Her gaze rose to Uzo again, and she gave him a little smile. "Indeed, it is something I pride myself on. I have an eye, and a taste, for only the finest things in life."

Uzo's brows rose almost imperceptibly. Loren looked back and forth between him and Kanja, and she almost burst out laughing as she realized what the smith was saying. Just to be sure, she cocked her head as if curious. "And do you have a husband who shares in those fine tastes?"

The smith's cheeks reddened slightly, and she dropped her gaze from Uzo demurely. "Who would want such a thing as a husband? It would be only a denial of other, mayhap better opportunities that present themselves."

Loren almost guffawed out loud, but she restrained herself. Instead she met Uzo's gaze and raised her brows. He glared back at her, and she could almost see him withhold a groan. Loren tilted her head and smirked.

Uzo gave a great sigh. Then he stepped forwards, flashing Kanja his widest smile. It was so bright, it even dazzled Loren.

"I myself have never thought to deny any of life's pleasures," he said, voice almost a purr.

Loren thought the steelsmith might bounce on her toes like a child. Behind them both, Gem looked between Uzo and Kanja with a scowl on his face. A little pang of guilt struck her, but she dismissed it. Gem looked more annoyed than devastated.

"I am glad to hear it," said Kanja, grinning at Uzo. "Mayhap I could arrange an introduction, then—after a fine meal spent together? I promise you that my tastes extend to wine as well. You look like a man of Feldemar, so you may not know fine Dorsean wine. We make it with rice, and it is clear and sweet."

Uzo inclined his head. "I shall look forward to . . . a new taste, then."

Loren and Annis turned away suddenly, both hiding their mouths behind their hands to stifle a laugh. Gem only snorted.

Kanja shifted on her feet. "I cannot wait. Come and see me before the sun goes down."

"It would be my pleasure," said Uzo. Then he actually drew her hand up and bent his lips to kiss it. Kanja shivered.

They left the shop and made their way through the streets back towards their inn. All were silent for a long moment. Annis and Loren kept sneaking glances at

Uzo, who stared stoically ahead. But at last he growled through his teeth.

"If you mean to say something, you may as well get it over with."

The girls burst out laughing, and even Shiun could not keep herself from a grin.

"I thought she meant to have you on the spot!" said Annis. "I wonder if she would have, if the apprentices were not in the room."

"What sort of dastardly woman is she?" grumbled Gem. "Why, she only *just* met you. Is no one else suspicious that she agreed to give up the secret so easily?"

"I, for one, am not," said Annis. "In the backroom dealings that take place between smugglers and thieves across the nine kingdoms, such transactions are neither rare nor frowned upon. Indeed, many welcome them, for there are darker deeds that can pay for goods and services."

Gem glowered in evident disagreement. Loren forced her smile away. "But of course, Uzo, you know you need not do this if you do not want to. It would be an aid to the mission, but we can find another way."

He heaved a sigh. "I do not prefer women, but neither do I loathe them. You are not asking anything I am not willing to give for the sake of our quest. But may I speak freely?"

Loren nodded at once. "Always."

Uzo stopped walking and caught her gaze. "Soldier

to commander, I expect you to get me very, *very* drunk before you send me out to my doom."

Loren could not stop a single loud bark of laughter, but she forced herself back to solemnity at once. "You have my word—commander to soldier. And when the bards sing the tale of our adventures, I will see to it that none of them forget the great sacrifice of Uzo the Spearman."

Annis doubled over and screamed with laughter while Shiun chuckled. And even Uzo and Gem wore reluctant smiles as they set off towards the inn again.

SEVEN

LOREN DID HER LEVEL BEST TO FULFILL UZO'S REQUEST, doling out precious gold to fill him with fine Calentin wine during their midday meal. Uzo drank deep and often, while Annis tittered and Gem shook his head ruefully. Uzo had not often complained during their journey, but as the wine set in, he began to make long-suffering remarks about his fate.

"Am I to blame for the way I look?" he said, the words slurring slightly. "I only ever sought to be a warrior. Yet all my life, lechers have eyed me like a mountain to be climbed."

"That is, mayhap, an unfortunate metaphor," said Shiun. "But come now. I know you had lovers on the Seat. You have never wanted for fine company."

Uzo slumped over the table and shrugged. "I suppose I have had my share of good companions in my time, yes."

"There, you see?" said Shiun, smiling as she sipped her wine. "Do not look so morose. We all honor your great sacrifice in the name of the High King."

Loren and Annis chuckled. Uzo's scowl deepened, and he pushed his chair back from the table.

"I suppose I have had enough fun poked at me. I shall go and get this over with."

"Fare well," said Gem, who had not looked up from his food in some time. "Be safe."

Uzo gave the boy a small smile. He ruffled Gem's hair before walking away. "I shall. Best to put the matter from your mind, little master."

Gem's head came up, and he watched the Mystic go. Then he lowered his chin to rest on his folded arms again, looking a little less forlorn.

There was little to do until Uzo's return. They went to their room after they had finished eating, and there Loren and Annis sat discussing the map while the others rested. Annis read the names of various cities to Loren and explained some of her thoughts about them, the pieces she had been trying to put together in their search for Damaris.

"As we traveled, I sometimes wondered if she

might be making for Bertram," said Annis. "But I thought that would be folly. Bertram is not the capital, but all the same, the King's law has a strong presence. She would attract notice here, no matter how stealthily she traveled. It might have made sense as a brief waystop before some other destination. But when she began to cut back and forth across the northern countryside, I thought that possibility had vanished."

"Could it still be possible?" said Loren. "We lost her trail in Sidwan. What if she evaded us long before that? What if we pursued her retinue for the last week or so while she made for Bertram and beyond?"

Annis frowned. "Anything is possible. But if that is the case, we have almost certainly lost her."

A while later, Uzo returned at last. His jaw was set in a firm line as he quietly entered their room. His clothing was mussed. When he stopped before Loren, he gave her a quick salute.

"I have returned, Nightblade."

"No need for formality," said Loren. "Do we have what we need?"

"We do," said Uzo. "Kanja waits downstairs, there to lead us to Wyle."

From the other corner of the room, Shiun looked at him with a carefully neutral expression. "And did Kanja get what *she* needed?"

Annis nearly died from trying to restrain her giggling, and Loren hid a smile. Gem looked morose. But

Uzo only glared at Shiun. "Even when it points in a less desirable direction, my spear is still strong."

Loren leaped to her feet and clapped him on the shoulder. "And that is all we need to hear about that, I think. Thank you again, Uzo. Now let us go and fetch the moon-eyed smith while she is still amenable."

They left Chet in the room again and went downstairs, where they found Kanja waiting for them. A beatific smile played across the smith's face. She draped an arm across Uzo's shoulders and kissed his cheek before nodding warmly to the others.

"Greetings, all. Let us do our business. It is a fine evening for it."

"Fine indeed," said Loren. "We are ever grateful for your willingness to make an introduction."

"Oh, I am more than willing," said Kanja, stroking Uzo's hair. "And please accept my earnest wish for many more favorable dealings in the future."

Several of the common room's patrons looked at Kanja and rolled their eyes. From the way they muttered into their drinks, Loren doubted this was the first time they had seen the smith conducting such business. Uzo gave Loren a weary look. She hid a smile and gestured Kanja out the door.

The streets were lit with strange lanterns like Loren had never seen before. Their sides were made with parchment, not glass, and they were open at the top and bottom, with a small cover a finger or two above the top to keep their flames from falling prey to wind or snow. The paper gave them a warm, soft glow, less harsh than a regular lantern, and it bathed all the streets and walls of the city as they made their way along.

There were few dancers or other street performers here, the way there had been on the Seat or in Dahab. But as the sky above grew darker, some people climbed to rooftop balconies built into many of the houses and shops. There they would stand, leaning on a railing, and sing. The words were in no tongue Loren recognized, and the tune was unfamiliar, though it sounded old. Then she noticed that the words and the tunes blended together from one singer to the next, with just enough difference to tell they were somewhat different songs. It created an odd sensation as they walked, for the same song seemed to shift and meld into different forms of itself the farther they went.

Most of the party looked up at the singers as they went, mouths hanging open slightly in awe. But Kanja walked as if she did not even notice them, and Loren supposed that might be true, since she likely heard them often enough. But Shiun tilted her head back, a pleasant smile tugging at her lips. It was the look of one meeting a friend they had not seen in a long time.

"Why do they sing?" said Gem. His voice was hushed with reverence.

"It is a farewell to winter," said Shiun softly. "The calendar of Underrealm says that spring has come already, of course, but tradition dictates that they sing it on this night. That custom was built on the fading of the snows, and not the marks of some scholars upon a piece of paper."

"What luck that we should be here," said Annis. "To think that they only sing like this once a year."

Kanja and Shiun gave a quick snort of laughter together. "That is not the case," said Kanja. "Soon they will sing the song to greet spring. Then they will sing another song to mark spring's peak, and then another to say farewell to spring, and then *another* to greet summer, and so on. If you spend any length of time in the great Dorsean cities, you will likely grow sick of all the singing."

"I do not see how I could," said Loren. "I hope I get to hear it again, and often."

They reached the point where the two rivers became one and spun away westward. Each current was spanned by a great bridge. In the center of the confluence was a massive pedestal built of unyielding stone, upon which were hung many lanterns. From what Loren could see, it was crafted out of a rock that had been in the water already. Atop the pedestal was a great statue of bronze, mayhap six paces tall. She was a woman, that much was certain, clad in armor and with her long flowing hair splayed out in the wind. On her shield was a device of the sun.

"Renna Sunmane," said Annis with reverence. "She resided here in Bertram during the Kinslayer War."

"She did," said Kanja. "But that statue was built a long, long while after those times. Now they say she stands guard over the riverboats that wind along the waterways. I myself think she is a great nuisance that too many ships crash into. But who would waste the effort to remove such a large rock from the river, especially when many of the simpler folk nearly worship her?"

Annis scowled at the smith's back.

They crossed to Bertram's eastern district, built on the wedge of land between the two smaller rivers. Shortly after that, Kanja stopped in front of a large building. It looked like a simple shop, but its front door was locked and barred shut. Kanja began to lead them around to the back of the building, but Loren stopped her, turning to Uzo and Shiun.

"Wait here," she said. "I will take Annis and Gem inside. Only come after us if you hear trouble."

Shiun nodded, and she and Uzo took position to either side of the alley beside the building. Kanja gave Uzo a little wave as she left. He returned it with a sickly smile.

They followed her around the back of the building, where a small door led to an apartment built in the building's rear. She knocked, and soon they heard a voice on the other side of the door.

"Who is that?"

Kanja smiled at Loren and winked. "It is Kanja, you rascal."

"I can see that, my dear. I am asking about the others with you."

Loren looked closer at the door. She could not see a peephole. How could Wyle see them?

"I have brought some new friends who wish to meet you. For business."

"Normally, new friends are my favorite people. But recent events have soured me on company. Mayhap another time."

Kanja drew back, looking nervously over her shoulder at Loren's party. "But Wyle . . . I vouch for them."

"And I trust you implicitly, my dear. Yet I do not trust them."

The smith pulled nervously at her collar. Loren licked her lips and stepped forth. "Trust is not always necessary for business," she said. "Especially when such business may fill your pockets for many months to come."

A long silence stretched from behind the door. "That is a mighty promise. You do not know how deep my pockets are."

"Yet I know what I have brought to fill them."

Another long silence. When Wyle spoke again, Loren thought she could hear some amusement in his tone. "Never let it be said that I do not respect confidence—even when that confidence borders on arrogance. Come in, then, I suppose."

They heard a bar sliding. Kanja breathed a sigh of relief and reached out to open the door. No one stood inside. Loren saw only a steep staircase leading up to the second floor.

"Where is he?" said Loren.

"Upstairs," said Kanja. "Come."

She led them up the stairs. The second floor was entirely separate from the first, and a half-wall divided part of the back of the room from the front. The place looked as if it had once been well furnished. The chairs and cabinetry were of fine craftsmanship, fine rugs were on the floor, and Loren spotted dishes with gold and silver inlay. But the apartment looked as though a disaster had struck it. There were bits of splintered wood on the floor, as though some furniture had been destroyed in a fight and no one had yet tidied up. There were stains on some of the rugs, and while they might be wine, Loren suspected blood.

In a blue, winged armchair sat a dark man with sharp eyes. He wore a black vest over a long, cream-colored tunic, and dark blue pants that went into high leather boots. His appearance was immaculate, utterly at odds with the state of his dwelling. In his hand was a glass goblet full of wine, which he set down as he rose from the chair to greet them. Loren thought to herself that that was entirely unnecessary, since he must have been standing when they arrived, and had only sat so that he could stand up again. His eyes roved across Loren's little group, studying each one of them with interest. His gaze lingered long on Annis, and he blinked more than once at Loren's striking green eyes.

"Greetings to all, and a good evening to you," he said, bowing low. "As Kanja has no doubt told you, I am known as Wyle—or, likely, you knew that already, for I heard that you have been searching for me. But I do not think I know you, or have heard of you, and you are a bit younger than the friends I am used to meeting." His eyes flicked to Loren again as he said it.

"But . . . but Wyle!" cried Kanja. "What on earth has happened here?" She gawked at the destruction all around them.

"Nothing you should worry your muscular self about," said Wyle. "It is a small situation with which I have only recently dealt. I shall have the place in order by tomorrow."

Kanja still looked upset. But Loren cared little for whatever trouble Wyle had had, as long as it had passed. She stepped forwards to speak before Kanja could ask further questions.

"We are friends and travelers passing through, and our age does not diminish the quality of our goods. We have some items that we wish to sell to you, if you are interested. They are of the finest quality, and nothing we would want to sell where certain . . . red-clad friends might catch wind of it."

Wyle's eyes widened, and the corners of his lips turned down in thought. "Of course, of course," he said. "Naturally. Well, if we are to do business, then I should don my business garments. A moment, if you would."

He retreated to the back section of the room, where the half-wall hid him from view. Loren and Annis gave each other an odd look. Gem looked at Kanja and frowned. "Business garments?"

"Some finery of his, no doubt." Kanja gave a little smile. "I have seen him in many fine clothes, as well as none at all."

From his expression, Loren thought Gem might be sick.

Then they heard the crash of a window from the back of the room.

"Dark below," growled Loren.

She ran around the half-wall. A window in the front of the building had been broken, and Wyle was nowhere to be seen.

"Gem, down the stairs!" she cried. "I will go after him."

Loren ran to the window. Wyle was already halfway to the ground. There were tiles and bricks set in the wall. Loren had thought them a decoration, but now she saw they formed a sort of ladder leading down. An escape route, in case Wyle found himself cornered. Loren admired the precaution.

She leaped out the window and took the same route down. Wyle jumped the last two paces to the ground. He landed in a crouch and came up running.

But he had not predicted the Mystics. Uzo leaped out of the alley, hands grasping. Wyle seized the spearman's arm and flipped him around, then kicked his legs out from under him. Uzo landed hard on his back.

But Shiun appeared, driving a fist into Wyle's stomach. He fell to the street, wheezing.

Loren reached the ground a moment later, and Gem appeared just after. Loren helped Uzo to his feet. He had hit the back of his head when he landed, and he rubbed it ruefully while glaring at the smuggler. Loren tossed her head towards the back of the building.

"Bring him back to his hideout," she said. "This is not a conversation for the open air."

They took him back to the door leading to the staircase, but Loren commanded Shiun and Uzo to wait again. "One of you remain here, and one at the front of the building. I will not let him try the same trick twice, but be ready just in case."

In truth, she had no wish for the Mystics to learn of her magestones. Uzo and Shiun nodded and went to do as they were bid. Loren put a hand on Wyle's shoulder. He tried to shake her off, but before he could react she pulled one hand up behind his shoulder blades and shoved him up the stairs.

"Be still. You will not escape me a second time, but I have no wish to hurt you."

"You are hurting me now," said Wyle. But to her surprise, his tone was affable. He stopped resisting and walked up the stairs without further trouble. Once they had entered the apartment again, Loren released him with a shove.

Kanja still stood where she had been, eyes wide and

head swinging back and forth. "I do not understand. What is wrong?"

"A sudden change of heart has come over me," said Wyle. "I decided—rather abruptly, it is true—that I would rather not do business with these new friends."

"But why?" said Kanja, blinking.

Wyle sighed and rubbed at his temples. "Kanja, you are a lovely woman—if too trusting—and a more than passable lover. But you are a terrible judge of people. Your new friends are the King's law."

Kanja gasped and took a step back. Her eyes grew panicked, and she seemed as if she might run.

"He speaks the truth," said Loren. "But you need not fear."

"Not her, mayhap," said Wyle. He shook his head with a sigh. "But I hold no illusions for myself. What a tragedy. I am too pretty and too clever to die under the knives of Mystics. And just after ridding myself of another gaggle of troublemakers."

Gem gave a loud snort. Loren shot him a glare.

"You have no reason to fear us, Wyle, nor was that little display of yours necessary," said Loren. "We are not here to kill you, nor to put you to the question. But I think I would prefer the rest of our conversation to be conducted in private. If you do not mind?"

She tossed her head towards Kanja. Wyle stared at her for a moment, and then a slow smile crept across his lips. He went to Kanja and put his hands on her shoulders.

"Whether she tells the truth or no, neither of us gains anything by your being here, my sweet," he said. "Go, and take care of yourself. I will see you soon, if I can."

Kanja gave Loren one last uneasy look, but she nodded. Then she pulled in Wyle and kissed him deep and long. Loren and Annis studiously averted their gazes, and Gem openly made a gagging noise. But the moment passed, and then Kanja left through the apartment's back entrance.

Loren waved a hand at the staircase. "That one hardly did much to guard your presence here. Whatever made you entrust her with the secret?"

Wyle shrugged. "Kanja is a fine woman, as I said. And when someone comes to Bertram looking for those who deal beyond the King's law, they never look twice at a steelsmith. I wonder, in fact, how you found her."

"How painful it must be to wonder," said Loren.

To her amusement, Wyle very nearly pouted. "Painful indeed." The pout turned into the same curious smile she had seen earlier. "But now we have wasted enough time on . . . shall we call them pleasantries? I wish to hear the real reason you sought me. Servants of the King's law, seeking to deal with a man like me? I begin to think you may be even better friends than I first thought."

"We may be," said Loren. "It has come to my knowledge that you deal in certain goods of inestimable price. And because of that, we know that *you* know a great deal about the family Yerrin."

Wyle's amused look fell away at once. He folded his arms over his chest. "I feel my mind changing again. On second thought—or rather, third, or is it fourth?—I think I would rather not have any dealings with you after all."

"How unfortunate for you," said Loren. "We have come to the point where your preferences matter very little to me."

The smuggler's eyes narrowed. "How *did* you come to be here, anyway? You seem to know a very great deal about me, but I only know that you are the Nightblade."

That took Loren aback. "You know who I am?"

Wyle shrugged. "Rumors are one of the most—no, *the* most important tool of my trade. Many people whisper about the green-eyed girl in the black cloak." He pointed at her face, and then her body. "Green eyes. Black cloak. And servant of the King's law."

"You know more about me than you make it sound," said Loren.

"Just because I hear rumors, does not mean I rely overmuch on them," said Wyle. "Many tales about you are obvious lies, like how you escaped a constable's prison with a magic cloak. I wish to learn a truth or two instead."

Loren well remembered Xain's warning: Wyle had no love for the wizard, and would not be pleased to find out Loren was his friend. "It does not much matter how I heard of you," she said.

"Come now. I am at your mercy. Who cares if I know how it came about?" Wyle began counting on his fingers. "Was it Torbrik who told you? He has never forgiven me for that mess with the Calentin ship. Or mayhap that girl Jessa. She has caused me more than a fair share of troubles, and all because of a little misunderstanding over hemlock. Ah, I have it. It was that idiot of idiots, Robb. If I hear one more word from him about that den of lovers—"

"Stop!" said Loren. "If it will cease your prattling, I will tell you. I learned of you from Xain, of the family Forredar."

Wyle's already annoyed expression turned to dismay. *"Xain?* Sky above. A trio of misfortunes has befallen me at once. A girl made out of rumors, sent by one of the worst investments I ever made, on some business concerning the Yerrins. No. That is three reasons for me to have nothing to do with . . . with whatever this is, and any of the reasons would be good enough on its own."

Loren felt herself at somewhat of a loss. The man clearly wanted nothing to do with her, and whenever she tried to argue with him, he only talked circles around her. But in the moment's silence, Annis stepped forwards.

"You need not have any dealings with the family Yerrin at all," said Annis. "We only wish to know what they are up to. A small group of Yerrins have been crisscrossing their way across Dorsea. We need to find them. Surely you must know something."

Wyle eyed her. "How much do you know about the family Yerrin, exactly?"

Annis' cheeks darkened for a moment. "Quite enough."

"Oh?" said Wyle. "I wonder. I wonder if you know what they do to anyone who attempts to interfere with their trade. No, not even interfere, but just to skim a small bit on the side. I have had friends who attracted their attention—*have had,* I say, for none of them still live. And they were not quick in dying. The Yerrins saw to that. No, I do not imagine you know very much about the Yerrins at all, or you would not pursue them in the first place."

Annis smiled, though the expression was devoid of humor and held only a clear threat. Loren shuddered at how closely she resembled Damaris in that moment.

"You guess wrong. I myself am of the family Yerrin. You have the honor of addressing Annis, daughter of Damaris."

Wyle's mouth opened at once, as if to reply by reflex. But once he heard Annis' words, his voice died in his throat. His skin went several shades paler. At last he choked out, "I . . . I had not heard that you still traveled with the Nightblade."

"Yet you can see that I do," said Annis. "And I would *ever* so much appreciate your help. But of course, if you will not give it, I shall be forced to send a letter to my darling mother."

"You . . ." Wyle swallowed hard. "I know you would not. They say you have sundered yourself from her. There are precious few rumors about you, but they all agree on that."

"If so, they speak the truth," said Annis. "And certainly we are on no friendly terms. Yet whatever opinion she holds of me, my mother—and in fact, all my kin—would be most interested to learn the name of a man dealing in magestones, and just where in Bertram he might be found."

Wyle stared at her for a long, silent moment. Then his gaze rose to Loren, and he flashed her a wide smile.

"The Nightblade of the High King," he said, giving her a deep bow. "I am most pleased to make your acquaintance. It will, of course, be my pleasure to serve you."

EIGHT

Wyle had a broad, solid table of oak, and across it he unfurled a map, holding down the corners with large tomes bound in leather. When that was done, he had Annis lay out their journey in Dorsea thus far. They started with riding south out of Feldemar and crossing the Sunmane Pass, and then the mad criss-cross through Dorsea's western towns, finally ending in Sidwan where they had lost Damaris' trail. Gem soon grew bored by the conversation and went to sit in Wyle's great armchair, where he promptly fell asleep. When they had finished telling the tale, Wyle pursed his lips and pulled at the thin scrub of beard on his chin.

"That is quite the journey, and I hear little information that may help," said Wyle. "She could have thrown you from her trail long ago, and you never realized it until Sidwan."

"We thought of that," said Annis. "But to a man so clever as yourself, surely such a setback would be merely a distraction."

Wyle arched an eyebrow. "You wound me, my dear, though doubtless you do not intend to. There are some kingdoms where the word 'clever' carries a more sinister connotation, and Dorsea is one such."

Annis' eyes went wide, and she tilted her head to the side like a bird. "Is it? I had not the slightest idea. You *must* forgive me."

The smuggler hid a smile. "I shudder to think how sharp your wits will be in adulthood."

"I will choose to take that as a compliment," said Annis, giving a perfect curtsey.

"I think you are right that Damaris would stay well away from Danfon and the other major cities," said Wyle, looking back at the map. "It would simply be too great a risk. But then again, an unexpected course is often the best way to accomplish something nefarious. And it is well known that Damaris is both crafty and devious—meaning no offense to her daughter, of course. Very well. I will send word at once to my friends in the city, and we shall see what may be seen.

But there is nothing else we can do tonight. After I send my letters I will retire, and I suggest that you do the same. We must all hope that the morning will bring news."

"Well enough," said Loren. "In that case, there is only one matter more we must discuss with you." She looked at Annis and tapped her cloak where an inner pocket held her magestones.

"Ah, yes," said Annis. "We did not entirely lie to you when we came here. We *do* carry a certain valuable cargo, and we *do* mean to sell it—or at least a portion of it."

Wyle drew up, looking back and forth between them. "Truly? Agents of the King's law, dealing in magestones? Wonders never cease."

"I think these are days when all of us will see many things we have never seen before," said Loren. "What price would you give us for them?"

For a moment Wyle did not answer, only pulling at his beard again and staring at the table in thought. "Let us see . . . I could give you mayhap fifty weights per stone."

Loren's knees went weak. With fifty weights she could make a pauper's journey from one end of Underrealm to the other, and with a hundred she could do the same thing but eat like a king the whole while. She had heard often that magestones were very valuable, but she had never known just how much so. She thought back to when she had found Damaris' caravan in Selvan, its wagons containing secret compartments holding hundreds of magestones each. She did not have a great enough command of numbers to calculate how much coin that cargo would bring, but she guessed it was enough to buy half a kingdom.

And then she almost fell over as Annis immediately replied, "Eighty weights."

Wyle frowned. "Are you mad? On my best day I cannot sell them for eighty-five, and five weights of profit is nowhere near enough for the risk I take."

Annis rolled her eyes. "You can sell them for nearly double eighty-five, you brigand. We will sell them to you for eighty if you will buy at least ten of them."

The smuggler's frown deepened. "Seventy-five—but I will buy fifteen."

"Seventy-six."

Wyle threw his hands up in the air. "You are a merchant's daughter," he cried. "You should conduct yourself with dignity. It is unbecoming to haggle for scraps."

Annis spread her hands with a disarming smile. "I must preserve at least some of my dignity as my mother's daughter."

Wyle rolled his eyes just as she had—but Loren thought she saw him hiding a smile as well. "Very well. Seventy-six, you beggar. I shall collect the coins tonight and have them ready for you in the morning."

Loren did not think her tongue would work. Visions of piles and piles of gold weights danced in her mind. But she forced herself to be calm again, and she gave Wyle a little half-bow. "Though at first our meeting was fraught with tension, I am glad to have made your acquaintance regardless. We shall see you upon the morrow."

Wyle returned her bow with a deeper one. "And you, Nightblade. If I am still uneasy about our association, I grant at least that it will be an interesting one. I beg only that you do not make it interesting in the same way that Xain did—leaving me alone and forlorn upon a riverbank without a copper in my pocket."

Loren raised an eyebrow. "It seems that you and I have had at least some similar experiences with Xain, then."

"Oh?" Wyle looked surprised. "You should have told me from the beginning that you and the wizard were not friends. It might have changed my opinion of you."

"Our road together was long," said Loren. "Things changed."

Wyle sniffed. "Very well. I hope to hear the tale some time. But that will have to wait for another day."

Annis gave him an even deeper bow than he had given Loren. They roused Gem and left. Shiun waited outside the apartment's back door, and she pushed herself from the wall with a raised brow.

"Since I have not had to chase him down again, may I assume that negotiations went well?"

"Well and better," said Loren. "He will begin gathering information at once, and we will return in the morning. I think we can trust him to do as we have bid him, but just in case . . ."

Shiun nodded at once. "I will remain here to watch the building and make sure."

"Thank you," said Loren. "I shall send Uzo to replace you after the moons have begun to lower in the sky. We are all of us weary."

They fetched Uzo from the front of the building and made their way back towards their inn. Gem was nearly asleep as he walked, and Uzo had to keep a hand on the boy's shoulder to prop him up. Loren took advantage of the Mystics' distraction to step aside with Annis.

"How did you do that magic with Wyle?" she murmured.

"Hm?" said Annis, raising her eyebrows. "I did no magic."

"You sold him the magestones for thousands of gold weights!" said Loren. "When we first met, you did not even know what the stones were, much less their price."

"Oh, that," said Annis. She dropped her gaze and smiled, brushing a lock of hair behind her ear. "It is simple, really. It would have been better if I *had* known their value to start with, for I likely could have fetched a better price. But I had to let him make his proposal first. I knew he would bid far, far less than they were worth. Once he gave his first offer, I picked what seemed a good amount higher and worked from there. And not that it matters much, but he is not giving us *thousands* of gold weights—not much over one thousand, in fact."

Loren scoffed. "You speak as though that is not simply *unimaginable* wealth to almost all in Underrealm. Sometimes I forget you are a merchant's daughter in truth."

Annis' smile widened but for only a moment. "We shall have to find some way to store them safely, of course. He will likely give us the coin in lockboxes, and we can spread them between all our saddlebags. At some point we should find a banker."

Loren hesitated a moment. Annis noticed it and looked at her curiously. Loren's mouth worked for a moment before she spoke, more quietly and slowly than before.

"Let us not spread the coins among all our saddlebags," she said. "Just yours, Gem's, and mine. It would be better if Chet did not know about it at all."

There was a long silence between them as Annis looked away uncomfortably. "This is about your dream, is it not?" she said at last. "I could understand Chet wanting to leave, after . . . after what happened. But do you really think he would rob us into the bargain?"

"I do not," said Loren. "But remember that Chet knows nothing about the magestones. How would we explain where the coin came from in the first place?"

"Ah," said Annis, nodding quickly. "Of course. That is very wise. I should have thought—"

But her words died as the night's silence shattered. Deafening as thunder, the city's bells began to toll.

The sound made them freeze in their tracks, and Loren's hand went to her dagger. In all their journeys, they had heard many bells tolling in alarm, and her first thought was that somehow she had been discovered. But she realized that was a ridiculous thought.

A second thought flashed through her mind to replace the first: *Damaris.*

"Something is happening," she said.

Gem had been startled to full wakefulness, and now he cringed every time the bells tolled anew. "Is the city under attack?"

Loren turned to Uzo. "Go to Shiun at once. Make sure that Wyle does not try to escape in the confusion. If you must, escort him to join the rest of us at the inn."

Uzo nodded and ran off while Loren turned to Annis and Gem.

"Whatever this is, I do not like it. We must reach Chet at once."

They set off at a sprint, only slightly hampered by Annis with her shorter legs and longer skirts. Soon they found the inn and ran inside. Loren had planned to dash upstairs and find Chet. But she skidded to a halt on the threshold as she saw him there in the common room.

"Chet!" she said. "Are you safe? We heard the bells—"

"As did I," he said, "and I came down to see what the fuss was all about. Then a crier come to the square outside. He . . . he told us the reason for the bells."

His words died, and one hand rose to scrub at his face. His skin had gone ashen, and his fingers were shaking.

"Chet?" She almost lifted a hand to reach for him, but she pulled it back at the last second. "What is wrong?"

"King Jun, the king of Dorsea," said Chet. "He has been murdered. The crier said he was assassinated by the High King. Dorsea has joined the war on the side of the rebels."

They stood there in silence for a moment, staring at him. Then Loren shook herself out of her thoughts. The common room buzzed, and no one seemed to pay them any attention. But that might change. She had to get them out of sight.

"Upstairs," she said. "Let us speak no further word until we are safe in our room."

Annis began pacing the room's length even before Gem closed the door behind them. "This cannot be," she said. "It *cannot* be. Dorsea pledged its support to the High King. Jun was one of only three kings to do so at once. Enalyn would never kill him when she so desperately needs the support of the other kingdoms."

"It is a ruse, then," said Loren. "It must be some work of the Necromancer. Only they stand to benefit from the tumult this will cause."

"And my mother must be behind it," said Annis.

Loren frowned. "Damaris? What makes you think so?"

Annis shook her head, looking miserable. "It is just as Wyle said. She has done the unexpected. We thought she would stay away from the capital, just as she wanted us to think. She went there and put this plan in motion, knowing we would be unlikely to follow her and discover her plot before she could carry it out. We thought she would avoid Dorsea's king, but all along she meant to kill him."

"But assassinating a king . . ." said Loren. "That is no small feat. And she has only been in Dorsea a scant few weeks."

"Oh, she must have set events in motion long before," said Annis. "I should have foreseen this. We wondered if she still served the Necromancer, and now we know. Seizing power in Dorsea was a part of the grander scheme. Now this kingdom is a strong foothold. Indeed, Dorsea's betrayal is far worse than Dulmun's. Dulmun's strength of arms may be greater, but it lies far to the northeast. Dorsea is in the center of Underrealm, and it borders more kingdoms than any other. There is some small comfort: this threat would have been even greater if Damaris had managed to capture and hold Yewamba. From that stronghold, she could have staged assaults into both Feldemar and Calentin with relative ease."

"At least we thwarted her there," said Gem. "And we will stop her here as well."

"It will not be so easy," said Annis, shaking her head. "Yewamba was a mighty stronghold, but Damaris was isolated. Now she is in Danfon itself. She will have the full support of whoever has taken the throne after Jun's death. Yet I do not know how they think to thwart the will of the senate."

"You mentioned that before," said Loren. "What is the senate?"

"A body of twelve representatives, two each from the six states of Dorsea," said Annis. "They govern most domestic matters within the kingdom, while the king has ultimate authority when it comes to war. But even in that, the senate may gainsay him if enough of them unite in common purpose."

Gem sniffed. "That sounds hideously inefficient."

"It is meant to be," said Annis. "A precaution so that no mad tyrant can lead the kingdom to ruin through warmongering."

"Yet Dorsea is the most warlike of all the kingdoms," said Loren.

Annis raised her brows. "Spoken like a true daughter of Selvan. They are often embroiled in battles, yes, but they content themselves with small border skirmishes. The senate is supposed to keep the king from doing anything too consequential."

Loren bit back her first angry answer and took a deep breath before answering in a calm voice. "The people of Wellmont would say that Dorsea's actions have been consequential enough."

Annis spread her hands. "No kingdom is perfect. Some are merely less terrible than others."

Gem looked back and forth between them with an uncomfortable expression. "Mayhap we should put aside philosophy for a moment and consider our next action. It seems clear we must stop Damaris, as well as the new Dorsean king."

Loren heaved a sigh. Gem was right. Her dislike of Dorsea mattered little in the face of their current predicament. "Who would that be? Who would turn this kingdom against the High King?"

"I do not know," said Annis. "Jun is of the family Fei, and it will be someone else in that house who takes his place. But I do not know the royal families of all the nine kingdoms very well. I know only that Jun has no siblings, and so it will be one of his cousins, or mayhap an uncle or aunt."

"So we mean to pit ourselves against a king, then?" said Chet quietly.

Loren looked at him. He sat on one of the beds, leaning against the wall beside it. His knees were up, his arms draped over them. He was not looking at any of them, but only picking at his nails.

"Only so far as we must," said Loren gently. "It seems clear we shall find Damaris in the capital, and she is our true aim."

We hunt Damaris, she thought, wishing he could hear the words. *You said you wanted to see it through, to catch her. Stay with me at least that long, before you tell me you mean to leave.*

He glanced up, meeting her gaze. His face filled with the sad smile she had seen too often lately. "Very well. It appears we ride for Danfon."

Loren nodded. "Thank you," she whispered. Then she turned to the others. "But not at once. We aimed to get a good night's rest, and I still mean to. Gem, go to Wyle's hideout. Tell Uzo and Shiun to split the watch between themselves, and that we ride from the city tomorrow. Then return here as quickly as you can, and get to sleep. We should try to be up before the sun."

Gem gave a quick nod and flew from the room. Chet readied himself for bed and fell asleep almost at once. Loren prepared to do the same, but Annis stopped her for a moment.

"We should bring Wyle with us," she said.

Loren's brows rose. "Why?"

"He is a smuggler," said Annis. "Danfon will be in great turmoil, and the guards at its gates will be vigilant. We must enter the city with all possible discretion, and I do not doubt he can sneak us in without anyone seeing."

"That seems wise," said Loren, nodding slowly. "We will bring him, then, though I doubt he will enjoy it."

Annis grinned. "I do not think he has enjoyed any part of his dealings with us yet. What is one more unpleasant duty?"

Loren smiled. "Thank you again, Annis. Our quest would be doomed without you."

The girl waved a hand. "You would muddle through somehow. You always do. I only do my best to make things a bit easier."

"And you do a marvelous job. Good night."

They went to bed, Loren on the floor and Annis on the pallet next to Chet's. But for a long while, Loren's thoughts would give her no peace. She had wondered why her dreams had led her here. Now she had a guess. They had a smuggler now, who could help them enter Dorsea's capital without being seen. That seemed a boon, but if the dreams were truly meant to help her, they would have led her to Danfon long ago, before Damaris carried out this coup.

Her hands tightened to fists. Chet's misgivings about her dreams wormed their way into her mind. Yet she could not bring herself to ignore them as he wished. How could she, when they were the only help she had?

Back and forth her mind whirled as she lay on the room's floor. When Gem and Uzo returned, she shut her eyes and pretended to sleep, but slumber came slow. At last, shortly before Uzo went to replace Shiun, Loren's eyes closed.

NINE

The next morning, they found Wyle no more excited about their proposition than they had expected. The merchant greeted them drowsily in a fine coat of blue with golden trim, but he walked around his apartment in bare feet. He had cleaned the place up somewhat during the night, and there were now several chairs upon which to sit. When Annis explained what had happened and what they guessed about Damaris' role in the rebellion, he waved his hand in dismissal.

"I have learned of King Jun's death already, of course, and furthermore I know who has succeeded him. The man's name is Wojin, and he is Jun's uncle. Was, I should say. And I had already guessed that Damaris might have played some small part, though I am glad, of course, to hear it corroborated by such a capable mind as the Yerrin girl's. Ah, well. Our meeting has been a blessed one, and I have enjoyed every instant of it. Your departure aggrieves me, but I suppose it is fate's cruel wont to force such bitter partings."

Loren gave him a faint smile. "Then let your poetic heart rejoice, smuggler. We do not mean to part ways with you at all. I need someone to get me into Danfon, and that person must be well acquainted with secret ways and passages that the King's law would not use. Who better for such a purpose than the great and honorable businessman, Wyle?"

Wyle tried to turn his expression into a smile, but it only became something of a grimace. "I might have guessed that would be your aim. But your words are truer than you know: I am great and honorable, but I am a *businessman* above all. You mean to end a rebellion. There is little profit in such a scheme, and therefore I decline to offer my further service."

"Only the poorest of merchants can find no profit in a war," said Annis. "Surely you can find some way to draw coin from a venture like ours."

All humor left Wyle's eyes. He leaned over his thick table, planting his hands flat upon it. "I enjoy my jibes with you, girl. But never insult me that way again. I am no warhawk."

The sudden vehemence in his voice surprised Loren, and she felt ashamed without truly knowing why. Even Annis was taken aback for a moment, and Gem stared at Wyle with wide eyes.

"Our apologies," said Loren carefully. "Indeed, I would not work with one who earned coin from the deaths of others. But we do need you, and our cause is honorable. We do not aim to join the war in Dorsea, but to end the far greater war across all of Underrealm. If you help us, you will be serving the cause of the High King herself. Can you not imagine that she would be grateful for such aid? How full might your coffers be after she expressed that gratitude?"

Wyle drew back for a moment, pinching his chin between two fingers. But then he shook his head. "My coffers are plenty full, and from dealings that are far less dangerous."

"Less dangerous, but still beyond the King's law," said Loren. "I am the Nightblade. I serve the High King directly. Imagine it, Wyle. Imagine me in her council chamber, speaking to her of your bravery. Imagine her scrawling a writ upon parchment—a writ of amnesty for your past . . . shall we call them indiscretions?"

Annis stared at Loren in surprise, but only for a moment before recovering. "Think of it, Wyle," she said. "A bank account full of the High King's gold, and a paper that absolves you from past crimes. You could become an honest businessman at last, making far more coin than you do now, and never fearing a constable's noose. Even my family would avoid you if you had the High King's favor."

Twice Wyle opened his mouth to answer, pointing his finger at them as if about to present a counter-point. Twice he closed his mouth again, looking off distantly as thoughts seemed to flit behind his eyes. In the end he tilted his head at them with a wide smile.

"I will admit you present an attractive offer, though you hide insults within it. I have *always* been an honest businessman. But in this, you have changed my mind. My heart sings at the opportunity to be of further service to Her Majesty."

Loren sent Chet and the Mystics to fetch the last of the supplies they would need for the journey. When they had gone, Wyle brought out eleven lockboxes full of gold coins to pay for her magestones. Each box was made of iron and had a small latch at the bottom through which a lock could be placed. All the locks had the same key, which Loren took from Wyle and put in her coin purse. Each box held four rows of twenty-five gold weights each, and they were packed tightly with velvet so that the coins did not jingle when the boxes were moved. Annis insisted on opening all of the lockboxes to verify their count, and Wyle seemed to take that as a great insult.

"As though I am a swindler," he complained. "As though I would have lived this long in my line of work if I had acquired a reputation of shortchanging my customers."

Annis inspected the lockboxes, and then the pile of gold weights that would go directly into Loren's coin purse. She pointed at the pile. "There are thirty-eight coins here where there should be forty."

Wyle's eyes darted to the pile. He picked it up and fingered through it before looking at Annis uneasily. "An honest mistake. My apologies."

He put the pile down and pulled not two, but six extra coins from the purse at his belt.

"By way of amends," he muttered.

"Most excellent," said Annis, clapping her hands. "Let us store them for travel, then."

Loren and Gem had stood silent through the whole exchange, gawking at the money before them. More than eleven hundreds of gold weights. Before leaving the Birchwood, Loren would have laughed at the thought of a single person owning that much wealth. Since then, of course, she had learned that some people had much more. But to see such riches laid out before her and know they were her own . . . she suddenly understood the gold-lust in the tales of Bracken, the old storyteller who came to her village in her youth. They closed the lockboxes, and Loren put six of them in Midnight's saddlebags. The other five went into the bags of the horse that Gem and Annis shared.

They ate an early midday meal and rode from the city just before noon. Loren feared that with the news from last night, they might face extra scrutiny at the gate, but the guards waved them on.

"A good thing, that," said Uzo, after they had passed well beyond earshot of the gate. "I do not think it will be wise to flash our Mystic badges any longer."

"Why?" said Gem. "The Mystics have no quarrel with Dorsea," said Gem.

Uzo scoffed. "Do you think our order is free from the politics of the nine kingdoms? Every Mystic vows to serve no king but the High King—and now the Dorseans have declared the High King their enemy."

Loren glanced over her shoulder. "What about the Mystics in Bertram itself?" she said. "Are they not in danger?"

Shiun and Uzo looked at each other uneasily, but this time it was Shiun who spoke. "I do not think so. Not so far from the capital. Not yet. Our holdings in Bertram are strong, and the Dorseans would be loath to assault them without a pressing reason. As long as the Mystics do not take overt action against Dorsea, they should be safe. In Danfon itself, things may be different."

That thought remained with Loren for a long while. She knew the Mystics had a presence in almost every great city across the nine kingdoms—a castle here, a fortress there, sometimes in the heart of the population, sometimes in long-distant wilderness. But now the Mystics in Dorsea were cut off from the rest of their order—and now that she thought of it, so were the Mystics in Dulmun. For three months now, they had been isolated in a kingdom at war with the High

King. If the Mystics here now faced a brittle peace, could such peace have lasted so long in the very heart of a treacherous nation?

Some referred to the Mystics as the Tenth Kingdom. Many in their ranks had held great power before donning the red cloak, and if unified that power would be no less than that of a true king. Yet Loren saw now that their power was scattered all across the nine lands. It would be near impossible to consolidate it in order to achieve any end, great or small. Sometimes she was not sure of her own feelings towards the Mystics. Some, like Jordel, served high ideals. Others, like Uzo and Shiun, were honorable enough soldiers, willing to follow orders and fight for the greater good. Loren had met others who were self-serving and hungry for power. But she did not relish the thought of small pockets of the red-cloaked warriors suddenly finding themselves isolated in rebellious kingdoms, there to wait until the king finally decided to eliminate them.

It was only a short ride from the gates of Bertram to the King's road, and from there they pushed their horses as hard as they dared. They ate their supper in the saddle, only stopping once the sun was well below the horizon and its last light faded from the sky. The hard ride brought them to the beginning of the Moonslight Pass, the southern route that would take them through the mountains to Dorsea's northeastern reaches.

The next morning they climbed into the Greatrocks themselves. As a section of the King's road, the pass was well tended. The road was laid in stone, and in many places it went straight through the mountains themselves, where large clefts had been cut as if by a giant's axe. But it was a steep climb even so, and in some places the road had no choice but to cut back and forth, following the contours of the land.

The mountains were beautiful in the last days of winter. The well-cleared road left the travelers a great deal of unused attention to study their mighty peaks and splendid valleys. It struck Loren how different this mountain range could be, at different points along its length. She had first seen the Greatrocks to the south, where they had ridden with Jordel. Those peaks were high, but they were somewhat gentle, and the summer sun had painted their grey cliffs and stones in hues of warm red. Then they had come to the Greatrocks in the north, searching for Damaris and the stronghold of Yewamba. There the mountains rose into the sky like knives, mighty and sheer, but still covered in green, for the jungle climbed even to their utmost heights. The range they rode through now was somewhere in the middle. Though the peaks had been tamed by human hands, they still stood proud and regal, and each was covered in snow like a robe of office. Indeed, when the sun bathed the slopes in amber at the beginning and ending of the day, Loren was reminded of the white and gold of the High King, and she wondered if this might be the place from which those colors had been drawn.

The day's end found them in the town of Midgar, which meant 'waystop' in the ancient tongue of Dulmun, from the days when Renna Sunmane had conquered this land in the name of the first High King. It was an entirely appropriate name, for the town had been built for the sole purpose of being a place for travelers to rest as they rode the Moonslight Pass. There was a Mystic stronghold just outside the town, a little farther up the slope of the mountains, as though it had been placed there to oversee the town. Loren stared at it as they entered Midgar. The shape of the stronghold was all too familiar. They had seen one just like it in the southern Greatrocks. Jordel had told her that all ancient Mystic strongholds were alike, so much so that he would know the placement of every stone within it. It was still disconcerting to see the truth of his words.

They stopped at one of the town's more modest inns. Midgar had several, and for a moment Loren had the wild thought of staying at the finest of them. She had a great deal of newfound coin, after all. But she doused the thought in an instant. She had riches, yes, but she would not hold them long if she spent them too freely. So she guided the party towards the meanest-looking inn, which was called the Jolly Rat, though Wyle protested mightily.

"I have visited Midgar before, and I can tell you the Jolly Rat is aptly named," he said. "The rats are so jolly because they are well fed, and that is because the innkeeper lets them run freely through her kitchen and the guests' rooms. Let us board at the Silver Boar instead. If they have the same cook as the last time I was here, you will never taste finer boiled carrots in all your life."

"We stay at the Jolly Rat," said Loren. "Though you may go and eat your supper at the Silver Boar if you wish, and pay for it as well."

Wyle sniffed. "I am no beggar who must accept free meals, especially when they are served in such a place. I will indeed eat at the Silver Boar, and stop by the blue door afterwards into the bargain."

Loren flushed. The blue door was known across the nine lands as the sign of a house of lovers. She had not thought there would be one here so far from any city. "What you do is your own business, as long as you use your own coin. But since I would rather not leave you alone to do it, take Shiun with you. You can buy her dinner as well."

Wyle scowled. Shiun smirked at him, but then she shook her head at Loren. "If I may make a suggestion, Nightblade, send Uzo instead. He will be just as fine as a guard, and he would likely get some use out of the blue door, whereas I would not."

Indeed, Uzo looked surprisingly eager. Loren nodded at once. "Of course. I am sorry I did not think of it already, Uzo, after your service in Bertram."

Uzo ducked his head. "Do not trouble yourself, Nightblade. And thank you."

Wyle's expression had darkened still further at the

prospect of paying for Uzo's lover as well as his dinner. But the smuggler took one last dark look at the Jolly Rat and turned on his heel, beckoning Uzo to follow him. Uzo threw a wink over his shoulder and went. With a little smile, Loren watched them go before leading the others into the common room of the Jolly Rat. They quickly secured a room and stables and then bought dinner. Loren thought it looked a bit meager, but nowhere near so bad as Wyle had made it sound. Indeed, they had stayed in far worse places in their travels.

Gem spoke up as they settled into their seats. "Is it wise to let Wyle go off, do you think? If he puts his mind to it, he might yet evade Uzo."

"He will not," said Annis. "The prospect of the reward at the end of this journey will keep him close. Indeed, Loren, you offered him more than I would have. A royal pardon is not something easily obtained."

Loren shrugged. "I am not wise in all the politics of the nine kingdoms. Yet it seems to me that whatever small mischief Wyle has gotten up to here in Dorsea, it pales in comparison to the threat of the Necromancer and the rebellion. If he can help us deliver Damaris, and even the kingdom of Dorsea, I do not doubt that Her Majesty will grant him a life as a honest merchant."

"And if she does, she will have removed a smuggler who traffics in illegal goods," said Shiun. "He may even begin to pay taxes on his dealings, furthering the king's and the High King's might. It is the wisest of generals who can defeat an enemy by turning them into a servant."

Loren laughed at that, as did Gem. But Annis did not join them, and now stared morosely at her meal. Loren saw it and leaned over, placing a hand on the girl's shoulder.

"Annis?" she said. "Is something wrong?"

The girl's head jerked up, and she shook her head too quickly. "Not at all," she said. "My thoughts are far away. Forgive me."

Loren frowned. She glanced briefly at the others around the table and then back to Annis. "Come. Let us take a walk together."

"No, we . . . we should eat," said Annis.

"Yet you have scarcely touched your food," said Loren, pointing into the girl's bowl. "Stand and walk before I am forced to drag you."

They rose and left Chet, Gem, and Shiun to their meal, fetching their cloaks and stepping out into the wintry night. Annis gasped at the chill and rubbed her arms.

"Step lively," said Loren. "You should get the blood flowing. It will loose whatever words you have bottled up inside yourself."

"It is no great matter, truly," said Annis. "I know I am only being foolish. Yet I still find myself shocked that Dorsea joined the rebellion. It is difficult to imagine a greater disaster for the High King, and it was orchestrated by my own mother."

"Your mother's misdeeds are not yours, and they never have been," said Loren.

"I know that. Yet we are in pursuit of her, and I have bent all my thought towards finding her. I should have seen this coming." Annis spoke faster and faster. "But then again, *should* I have been able to predict it? Why should I? My mother is much older and, it seems, infinitely more cunning. I have begun to think this is a fool's errand. The two of us chasing her across the kingdom, I mean. It seems that we run off on one mad course of action after another. Yes, it seems like the right thing to do every time. But what if we are only making things worse? I—"

Loren put a hand on Annis' shoulder and squeezed. Not hard, but just enough to get her attention. Annis' words cut off at once, and she looked up. Loren smiled gently.

"I am sorry," said Annis. "Babbling is a difficult habit to break."

"You are being too harsh with yourself, as usual," said Loren. "It is as you said: Damaris must have been planning this rebellion for some time. If we had not followed her to Yewamba, and then to Dorsea, this still would have happened. And furthermore, she would be sitting safe in a stronghold of power, one that even the High King's armies might have had trouble removing her from. Mayhap our actions have forced her hand sooner than she wished to reveal it. Her strength now—and the strength of the Dorsean rebels—is likely less than it would have been if we had not remained on her trail, nipping at her heels."

Annis ran her hands through her hair, mussing it for a moment before pulling it back into place. "You are right, of course. And these things are what I keep telling myself. But after such a long pursuit with nothing to show for it, I am becoming a bit discouraged."

At those words, she glanced back at the inn. Loren frowned, and then she thought of Gem sitting inside. She shook her head and wrapped an arm around Annis' shoulder, pulling her close.

"It would be good to have *some* sort of victory," said Loren. "I agree with you there. Let us hope that one is just around the next corner—or the next turn in the mountain pass, as it may be."

Annis looked up at her and smiled. "Thank you, Loren. But now let us go inside and finish our meal, before I either starve or freeze to death. I am not sure which would come first, and I have no wish to learn."

Loren chuckled and led her back inside the Jolly Rat.

TEN

On the third day of their journey, they rode down the other side of the Moonslight Pass to find the city of Danfon laid out before them.

Dorsea's capital had been built at the very feet of the Greatrocks. There the River Marsden spilled from the foothills, winding its way north and east until it joined the Skytongue to form the border between Dorsea and Feldemar. The Marsden flowed throughout the year, for winter's chill was too weak to tame its mighty current this far north. Danfon sprawled wide across the landscape on both sides of the river, and beyond its walls, farmlands reached almost to the horizon. Loren had traveled the countryside east of here and knew it for a brown and arid place, but here the soil was rich and loamy, and it gave the capital a fine yield.

They paused as they reached the final bend in the pass out of the mountains. Now they stood on a flat place in the land that seemed built for the sole purpose of observing the city, which seemed only a stone's throw away. The streets, like Bertram's, were laid out in neat rows that crisscrossed each other in a simple pattern. Near the western walls was the king's palace. Its red tile roofs were free from snow, either because they were swept by attendants or because their height left them more open to sunlight. The tiles shone proud in the midst of the city, like a pattern of rubies set on a veil of white lace.

Loren was struck by a feeling both unsettling and all too familiar. She had seen the palace before. Her dream had not shown it from this angle, but still she knew it. And when she turned, she saw the Greatrocks looming above her just the same. The world seemed to spin around her for a moment, and she clutched tight at the horn of Midnight's saddle. The mare blew a loud snort as though she sensed Loren's disquiet.

"Welcome to Danfon," said Wyle. Despite the city's splendor, the smuggler looked at it with an upturned nose and a frown. "A city that I thought not to visit for a long time, if ever I returned here. We will ride around it to the river on the other side."

That distracted Loren from her thoughts, and she frowned at him. "The east? Why?"

Wyle arched an eyebrow at her. "Did you not hire me to sneak you into the city unnoticed? There are secret ways that only I and others like me know of, and I mean to lead you to them. But they cannot be traveled on horseback. To the east is a town called Yincang, and there I know a man who will care for our steeds while we see to our business in the capital. We should reach the town just after nightfall, and there I suggest we remain for the night."

"We should enter the city overnight," said Loren. "Doubtless we will attract less notice that way."

But Annis shook her head. "The capital will be in turmoil after the death of King Jun," said the girl. "This new king, Wojin, will have established a curfew. We will attract more notice if we are on the streets after dark."

"Just so," agreed Wyle. "And as for the secret passages, we are no less likely to be seen there after nightfall than during the day. Thieves and scoundrels—for so I am often called, very unjustly—do not keep the same hours as more honest folk."

After they came down out of the mountains, Wyle led them off the King's road to a smaller courseway that curved through the farmlands. The plots of land were all sunken into the earth, and there were no people out working them. Loren knew little of farming, but at home in the Birchwood there were many crops that could be planted even in winter. This stillness was strange to her.

"What do they grow here?" she said.

"Rice, mostly," said Wyle. "They will begin planting a bit late this year, for winter has lasted longer than it usually does. But the capital does not lack for food stores, and the king takes good care of his people when the seasons are unkind." He paused for a moment and shrugged. "Or at least, King Jun did. I know very little of Wojin's temperament, nor how he will care for his citizens."

Loren scowled, and her hands tightened on the reins. "I am surprised to learn that the Dorsean king cared so much for his own subjects. He gave little enough thought to the suffering of other kingdoms."

Wyle glanced at her. "You were no admirer of Jun, I take it."

"I did not know his name until only recently," said Loren. "Yet if he was the king of Dorsea, then no, I had no love for him."

"You refer to Wellmont, I assume," said Wyle. Loren jerked in her saddle and looked at him. Wyle nodded. "Your Selvan accent gives it away—and that is something you should try to rid yourself of, by the by. It is always better when others cannot guess everything about you simply from the way you sound."

"Why does everyone insist I have an accent?" growled Loren. "How can I rid myself of it if I cannot even hear it?"

"Surely you can recognize that your voice is different from mine, and from the Yerrin girl's," said Wyle. "Even the boy's voice is harder to place than yours. In any case, you do yourself no favors with your concern for Dorsea's border squabbles. The Battle of Wellmont was little more than an overenthusiastic war holiday for our great king. Former king, I should say."

"You say those words easily," said Gem quietly. His gaze was far away. "But we were in the city when it was attacked. It was far from a holiday."

Wyle only shrugged, increasing Loren's irritation. "Battles rarely seem so to those who experience them, which is why I make a habit of avoiding them. But all manner of mad rumors have been spun about Wellmont since that attack. Something happened there, they say, that has turned the greatest heads in all the nine lands."

Annis arched an eyebrow. "I presume you include yourself in that company?"

Wyle shook his head quickly. "Oh no, dear girl. I count myself an honest man of great wit, but I am aware of my own insignificance. I am no mighty figure in the affairs of the nine kingdoms, nor would I wish to be so. A life of good food and good wine and some little excitement is enough for me."

Loren did not wish to speak further of Wellmont, but Gem turned to the smuggler with interest. "What did you mean before?" he said. "What happened at Wellmont?"

Wyle shrugged. "Rumors and speculation fly, but the truth is not so easily found. It seems that certain powerful parties have been trying to conceal the truth of the matter, and that is most interesting. I do not suppose you noticed anything unusual while you were there?"

"Other than the battle itself?" said Gem. "That was unusual enough for me."

"Enough of this talk," said Loren. "I do not wish to hear more about Wellmont."

"As you wish," said Wyle. The party fell silent for a time.

They followed the road in its wide loop around Danfon to where it met the Marsden half a league to the east. There they found a great construct of stone and iron, with many great pipes sticking out of the riverbank to empty into the waters, pouring a steady stream of refuse. The smell of it struck them hard even in the cold air. Gem turned away and pinched his nose, shoulders heaving.

"There you have it," said Wyle. "The secret passages. Danfon's sewers are some of the best in the nine kingdoms, and one can get entirely lost inside them. Which means, of course, that it is easy to avoid being found."

"Sewers," muttered the boy. "I had hoped I had escaped sewers forever when I left Cabrus."

Wyle laughed and shook his head. "For those who skirt the King's law, sewers are like a second home. You should enter a new line of work if you seek to avoid them."

Uzo glared at the smuggler. "We *are* the King's law."

Wyle gave Loren a broad wink. "Of course you are."

He turned them away from the sewers and took them back to the road, which went east for a ways before turning south to reach the little town of Yincang. The sun had disappeared over the Greatrocks by the time they reached it, and twilight had set in. Yincang had no wall, and so they came unchallenged to its streets. Wyle took them straight to the inn. It was a small, nondescript building with only one floor, smaller than the stable at its rear.

"Many travelers like us leave their mounts here while they do business in the city," said Wyle. "This place was built to take better care of horses than humans."

The innkeeper, a spindly man with a thin beard, took their coin without comment and directed them to three rooms where they spent the night. They woke before dawn, dragging Gem from bed as usual, and set off for the capital.

It was an hour's brisk walk to the sewers. A small staircase led down from the riverbank to the opening of the pipes, but there was no platform leading directly inside. They had to take a few precarious hops from the end of the staircase along the water's edge before they could get a handhold on one of the pipe's edges.

One by one they pulled themselves up and into the dark tunnel. Loren helped Annis make the climb, but Gem leaped up by himself, eschewing her help. His foot slipped, and his shoe came down in the sludge with a *splash.*

"Ugh!" he cried, lifting his foot up. "What do the people of this city eat? That smells ten times worse than the sewers of Cabrus."

Wyle flashed an easy smile. "We spice our foods well in Dorsea, and nowhere more so than in the capital. Alas, our concern has never been what some foreigner will think of the smell of our shit."

Annis blushed at the smuggler's frank words. Wyle seemed not to notice, and he led them on through the sewers without a pause. The passages twisted and turned, intersecting with each other in such a confusing manner that Loren was lost almost at once. Soon the smell of the tunnels became little more than a background sensation in her mind. She focused on keeping one hand on the wall and her feet out of the muck that ran just below the narrow walkway.

After a time, she became aware of a noise. It grew steadily the farther they walked: a low, murmuring hum that echoed gently from the stone walls around them. Soon she placed it. It was the sound of many voices, human and animal both, as well as the low rumbling of wagon wheels. They were under the city.

"Have we passed beyond the walls?" said Loren. "When will we surface?"

"Soon enough," said Wyle. "But I do not want to lead you back into the sunlight in the middle of some busy thoroughfare. It would not do to have King Wojin's soldiers catch sight of us climbing out of the sewers in the middle of the street. There are back alleys where no one will observe us."

"And the smell will be worse there, I imagine," grumbled Gem. Loren shushed him.

The smuggler was as good as his word, and soon he led them up a ladder that took them into the open air. They had been in the sewer for hours by that time, and Loren gasped at the smell of cool, fresh air again. She could almost taste it on her tongue, and it seemed sweeter than honey.

Wyle paused for a moment to get his bearings. "There is a place not far from here where we may settle in," he said. "The innkeeper always has a warm bath ready with perfumes on hand, and she knows better than to ask me very many questions."

They came to the inn shortly, and Loren paid for their rooms. Some of the patrons in the common room turned their noses up as the party walked through, and the innkeeper offered them baths without being asked. They took turns, for there were only four tubs, but Loren commanded them to hurry.

"I wish we had not spent a night in Yincang," she told them, "and I want to make up for it by getting straight to work. I would rather not rest until we have spent at least some time in the city learning what we can."

After they were refreshed, they ate a quick meal and planned their next move. Wyle had many contacts in the city, but he did not think it wise to bring a large party with him when he went to visit them.

"Take Shiun with you," said Loren.

Wyle put a hand to his breast, frowning. "Do you not trust me? I would neither run off on my own nor betray you, for I have always been—"

"—an honest businessman. Of course," said Loren, raising an eyebrow. "My assurances, smuggler, that she will only be there for your own protection."

His smile grew somewhat forced, but he bowed gracefully in his chair. "Of course. How thoughtful of you."

"The rest of us will get a feel for the city's mood," said Loren. "Chet and Uzo, visit some taverns and inns, any place that the city folk gather to have a drink. See what they think about the new king, and whether or not anyone has noticed the presence of the family Yerrin within the city walls. I will take Annis and Gem with me and visit shops. We can tell them we are gathering supplies to go on a journey. Let us try to get a few tongues wagging while we barter for prices."

ELEVEN

With their plan formed, they quickly finished their food and set off into the streets. Loren took Annis and Gem to a marketplace near the inn.

They had lodged in one of the city's finer districts, which must have been a deliberate choice of Wyle's; the smuggler enjoyed a good bed and good wine. Now they passed between stores with fine luxury crafts displayed in the windows, which were often paned with glass and framed by ornamented wrought iron. Annis took the lead at once and led them towards the first shop—a tailor. Just before they reached the door, Loren paused and turned to her.

"Barter hard for everything we purchase," she said. "And if the price is too high, let us take our business elsewhere. We are only here for information, and it looks like the goods here are expensive."

Annis tilted her head. "We will have to spend some coin, Loren. We have plenty of it now, and a merchant's tongue never wags so freely as when their purse is being filled."

"We do have coin, but that was not the case a few days ago, and I did not enjoy it," said Loren. "Our gold may have to last us a long while. I do not have an endless supply of magestones to sell, after all."

Annis arched an eyebrow at her. "Do you think I would waste our funds? I am a Yerrin, Loren. I can buy information without emptying our purse. My mother taught me that much, at least."

"Oh, let her handle it, Loren," said Gem. "I should so love a new suit of clothes."

Loren frowned. "You will only get them filthy. Indeed, I think you know some spell to coat your garments with grime, for it seems to happen instantly."

Gem scowled. Annis giggled at them both. "Trust me, Loren," she said. "This is why you have brought me along, after all."

Loren sighed. "Very well. Of course I trust you—and I brought you because you are my friend, not just because you are useful."

Annis smiled and led the way into the shop. Inside, they found the tailor to be a man both portly and incredibly short, a finger shorter even than Annis. At first he looked at them with disdain; though they had just bathed, their clothes were still worn from long leagues on the road, and were modest besides. But when Annis flashed a pair of gold weights in her palm, his demeanor changed at once.

"Of course it would be my pleasure to serve you," he said, beaming a smile. "Do you want new clothes for further travel, or something a bit more elegant for functions within the city?"

Annis eyed the fine gowns displayed on mannequins along the walls. But after a moment she turned from them with a quiet sigh. "Indeed, we mean to ride from the city soon," she said, "though it pains me to refuse such dresses as yours. Such fine craftsmanship is rare to see, though I should have expected it from an establishment as well kept as this."

The merchant's smile grew still wider, and he bowed. "You learned your manners too well, for they compel you to be overly generous. Mine is a humble shop. But let me see what insufficient garb I can clad you in. My only hope is that you remember this mean little place with some fondness."

Shelves of fine cloth ran along the shop's back walls, and there were more standing shelves in the center. He led them along the rows, bouncing on the balls of his feet and pointing out this or that weave and color, inviting them to feel the textures. Loren was glad she had just bathed, or she would have feared to smudge dirt all over the bolts of fine fabric.

Annis appraised everything in the shop with an expert eye. Loren remembered how they met almost a year ago, when she had snuck into a Yerrin caravan just south of the Birchwood. The wagons had been filled with fabrics, for the Yerrin's chief trade was textiles—at least on the surface. Loren did not know much about clothing, but she guessed that the Yerrins trafficked in only the best, which must have been why Annis' interest alighted only on the shop's most precious samples.

At last Annis selected a few different materials. Once she had, the tailor took them back to the mannequins. He offered suggestions of various cuts, pointing to some riding dresses for her and a suit of clothes for Gem. The clothes were far too large for the boy, but the tailor promised he could deliver the same look on Gem's slighter frame.

"And for you?" he said, turning to Loren. "A riding dress as well, mayhap? Or a shirt and trousers?"

Loren balked. "Me? I do not require anything new," she said.

"Oh, yes you do," said Annis. She pursed her lips, tapping them with a finger. "But something quite different for her, I think. Not a dress, certainly, but not a suit like Gem's, either. Here."

She went to the back corner of the shop. There stood a mannequin in fine clothes that yet seemed entirely useful—somewhere between a peasant's garb, meant for hard work on a hot day, and a suit that a noble might wear. Loren could see at once that the tunic and pants would be easy to move in, and yet they had an elegant sort of flair. There was also a vest with many stylish pockets that buttoned shut.

The tailor turned to Loren with wide eyes, and a little smile played at his lips. "Ah, I see it at once," he said. "Yes, of course. Perfect. And the material?"

Annis took him back to the shelves. She must have anticipated this, for she immediately pointed out a few bolts of cloth that were all black or dark grey. But then she went to the next shelf over and pointed at a bolt of muted green velvet.

"Trim it in this," she said. "For the eyes."

"Of course, of course," said the merchant. To Loren's surprise, he was very nearly bouncing in anticipation. "And might I suggest this for the inside of the vest? You will see only a flash of it when she moves, of course, but that will make all the difference." He put his hand on a bolt of satin, green as well, but closer in color to the sea.

Annis gave a sharp clap, her eyes shining. "Sky above. It is perfect. Mayhap on the inside of the collar as well?"

The tailor snapped his fingers. "Just so. It is the final piece to make it perfect. You have a fine judgement for this, my lady. I am further humbled by your presence in my modest place of business."

"Modest you may be, but not deservedly so," said Annis. From the pouch at her waist she pulled four gold weights. These she placed in the tailor's hand, and then she deliberately pulled forth another and added it to the pile. "I hope we can retrieve the clothing tomorrow."

"I will delay some other orders to ensure it," said the tailor. "But your offer is far too generous." Yet Loren noticed his fingers closed over the gold at once.

"Not at all," said Annis. "For the quality I see here, I think I make a more than shrewd bargain."

The tailor bowed lower than ever before and drew them to the back of the shop to take their measurements. Annis went first, holding out her arms while he pulled out a ribbon and ran it along her limbs. She smiled as he did it, but then her brow furrowed for a moment.

"I do so hope the road is safe to the west," she said. "What a shame it would be for our new garments to be endangered by bandits."

The tailor frowned at that. "Things are uncertain these days, to be sure."

Annis nodded. "Still, I am certain that Wojin—pardon me, King Wojin—will maintain order."

That drew a snort from the tailor. But he quickly suppressed it, and Loren saw him look askance at Annis. He tried to pass it off by coughing quietly.

"It sounds so strange to say." Annis shook her head. "King Wojin. My heart breaks for King Jun. I saw him once, you know. He was a good man."

"He was that," said the tailor fervently. "It was my

great pleasure to make clothing for many members of the royal family—though never King Jun himself, of course. I was invited to the palace more than once, and though I never had the honor of meeting His Grace, I saw him on occasion. He was a regal man, and so handsome. Not like . . . well, I mean to say that we will not see his like again for a long time."

"I can only imagine your sorrow at his passing," said Annis. "Yet at least his kinsman sits the throne."

"That is a blessing, I suppose," the tailor grumbled. "And Wojin has what he wants, in the end. That is all for you, dear. Young master, if you would?"

Gem stepped into Annis' place, his chest puffing out at the title of "young master." Annis drew aside, her eyes widening.

"Do you mean to say that Wojin desired the throne already?" she said. Her voice dropped almost to a whisper. It was the voice of a girl sharing some bit of scandalous gossip with a close friend.

The tailor responded in kind, looking over his shoulder at her and giving a wink. "That is the most ill-kept secret in Dorsea, and mayhap all the nine kingdoms. Wojin was the youngest brother of King Jun's mother, Min, of course."

"Of course," said Annis, nodding as though everyone knew it. Loren hid a smile.

"Well, everyone in Dorsea knows Wojin resented the throne passing to his nephew when Min passed away. Later, when King Jun's son, Senlin, was born, they say Wojin flew into a rage that lasted for days." The tailor sighed and shook his head. "Still, that was a long time ago. Long before King Jun met his end—at the hands of agents of the High King, or so they say." He snorted again, louder this time, and rolled his eyes.

Annis' eyes grew still wider. "Do you not believe it?" she said, her voice a sing-song.

The tailor's eyes narrowed, and he paused before answering. "The intrigues of palace life are far above my station," he said slowly. "Keep your head from the clouds lest it be removed, or so they say. Yet I have my doubts."

A thought struck Loren all at once. "And what of those others?" she said. "They say Wojin has the support of some foreigners, recently arrived here at the capital. I heard the family name, but it escapes me . . . Yamen? Yarvin?"

The tailor went still. "Yerrin? The family Yerrin?"

Loren snapped her fingers. "That was it. Yerrin. Did they not arrive here only just ahead of King Jun's death?"

"I had not heard that." The tailor pursed his lips. "I wonder . . . hm."

Over the tailor's shoulder, Annis gave Loren a small smile, but she also shook her head. Loren shrugged and turned to look out the shop's window. "I do not mean to suggest anything untoward, of course. I am a stranger to this city, after all. I only repeat what I have heard."

The tailor went silent after that, and Annis deftly turned the conversation to talk of lighter matters. But after they left the tailor's shop, she fixed Loren and Gem with a look.

"That was most telling," she said. "If the first shopkeeper we met was willing to whisper of such rumors, that means many in the city must secretly believe them. And what a stroke of genius, Loren, to plant the idea of my family's involvement. Dorseans are not fond of foreigners meddling with their kingdom. Word will spread, and when it returns to us we may learn something of my family's plans."

"Indeed," said Gem quickly. "I had thought of doing the same thing, of course, but you beat me to it."

"Of course you did," said Loren, arching an eyebrow. "But what can we do with such information?"

Annis shook her head. "Nothing yet. But it is a start. Let us go to a few more shops and see what else we may learn."

As it turned out, there was little else. They went to a cobbler, a carpenter, a steelsmith, and some other little shops of various trinkets and oddities. Most of the owners seemed to hold a similar opinion to the tailor, but none expressed it so plainly. Loren wondered if that might be because they did not spend their coin so freely at the other shops, but she did not encourage Annis to spend more. The girl clearly knew what she was doing.

A few hours before sundown, they made their way

back to their inn. Uzo and Chet sat in the common room, and both had clearly had a few cups of wine. Chet's nose and cheeks were ruddy, and when Loren asked Uzo how they had fared, the Mystic blinked three times before answering.

"We did well enough," he said slowly. He leaned closer and dropped his voice. "Certainly there is some disagreement in the city about Wojin taking the throne. No one was willing to speak very plainly, but there was much to be read in their quiet words and sidelong glances. It seems King Jun is greatly missed."

"It was much the same with us," said Loren. "That is good for our purposes, I think. If we faced a happy populace with great love for their liege lord, I think it would be harder to seek information about the Yerrins."

"I find myself ever more curious about the senate," said Annis. "If the kingdom does not support King Wojin, the senate may be persuaded to take action against him. Hopefully Wyle's contacts will know something of that. I am interested to hear what he has to say when he returns."

Loren nodded—and then she noticed Gem sitting very still, his eyes darting furtively over her shoulder. She barely stopped herself from following his gaze.

"Gem?" she said quietly. "What is it?"

He frowned. "Mayhap it is nothing. Only there is a girl over there—no, do not turn and look, any of you. She seems very interested in us. I have caught her looking at our table often."

Loren's stomach lurched. What if it was some spy of Damaris'? That seemed impossible. The merchant could not have heard about their presence in Danfon so soon. Yet Loren had learned long ago that the Yerrins could not be underestimated.

"I will fetch us some wine," she said. The others nodded.

Loren stood and made her way towards the bar. As she did, she stole a surreptitious glance at the girl. She wore the simple garb of a Dorsean peasant, loose pantaloons and a tunic that gathered at the wrists. She wore a wide-brimmed hat like many in the city, and her hair was black, as was common here. Yet her features were a bit softer than a typical Dorsean's, and her freckles were unusual in this kingdom. The girl did not look up—indeed, she studiously turned her gaze away. But Loren sensed a tension in her.

Loren bought a bottle of wine and returned to the table. "She does not look dangerous, at least," she said quietly. "If she is a spy, what then?"

"We should capture her," said Annis. "She may be able to help us find my mother—if indeed that is who sent her."

"Agreed," said Loren. She gave Uzo a quick look. "But we must be careful. We need her alive."

Uzo rolled his eyes and nodded.

"Very well," said Loren. "Everyone come with me."

She rose, leaving her cup and the wine. Quickly she went towards the inn's front door, and the rest hastened to follow. Just before stepping outside, Loren saw the girl shoot up from her table.

Loren darted to the corner of the inn and directed the others to file around the side of the building. She went last, waiting until the girl started to emerge through the front door. She timed it so that the last flap of her cloak was just visible as the girl stepped outside.

Quickly she directed the others to hide in the alley's dark corners. She herself stood behind a stack of crates. Soft footsteps sounded from the street. Loren drew a throwing knife from her belt.

The girl stepped into view. Loren threw the dagger, but aimed wide. The blade plunged into the wall near the girl's face, making her jump. Uzo pounced, snatching her arm and clapping a hand over her mouth. Loren stepped up beside him and slowly tugged her dagger free to sheathe it.

"Hello," she said amiably. "You seem most interested in our little party. Why?"

The girl only stared at them with wide, terrified eyes. Uzo withdrew his hand slowly, ready to replace it if she tried to scream. But the girl made no sound at all.

Loren sighed. "How long have you been following us?"

That made the girl glance at Uzo and Chet. "I was not following you. I was following them."

"Fair enough," said Loren. "Why?"

"I . . . I heard them asking questions about Wojin."

"And do you work for him?" said Loren. "Or do you work for the family Yerrin?"

The girl's brow furrowed. "Who?"

Loren glanced at Annis. The reaction seemed genuine. Mayhap the girl was a skilled liar, but Loren did not think so. Annis gave a barely perceptible shake of her head.

"What is your name?" said Loren.

"I . . ." The girl's voice faltered. She drew herself up straighter. She had some spirit then, and not just a pretty face. "I am Keridwen, of the family Ogun. Why are you in Danfon?"

Loren cocked her head, unable to keep herself from a small smile. "That is a proud question to ask ones who hold you captive."

Keridwen blushed, but she did not relent. "Are you here to help the king?"

"We do not know Wojin."

Keridwen shook her head quickly. "Wojin is not the true king."

Annis stepped forwards. "Yet he sits upon the throne, for King Jun is dead."

The girl's eyes widened and darted around nervously.

Sky above, thought Loren.

She gently pushed Uzo aside. He moved, if somewhat reluctantly, and Loren stepped within a pace of Keridwen. From her cloak pocket, she pulled her writ from the High King.

"Can you read?"

Keridwen stared for a moment before nodding slowly. Loren handed her the writ. Keridwen opened it and read it. Loren saw the color drain from her face and then come rushing back in a flush.

"You serve the High King," she said. "I hoped, but I could scarcely believe . . ."

"And now I ask again," said Loren. "Why did you follow my friends?"

Keridwen seemed to steel herself, and she drew up even straighter than before.

"King Jun was not killed," she said. "He is still alive. And if you truly serve the High King, I will take you to him."

TWELVE

After they had recovered from their shock, Loren sent Gem to check the inn. But he returned to report that Wyle and Shiun had not yet returned. At first Loren wanted to wait for them, but Annis counseled against that.

"The city has a curfew now," she said. "Nightfall is close at hand, and we will have a harder time of it if we do not go at once."

"And I do not think you should go at all," said Chet. "If this is a trap, you will be in grave danger. Send one of us as an intermediary instead."

"It is not a trap," said Keridwen, frowning.

"And besides, I *am* the intermediary," said Loren. "Though I think you are right in one respect. Not all of us should go. I will take Annis. The rest of you remain here in case something goes wrong."

"I am coming as well, of course," said Gem. "But you knew that already."

Loren sighed and turned to Chet and Uzo. "Wait here for Wyle and Shiun to return, and tell them what has happened. We will send for you as soon as we know it is safe."

"Yes, Nightblade," said Uzo.

Chet's eyes were troubled. "I do not like this."

Loren gave him a smile. "This could be the best news we have had in some time. If Jun remains alive, he can doubtless help us get to Damaris. I must at least try."

He turned away. "I see that. But please, return as quickly as you may."

Loren nodded. She had to stop herself from reaching out to take his hand. In the back of her mind, a voice whispered. *He did not insist on coming with you. Is this when he plans to leave?*

She forced the thought away and turned to Keridwen. "After you."

Keridwen nodded and raised her hood before leading them into the street. Loren and the children did the same as they passed through the crowds. They made their way south and west, and soon they had come very close to the place where the river entered the city. Not far away was the palace itself, but Keridwen turned from it and took them due west. Here the homes were all grand and towering, with multiple floors and little courtyards walled off from the rest of the city. This must be where the mightiest families lived. It had been the same on the High King's Seat and the other great cities Loren had visited: power gathered to power, and wealth to wealth.

Soon they came to a manor with a hipped roof and two great wings stretching forth from either side of the front door. Surrounding it was no stone wall, but only a wrought iron gate. Guards watched them as they went around the side. Two more guards stood at the smaller rear entrance. When Keridwen threw back her hood, they nodded in greeting.

"Welcome back," said one of the guards. "But who are these with you?"

"Friends," said Keridwen. "They are here to help the mistress's special guest."

The guard looked at her companion. He shrugged, and she turned back. "We shall have to send word."

Keridwen nodded. "Of course."

The second guard left to deliver the message. Keridwen stood back, folding her arms to keep warm. Loren appraised the manor.

"Whose home is this?"

Keridwen glanced at her and then at the home. "She is a merchant. Her name is Yushan of the family Ying. She remains loyal to—" She paused to look around, but the street was empty save for the guard. "To King Jun. She has helped us conceal him since Wojin's betrayal."

"Is she trustworthy?" said Annis. "Wojin knows the King is alive, of course, and I imagine he has offered a considerable sum for his capture."

"I imagine he has, but we have heard no word of it," said Keridwen. "It is not exactly something he can publicly declare, since his right to the throne depends on His Grace being dead already."

Soon the second guard returned, and he gave the first a curt nod. She opened the gate and motioned them all inside, and Keridwen took them in through the manor's service entrance.

Just inside, they met the merchant Yushan. She was tiny and fat, her round head balanced on her round body like a snowman's. As Loren and the others shook the snow from their clothing, she took them in with sharp eyes.

"Well met. I am Yushan, of the family Ying. I was told you are here to help?"

"And to receive help in return," said Loren. "We serve the High King Enalyn."

Yushan's eyes flashed. "I trust those who are here in my employ, but even my trust only goes so far. I would ask you not to speak so plainly—not of whom you serve, nor of anything you might see while you are here. Absolute discretion is the only thing that has kept my special guest alive so far. Do you bear any proof that you are who you say you are?"

Loren produced her writ, and Yushan scanned it quickly. But her hard look softened not a whit. "It looks to be in order," she said. "Yet I still find myself suspicious. We only sent for aid a few days ago. How did you respond so quickly?"

"That is easily answered," said Annis. "We did not respond at all, but were traveling on other business when we heard of the turmoil in the capital. We came to Danfon with no idea that your special guest was alive, for we pursued another goal entirely."

Yushan sniffed. "That has the ring of truth to it. Very well. Follow me—but be warned. I have guards aplenty, and not only the ones you can see. You will not come too close to my special guest, or they will cut you down. The fact that two of you are children will not stay their hands."

"Children?" said Gem, lifting his chin. "I would wager I have seen more battles and traveled more miles than you have."

Loren slapped his shoulder hard. But to her surprise, Yushan's face finally cracked into a smile.

"I like you, boy," said the merchant. "Come, then."

She snatched Gem's hand and drew his arm into her own as she led them into the manor. Gem looked back at Loren in a small panic as she forced him along, but Loren only smiled at him and shrugged.

Keridwen walked beside Loren and Annis as

Yushan took them through the rear entry hall into the kitchen, and then opened the door to a staircase leading down. At the bottom of the staircase was a pantry with shelves along the walls. But no one waited within. Loren's hackles rose, fearing a trap.

Yushan turned to them. "Keridwen, if you would? My bones are old."

Keridwen nodded and went forwards to one of the shelves. She knocked on the side of it, thrice and then twice. After a long moment's pause, four knocks sounded from the other side. Keridwen squatted and took one end of the shelf, heaving it from its place.

"Let me help," said Loren. She seized the shelf, and Keridwen gave her a grateful smile that made her freckles dance. They swung the shelf out together.

Behind the shelf was a small doorway that Loren had to stoop to get through. A chamber lay beyond, with rugs on the floor and chairs and a table in the center. But the room was empty. Loren wondered briefly who had knocked on the back of the shelf, but then Yushan led them through this chamber to another door. This one she opened without knocking, and inside they found their prize.

The chamber into which the door opened was far larger and grander than the first. Leading off from it were four more doors, but Loren had eyes only for the people in the room. Two guards stood before the party, clad in armor of leather and chain. They had their hands on the thin swords at their belts, but they had not yet drawn them. Behind them was a larger man with a short beard whose hair was cut close to his scalp, revealing a long scar that ran back from his forehead. But behind them all was a man who Loren knew at once must be King Jun.

The king was not as tall as she might have guessed, certainly not as tall as any of his guards. But he had an imperious air that commanded attention. It was not only in the immaculate cut of his hair, nor in the fine robes that he wore, though Loren guessed they were worth more than all the cloth in the whole tailor's shop she had visited that day. Nor was it in his eyes, though they were piercing and wise in equal measure. It was the way he held himself, the subtle pose of his body that somehow elevated him above the others in the room. Loren had seen such presence before; the High King Enalyn was much the same. She almost felt compelled to take a knee.

But then she thought of Wellmont, and her thoughts soured. She inclined her head instead. "Your Grace."

King Jun did not answer her. Instead, the man with the long scar stepped forth. "And who are you?"

"I am Loren of the family Nelda, Nightblade of the High King." Loren pulled the writ from her cloak. "This letter bears her seal, and will show I speak the truth."

One of the foremost guards took the writ and handed it to his commander. He did not even glance at it before handing it back to King Jun. Loren guessed that he could not read any better than she could.

Jun took the writ and unfolded it. Each movement of his fingers was graceful, and he did not lose his poise even when he held the writ close to read it in the dim light of the room's candles. After a moment his brows rose, just a hair. He handed the writ back to his guard, and it was passed forwards to Loren.

"Greetings, Nightblade," said King Jun. His voice was like silk, and though he was quieter than his guard had been, it only served to make them listen more closely. "You have my gratitude for coming to my city."

Loren bowed her head again on instinct, but she looked up at once to match his gaze. "Of course, Your Grace. But as we have told the lady Ying, I did not know you were alive when I came to Danfon. It was only by fortune—and by the wits of Keridwen here—that we discovered you at all."

"I see," said Jun. "Why, then, did you come?"

"We seek the merchant Damaris, of the family Yerrin," said Loren. "We believe it was she who backed Wojin in his bid for your throne."

Jun frowned. "The family Yerrin. That makes some sense, I suppose. Wojin is too much of a craven to plot rebellion without powerful aid."

"Though it should be noted that Damaris does not speak for all the Yerrins," said Annis. "She has been cut off from the family. Though she is dangerous enough on her own, we do not contend with all the might her clan could bring."

The large guard with the scar glared at her. "You speak of 'we.' But who are you, girl?"

Annis gulped and lifted her chin. "I am Annis, of the family Yerrin. And I am Damaris' daughter."

All three guards tensed, but Jun lifted a hand at once. "Stay yourselves. I have heard of this girl. She sundered herself from her mother, just as the rest of the family did. We have nothing to fear from her."

Annis bowed her head. She had gone a shade paler, and her voice quivered. "Thank you, Your Grace."

Jun inclined his head. "But that makes only two introductions. The Nightblade has a second companion."

For a moment, all was still, and then Gem jerked upright as he realized Jun was talking about him. "Oh, I—yes. I am Gem, of the family Noctis." He smiled weakly, and then after a moment he added, "Your Grace."

Jun pursed his lips. "Well met. And what purpose have you here?"

Loren was about to answer, but Gem stood forth and threw out his chest. He actually had the audacity to stare down his nose at the king.

"I? I am the Nightblade's bodyguard."

The room was dead silent for a moment. King Jun's guards stared at Gem, the corners of their lips twitching, while the large one with the scar frowned. But Jun showed no trace of a smile when he nodded. "Then you are most welcome. Loyal servants are worthy of the highest honor."

Then he flapped out his robes and took a seat on the chair behind him. "Very well. Whatever your reasons for coming to Danfon, Nightblade, I am glad you are here. I know that I can rely on your help to retake my throne—not only for my sake, but for the sake of my son."

He waved an arm at Keridwen. She bowed and went to one of the room's doors, ducking within for a moment. When she emerged, she had a young boy in tow. His resemblance to Jun was obvious at once. But where King Jun had an imperious and commanding air, the prince's eyes shone with curiosity as he looked at Loren and her friends. He went to his father's side and then gave them all a deep bow.

"My son, Prince Senlin of the family Fei," said Jun.

"It is an honor to make your acquaintance," said Prince Senlin.

Annis bowed in response. Gem stood stricken for a moment, his mouth hanging slightly open, before he did the same. But Loren only inclined her head again.

"Well met," she said. "But Your Grace, I must correct you on one point. I was sent here on a mission from the High King. That mission has not changed. I am sure we all hope Damaris's capture will help you regain your rightful place as king—but her capture is my only purpose in the city."

Jun frowned—barely a small turn of the lips, but it chilled the air in the room. Annis tensed and put a hand on Loren's arm, but Jun spoke before she could. "As an envoy of the High King, and a servant of her laws, you have a duty to help me restore order."

"I know my duty," said Loren. "Her Majesty herself was the one who gave it to me, Your Grace."

The room was silent for a long moment, silent enough for Loren to hear her own pulse in her ears. Her hands had formed fists without her realizing it. Jun studied her for a moment. Then his eyes widened, and he cocked his head.

"Ah. I believe I understand. You are a girl of Selvan, are you not? I can hear it in your voice. No doubt you resent my kingdom's role in the Battle of Wellmont."

Loren frowned. "Who would not? I was in the city when your forces attacked. I watched its buildings burn and its citizens roast alive in flames—not only the warriors, but the simple folk as well. And it is not the first time you have attacked Selvan without provocation."

To her mounting irritation, Jun nodded. "Of course I understand. And who could blame you? Yet I am a king. It is part of my duty to bring prosperity to my people, and to keep them happy."

"You . . . you do not even deny it."

Jun spread his hands. "What would you have me deny? I have made war with the blessing of the senate, and my people have prospered as a result."

Annis held up a hand. "Mayhap we could turn our discussion to the matter of—"

"Your people have prospered, have they?" said Loren. "Yet some of them—many of them—died for it. And so have my people. If your son were on the battlements, I doubt you would think so lightly of war."

"I have fought in war myself," said Jun. "When he is of age, Senlin will do the same. If his fate is to die, that is as it shall be. The nine lands make widows and orphans of us all in the end."

Loren snorted and gave him a savage grin. "I have heard that wisdom before. It came from Damaris of the family Yerrin, who took your throne from you."

Jun frowned. For the first time, Loren thought she saw a flash of anger in his eyes. But Annis stepped forth and spoke loud enough to quell the conversation.

"If I may," she said. "Much has happened to us this day, Your Grace, and we are only recently come from the road. I must take a moment to speak with my compatriot. May we retire to the outer chamber, for a moment only?"

Jun blew a small sigh through his nose. He looked away and waved a hand in dismissal. Loren almost refused—but Annis took her arm and gripped it tight. Relenting, Loren followed her into the sitting room outside, and Gem came at her heels. Thankfully, none of the bodyguards followed, nor did the merchant Yushan. Behind them, someone closed the door with a soft *click.*

Annis fixed Loren with a stern glare. "You must control yourself."

Loren's nostrils flared, and her jaw worked. She wanted to argue against Annis—in fact, she wanted to shout at her. But she restrained herself to terse words through gritted teeth. "He speaks of death and killing the way a sane man speaks of cutting his fingernails."

"I know," said Annis. "You know I agree with you. I, too, was at the Battle of Wellmont. Yet you must realize that Jun is not entirely in control of his own position. He must do as the people expect, and he cannot thwart the will of the senate, for they would make things very difficult for him. Power comes with laws that Jun must obey—and one of the most important laws is that might always requires sacrifice. He does what his position forces him to do."

"Do you think that makes him blameless?" said Loren. "Your mother taught you to be cruel, and a killer. Yet you rose above it."

"And many others have not," said Annis. "It does not earn them forgiveness—yet it can give us some sort of understanding. Whatever Dorsea's faults, one of Jun's chief loyalties aligns with ours. He is a servant to the High King. Wojin serves only himself—and he is allied with my mother."

Loren held her gaze. "What will happen if we put Jun back on the throne?"

Annis' mouth opened with a quick reply—but then she paused and sighed. "In truth? One day, he will likely make war on Selvan again. Yet Wojin will certainly do the same. And restoring Jun's kingship will stave off the greater war—the one between the High King and the Necromancer. Jun and the senate may be dealt with later, when Underrealm itself is no longer in danger. Indeed, if we survive this mess, I will help you fight him."

Loren turned away with a frown. Then she pushed past Annis and made for the door to Jun's chamber.

"Loren—!" Annis reached for her arm, but Loren threw off her hand and opened the door.

The bodyguards looked up. The one with the scar had gone to Jun's side and was leaning over him, muttering. He straightened, and Jun turned to Loren. She stopped at the front of the room, feet apart, hands at her sides.

"I will return you to your throne, Your Grace," she said. Behind her, she felt Annis freeze in place. "But once I have, I will expect you to remember that it was the Nightblade—a woman of Selvan—who put you there."

"And her friends!" said Gem brightly. Loren did not turn, but she heard Annis cuff the boy's arm.

Jun met her gaze, unflinching. Then, after a long moment, he inclined his head. "If you manage it, I will not forget—and I will see to it that the senate does not forget, either."

Loren nodded. "Very well. I suppose we had better get to planning."

"Actually," said Annis, holding up a finger, "while I appreciate our eagerness, we are all of us weary, as I said. And doubtless His Grace must spend time considering how our arrival may work into whatever plans he had already begun to concoct. I recommend that we retire to our other friends and resume this work on the morrow."

"A sensible proposal," said Jun. "I accept."

But the bodyguard with the long scar scowled. "You cannot take lodgings in the city," he said. "It poses far too great a risk to you, and now, therefore, to His Grace. I will have one of my men fetch your companions, but you will bed here."

Loren glanced at Annis. The girl tossed her head slightly and nodded. "Very well," said Loren. Then she turned to the merchant, Yushan. "And I thank you for your generous hospitality."

Yushan bowed low, and her sharp look softened with a smile. "It is my honor. I am only ashamed that His Grace must bed here in my basement while I continue to move about my house in freedom."

"You have nothing to be ashamed of," said Jun. "It is only by your loyalty that we have survived this far. When I am restored to the throne, you and I may discuss how best to fill Wojin's position in the senate. He will have difficulty holding his seat when he is a corpse."

Yushan bowed still lower. Then she beckoned Loren and her friends out of the room and led them up into her manor. One of the bodyguards came with them and then ducked out the manor's rear entrance to fetch their friends.

Loren pulled Annis aside to murmur to her. "Why did you call an end to the meeting?" she said.

Annis blinked at her as if it were obvious. "Because of the exact reasons I said. Mayhap *you* are not ready to fall over from exhaustion, but I am. At the moment, I could hardly plan an escape from this manor, much less the overthrow of a king."

Gem snickered—but ahead of them, the merchant Yushan turned on them sharply. "You shall not need to plot any escape from me, but if you do I hope you will not damage my tapestries. They are expensive. And remember that we who are old have not necessarily taken leave of our senses. My ears, in particular, are still sharp."

Loren barely hid a smile. Annis flushed and bowed low. "I will remember it, my lady."

"Hmf." Yushan turned and led them on down the hall.

THIRTEEN

WHILE THEY WAITED FOR CHET AND THE OTHERS TO arrive, Loren looked around the rooms they had been assigned. Yushan had put them in one of the manor's front wings, where four rooms had wide windows that overlooked the surrounding streets. Yushan had a servant draw drapes across these. "I doubt many in the city would recognize you, but it is best to take precautions," she said.

"Thank you," said Loren.

"Think nothing of it," said Yushan. "I will have my servants fetch you something to eat. Do you take wine?"

"As much of it as we can," said Gem. Loren glared at him, and he flushed. "And, of course, we thank you for your generosity."

Yushan chuckled. "Oh, I *do* like you, child. Someone will be along shortly."

The food arrived just before their friends. Chet looked around cautiously when he was shown into the apartments. Uzo and Shiun went straight to their room once Loren pointed it out. But Wyle stood in the common room of the wing, looking about with pursed lips.

"Passable, I suppose," he said. "At least we are not paying for it."

"Oh, be silent," said Annis. "You will be glad to learn you have a room to yourself—not out of courtesy, but because no one wishes to share it with you."

"I am glad indeed," said Wyle. He went to the meal that had been laid out for them, ate a few bites and drank a cup of wine, and then made for the room Annis had indicated. "And with that, I bid you all good night."

"Wait!" said Loren. "You went out seeking information today. What did you learn?"

"Nothing," said Wyle, shrugging. "I merely sent out word and asked for information to be gathered. These things take time, my dear."

Loren suppressed a growl as he went into his room and closed the door. She sat with the others and picked at the food, but her appetite had suffered after her angry words with Jun. She had not been sitting long, however, before a knock sounded at the door. Loren glanced at Annis, but the girl only shrugged.

"Come in," said Loren.

The door opened to reveal Prince Senlin. Just behind him were Keridwen and the large bodyguard with the scar, who pushed into the room first, looking all around. When he was done, he ushered Senlin inside. Gem shot to his feet at once, bowing to the prince, and Annis and Loren did the same a moment later.

"Your Excellency," said Annis.

"Lady Yerrin," said Senlin. "I wonder, Nightblade—might I have a private word with you and your companions?"

Loren's brows rose. "Of course, Your Excellency. Although there are more people than I think would fit comfortably—Uzo and Shiun, would you remain here?"

Shiun nodded at once. "Of course, Nightblade," she said.

Loren motioned towards her room. Senlin made for the door, and Loren followed, with Annis, Chet, and Gem behind her. But at the threshold, Senlin stopped and looked up at the bodyguard behind him.

"I wish to speak with them alone, Jo."

The bodyguard frowned down at him. "My duty is to see to your safety, Your Excellency."

Senlin gave the man a frigid look—an odd expression on his soft, youthful face. "There is only one way into the room. They are no threat, and no one else can harm me if you guard the door. You will remain here."

Jo's face darkened, but he bowed his head and took a step back. Keridwen, however, remained by Senlin's side, and he did not order her away. They stepped into Loren's room—Gem scampering in even though Loren had not asked him to—and closed the door behind them. Inside were two fine armchairs. Senlin took one. But when Keridwen went to stand at his side, Loren shook her head and waved towards the other.

"I will sit on the bed. You may have the chair."

Keridwen blinked in surprise. "I thank you, Nightblade." Quickly she went and sat next to the prince, looking somewhat uncomfortable.

Loren and Annis sat beside each other on the bed while Gem sat on the floor by their feet. For a moment Loren merely looked at the prince, and Senlin studied her in turn. The prince was little more than a boy—Gem's age, or mayhap a year or two older. He had a thin build. Everything about him looked scholarly and thoughtful, rather than noble and dashing. But Loren could see a keen wit and a deep mind behind his eyes. She suspected they rarely missed a detail. Indeed, Senlin seemed somewhat akin to Annis, though he carried himself with greater confidence—likely the result of a lifetime where every need was attended to without question, to a degree that even Annis had never experienced.

Senlin spoke first. "I have heard tales of the Nightblade for some months now. I thought you would be a bit older."

Loren tilted her head. "I mean you no offense, Your Excellency, but you yourself are hardly a grown man."

Senlin smiled. "Pardon me—that must have sounded like an insult. Indeed, I am heartened to find you so close to my age. And that goes double for your worthy companions." He gave Annis and Gem each a nod in turn, and they returned it—Gem somewhat more eagerly. "I often feel that my age limits the influence I can have. It is heartening to meet people like you, who have managed to do so much good in so short a time."

It might have been only flattery, but Loren blushed all the same. "Thank you, Your Excellency," she said. "You are not lacking in kindness or grace."

Senlin sighed and leaned back in his chair. "Yet mayhap I lack in effectiveness. I came here to tell you that I do not disagree with what you said to my father."

That piqued Loren's interest. "Oh? I fear my words may have been overly frank. Even harsh."

"They were, yet they were not unearned," said Senlin. "I am no fan of warfare, nor of fighting in general. And I do not think Dorsea's wars serve the greater good."

Loren gave Annis a look, recalling their conversation in the basement. Senlin must have been brought up learning the same laws of power as his father—yet he rose above them, or tried to. That, at least, was heartening.

"I thank you for your agreement," said Loren. "Yet

I do not entirely understand how it helps. Will your father listen to your counsel, if that counsel is to cease his wars?"

Senlin sighed. "He will not. Though I disagree with him, he does as he believes he must—and as the senate pressures him to do. Victory in battle pleases them, and for the most part it pleases the people they serve. Without the senate's support, my father's rule would be toothless. Because it is not, he is able to do great things for our people."

"So he does great good, but pays for it by doing great harm?" said Loren. "That is a weak justification in my mind. I will take a benevolent king, like King Anwar of Selvan, who can help his people without having to kill strangers."

"I have heard that Anwar is a good king," said Senlin. "But what of his daughter? She will take the throne from him one day. What if she is mad? Or cruel? There will be no senate to stay her hand from evil."

Loren folded her arms. "Your senate has done nothing to stay Wojin's hand."

"Give them time," said Senlin. "We will depose Wojin with their help, or not at all."

"And then your father will resume his border wars, in order to please his *people* and his *senate,"* said Loren, growing ever more irritated. "And even Dorseans who are brave enough to object will have to shrug their shoulders at the same time, because that is how Dorsea works."

"It is," said Senlin. For the first time he ducked his gaze as though ashamed. "When I myself hold the throne, I hope to do things better—though I also hope it will be a long time before that happens, for I wish a long life for my father."

Rather than soothe her, Senlin's words only made Loren more angry. "I am not you, Your Excellency, and I cannot know what your life is like. But I like to imagine, at least, that I would not be content to sit and watch as my father waged endless war."

"I am not content with it," he said. "And I advise when I can. But I cannot stop him. I mean that in the strictest sense of the word—I *cannot* stop him. Therefore I do not choose to spend my time complaining about how things ought to be. I do what I can from my station." He must have seen Loren tense, for he went on quickly. "Please do not misunderstand me—I know it is not enough. That is why I find your story so heartening. No doubt you were raised in other circumstances, ones where you could act more directly."

Loren felt her wrath deflate at once. Senlin's words were far from accurate. She had been raised by cruel parents, and until her sixteenth year she had taken no action to change things. True, her parents' evil was directed only at her, not at any others. But she remembered the way they had treated her, the way they had quashed even the slightest sign of rebellion. What if they *had* harmed others? Could she really have stood up to them? It would have been hard, though she hated them and knew they hated her in turn. What if they had raised her with kindness and love, as Jun clearly had done for Senlin?

Chet spoke, his words clipped. "Forgive me, Your Excellency. But I think you underestimate just how sky-blessed your life has been. You say you cannot change things in your kingdom. But mayhap you would not feel the same way if you yourself were threatened with the consequences of your father's wars."

"That is enough, Chet," said Loren quietly.

The room fell silent for an overlong moment. Senlin bowed his head and folded his hands over each other. "I fear I have cast a shadow over our meeting. I apologize, for that was not my intent. I look forward to seeing you again upon the morrow, and I hope that we may all find a way to achieve our ends together. That is all I wished to say."

He stood, and the others did the same. But before he could go, Loren stepped forth and put out a hand. "I thank you, Your Excellency. And forgive us if we spoke too harshly—now, or before. I often forget that the world is nowhere near so simple as I would like it to be."

Senlin's thin brows rose. Then he reached forth and took her wrist. They shook once, firmly. "Thank you, Nightblade. I think we both have a great deal to learn from each other, you and I."

He turned to go. But Keridwen stepped forwards quickly and spoke. "Your Excellency. Might I remain for a moment?"

The prince looked at her in surprise. "Of course," he said. "You are no servant, Keridwen, though my father and I greatly appreciate your aid in these dark days."

Keridwen nodded, and Senlin finally left them. Loren caught one glimpse of Jo, the bodyguard, outside the door. He appeared to have been engaged in a staring contest with Uzo and Shiun in the common room. When Senlin emerged, he quickly moved to escort the prince out of the room. The door shut behind them, and Keridwen turned back to Loren.

"I have heard many stories about you. Are they true?"

Gem's eyes lit up like the moons. Loren tried to ignore him. "I do not know what stories you have heard. Likely some are truer than others."

"Is it true that you saved the High King and the Lord Prince?"

Loren's cheeks flamed. "I found a way out of the palace when it was attacked. But many others helped in the escape. Some gave their lives. Before that, Chet took a dagger in the chest as he defended the Lord Prince."

"It was nothing," said Chet at once. But he lifted a hand, tracing his fingers over the place where the dagger had nearly pierced his heart.

Keridwen slumped. She moved to the armchair that Senlin had been in and sank into it. "I wish I could have done something like that. When Wojin attacked the palace, I mean, and we were forced to flee."

That gave Loren pause. She had spoken to few enough people about her actions upon the Seat. Mostly it had been Kal, who seemed to think she might have done a better job of her rescue. "Yet King Jun and Prince Senlin survived, in the end."

"No thanks to me," said Keridwen. "It was Jo—the king's right-hand man, and the one who came here with Senlin and me—who rescued all of us. I only followed along, protected by others but protecting no one."

Loren gave Annis a pointed look. Annis had often spoken similar words—bemoaning her own role by Loren's side and her uselessness in a fight. Annis' mouth twisted, and she shook her head. Loren smiled and went to sit in the armchair beside Keridwen.

"And who are you, exactly?" said Loren. "Are you some kin of the royal family?"

Keridwen shook her head and held up her arms. "In these clothes?"

"I have often worn disguises when I did not wish to be recognized, and you have been walking the city's streets."

"That is true enough," said Keridwen. "But no. I am only an apothecary, and from my parents I have learned some skill in healing."

"But there you have it," said Loren. "You have no reason for shame. If you have been practicing for any time at all, you have probably rescued more people than I have. I can only save lives by fighting. The world would be a worse place if everyone were like me, but a better one if all were like you."

Keridwen laughed. "I agree with you there. Yet still I wish I could do more—or that I could have done more than I did." She paused for a moment, fixing Loren with an appraising look. Loren met her gaze, feeling a twisting in her stomach. "I agree with you, you know. I know that His Grace's actions are wrong."

Loren frowned. "So does Prince Senlin. Yet that does nothing to stop King Jun."

"I do not agree with His Excellency either," said Keridwen, shaking her head. "War has never come to Danfon in my lifetime, yet we feel its effects even this far north. Often our warriors return from battle gravely wounded or even without limbs. Sometimes they have a sickness of the mind instead, a memory of death and pain that they can never banish. Dorseans honor our soldiers above all others. They risk their lives for the good of the kingdom—or at least that is how they see it, no matter how misguided our wars. Yet those wars often leave them a wreck, in mind as well as in body. I am put face to face with such maladies. The prince is not. I think it makes him more complacent than he might be. He contents himself with his principles, though they accomplish no tangible change."

"And what do you do?" said Annis quietly. "When you see these soldiers, I mean. What is your answer to King Jun's wars?"

"In one respect, Prince Senlin is right," said Keridwen. "I can do nothing to stop His Grace from waging battle. And I know he faces pressure from the senate. Yet neither am I content to wait, as His Excellency is. Instead I tell myself that I will grow. I will learn more, I will gain more influence. And I will do better next time. I hope that one day it comes true, if we survive all of this."

Loren nodded slowly. "I think I prefer your way of thinking to the prince's."

Keridwen smiled and cast her eyes down. Then she stood abruptly from the chair. "I had better leave and let you get your rest. But I thank you for the opportunity to speak."

"Of course," said Loren, rising to see her out. "I am glad you found us, Keridwen. And I hope you will come speak with us again, any time you wish."

"I would enjoy that. Only please, you must call me Kerri. Only His Grace and His Excellency call me Keridwen, and as a consequence it seems frightfully formal."

Loren smiled. "Very well, Kerri."

She held the door as Kerri left and then closed it softly. Turning to Annis and Gem, she raised her brows.

"Today has been a day," she said.

"It has been that," said Annis. "These people are somewhat strange to me. Yet I think I like Keridwen—Kerri, I suppose—the best."

"And I," said Loren. Then she noticed that Gem

wore a grin that split his face from ear to ear. "What are you giggling about?"

"She had heard of you," said Gem triumphantly. "She had heard tales of the Nightblade."

Loren shook her head, trying to ignore the flush that crept up her neck. "Be silent, Gem."

FOURTEEN

In the common room, they ate a small meal before retiring to their beds. Loren had put Chet and Gem in one room, with Annis and herself in another. Almost at once, Annis went to bed and fell asleep. Loren soon joined her.

They rose before dawn—all but Gem—and broke their fast on eggs and rice. Soon a messenger arrived, requesting their presence in the king's chambers.

Loren turned to the party. "It is cramped down below. I will take Annis, Wyle, and Chet with me, but the rest of you should remain here."

Wyle pulled at his collar. "Must I come?" he said. "The king has never seen my face, and I see little benefit in changing that now."

"You are here to help secure his rescue," said Loren. "If he never meets you, how will he know who to pardon when this is all over?"

Wyle held up a finger. "You promised me a pardon from the High King, not Jun. I will not forget it. And besides, I expect an open pardon—one that absolves the crimes of anyone who holds it." Wyle paused and pulled at his thin beard. "Sky above. I wonder what such a document would be worth to the right buyer."

Annis rolled her eyes.

"But you must bring me as well!" said Gem. "There is no more cunning mind in our little party."

Before Loren could argue, Chet smiled and shook his head. "Take him," he said. "I will remain behind. It is as it was in Bertram—I shall prove no more useful than a third shoe."

"The same might be said for Gem," said Loren, scowling at the boy with mock severity. But he only grinned as he accompanied her to the manor's basement.

Jun sat in the same place he had yesterday; it seemed he had adopted the chair as his temporary throne. A guard stood to either side, and the larger bodyguard, Jo, sat just in front and to the side of his king. Prince Senlin was there as well, partially hidden behind one of the bodyguards.

"A good morn, Nightblade," said Jun. "Let us now take counsel and determine our best course of action."

"Of course, Your Grace," said Loren. "I have brought Annis with me. She has a brilliant mind for strategy and politics both. I think you will find her advice far more useful than mine."

"Then I welcome her," said Jun. He gave Annis a grave nod, which she returned.

Loren motioned for Wyle to step forwards, and he hesitated only a moment before complying. "This man is called Wyle. He is a business associate, hailing from Bertram. It was he who helped us enter the city without being seen. He knows many secret ways and has friends in the capital."

From the way Jun looked at Wyle, Loren thought he must know exactly what sort of "associate" the smuggler was. But he said only, "Welcome. If you can indeed be of help, you will have my gratitude."

"I am counting on it," said Wyle, giving the king an easy grin.

A table had been put before Jun's chair, and a map was laid upon it. Chairs were brought for Loren and Annis, and they sat opposite the king. The map depicted the city—not all of its streets and alleys, of course, but its layout around the river, as well as the locations of some important buildings. Wyle bent over the map, his hands folded before his chin. But it was Annis who spoke first.

"As has been mentioned, Wyle escorted us into the

city on a route that few know about. He should be able to lead us out the same way."

"Yes, of course," said Wyle. "We will be a larger party now, but we can still avoid detection if we dress you up as beggars."

Jun tilted his head. "Lead us out? Why would I leave the city?"

The room went still. Loren and Annis looked at each other. Wyle studied King Jun for a moment, and then he sighed quietly.

Annis cleared her throat. "Your Grace, you are in grave danger while you remain here."

"That will not change if I depart—not unless I leave my kingdom entirely. Wojin will not stop hunting me just because I pass beyond Danfon's walls."

"But he will have a harder time of it," said Loren. "I said I would help you take back your throne, but I cannot also keep you safe if you remain here."

"Nor would I ask you to," said Jun. "I have my guards. But I mean to take back my throne, not merely survive. If I leave, I will look far too weak in the eyes of the senate."

Loren looked to Jo. The large bodyguard's face had darkened, making the white of his long scar stand out in stark relief. "If it is not too presumptuous, I would ask Jo's opinion on this matter. Your safety is his responsibility, after all."

"I serve at the pleasure of His Grace," said Jo.

But King Jun shook his head. "Jo does not wish to

gainsay me in front of others. But I will tell you what he has said in our private meetings: he agrees with you. He wants to get me out of the city, where he believes he will be able to protect me more easily. But I have told him what I tell you now. I will not leave Danfon while I still have claim to its throne. On this matter, my mind is resolved."

Loren looked to Annis. The girl shrugged.

"Very well, Your Grace," said Loren. "If that is the case, tell us where you would like us to begin."

"We must unite the people behind me," said Jun. "Wojin is not well loved, neither by my citizens nor by most of the senators—only a few of them were in his pocket before the revolt. If we can inspire a popular uprising, the senators will rally behind us, and Dorsea itself can overthrow the usurper."

Loren had to fight hard to keep from rolling her eyes. But to her surprise, she saw Annis and Jo both nodding at the king's words. "Do you think such a plan is wise?" Loren asked Annis. "We speak of ordinary citizens, not trained soldiers. Would they risk their own lives in a battle?"

"I think they might," said Annis. "Even as far away as the High King's Seat, I heard how His Grace is beloved by the Dorseans. Nowhere is that more true than here in the capital. Yet Loren strikes upon a truth—by and large, the citizens of Danfon are *not* trained soldiers. If you reveal yourself, there is a strong possibility that Wojin will manage to kill you before you can rally enough support. A determined force of soldiers could cut their way through even a great mass of loyal citizens in short order."

"Yet the states have their own standing armies, and the senators can control them," said Jo. "And while senators can be conniving, they generally bow to the will of their people. Several senators are in the capital now, as it happens. If we can gain their support, we will have more than enough trained soldiers to resist Wojin."

"That could work," said Annis, tapping her teeth. "But still, at least for now, His Grace must not reveal himself. It would be far too dangerous."

"Then we must fight from the shadows," said Jo. He lifted a hand to scratch at his scar where it met his temple. "The people must know their true king is alive, but his location can never be known."

"That seems a tall order," said Loren. "If they cannot see you, how can you unite them?"

"We will have to proceed slowly," said Annis. "Plant the seeds of rebellion one at a time, the way a farmer turns crops—first doubt, then distrust, and finally anger. When the whole city has come to believe in Wojin's treachery, *then* His Grace may reveal himself. You will have a popular revolt already in progress, and a trained army awaiting your orders."

Prince Senlin leaned forwards suddenly. "Yet even that plan requires some level of exposure," he said. "People spread rumors all the time. But no one places much faith in such rumors unless they come from a strong source."

"You could reveal yourself," said Loren, pointing at Senlin. "If the people saw you, even briefly, *that* rumor would fly far and fast."

"No," said Jun, Annis, and Jo all at once. Jun shook his head furiously and went on. "No. I will not risk my son."

"If anything were to go wrong, it would be disastrous," said Annis. "This is not yet a battle of swords, but one of hearts and minds. If Prince Senlin revealed himself, that might stoke the flames of hope in some citizens. But if Wojin managed to capture or kill Senlin, that would quench such hope beyond chance of rekindling."

Gem smiled. "It should be the Nightblade."

They all paused. Loren turned to him with a frown. "Gem, still your tongue if you have nothing useful to say."

"But that *is* useful," he insisted. "Loren, it should be you. The people will have heard tales of you. It was not only His Grace who knew of your exploits. Keridwen knew of you, and I am sure many others in the city do as well. You can be the one they rally behind. And if Wojin should try to track you down, he will have a hard time of it. There is no one better than you at escaping danger—except for me, of course."

Loren opened her mouth to argue again, but Annis spoke first. "I think he may be right," she said. "If the

Nightblade tells them that King Jun is still alive, that would be worth more than whispers from a gossiping neighbor. You could tell them Wojin is an impostor and a liar. You would be a messenger of the king himself."

"I like it," said Wyle. Loren shot him a dirty look, but he only beamed back at her. "I myself would never do something so ostentatious, but I appreciate that it has a certain . . . grandiose style. What did I tell you, Nightblade? I place a high value on courage."

Jun nodded and held up a hand. On it was a ring in the shape of a dragon, twisted around a great ruby. "I will give you this. It is one of the emblems of my office. I would wager the fact that Wojin does not have it rankles him. It will lend credence to your words."

But Loren shook her head. "You cannot be serious. I am a spy, not a general."

"You are more than a spy," said Gem. "You are a legend."

Annis silenced him with a sharp look and put her hand over Loren's. "Gem speaks with words that are more flowery than useful, but he is not wrong. He is too eager to overestimate your worth, but you are too eager to dismiss it. Let my voice be the middle ground—you cannot singlehandedly save the nine kingdoms, but you can do this."

Loren frowned. "I do not share your confidence."

Annis' eyes sharpened. "Sky above, Loren. You claim to keep me by your side because you value my advice. I am giving it now. Will you not heed it?"

Loren sighed and looked towards the ceiling. "Very well."

"Very good," said Jun. "And I believe I know what your first task must be. Wojin means to address the public tomorrow. It shall be a large event, carried out in a great square. We can expect many hundreds of people to gather. No doubt he means to lament my untimely death and decry the High King. He has not properly done so since he took my throne. We could hardly design a better place for you to reveal yourself."

"That should work well," said Annis. "If you interrupt his address, you should have just enough time to tell the people that Jun is alive and Wojin is a traitor."

Loren's throat had gone dry. "And then? I will be a poor figurehead if soldiers fill me with arrows."

"You shall have to be fast, and you shall have to escape quickly," said Wyle. "I can help you with that. My knowledge of secrets is not limited to ways in and out of this city. I know its streets as well."

"We should go there today," said Annis. "Scouting the place first will give us a greater chance of success—as well as a greater chance of getting out alive."

Jun turned to the back of the room and beckoned to Kerri, who came forth at once. "Take Keridwen with you," he said. "I do not doubt the craftiness of this man Wyle, but if I understand right, he has not been in the capital for some time. Keridwen lives here, and will no doubt have useful insight."

Kerri inclined her head towards him. "It will be my pleasure, Your Grace."

Loren nodded and stood. "If we mean to do this, we should not delay. I shall return before nightfall, Your Grace."

Jun nodded and stood. The others were quick to follow, and Loren led them from the room.

"This is glorious," said Gem. "I knew that tales of you would one day turn to legend, but this is something beyond what I had hoped."

"Stop treating this like a lark," said Loren. "It seems to me that your whispered rumors have only led me—and all of us—into greater danger. Some bodyguard you are."

Gem ducked his head, but Annis smiled at him. "That may be true—but only because his tales have added to your power. You wish to do great things in Underrealm, Loren. But great actions always carry at least some danger. You cannot have the one without the other. We all play by the same rules in the end."

Loren's scowl deepened, and she waved her hand sharply. "Let us get on with this, then."

FIFTEEN

Loren sent Gem to fetch Chet and the Mystics before they left. Once the party reached the streets, Kerri took them southeast on a path that briefly drew near the palace. Loren eyed the place with distrust. It was familiar from her dream, and this close the resemblance was even more clear. The mountains loomed above, just as she had seen them in slumber. She thought she could even see the street down which the faceless, masked army had marched, flowing into the front courtyard and breaking around Damaris and Gregor.

They passed the palace, and soon Kerri led them to a town square. In the center was a statue of a man Loren did not recognize, a man with a full beard and long, flowing robes. He had one hand raised to the sky. But before Loren could ask about him, Kerri pointed. A large manor dominated one entire side of the square, far more impressive than Yushan's home where they had spent the night. The manor looked to be of the same sort of construction as the palace itself. Two of the square's other sides were composed of shops, while directly across the way were four more manors, though they were far smaller and less impressive than the first.

"Wojin will speak from there," said Kerri, still pointing at the largest manor. Set in its side was a wide marble balcony that stretched a few paces out into the air, overhanging the cobblestones below.

Even as Loren studied it, her attention was pulled away by the people milling about. Passersby gave the manor an uneasy look. The merchants hawking their wares seemed to studiously avoid looking at the place, as though they wanted their customers to forget it was there. Loren saw two children running along, and one of them stopped to spit on the building's wall. A nearby guard gave a cry and came after the girl, but she laughed and scampered off.

"I am no great judge of people," said Wyle, making it clear in his tone that he did not think that was true. "But I would wager that these citizens do not enjoy that building."

"That is Wojin's home," said Kerri. "Or at least, it was before he moved into the palace."

"Then why would he not give his speech from the palace?" said Chet.

Kerri glanced about to make sure no one was close enough to overhear them. "King Jun used to do so," she said. "But it required opening the palace gates so that the people could fill the courtyards inside. They loved Jun, and so he did not fear to do so. I doubt Wojin feels the same. It would surely make him anxious to have so many thousands of citizens inside his very walls."

"This is heartening," said Wyle, grinning. "These people seem to be half revolting already."

Annis frowned at him. "That was a poor joke. And we should not grow overconfident. Let us craft our plan."

"The crowd could hear me from the statue," said Loren. "It stands on a pedestal in the center of the square."

"Yet you would be surrounded," said Wyle. "The crowd would hamper the guards from coming to attack you, but it would not stop them completely. And the people would be a hindrance to your escape as well. Also, there is no cover to stop an arrow."

Loren grimaced. "Of course. My first thought was that Wojin would not have his soldiers shoot at me if I stood there, for a miss might strike the crowd. Yet from what I hear of him, he might not be deterred."

Kerri's expression grew dark. "No, Wojin would care little for that."

Gem bounced on his feet. "The rooftops!"

He pointed to the manors across from Wojin's. Their roofs were the same red tile as most in Danfon, and each a gentle slope meeting in a peak. And Loren saw now that while they were far shorter than the manor across the square, they were almost of a height with the balcony from which Wojin would deliver his speech.

"That would do," Loren mused. "But I should like to get a better look."

"I will find us a way up," said Gem, and scampered off to do just that. It was only a few moments before he returned. "Follow me."

Just beside the middle building was a huge pile of fresh-cut lumber. It was stacked neatly and formed a sort of staircase leading to the roof's edge.

Loren nodded. "This is perfect. It will let us get up and down from the roof, and I can address the crowd from there."

"Yet it still proves a poor means of escape," said Wyle. "If the space is indeed packed with the citizenry, you will not be able to get through them after climbing down."

"There is likely another way off the roof," said Gem. "Let us climb up and see."

He leaped up the piles of timber like a satyr, and Chet started up behind him. But Wyle took a quick step back and raised his hands. "I shall leave such exertions to you. I have a physique built for cleverness and charm, but not for climbing."

"That goes for me as well," said Annis. "Besides, someone should keep an eye on the smuggler."

Wyle held up a finger. "Ah, ah. I work for the king now. That means I am an honest businessman."

Loren arched an eyebrow. "Indeed. But all the same, I think Annis is right—Uzo and Shiun will remain here with the honest businessman."

"Certainly," said Shiun. She took a step closer to Wyle, as though she were ready to catch him if he tried to sneak away. Uzo stepped up on the smuggler's other side.

Wyle shook his head with an air of long-suffering dignity. "Always so distrustful," he said. "But I forgive you. Who could blame such an upstanding servant of the King's law?"

Loren smiled and turned to climb the pile of timbers. But to her surprise, she saw Kerri starting the climb as well.

"It might be better to remain here," said Loren. "There is no need to risk yourself."

Kerri raised an eyebrow, but she did not stop making her way up. "You think this is a risk? I think the danger will come during Wojin's speech. If you fear I cannot keep up, do not worry. I am as much a city child as you are."

Loren laughed at that, and so did Gem. The boy

had reached the rooftop already, and had lowered a hand to help Chet make the last few steps. "She is no daughter of a city," said Gem. "Loren came from the forests."

Kerri seemed surprised—so much so that her foot slipped. Loren quickly caught her hand and steadied her. "Thank you," mumbled Kerri. "And forgive me for assuming. You are more refined than I would expect from a backwater bumpkin."

Loren's cheeks flushed. "I am only pleased you have not made fun of my accent, the way most people do. As for refinement, I would not say that I possess much, though I have had many experiences since leaving my home."

"She has indeed," said Gem. "You should have seen her when we first met in Cabrus. She stared in wide-eyed wonder at all the buildings, and her accent was even worse than it is now."

Kerri laughed. "I think it is lovely." Loren's cheeks flamed still further.

Chet helped Kerri make the last few paces of the climb. The girl was not quite as agile as she had boasted, though she was no bumbler, either. They took a few cautious steps on the roof. Loren was pleased to find the red tiles were firm under her feet—they would not slip and make her lose her footing, and she doubted if they made any noise that could be heard in the manor below. Gem bounced close to the front edge of the roof, making Loren's heart skip nervously. She always had to remind herself of Gem's familiarity with heights, for he took risks and balanced on perches that she herself would not have dared. Chet stopped a pace behind the boy, looking at the square below.

"It is a bit more exposed than I would like," said Chet. "They might still be able to shoot at you."

"The lip of the roof will give me some cover from the street," said Loren.

"I do not mean down below," said Chet. "If he has any archers on the balcony with him, or in the building, they will have a clear shot."

Loren looked at Wojin's manor. There were, indeed, many windows with a good view of her, and the balcony was more than wide enough to allow for archers. "I had not thought of that. I suppose I shall have to keep my words brief, then."

"But at least there are many routes of escape," said Gem. "And not just to the sides, but behind."

He pointed, and Loren could see that there were indeed many rooftops leading directly away from the square. There were not many gaps, and all were an easy leap.

"That shall be my route of escape," she said. "But we should find a place to climb down. I would rather know just where to go, rather than have to discover a ladder in the thick of things."

Gem led the way, jumping from one roof to another, and they all hurried to follow him. But it was almost no time at all before he stopped and pointed again. There was a drainpipe against a solid shop wall, anchored to the building with thick iron bands that would form perfect handholds.

"There," he said. "And we are far enough from the square that I doubt they will be able to reach you here."

"It is perfect," said Loren. "Though just to be safe, let us all climb it, to make sure it will hold."

It did, and when they had reached the cobblestones, Kerri led them back towards the square. When they came around the corner of the manor, Annis and the others turned to them in surprise.

"Back so soon?" said Wyle.

"Will it work?" said Annis.

"It will," said Loren. "It is as good a place as any to address the crowd, and there is an easy way to escape once I have done so."

"Most excellent," said Wyle. "Though while you have been scampering about having an adventure, I have turned my considerable mind to our plan. I think there is a way to make your appearance do more for our cause."

Loren folded her arms. "Oh?"

Wyle flashed his easy grin. "You are an impressive woman, Nightblade, and your black cloak will do you many favors in capturing the people's minds. I think King Jun is right, and his people have no great love for the usurper. Yet while the masses love to believe in a figurehead, they are reluctant to follow them unless they see their fellows already doing so."

"Speak plainly, smuggler," said Loren. "I do not enjoy parsing the meaning from your words."

"He means that a crowd will follow a crowd," said Annis. She turned to Wyle. "That wisdom is known to many. But how do you mean to use it?"

"In the simplest way possible," said Wyle. "When the Nightblade addresses the people, no doubt some of them will listen to her. But if some of them give voice to their support, and loudly, that will sway even more hearts."

Annis' eyes lit up, and she nodded eagerly. "Agents. Plants in the crowd to raise a cry."

"I do not understand," said Loren.

"Wyle will hire some few people—beggars, mayhap—to cry their support for you as you speak," said Annis. "That will encourage others to do the same. It is one thing to whisper gossip in your own shop. It is quite another thing to shout down a king—even a false one—when his guards are close at hand, and armed."

"But even the meek will rise up if they think they have the support of their fellows," said Wyle. "If we are agreed, then, I will see to the specific arrangements."

"More of your friends within the city?" said Chet.

Wyle cocked his head with a smile. "But of course. The meaner sort—not quite beggars, as the Yerrin girl said, but close enough. They will require payment—but I do not doubt that King Jun will be willing to accommodate that. As well as a fee for business honestly conducted, of course."

Loren fumed. Wyle confused her sometimes, when he seemed so eager to help them—but only until she discovered how he meant to profit from it.

"Very well," she said. "I will speak to King Jun and secure your payment—once he has the city. In the meantime, send your messages and have your friends ready to act."

"My pleasure," said Wyle, bowing low. "I imagine one of the Mystics will accompany me, to ensure there is no wrongdoing? Which one shall you send—the handsome one, or the quiet one?"

Loren looked at Shiun. The woman barely restrained a sigh as she went off with Wyle. Loren turned to Annis and the others. "Let us return to the manor and tell the king our plan."

"Later," said Annis. "Before we do, we have some goods to retrieve. Did you forget the tailor?"

Loren's eyes widened as she stared at her friend. "You cannot mean to fetch a dress now, Annis. There are more important things to be done."

"My dress is unimportant, but your new clothes are not." Annis' tone brooked no argument, and she stepped forwards to take Loren's arm. "One cannot take too much care with one's appearance when one is about to become a legend."

"She is already a legend," said Gem brightly. Annis ignored him and led Loren northeast into the city.

SIXTEEN

The dream took her.

Loren was in the sewers, and the man was there. The one whose hair was cropped close, who dressed in black leather, who had scars along his arms. His eyes still glowed with that strange light, akin to magelight and yet somehow different.

He leaned against the passage wall and put a finger to his lips, though Loren had spoken no word. She spun, looking around. They were in Danfon's sewers, but she could not place their exact location. Then she thought she heard a noise—a great deal of running water. The river. They must be near the place where Wyle had first led them into the sewers.

She turned back to the man with the scars. He still held a finger to his lips, but now he lowered it and stepped around the corner. Though she had not willed her body to move, Loren found herself following him. She stepped around the corner and almost bumped into his back. The man motioned her to silence and then stepped aside for her to see.

There were Damaris and Gregor, just a little way down the tunnel. But there, too, was a woman Loren did not recognize. She had the look of a Dorsean woman, and she sat in a chair facing Loren. Damaris and Gregor faced her, away from Loren. Then Loren realized that the woman was bound and unable to move.

For the moment, Damaris and Gregor seemed content to ignore their prisoner. Gregor strode up and down the sewer, studying its walls, its ceiling. "This is how Loren entered the city," he said. "I know that she and her party came this way, but my agents could not discover her whereabouts above ground."

"That is no matter," said Damaris. "Maintain a guard so that they cannot escape the same way. But I do not think she will try to flee. I think she came here seeking us. If that is true, then it is only a matter of time before she reveals herself, and that is when we may strike."

Loren's knees shook. Damaris knew she was in the city. Of course she would know eventually—Loren meant to reveal herself to the whole populace the next day. But how had she found out in advance? Or was this a vision of the future?

Her terror increased tenfold as Damaris turned to look into her eyes.

"Hello, Loren," she said softly.

"I . . . this is a dream," said Loren.

How did she know that? She had never realized it before—not while she was in the dream, at least. Or had she? Her mind was muddled.

Damaris did not acknowledge Loren's statement. She only came forwards, walking up until she stood less than a pace in front of Loren. Gregor did not follow, though Loren could almost feel the bodyguard grow tense.

"Thank you," said Damaris, "for bringing Annis to Danfon."

Loren wanted to flee, but she could not move. "She is not here. You have been misled."

The merchant smiled. It was a sad, lonely expression, but her eyes were warm. She stepped forwards. Loren tried to jerk away, but she still could not move.

Damaris embraced her, arms wrapping around her back to rest on her shoulder blades. She laid her head on Loren's shoulder, face turned away, and squeezed her tight—not to harm, but only to give comfort. Loren had almost forgotten that the merchant was nearly a hand shorter than her.

"You have taken such good care of her," said Damaris softly. "I know now that if she had joined me in the Greatrocks, I would have regretted it. Everything had happened so fast. My hasty decision would have been my ruin. The Necromancer would have taken her from me. They have leverage over me already, but they always want more. Thank you for seeing to her safety."

Despite herself, Loren relaxed in the merchant's embrace. Why did she feel so safe? She knew Damaris' evil—knew her love of others' pain, her desire for control.

Yet after a moment, Loren recognized the truth. This was not the embrace of a friend. It was the comfort of a parent. It was something Loren had no memory of. Jordel had given her only a pale shadow of it, more akin to a battlefield commander than to a father. Loren was always expected to look after Annis, after Gem, to console them when the world was cruel, to see to their safety. Now, for just a moment, a part of her mind could pretend that Damaris' embrace promised the same. Reassurance. Security. Protection.

"Do not forget what happened at Wellmont," whispered Damaris.

Then she pulled away, and Loren's wits returned. It was the dream. It made her see things—think things—that would never happen in the waking world. This was another lie. Another trick.

Damaris stepped back until she stood by the woman in the chair. The woman's head had hung, but now she lifted it. Loren studied her. Sharp and severe features, thin eyebrows and regal lips. But she had been beaten terribly, and one eye was almost swollen shut. Far worse than that, her clothes were soaked in blood. Loren knew it came from a thousand torturous cuts, the sort that Damaris liked to give her victims as she pried information from them.

The woman tried to speak, but a bubbling cough came out instead. She hacked for a moment and tried again, her voice like steel.

"Never again will Jun sit the Dorsean throne."

Damaris drew a dagger and cut the woman's throat. The dagger was—had been—Auntie's.

Loren took a step back, horrified. Then she heard a noise behind her and turned. The man in black had gone, but someone else stood there.

Kal.

The grand chancellor was resplendent in his red cloak, which was free from any of the sewer's grime. Behind him were many Mystics, all of them armed and armored.

Loren almost melted in relief. "Damaris is here!" she said. "We can capture her!"

Kal did not answer. He raised his sword and leaped to attack her.

She barely scrambled out of the way in time. At the last moment she fell and struck the wall—but then she fell through it. Loren looked up in shock. What had seemed a small alcove was actually a side tunnel entrance. It led off into utter darkness—but in the main tunnel were Kal and his bloodthirsty Mystics.

Loren ran as fast as she could. Away from Damaris. Away from Kal and his Mystics who howled for her blood. But more red-cloaked warriors appeared in the sewers ahead. Again Loren had to turn down a side tunnel. She was hopelessly lost. Where was the city? Where was escape? She had no idea. She could only keep running.

A figure leaped out of the darkness ahead, and Loren recoiled. But it was no Mystic—or at least, not a real one. It was Niya.

Loren turned to flee again, but Niya snatched her arm.

"Quickly! We must escape!" she cried.

The Mystics were now close behind. Loren hesitated just a moment too long, and Niya's grip was strong. Soon they flew side by side. They came to a junction.

"Bent grate!" cried Niya, pointing. Loren saw it—twisted and bent, as though it had been struck by something heavy.

"Left," said Niya, and turned to follow her own direction.

The cries of the Mystics were still close, but now at least they were out of sight. Loren almost stopped following Niya, but then the woman spoke again.

"Bronze plate. Right." She pointed again, and Loren saw a bronze plate set in the ceiling. It had drainage holes, but beyond that she could not guess at its purpose. Niya turned right, and soon they had reached a heavy iron door.

"Help me get it open," she said. She seized the door and grunted as she heaved at it. Once again Loren lost control of her own body, and she moved to help. Together they heaved the iron door open. Its hinges groaned.

Sweet, fresh air rushed in to greet them. They darted through the doorway, and Loren found herself on a low wooden dock built on the river's edge. Looking up, she could see they were in the city again. They had made it back to Danfon. But Loren had wanted to escape the city.

"This is the wrong way," she said.

"It is the only way," said Niya. "Come, or they will catch you."

Loren glanced back the way they had come. Many Mystics rounded the corner. Battle cries poured from their lips as they chased her. With no other choice, Loren turned to follow Niya. The woman climbed the riverbank and ran towards a small, nondescript shop nearby. She flung open the door and ran inside, with Loren only a pace behind her.

She was in the king's palace. Confusion struck her like a hammer blow, and for a moment she froze in her tracks. The halls and mighty pillars were familiar from the last dream. Turning, she saw the shop door behind her. It was set in the wall, and beyond it was the river. It was like a portal to another world, and her mind could not reconcile the difference.

"They nearly killed us," said Chet.

Loren whirled. When had Chet appeared there? He was within arm's reach. His limbs shook, and his eyes darted everywhere, mad with fear.

"They . . . they were so close," said Chet. Even his words quivered. "If any of us had made a misstep . . . if I had fallen . . ."

"We are safe," said Loren. "They did not catch us."

"How long?" said Chet. "How long can we keep running? How long before I stumble in the chase?"

Loren opened her mouth, but no words came out. She only shook her head.

"You cannot follow me anymore," whispered Chet.

"But you have followed *me,"* cried Loren in frustration. "And I know you cannot do it anymore. It is killing you, Chet. I can see it, and I know you can as well. I only wish you did not feel the need to try."

Unthinking, she stepped forwards and tried to embrace him. But he screamed and pushed her away. Loren recoiled, cursing herself as Chet fled weeping. Loren went after him, crying for him to wait, that she was sorry. But he kept running until he had led her to the passageway—the one she knew well, the one where her dreams always led her. Ahead was the dining hall. Chet fled through it. The way beyond was clear, and an open gate led to the city. Almost Loren followed him.

Then she heard cries behind her and turned. The Mystics were there. They had found her again, and their swords hungered for her blood.

She had to lead them away. Had to keep them from Chet's trail. If she followed him, he would die.

But if she went into the secret passageway, *she* would die. Gregor would see to that.

Loren threw open the small iron door and ducked inside the serving room. She seized the cupboard and heaved—it fell to the ground with a crash, scattering broken dishes everywhere. Beyond was the dark passageway, and she ate a magestone so that she could see. There was the ladder, and at the top was the second hall. Soon she came to the tapestry and moved it aside.

It was the apartment. The same as last time. She had half hoped the dream would play a trick on her again, that she would find herself somewhere else entirely. But it was the same. In the far wall was the door leading to the balcony, and before it stood Gregor. His eyes fixed on her, and she could not move as terror filled her body.

"The Elves told you." Niya's voice floated from nowhere. Loren was alone as Gregor stepped forwards, drawing his sword.

The dream released her.

Loren started awake in her bed and sat up. For half a moment she forgot where she was, and fear coursed through her as she imagined herself in the Danfon palace. But her wits soon returned. She was in the manor of the merchant Yushan, and Gregor was far away. Annis lay within arm's reach, but the girl did not stir. Slowly Loren's breathing returned to normal. She hung her head, resting it in her hands.

The dreams were more vivid, more detailed, and yet they still brought less terror each time. That was good. Whether or not the dreams were meant to help her, she could do without the dread they always left behind. Mayhap soon they would leave none at all.

But though the fear soon passed, it left her anxious and jumpy. She needed to move, to work out the sudden tension in her limbs. So she rose and dressed herself, wearing her regular, simple garments, and not the new clothes from the tailor. She did not bother to pull on her boots. The door opened silently, and she slipped out into the common room.

To her surprise, she found Shiun there. The Mystic sat in a chair by the door that led to the rest of the manor. Loren paused for a moment, and the two of them stared at each other. After a moment, Shiun raised an eyebrow.

"Can you not sleep?"

"I . . . did, but something woke me," said Loren. "What are you doing?"

"Sitting watch," said Shiun. "Uzo and I have done so since we came here."

Loren cocked her head as she went to one of the room's armchairs and sank into it. "Do you suspect Yushan might betray us?"

"I do not. But one can never be too careful. Call

it an old habit—technically we are still on campaign, after all."

Loren sighed. "You are right, and I thank you for it. It is only one more detail I should have thought of."

Shiun sighed and looked away, picking at her trouser leg with her fingernails. Loren felt shame rise in her breast, and she, too, turned away. Shiun deserved better than her. The whole party did. Too often, Loren forgot that she was only a girl. The next day—or, she supposed, later this day, for it was the small hours of the morning—Loren would play at being a legend, a master thief of great renown. Yet she could not even remember to do simple things like setting a watch.

"I am sorry you were assigned to me, Shiun," she said softly. "I know you would rather not have been. I am sure you and Uzo must be frustrated by me. I should have caught Damaris long ago. A smarter woman would have. I should never have followed her to Yewamba. Sometimes—that is, I do my best, but sometimes I feel as though I am just stumbling from one mess to another, and making each one worse as I do."

Shiun's lips pressed tight. She turned back to Loren, studying her in the dim light of the room's lamp. Then it seemed to Loren like she came to a decision, resolving something in her own thoughts.

"May I speak to you openly, Nightblade?"

"Of course," said Loren. "I am your commander in name only."

"You are *not,*" said Shiun sharply—so sharply that Loren jumped a bit. "You are who I was assigned to follow, and the same is true for Uzo. Yet all the long while we have ridden together, you have . . . well, you have whined and complained and moaned to us. You speak too openly and listen too eagerly."

Loren straightened somewhat in her armchair. "I . . . you do not want me to listen to you?"

"I understand your situation, at least somewhat," said Shiun. "You are young. Few are given a command at your age, even in the Mystics, where we recruit some fine soldiers of your years. You are nervous that you will make a mistake. And before you rode with Mystics, you rode alone—or with a small group of friends. And you treat them as friends. You speak to them openly, sharing everything."

"Of course," said Loren, feeling a little defensive now. "They *are* my friends."

"But I am not," said Shiun flatly. "Do not misunderstand me. I think you are a fine woman, and honorable. I do not tell you all this only for my own sake and Uzo's, but for *everyone* you may lead in the future. Sky above, act like a commander for once. Let those who serve you *serve* you. We do not need to hear the smallest details of every thought that crosses your mind. Some information can be helpful, but too much debate gets tiresome. Uzo and I are not your friends. We are here with one purpose: to carry out your orders. That is the lot of a soldier, and that is why we joined the Mystics."

"I did not join the Mystics," said Loren. "I am—"

"Stop," said Shiun. "You did not join the Mystics, but you accepted your assignment from the High King. That grants you privileges, but it also comes with responsibilities. I swear on the darkness below that I will pull my hair out if you seek reassurance from me one more time. That is not my duty. It is *your* duty to reassure us—or rather, to reassure Uzo, if he should need it. I require little for myself."

Loren found herself on her feet, fists shaking by her sides. "How do you think I can promise him that all will be well? I have little faith in myself, much less our mission."

Shiun, too, stood, matching Loren's glare with one of equal fury. "Never say that again," she hissed. "Not to any soldier who follows by your side—and, if you *do* want my advice, which you should not, then never say it to the children, either. If you believe in some Elf-tale where you are all friends on a grand adventure, I assure you that they do not. They see you as their leader, even if you do not act like one."

Loren almost argued. She wanted to. But her mind flashed back to her dream. She saw Damaris standing before her. She felt the merchant's embrace and the peace it had brought her. Reassurance. Safety. Comfort. Things she had not felt for so long, not since Jordel had died.

Shiun was studying her, and now the woman tilted her head with satisfaction. "Yes, Nightblade." Her voice was no longer angry, but quiet—and mayhap even a little sad. "That is your place. I take no more pleasure in it than you do, I am sure. But that is the way of it all the same."

Almost, Loren apologized. But then she thought better of it and nodded instead. "You . . . you are right."

Because of course Shiun was right. Loren rarely stopped to consider her own actions. That was partly because there was little time. But, too, she did not always like what she saw. She had left the Birchwood with dreams of becoming a great thief, a woman who could bring fear to kings and succour to the oppressed. Yet sometimes she still acted like a young girl, one who longed for the kindness and love of a mother and father who had never shown her either.

"You are right," she said again, slowly. "I will do better. And I thank you and Uzo for your patience with me. I could hardly have asked for better soldiers to serve in my first command—all of you but Niya, of course."

Some of the tension seemed to flow out of Shiun, and she nodded slowly. "Now *that* is the sort of thing a commander might say. And as for Niya, I hope that sow has felt all the torments of the darkness below."

Loren nodded, passing a hand over her eyes. "I . . . I should return to sleep. Do not stay up all night. Make sure you wake Uzo to replace you."

Shiun resumed her seat. "I will. Sleep well, Nightblade."

Loren returned to her room and lay down. But she could not find sleep. Shiun's words echoed in her mind. She dreaded the thought of becoming a hard-bitten commander like Kal. But then, he did seem the sort of leader whom soldiers would follow into battle. Loren pictured herself in the role and wanted to laugh.

Annis still slept, her mouth open slightly. Loren studied her. Did the girl see Loren as a commander, the way Shiun said? It seemed ridiculous. Yet the children had followed her into dangers more deadly than most soldiers faced on a battlefield. But then again, they had done so while Loren acted like herself, and not the war commander Shiun seemed to want.

She sighed, pinching her chin. Her thoughts spun around each other and seemed determined not to sort themselves out. One more worry. One more crushing weight atop all the others, threatening to snap her in two.

She could not sleep, at least not yet. So she sat up in the bed and thought about what she would say the next day. Words came slowly, and she fumbled over them. Eventually she rose and began to pace. The motion helped her, and she began to form some semblance of a proper speech. She only hoped that the plan would go smoothly, and she would in fact be able to deliver it.

Moonslight peeked through a gap in the curtains. Loren went to the window and leaned against it, pulling the cloth aside to look out. The red roofs of Danfon were silver in the night, accented in red by torches set in the walls of the buildings.

Ever since she could remember, she had dreamed of becoming a thief of legend. Something from campfire stories. Tomorrow might be the most significant single step she had yet taken on that road. It frightened her, as she knew it should. But far more than that, it excited her, if she was being honest. She often cuffed or chastised Gem when he made too much of the stories that surrounded her. The tales were embellished, made to sound like extravagant adventures when in truth she had struggled just to survive. But now she meant to pit herself against a false king before the eyes of an entire city—indeed, an entire kingdom.

"What under the sky has my life become?" she whispered.

And who was the Nightblade? A thief in the night, gallivanting across Underrealm with her band of merry companions? Or an agent of the High King and a commander of Mystics?

She blinked, and her lids were slow to rise. Weariness had come at last. She lay down in the bed once more and drew the covers over herself. At last her head settled comfortably into her pillow, and sleep claimed her quickly.

SEVENTEEN

The morning dawned bright and fair, the air as warm as one could expect in winter. Loren woke the moment Annis began to stir. When dressing, she almost reached for her normal clothes, the white shirt, green vest, and brown trousers she had worn ever since she left the Birchwood. But her hand paused on the garments. Today was not a day for simple clothes. Today she would don the new clothes Annis had bought for her.

Carefully she untied the string that held the brown cloth package together. New boots were wrapped around the rest of the clothes—not made by the tailor, but procured by him from a nearby cordwainer to go with the outfit. Loren did not think they were all that different from her old boots, though certainly they were less worn and had a few more buttons running up the calf.

The new trousers were a bit tighter than she was used to, but they still let her move about with ease. The shirt buttoned twice, inside and out, and had more buttons at the wrist. The sleeves hung somewhat loose, and they fluttered when she moved her arms. Over the shirt was a long waistcoat with many pockets on both the inside and outside. Loren thought it looked somewhat ridiculous, but the green velvet trim did catch the eye.

When she had finished dressing, she turned to find Annis staring at her. Loren had no idea how long the girl had been watching, but now she smiled with satisfaction.

"And the cloak," she said. "Put that on."

"Why?" said Loren. "It is warm in here."

Annis rolled her eyes. "Oh, come now, Loren. Let me *see* it. I picked these clothes, after all."

Loren sighed and went to the wall, fetching her cloak and putting it on. When she turned back to Annis, the girl squealed and clapped her hands.

"It is perfect. Every stitch of it. That merchant is worth twice what he charges. If we survive all of this, I shall have to send him a mighty gift of gold."

Loren looked down at herself. "Annis, I think I look ridiculous."

"Of course *you* think so," said Annis, sniffing. "You have never had good taste when it comes to the finer things in life. Do not worry how you *think* you look, for I assure you that you are wrong. Are the clothes comfortable?"

She had not thought about it. Loren crouched, then gave a jump, then twisted all around. "Actually, yes. Very comfortable indeed. Is this silk?"

Annis rolled her eyes again. "Honestly," she whispered, before speaking in a normal tone of voice. "No, it is not. Do not trouble yourself over the fabrics. We have more important things to worry about today."

Once Annis had donned her own new garments, she and Loren stepped out into the common room. The moment they stepped into view, everyone in the room froze. Loren stopped as well, pausing on the threshold. Chet and the Mystics were looking at her, their eyes wide. Kerri was there, too, and she had her head cocked, as if Loren were a stranger she did not recognize. Even Wyle paused in eating his breakfast, his eyes traveling up and down her new garments. Gem's mouth hung open.

"Sky above," breathed the boy. "You look like the Nightblade now, and no mistake."

Loren ducked her gaze, fidgeting with one of the cuffs of her shirt. "I think you are an idiot," she muttered. "Besides, I am not the only one in new clothing."

Gem looked down at his own little suit. Somehow he had rumpled it already, but its fine cut was still eye-catching. "I like it," he said simply. "But it is nowhere near as impressive as yours."

Chet stepped up before her, smiling. But Loren could see the sadness and doubt in his gaze. For a moment she thought of her dream, but she forced that thought away.

"It suits you."

"Thank you," said Loren. "But we should be off."

They all left the manor, making for the square where Wojin would deliver his speech. It was somewhat late in the morning, and the streets were busy. Wojin's address was scheduled for midday. They had intended to give themselves some time to prepare, but Loren suddenly worried that the crowds might make them late.

She touched Kerri's arm briefly, drawing the girl's attention. "Is there a faster route?"

Kerri glanced at her. "I can take us down some side streets if you wish."

"Please," said Loren. "I would rather not be late."

Kerri smiled, and her gaze darted down to Loren's outfit. As they ducked off the main thoroughfare down an alley, she looked at Loren again. "Your outfit truly does look wonderful."

Loren tried to suppress the burning in her cheeks. "Not you, too."

The girl only chuckled, a light sound that played

musically on the morning air. "Do not look so flustered. I told you when I met you that you were not quite what I expected, from the stories I had heard. But now you look much closer to the mark."

Loren chose not to answer that, and instead only urged them on to greater speed. Soon they reached the place where Loren would climb down from the rooftops. There they left Kerri, who would guide them in their escape. Loren and the others pressed on, crossing the last few streets that took them to the square.

A large crowd had already gathered. Some were there to trade, and made their way among the merchant stalls that lined two sides of the square. But most had clearly come for Wojin's speech, for they stood expectantly, looking up at the manor from which he would address them. Loren saw more than a few of them frowning and muttering to each other. She wondered if they were agents Wyle had placed in the crowd, or merely dissatisfied residents of the city. She hoped it was the latter.

"Up we go," said Gem.

He bounded up the pile of timbers, which was unchanged from the day before. Loren followed quickly, as did Chet. Shiun and Uzo remained on the ground, there to support Loren if she should need it. If all went well, and Loren escaped on the rooftops, they would vanish into the crowd and rejoin the party at Yushan's manor. Annis and Wyle had remained there, for they would be little help today.

Atop the roof, Gem bounced on the balls of his feet. When Loren and Chet reached the top, he turned to them with a grin. "I am glad to be here," he said. "Today is the day the Nightblade turns from a campfire story into a true legend."

"Be silent, Gem," said Loren. "And get down." She followed her own directions, lying on the rooftop so that she was nearly out of sight of the square below. For a moment she worried that she might be getting her knees and elbows dirty, but she quickly shook the thought away. Darkness take her if she would become someone who always worried about her appearance.

"I am worried," said Chet. He frowned down at the crowd. "There are many guards down there. The moment they see you, they will try to find a way up. It will not take them long."

"Then I will be quick," said Loren. "By the time they reach the building, we will no longer be here."

"Of course," he said, forcing a quick smile. Loren returned it, hoping hers looked more genuine.

Suddenly the crowd below them quieted. It left the air feeling empty, yet also charged with power. Loren turned. Across the square, the balcony door opened. For a moment she was uncomfortably reminded of her dream, of the balcony where she always found Gregor.

But then figures stepped through the doorway, and she shook off the thought. First came four guards. They wore armor and carried swords, but Loren noted that they did not have bows.

Then Wojin stepped into view. His robes were red trimmed with yellow, the colors of Dorsea. Upon his head was a thin circlet of gold set with many rubies. He was thinner than she had thought he would be, and his chin came down in a severe point. The point was not lessened by his thin beard, which was combed into an even sharper angle. He wore no weapon as the High King often had, not even an ornamental one. Apparently his guards were enough of a show of force for him.

Just behind Wojin came a younger man. Loren guessed that he was Prince Shun, Wojin's son. He wore robes like his father's, but a little less ornate. His head was bowed, and he kept his eyes averted from the crowd, almost as if he was ashamed to be there. Loren wondered at that for a moment, but then all her attention was taken by the next figure stepping through the door.

Damaris of the family Yerrin emerged into the sunlight. Gone were the kindness and concern Loren had seen in her dream. Damaris strode with purpose, her head held high and haughty. She was imperious, commanding. Loren did not doubt that many in the crowd ignored Wojin to study her. Some had to wonder who she was, and what had earned her the right to stand at their king's side.

A plan began to form in Loren's mind. She watched the balcony door a moment longer, but Gregor did not appear there. She smiled to herself.

Wojin paid no attention to Damaris. He stepped to the balcony's railing and raised his hands. The crowd, which had begun to buzz below them, quickly fell silent. Wojin looked solemnly down at them all, no trace of a smile touching his features as he gradually lowered his hands.

"My people," Wojin proclaimed. His voice was powerful, Loren had to give him that. She thought she could almost feel it in the tiles beneath her hands. The words hung on the air for a moment, and the last mutterings of the crowd faded to silence. "My people," he said again. "I give you my blessings, just as the sky has given us this beautiful day. But my heart is no less heavy. Day and night, I mourn the loss of my dear nephew. No parent should have to bury their child, and though Jun was not my son, I feel his loss no less keenly."

Gem snickered aloud. Loren shot him a glance, and he shrugged. "Oh, come, Loren. The man is a pompous fool."

"Silence," she whispered.

Wojin leaned forwards, his hands gripping the balcony's railing, and his brows drew together in a frown. "But with that sense of loss comes a sense of duty. My nephew's death must not go unavenged. For the so-called High King Enalyn, there can be no forgiveness. No amends or reparations can return what we have lost. The debt can only be repaid with blood!"

He paused for a moment, as if he expected the

crowd to roar in approval. They did not, and Loren thought she saw Wojin swallow.

"That is why I have joined Dulmun," he went on. His voice rose, as though he was shouting to be heard, but no one else had made a sound. "Enalyn's tyranny has had its day. For the last time, she has interfered with our sovereignty and that of the other kingdoms. No longer will we let her meddle in our affairs, keeping us from reclaiming our birthright. Dorsea should command all the southern lands that Selvan now calls their own. We did once, and we will again. Are any of us surprised that Enalyn would intervene on behalf of the kingdom she once hailed from? Underrealm is a strong nation of proud laws—but Enalyn has corrupted those laws. She calls us rebels, as she calls the kingdom of Dulmun. But I say that we 'rebels' uphold the true ideals of Underrealm!"

The time had come. Loren could feel it. She leaped to her feet and threw back her hood.

"And do those ideals include kinslaying?"

The air fell deadly quiet. Wojin gaped at her, stunned to inaction. Every head in the square turned to look. But Loren kept her gaze on Damaris. The merchant was as surprised as Wojin—but where the king stood staring at her in wonder, Damaris wore a look of open hatred. If her eyes had been longbows, Loren would have been pierced a dozen times in the space of a heartbeat.

Loren smiled briefly at Damaris, hoping the merchant could see it from such a great distance. But then she dropped her gaze to the crowd below. For a moment, she froze. They were all staring at her, many of them as dumbfounded as their king, but all of them clearly expecting her to say something. Panic struck, and her mouth worked without producing any sound.

Say something, she shouted in her own mind.

"Wojin is a usurper," she cried. They were not the first words she had planned the night before, but they seemed to do the trick. She could see a ripple move through the crowd. It was as though her words were traveling through the people like a wave. Some of them cast dark looks at Wojin where he stood on the balcony.

"A usurper, a murderer, and a would-be kinslayer," said Loren. Now that she had managed to speak, the words began to come more easily, and she remembered her speech. "Yes, I say would-be, for Wojin was not even powerful enough to bring his plans to fruition. He may have overthrown King Jun by force, and he sits in the palace now. But he is no king. King Jun is alive, and he will soon return!"

The crowd gasped. Some of them began to mill about. Glancing around, Loren could see some figures fighting to push their way through the press—guards of Wojin's, no doubt, trying to reach the base of the building upon which Loren stood. For a moment she had almost forgotten that she would need to escape.

"Liar!" cried Wojin, capturing the attention of the crowd again. "This girl tells you falsehoods!"

"Oh?" said Loren. She reached into one of the many pockets of her new vest and drew forth Jun's ring of office. Its ruby glinted in the sun as she held it up. "Then where did I get this?"

The crowd's murmur swelled as they beheld the ring. Wojin's mouth opened, but no sound came out. Loren smiled. Then a woman jumped up on the base of the statue in the square's center. She threw a fist in the air and cried out.

"Long live King Jun! Down with the usurper!"

"Down with the usurper!" yelled someone else. Loren could not see who it was, but soon a few others took up the call.

Wyle's agents, she thought. *Bless that smuggler.*

Wojin rallied himself at last. "My people!" he cried. "Do not listen to this woman. Who is she? A foreigner, and a liar! Jun is dead, murdered by assassins of the false High King! For all we know, this girl is the one who killed him! That is how she got the ring!"

Damaris' face went a shade paler, and Loren laughed out loud in what felt like a moment of madness. The laugh seemed to shock Wojin, for he fell silent again. Loren, murder Jun? She had never willingly taken a life. Wojin could not know that, but Damaris would.

Loren's laughter died, and she shook her head. "I am no murderer, Wojin. Not like you. I am a simple woman of Selvan." The crowd muttered, and she lowered her gaze to address them once more. "Yes. My kingdom has no great love for yours. But the petty differences of kings are as nothing now. Before I am a woman of Selvan, I am first a citizen of Underrealm. A servant of the High King. I did not kill Jun—I spoke with him only last night. And I will not rest until the High King's justice finds this false king—him, and the woman by his side who holds his strings. He calls me a foreign meddler? What of her? Ask yourselves, people of Danfon: why would a merchant of the family Yerrin support a man who killed his own nephew in a mad quest for power?"

Wojin was muttering to his guards and making sharp gestures towards Loren, but they had no bows with which to shoot her. Loren looked at Damaris again. The merchant's face had gone dark, and there was an evil glint in her eyes. She looked right back at Loren, her expression holding a grim promise.

I will find you, Nightblade. And I will end you.

The crowd was chanting now. "Long live King Jun! Down with the usurper! All hail the Nightblade!" That caught Loren's attention. She had not proclaimed herself to be the Nightblade at all. Wyle must have taken liberties when he gave orders to his agents.

She almost opened her mouth to speak again, but she felt a sharp tug on her pant leg and glanced down. Gem was lying flat so that the crowd could not see him, but every so often he had poked his head over the roof's edge to peer at the throng.

"The guards are close," said Gem. "It is time we left."

Loren looked and saw he was right. The guards had neared the bottom of the building where they stood. They would soon find a way up, and she did not want Uzo and Shiun to be drawn into a fight as they tried to protect her.

One last time, she turned to the crowd. "Ready yourselves for King Jun's return!" she cried. "It will be soon, and he will be wroth. For Underrealm and the High King!"

She threw a fist into the air, and many in the square cried out as they did the same. Then Loren turned with a whirl of her cloak and scampered away across the rooftop. Gem and Chet slithered away from the roof's edge, then rose to follow her.

"That was the single most glorious thing I have ever seen," said Gem with excitement. "And considering the leagues we have ridden together, that is saying a great deal."

"Oh, be *silent,* Gem," said Loren sharply. But she could not wipe the grin from her own face—even when she saw that Chet kept his gaze low, his eyes troubled. She ignored him. Mayhap she did indeed trip from one disaster into the next. But now, for the first time in a long time, it felt like she had finally gotten one thing right.

EIGHTEEN

THEY DARED NOT RETURN TO YUSHAN'S MANOR STRAIGHT away, in case someone spotted them. Therefore they spent some time wandering in back alleys and deserted streets, constantly searching to make sure no one had followed them. By the time they finally reached the manor, the sun was low in the sky.

In the basement, they reported the day's events to King Jun. Their news was met with celebration. Senlin's eyes shone as Gem told them of Loren's speech—Loren had not thought it necessary to give them details, but Gem insisted—and Jun wore a fierce smile.

Yushan herself actually clapped her hands when they were done, and immediately she beckoned for servants to bring them food, as well as some of her finest wines.

"A good day's work," said Jo. The bodyguard pulled at his close-trimmed beard, and though his face was characteristically dour, there was an uncommon energy in the movement.

"How many would you say spoke in support?" said Prince Senlin.

"Very many," said Gem quickly, before Loren could answer. He bounded up to the prince and bowed low. "I half thought the crowd would rise up on the spot and storm Wojin's manor. Mayhap they did, after we left."

"They did not," said Uzo. "It took us a while to withdraw from the press. Wojin departed almost immediately, and the crowd dispersed soon after."

Gem looked crestfallen, but Senlin smiled and put a hand on his shoulder. "That is no matter," said the prince. "The important thing is that they know we are alive. You have performed a great service—not only to us, but also to the High King herself."

This time Gem not only beamed, but blushed as well. "I suppose it is not the first time we have done so. But I thank you nonetheless, Your Excellency."

The servant arrived with a tray holding three bottles of wine. Yushan quickly unstopped one and poured a glass, which Loren accepted gratefully. But she paused as she caught King Jun's eye. He studied her with pursed lips and a furrowed brow.

"Today was a good start," he said slowly. "Yes. A good start. But *only* the start. We will not retake the kingdom on the strength of one victory."

The room went quiet. Loren's mood dampened at once as she recognized the truth in his words. But after he had let the gravity of it settle for a moment, Jun took another glass from Yushan and filled it himself. He raised it slightly in toast to Loren.

"Then again, mayhap even a small victory deserves some acknowledgement."

Jo grunted a laugh at that, and Loren's smile returned. She touched her glass to Jun's, and the two of them drank deep.

Jun turned to speak with Senlin in a low voice, and Loren studied them for a moment. She still had little love for the Dorsean king and the wars he had brought to Selvan. But she had to admit—if only to herself—that he was not so simple a man as she had imagined him to be, back when she had been younger and had seen so little of the world.

What would I have thought a year ago in the Birchwood, to see myself drinking with a king? she thought. *Indeed, he is not even the first king I have shared wine with.*

They all made merry in Yushan's basement for a short time, but Loren soon ordered her party to return to their quarters. Jun had been right on one count: they still had much to do, and the sooner they began, the better. They spent the day resting, and retired early.

Loren spent a dreamless night in sleep and woke before the sun, rising to break her fast in the common room with the others. But before she had finished eating, an urgent knock came at the door, and a messenger summoned her to Jun's side.

Annis had risen, and together the two of them made their way to the basement. There they found Jun ready to receive them—indeed, he and Senlin scarcely seemed to have moved from where they had been the night before. If they had not been wearing different clothing, Loren might have thought they had slept in their chairs. For a moment she was struck by the ludicrousness of the king and his son and their little court in this basement. Beside them, Yushan looked like a court scribe ready to take notes of the king's proclamations. But such thoughts fled her mind as Jun looked up at her gravely.

"We have received a message, relayed through many ears," he said. "Someone in the city wishes to meet with me."

Loren balked and shot a quick glance at Jo. The bodyguard's face was grave. Beside Loren, Annis spoke carefully. "That does not seem wise, Your Grace."

"Of course His Grace will not take the risk," said Jo.

Senlin glanced at the bodyguard. "Yet neither can we allow this opportunity to pass us by."

Loren held up a hand. "Pardon me, Your Grace. But *who* wishes to meet with you?"

Jun shifted in his seat. "Her name is Duris, of the family Fei. She is a senator, and she is my kin, though somewhat distant."

Annis arched an eyebrow. "And Wojin has allowed her to remain free? Why would he do that, unless she is loyal to him?"

"I have thought much the same thing," said Jun. "Yet Wojin could hardly have had time to thoroughly test the loyalty of every senator. Most likely, he hopes that they will accept his new position because it would be too difficult to resist him. The senate's purpose is to provide a check on the power of the king in domestic matters, but that power has not been strongly tested in many years. And Dorsea has not seen anything like Wojin's treachery in centuries. If he is willing to assassinate me to take the throne, would he hesitate to kill a senator? He hopes they will obey him out of fear of being replaced, or worse."

"Yet that fear may bind them to our side instead," said Jo. "They have their own states' armies, but they would not risk using them against Wojin—unless, mayhap, they think they can win. It is not the most honorable course, but it is prudent."

"And this woman Duris?" said Loren. "Is she the sort of woman who would act with such . . . prudence?"

"We do not know for certain," said Jun. "She does not normally reside in the capital, and we have had few reasons to meet each other. She only happened to be here on state business when Wojin took control.

Normally she serves in the southeastern reaches alongside that state's other senator—Shen, my cousin, and a good man. But he fell in the Battle of Wellmont."

Jun abruptly stopped talking, and his eyes flashed as he looked at Loren. He must have wondered whether it was wise to mention that battle in her presence. But Loren's thoughts went elsewhere—to something in her dream she had scarcely remembered until Jun's words brought it to the fore.

Do not forget what happened at Wellmont.

Did Damaris' words refer to the death of this senator? But how could they? How could Loren forget Shen's death, when she had never heard of it before this moment?

Her thoughts had begun to wander, and she reined them in. "It seems clear what we must do," she said. "A meeting must be arranged with Duris, though His Grace cannot attend it."

"I will go," said Senlin. "I know enough, I think, to act on my father's behalf."

"Absolutely not," said Jun. "I fear for your life more than mine. If anything were to happen to me, you would be the last of our line—except Wojin himself, and that does not bear thinking about."

"It should be me, of course," said Loren. She spread her hands. "Is that not why you have summoned me here?"

Jun lifted his chin for a moment, studying her. Loren had the feeling that he had not expected her bluntness. "It is," he said at last. "I would consider it a great service."

"I have already pledged myself to helping you reclaim the throne," said Loren. "This seems but one small step on that road."

Annis pursed her lips. "It could be dangerous, Loren. If it is a trap, this Duris may well spring it on you instead. She will think she can pry the king's location from you through torture."

"Then I will not let her catch me," said Loren. "If there is one skill I possess, it is the ability to escape the traps my enemies set for me."

She meant it as a jest, but Annis' frown only deepened. "That is what the tales say about you. Take care that you do not believe too strongly in your own myth."

Loren nodded gravely. "I will not. It was a poor jest, for I know only too well how dangerous our enemies are." She turned back to Jun. "What should I seek to gain from this meeting, Your Grace?"

"That depends very much on what Duris plans to offer," said Jun. "For now, meet with her and hear what she has to say. As I have mentioned, I know little of her directly. I hope she means to pledge her loyalty and offer help. But we must be cautious. She may seek to turn me over to Wojin, thereby earning his favor."

Annis perked up. "I should go with you," she said. "If Duris wishes to negotiate—or to plan—you will need me."

Loren's mouth twisted. "I would prefer to have you by my side, certainly. Yet it seems too dangerous. If Duris is working with Wojin, she is also working with your mother. If Duris should bring word of your presence back to her, that would be disastrous."

And she fought back a thought: *unless Damaris already knows you are here, as she said in my dream.*

No. You do not see the future. Auntie was proof enough of that.

Annis shook her head at Loren's words. "I need to be there. Forgive me, Loren, but you are simply not qualified. When it comes to a fight or to gathering information, of course you are the right choice. But not when it comes to negotiation."

"That seems to make you an even more valuable asset," said Prince Senlin, frowning. "Mayhap the Nightblade is right, and you should remain here."

Frowning, Annis thought for a moment. Then she brightened. "We will take extra precautions. We will arrange the meeting at the safest location we can manage. At the beginning, someone will meet with Duris alone while others of our party scour the surrounding area, searching for any sign of an ambush. If they find nothing, they will alert Loren, and Loren will fetch me to handle the details."

They all paused. Even Loren thought that idea had some merit. "Very well," said Jun. He turned to Yushan. "Have you any idea where such a meeting might be arranged?"

Yushan thought for a moment. "I may know a place," she said at last. "It is a warehouse owned by the family Jinso. Their trade has fallen in recent months, and the warehouse has seen little use. There will be no one around to snoop about and expose us."

"We should tell her to meet us somewhere else," said Annis quickly. "Mayhap a tavern—not too close to the warehouse, but not across the city, either. We will send an agent to meet her there and then lead her to the warehouse. That way Duris will have no chance to set a trap, if that is indeed her intention."

Jun paused for a moment, looking at Jo. The bodyguard nodded slowly before turning to his liege. "It seems wise to me, Your Grace."

"Very well," said Jun. He clapped his hands to settle the matter, and Yushan scuttled off to send the message wending its way back to Duris. When the merchant had gone, Jun turned back to Loren. "Now let us determine what your goals in the meeting should be."

"I thought I was to hear Duris out," said Loren.

"That, certainly," said Jun. "The best we can hope for is that Duris wishes to help me reclaim the throne. If that is the case, the most important thing we need is the support of as many senators as we can muster."

"Agreed," said Annis.

"And I will need their full-fledged support once I have taken the palace," said Jun. "It will do me no good to reclaim the throne if I do not have the senate ready to act on my behalf."

"Forgive me, Your Grace," said Loren. "But that seems a weak method of persuasion. Right now, Wojin holds all the power. Would the nobility not be wiser to pledge their strength to him?"

Jun smiled. It was a grim expression, fell and cold, and Loren had to hide a shiver. "Not necessarily," he said, his voice tight. "Anyone who takes a throne by force must first rally support—just as we are doing now. How do they gain that support? By promising rewards. And where do they get the rewards?"

Loren frowned. After a moment's silence, Annis answered. "They eliminate possible opponents," the girl said quietly. "Then they divide the spoils of conquest up between those who supported them in their rebellion."

"Just so," said Jun. "Until Wojin is removed from power, every senator who did not directly aid him is at risk. Duris will likely know this, Nightblade. But if she does not, you must remind her."

"I will, Your Grace," said Loren.

"Then go. Sky keep you safe."

Loren bowed, and then she and Annis returned to their quarters upstairs. The others were just rising—all but Gem, who had to be roused from bed as usual. But as the rest of them woke and broke their fast, Loren sat in her own armchair in the corner and stared into the low fire burning on the hearth, her thoughts far away.

NINETEEN

The meeting was arranged for the next day—at midday, the time when their enemies would have the most trouble pursuing Loren through crowded streets, if it should come to flight. This time Loren's whole party came, and once again Kerri guided them. She was curiously quiet as she took them through the streets, following the directions Yushan had relayed to her. At last she glanced over at Loren.

"Do you think this will work?" she said, too quietly for the others to hear.

Loren looked at her in surprise. "You were not

there when we made our plans. How do you know what we mean to do?"

"Prince Senlin told me," said Kerri. "He trusts me, and he confides in me when he has some doubt about his father's course of action."

"And does he doubt this one?"

Kerri shrugged. "He is not sure. But I did not ask about the prince. I asked about you."

Loren replied with a shrug of her own. "I do not know if it will work, but it is what we must try."

That only deepened Kerri's frown. She glanced all about, as though she expected to find Wojin's agents lurking nearby. "I am less optimistic. In all the time I have spent in Jun's household, I have learned one thing about senators: they all seek to increase their own power, no matter how much they have already. It is that exact attitude that led Wojin to rebel against his rightful king. I am leery of those who offer help for no reason."

"Yet Duris may have a very good reason," said Annis suddenly. Kerri and Loren both jumped and turned to the girl. Annis arched an eyebrow. "Yes, I heard you. By all accounts, and according to everything I have learned growing up, King Jun's rule has caused much coin to flow into the purses of his senators. Nowhere was that more true than in the kingdom's southeastern reaches, which have often borne the brunt of Jun's wars, but also benefited the most from his pillaging. With uncertainty in Danfon, and indeed across all of Dorsea's northern reaches, the south is now exposed, and it faces the wrath of neighbors who have no love for the kingdom. Furthermore, those kingdoms will now have the High King's blessing to pursue war, since Dorsea has joined the rebellion. Wojin would care little for any of this—he only wishes to strengthen his grip on the throne. Duris' homeland is threatened. Jun offers an end to that threat."

Kerri looked at Annis, studying her for a long moment as though appraising her. "That is a somewhat . . . cynical way of looking at things."

Annis shrugged. "Yet it is how our enemies view the situation," she said. "We cannot ignore that fact and expect to win in this little game."

Loren frowned. "How close are we, Kerri?"

"Not far now."

Indeed, they came to the warehouse soon after. The street was deserted, just as Yushan had thought it would be. Together the group filed around to the back of the building. There was a large iron lock on the door, but it broke after a few sharp blows from the butt of Uzo's spear. Loren went inside and inspected the place. It was nearly empty, with only a few crates scattered around. She returned to the others.

"It will do nicely," she said. "Kerri, go and fetch our friend."

Kerri nodded and left. Annis went with Gem to hide in a nearby alley, while Shiun and Uzo took up position near the warehouse, where they would watch from hiding places. Chet entered the warehouse with Loren.

While they waited, Loren found a small box and sat upon it, resting her back against a much larger crate. She indicated the other half of the box and raised an eyebrow at Chet. "You might as well sit," she said. "I think we have a little while to wait."

"I would rather stand," he said quietly. He began to pace back and forth, his steps quick. "I feel restless."

Loren eyed him carefully. "No one could blame you. Our situation is hardly free from peril."

He paused and smiled at her. "Yet you seem to be facing it easily enough."

Loren waved a hand expansively. "Long exposure has let me grow used to it."

"You said much the same thing before Yewamba." Chet's voice had gone quiet, and he stared at his boots. "I was terrified, then, too, but it is different now. I am not just afraid, I am . . . weary. And it is a weariness that does not leave me, no matter how long I sleep."

His words struck Loren's heart. She had noticed it, of course—the long hours he spent in bed, the ever-growing bags beneath his eyes. She could see it in the slow way he blinked, the way he jumped at sudden sounds. The way he recoiled from her touch.

"Chet," she said softly. "We have all seen much darkness. You more than most. I do not know how to make it any easier. But I do know that you need not feel guilty about it."

He looked up at her, his eyes glistening. But he smiled through it and shook his head with a sudden sniff. "Thank you. But even though you say that, I cannot rid myself of such a feeling."

She opened her mouth to answer, but a sudden knock came at the warehouse's back door. Loren shot to her feet and glanced at Chet. "You should hide yourself."

"No." He shook his head. "Let us get it over with. If they mean us harm, it will do me no good to hide in the shadows. They will find me regardless."

Loren nodded. Then she turned to the back door. "Come."

The door opened, and Loren's dreamsight struck her like a hammer blow.

Through the door stepped a woman she had seen before. Features sharp and severe, thin eyebrows and regal lips. Loren had seen her in the sewers below Danfon, and she had been a prisoner of Damaris and Gregor. Damaris had cut her throat.

But Loren had seen something like that before. Damaris had cut Chet's throat, too, in her dreams.

Was this woman—she must be Duris—was she a weremage? As Auntie had been? No, as *Niya* had been. It was Niya all along, not Auntie. No. Niya had *been* Auntie. Was Damaris a weremage as well? Who would cut Duris' throat, if not she?

"Loren!"

She was on her knees. Her shoulders heaved, and her breath came in ragged gasps. At the door of the warehouse, Duris stood in shock, looking down at

Loren. Kerri dashed forwards from beside the noblewoman. She knelt at Loren's side and took her shoulder, putting a hand to her forehead.

"What is it?" she said. "Tell me what is happening."

Loren glanced up. Chet stood two paces away, hands raised as if he wished to go to her. But he held back, his fear keeping him from touching her.

"I . . ." said Loren. The words ended in a gasp. But then she forced her breathing to calm, and she got to her feet with Kerri's help. "I am fine. A . . . a spell. Nothing more."

"A spell of what?" said Kerri. Her voice was uncharacteristically sharp, and her eyes were hard as steel. "I cannot help you if you do not tell me what is wrong."

"I said I am fine," said Loren. She pushed Kerri away—but gently. Then she turned to Duris and forced a smile. "My apologies, Lady Fei. The road here has been long, and the city has not lacked in excitement since my arrival."

Duris studied her for a moment, one eyebrow raised. "Yes," she said slowly. "I have heard of your . . . performance in the city square. I cannot say that that was a wise course of action, but it has certainly had some effect on the people."

Loren was still light-headed, and her hands felt clammy. But she forced her smile to widen as she bowed. "I have never had much trouble attracting attention. Indeed, sometimes I attract more than I would wish."

Duris sighed. "I find that easy to believe." She stepped into the warehouse and closed the door softly behind her. As she came forwards, she glanced around. "Are there any guards nearby I should be worried about?"

"Why should you worry about them?" said Loren. "I thought you were here to offer your aid to King Jun."

"I am," said Duris. "And my aid will be hard to lend if someone shoots me with an arrow because I made some sudden movement towards you."

Loren cocked her head. "Then mayhap you should not make any sudden movements."

Duris gave an exasperated sigh. "I . . . I am loyal to King Jun, but I am not one for intrigue. I beg you not to bandy words, but to speak plainly. Is my aid welcome or not? I am nervous enough just being here."

That took Loren aback. She spread her hands disarmingly. "Let us speak plainly, then. I have guards nearby, yes, but you will not see them. They will not act to harm you unless they have a very good reason. They can tell when I am in danger, and they know that *you* are no great danger to me on your own."

But she remembered the words that Duris had spoken in her dream: *Never again will Jun sit the Dorsean throne.*

A long breath came rushing from Duris' mouth. "Very well. I am relieved to hear it, and I suggest we do our business quickly so that I may leave. You are, I presume, the Nightblade of the High King?"

"I am."

Duris took an eager step forwards. "And you swear your words are true? You have seen Jun? He is alive?"

"He is," said Loren. "And he is eager to learn how you may be of service."

Duris sagged. It looked as though relief had made her limbs suddenly weak. "Thank the sky. I understand, of course, that you cannot tell me where he is. I am no friend of Wojin's, but you have no way of knowing that. He must remain secret to remain safe."

"As you say," said Loren. "But as you and I have both said by now: let us get to the point. Why did you ask for this meeting, Lady Fei?"

Before she could answer, there came a knock at the warehouse door. Duris jumped and turned in a panic. But Loren held up a hand to calm her.

"Do not worry. That will be one of my agents. Kerri?"

Kerri hastened to the door and opened it. Gem poked his head inside and caught Loren's eye. He nodded.

"Excellent," said Loren. "Show her in."

Gem opened the door wider, and Annis stepped inside. Duris gave a start at that. Annis ignored her, striding across the warehouse to stand beside Loren. Gem followed close on her heels. Duris stared at the lot of them, her head tilted in confusion.

"Who is this?"

Annis bowed low. "I am Annis, of the family Yerrin," she said. "My mother is Damaris. You may know her as the merchant who has taken residence in the palace and pledged her service to Wojin."

Duris' skin very nearly went as pale as Loren's. "I . . . but you . . . I swear that I—"

Loren raised a hand to silence her. "Be calm. She does not serve her mother. I am an agent of the High King, remember? Annis is the same. We came to this city to capture her mother, not to help her."

But Duris hardly seemed reassured. She put a hand to her forehead and stumbled. Loren leaped forwards to take her arm and helped her to a sitting position on the same box where she herself had rested a moment before. Duris fanned herself with a hand.

"I . . . I apologize," she said. "I . . . the shock. I fear I am ill-suited for this sort of thing. And Damaris is . . ."

She trailed off, looking uncertainly up at Loren. Annis took a step forwards.

"Damaris is what?" said Annis.

"She has her claws in Wojin," said Duris. "He rules in name only. I and the other few senators here in the capital can see it, but we can do nothing. She disregards us entirely. I had thought—hoped—that Wojin might have some respect for the senate. He was one of us before he took the throne. But he ignores us at Damaris' urging. And she is ever wary of betrayal."

"She does not like being double-crossed," said Annis, raising her brow. "I can tell you that much."

Duris studied her. "I believe it. If . . . if she were to

learn that I am here . . ." She covered her eyes with a hand. "Forgive me. As I said, I think I am ill-suited to this sort of thing."

"I was about to say the same thing," said Gem brightly. "What on earth prompted you to pursue this meeting, anyway, if you are so afraid of her?"

"Gem." Loren shoot him a look, and the boy subsided. But his words made Duris look up at them, and a fire burned in her gaze.

"She is a foreigner," said Duris, all weakness gone from her voice. "Dorsea is a proud kingdom. We do not serve at the will of outsiders."

Loren crouched before Duris, resting her arms across her knees. Her new clothes accommodated the motion easily. She hated to admit it, but she was growing quite fond of how smooth they felt on her skin.

"We have had enough shock and excitement for one day—or for many days, I think. Let us get on with this quickly, Lady Fei. What do you have to offer?"

"I . . ." Duris swallowed hard. "Well, I and many of the other senators like me, that is—we wish to help Jun retake his throne."

"His Grace hoped that that might be the case," said Annis. "Yet he was also somewhat reserved in his excitement. By his account, the two of you have never been especially close. In fact, you are just as closely related to Wojin."

Duris' breathing had returned to normal. Now she gave Loren a careful look. "From what I have heard about your speech in the square, you are a woman of Selvan. Is that right?"

Loren nodded slowly. "It is. Why?"

"You know, then, how the other kingdoms perceive Dorsea. Many of them see us as warmongers—and they are not wrong. Jun enjoys battle, and many in the senate are of the same mind. Yet that is primarily because of Wojin himself."

That gave them pause. Loren looked at Annis in surprise, but the girl only shrugged. "I had heard nothing of that."

Duris waved a hand. "Oh, Jun would be reluctant to admit it. Every king wishes to be seen as a strong leader, one who chooses their own path. And particularly here in Dorsea, our king wishes to be seen as the ultimate authority when it comes to war. Yet Wojin is far more warlike than Jun has ever been, and he coaxes the other senators to put pressure on Jun. When Jun commanded us to war—us in the southern states, I mean—he would never overextend his own forces. And he would never force the issue beyond wisdom, lest other kingdoms strike back. Even so, his wars cost many lives. That is why I came here in the first place—to urge him to pursue peace after the war on Dulmun."

"It is as I suspected," said Annis. "Now that Wojin is on the throne, you fear that things will be worse, not better."

Duris nodded. "It is not only a fear. I am certain of it. Wojin is concerned with northern politics now, of course. But after he has gathered his power, he will order the south to war again. But not just border skirmishes—a true war, a war of conquest against the other kingdoms. It is a war we have no hope of winning."

Loren wondered if that was true. Damaris served the Necromancer, and Dorsea now did the same. That dark wizard had clearly been plotting this rebellion for a long time, and their Shades were part of it. She doubted they would have started the war with no hope of victory. Now Loren wondered what other schemes were in place, what next would befall the nine kingdoms.

But she could say nothing of this to Duris, of course. She needed to secure the woman's support, not make her think that Wojin would soon have even more allies on his side. "King Jun thought much the same thing," she said. "But that leaves us with the same question, which you have not answered with any great exactitude. What, exactly, do you propose to do to help your rightful king?"

"We have very little in the way of exact plans yet," said Duris. "Indeed, until the day before yesterday, we did not know that Jun was still alive. But I—and those other nobles who feel the same as I do—what we do know, is that our plans must begin with the army. Wojin controls the capital's forces, but only a small portion of the soldiers are truly loyal to him. Another small portion will be loyal to Jun, once he reveals himself. They must hide their hearts now, but they wait for the right moment to reveal themselves. My daughter is one such."

Loren drew back, surprised. "Your daughter?"

Duris lifted her chin, fierce pride shining in her eyes. "Yes. She is Morana, of the family Fei. She is a captain within the palace. Right now she serves Wojin, for she believes that is her duty. But if it was confirmed that Wojin is a liar and a murderer, and that King Jun is alive . . ."

But Annis frowned. "I am sure she is an honorable woman," she said carefully. "Yet I think Jun and Wojin must command an equal number of soldiers who are loyal to them. If anything, Wojin likely has the advantage, for his warriors must have killed many of Jun's when he took the throne."

"Yes," said Duris. "But both of their factions together are only a small part of the army. The rest of the soldiers serve the same master they have always served, the same master *most* soldiers serve—simple coin. Even if Jun were to reveal himself now, most of the army will be confused at best. They may even be swayed to Wojin's side in the end, since he is in command of the treasury."

"Then we seem to face an obstacle," said Loren. "What plans have you devised to overcome it?"

Duris shook her head. "None. But if you can solve the problem of Wojin's coin, I will continue to raise support among the other senators. They will be ready to act in Jun's favor when he reveals himself, and together we can cast Wojin from the throne."

Loren glanced at Annis, and the girl nodded. "Very well," said Loren. "I will return to His Grace with this news."

Duris stood. "Thank you, Nightblade. Forgive me for my moment of fright. I am glad to have met you, and I wish us both well."

"As do I," said Loren. She made no mention of her own moment of weakness. Hopefully Duris would forget all about it. She extended a hand, and Duris clasped her wrist. Then the noblewoman let herself out through the warehouse's rear door.

Loren turned to the rest of them. Annis gave a little smile and shrugged. "An army to persuade, and a treasury to pilfer. What could be simpler?"

"A great many things, I think," said Gem. "But who wants simple deeds? That is not what builds a legend like that of the Nightblade."

"Oh, be *silent,* Gem," said Loren, and she led them all from the warehouse.

TWENTY

THEY RETURNED TO JUN AND MADE THEIR REPORT. THE king seemed heartened by the news, and he nodded thoughtfully when he heard what Duris had proposed. But Loren could not help a strong feeling of doubt. She could not fully rid herself of the memory of her dream, nor what Duris had said in it.

Never again will Jun sit the Dorsean throne.

Did Duris mean to betray them? Was she serving Damaris in truth? But no, in her dream, Damaris had killed the senator. Yet those who died in Loren's dreams did not always do so in life.

Jun seemed to sense her mood. "You seem troubled," he said. "More troubled than I would expect, for I think this meeting went very well indeed. What is it?"

"I . . ." Loren considered her words carefully. What could she tell him, in truth? "I am not entirely certain we can trust her."

Jun glanced between Jo and Senlin, but they only looked bemused. "I do not understand," said Jun.

"It seems suspect," said Loren. "Mayhap her offer is too good to be true. Call it a hunch if you like, but something feels wrong."

Jun's frown deepened. "Did she do something suspicious? Could you hear some hidden meaning in her words?"

Loren flushed. From the corner of her eye she could see Annis looking at her strangely. "It is nothing so precise, Your Grace. But I have a . . . a sense for people. I only ask that we proceed with caution."

"We will do that, of course," said Jun. "But for now, this is the only path we have. We must take it, or waste away here with inaction."

Loren bowed her head. "Of course, Your Grace."

How could she explain herself more clearly? There was no way to do so without telling Jun of her dreams, and she knew that would be a mistake. She realized suddenly that she had not told Annis, Gem, or Chet of the most recent vision. That would have to be remedied, as quickly as possible. Mayhap Annis could help her devise a way to convince Jun of the need for caution.

"It seems that our next task is clear, then," said Wyle from his armchair in the corner. "We need to empty your treasury, Your Grace."

"We had already thought that might be necessary," said Senlin. "My father knows as well as anyone that many of his soldiers serve him for pay."

Gem piped up. "But how to do it? I have stolen coins before, but I do not think all the kingdom's wealth is contained in a single purse." The boy had seated himself upon the floor about a pace away from Prince Senlin's chair. Loren had noted it with some surprise; Jo and the other guards made no mention of it, though they were hesitant to let Loren get near the king and prince.

"Indeed not," said Senlin. "Our treasury is sizeable—a building near as large as a warehouse, and filled with many treasures besides mere coin. Even if we could somehow remove all the coins—which would be a considerable enough feat—Wojin would yet possess a great deal of wealth. Many of the treasures are bulky, all are difficult to remove, and they could easily be sold in order to continue paying the army."

Jun said nothing, but sat pensively in his chair with his chin in one hand. Senlin watched him for a moment, seeming to expect him to speak. But the king said nothing.

"It seems that our problems are access and time,"

said Loren slowly. "Might I ask, Your Grace—do you have any alchemists who are loyal to you?"

Jun frowned at the question. "One served me, but he perished during Wojin's attack."

Loren looked to Gem. "Fetch Shiun. We may have to reach out to the Mystics here and see if they have an alchemist to help us."

The boy leaped up at once to obey, but Jo stopped him with a raised hand and leaned forwards. "I do not understand. Why do you want an alchemist? If you are thinking of storming the palace, you would do better to have a firemage or mindmage at your side. But I doubt even a wizard could help us here, unless they were uncommonly powerful."

Loren could not help a little smile. "My strength is not as a warrior, but as a thief," she said. "An alchemist might help us where a firemage cannot. If Wyle could lead us to the sewers beneath the treasury, an alchemist could tunnel up through the stone into the treasury itself. From there, with enough help, we could remove the treasure without anyone being the wiser. It would still take time, of course."

"That would not work," said Senlin flatly. "Forgive me, Nightblade, but you are hardly the first to think of such a scheme. The walls, ceiling, and floor of the treasury are all enchanted against such magic. Indeed, we even have guards posted in the sewers below the treasury to ensure no one can even make an attempt, and Wojin will have maintained those guards."

Blood flooded Loren's cheeks, and she ducked her head. "My pardon. I am less educated in ways of magic than I should be, it seems." She motioned Gem to sit again, and he sank to the floor with a dejected sigh.

"There are two things you can do to remove a man's wealth," said Wyle suddenly. His voice was filled with sudden eagerness, and Loren glanced at him. He leaned forwards in his chair now, hands on its arms, no longer slouching. "Did that man Xain ever tell you how we met, Nightblade?"

Loren arched an eyebrow. "He did not, though you hinted at it before. I gathered you did not part as friends."

Wyle snorted. "That we did not. I hired him and a riverboat captain to assist me with—" He paused suddenly, eying King Jun. "Well, with a certain business transaction. Yet when Xain discovered my aim, he misunderstood entirely, and he and the captain destroyed the goods I had intended to sell."

Annis' eyes flashed. Loren raised an eyebrow at her, but the girl held her peace for the moment. "I do not entirely understand," said Loren. "What are you saying?"

"If we cannot steal Wojin's gold—or, more properly, King Jun's gold, of course—we can destroy it."

That gave everyone in the room pause. Prince Senlin frowned in thought. "I do not see exactly how," he said slowly. "Even if we were to . . . to melt it somehow . . . Wojin could simply re-melt it and cast it into new coins."

Gem spoke quickly in Senlin's support. "And I do

not see that it removes our earlier problem—namely, that there is a great *deal* of treasure. How could we hope to melt it all without alerting the guards?"

"We could burn it," said Annis. "We could burn it with magestones."

At the word *magestones,* the king and prince gasped. Wyle very suddenly looked as though he would rather be somewhere else.

"Do you mean to say that you are carrying those cursed stones?" growled Jo. His hand fell to the hilt of the blade at his hip.

"Of course not," said Annis smoothly. "Yet my mother may have some on hand."

Jun's eyes narrowed. "There have long been rumors that the family Yerrin traffics in magestones, but they have always denied them. Do you mean to say that it has been true all along?"

"I would never suggest such a thing," said Annis. "What wise family would condone it? Yet we all know that my mother has been sundered from the family, and I from her. Did you not know that was the reason?"

That gave them pause. "A different reason was given," said Senlin. "It was said that she aided the Shades in their assault on the Seat."

"Sometimes the High King cannot be entirely plain in her proclamations," said Annis. "Sometimes she must give a reason for her actions that is—not a falsehood, of course, but not the entire truth."

Loren's heart thundered in her breast. Annis walked on the edge of a knife. Revealing Damaris' involvement with magestones brought a dangerous amount of attention to all of them. If Jun learned that they had trafficked in the stones, or worse, learned that they still bore some, all their lives would be forfeit. Yet Annis seemed utterly calm.

The coin was cast. If they were to remain safe and avoid suspicion, Loren had to help. She nodded slowly, as though she had been considering Annis' words and had now come to a conclusion. "I think this is the best course, Your Grace. If we can steal Damaris' magestones and use them to destroy the treasury, we will accomplish two ends: we will remove Wojin's ability to pay your soldiers, and we will remove a great store of dangerous and illegal goods forbidden by the King's law."

The room went silent. Jo studied Loren and her friends with a stony expression, while Senlin looked to his father, gauging his reaction. But King Jun looked straight at Loren. She felt as if he was trying to read the truth in her face, and she was grateful that her upbringing had taught her to lie so well. Even Damaris had praised Loren's skill at telling falsehoods.

At last Jun nodded. "If you believe she has a store of those accursed stones, then I think there may be some merit to this plan."

Gem wore a wide grin. "Do I understand our plan aright? First steal magestones from Damaris, then use them to destroy the treasury?"

Loren matched his smile. "You must admit it is audacious."

"Audacious?" said Gem. "It is brilliant!"

"We would not even require very many," said Annis. "When magestones burn, they burn with darkfire. It will not only melt the gold, it will destroy it—and the fires will last until they have consumed everything they have touched. We will have to set the flames carefully to see that they do not spread too far, but once we start them, Wojin will have no way to put them out."

But Jun held up a hand, his brow furrowing. "Yet one detail still remains to be resolved. Namely, once I have reclaimed my throne, how can I expect to pay my soldiers any better than Wojin could?"

"We would be in just as precarious a position as Wojin is," said Senlin. "Damaris—or any other foe—could overthrow us just as easily as we now plan to overthrow him."

"When my friends and I enter the treasury, we shall bring packs with us," said Loren. "We will fill them with as much gold as we are able to carry. That can be your soldiers' pay, at least for a little while."

Jo's mouth twisted in a grimace. "You overestimate yourselves—or you underestimate the size of our army. Even if you took as much as you could carry—which would be so heavy that you could not escape afterwards—that would not last us a week."

But Annis only smiled as she turned to Wyle once more. "You have wealthy friends within the city."

"I do," said Wyle cautiously. "Many of them."

"Surely they have gold on hand. And I would wager they have a considerable amount of it."

Wyle's eyes grew shifty, and he did not reply.

Annis sighed and adopted a more careful tone. *"If* your friends happen to have gold on hand, and *if* they were to use it to supplement the king's ability to pay his soldiers for a time, I am *certain* His Grace would extend his forgiveness to your business associates."

Wyle raised an eyebrow. "Mayhap he would. Why do you speak to *me* of this, when it seems only to help my friends?"

Annis snorted. "Very well. And I am certain he would repay the gift as soon as he was able—with, mayhap, a bonus of two percent for the honest businessman who made it possible? As a reward for your exemplary assistance to the kingdom?"

The smuggler's eyes narrowed. "Five percent."

"You remember what happened the last time we bartered," said Annis. "Do not toy with me."

Wyle spread his hands with an easy smile. "What was it you said to me then? I accused you of haggling for scraps, and you told me you were only trying to maintain your reputation as a merchant's daughter. I am trying to maintain my standing as an honest businessman."

"You will wind up an honest corpse if you do not aid us," snarled Jo.

Wyle eyed him uneasily. "Three percent," he muttered.

"Done and done," said Annis. She relaxed into her chair and drummed her fingers on its arm, smiling.

"You seem to have bartered on my behalf without consulting me," said Jun, though his tone was not very severe. "You speak of repayment—yet how am I to repay Wyle? I will still have no coin in my treasury, and I cannot raise such a heavy tax so quickly. There is enough instability in the kingdom as it is."

To Loren's surprise, Prince Senlin leaned forwards to speak. "Yet you will have the throne, Father. That is the only thing that truly matters. You, unlike Wojin, are loyal to the High King. Once you have reclaimed your seat and rallied Dorsea to her side, I am sure she will compensate us for our loss. Especially if the Nightblade should speak on our behalf. It is a small price to pay for having the might of Dorsea on her side again."

King Jun sat silently for a long moment. He drummed his fingers on his chin, deep in thought, but he did not look at any of them. His gaze was far away, seeing something Loren could not. Mayhap he imagined the future, thinking through the advantages and disadvantages of such an arrangement. Frankly, Loren's head spun at even the limited discussion they had had here in this room. She did not think that hers was a mind for the politicking of the nine kingdoms, and once again she felt an enormous wave of gratitude for the presence of Annis by her side.

"Very well," said Jun at last. "We shall follow the

plan of the daughter of Yerrin." He inclined his head towards her.

"Thank you, Your Grace," said Annis, standing to bow in response. Loren thought that was a bit of a joke—she was helping him, and not the other way around. Annis should have been the one to receive gratitude.

Jun excused himself from the room, taking Senlin with him. With a forlorn expression, Gem watched them go. Jo stood as well. But rather than leave, he fetched a map from a cabinet across the room and spread it on the floor between them. Loren studied it for a moment, but could make little sense of it without being able to read the words.

"This is the palace," said Jo. "This building here is the treasury." He pointed to a building drawn on the palace's northern side. "There is no entrance but the front door. There are windows, but they are very high. I do not know if you could sneak in that way."

"We will see when we get there," said Loren. "I am quite good at getting into places when people do not want me to."

"And how often have you had to sneak into a well-guarded palace?" said Jo.

Loren fixed him with a look. "I once strode into the middle of a mercenary army and stole a horse I liked, then set the rest of their mounts to stampede. This seems a small feat by comparison."

Jo grunted. "Very well. But we have not been in

the palace for some time. If the Yerrins are not keeping their supplies of magestones in the treasury, we have no way of knowing where they would be."

"They will be close at hand," said Annis. "My mother would not risk letting the stones out of her sight."

Loren thought back to Cabrus. There, just before she had fled the city, she had infiltrated the apartment Damaris kept at one of the inns. There she had found the woman's magestones, all kept together in a great wooden chest with a lock. It had been one of her first thefts—though she had not stolen the stones at all, but had destroyed most of them and scattered the rest for others to find, bringing the King's law down on Damaris' head. That move had been meant to remove Damaris' threat forever, though of course things had not worked out that way.

"She will have them wherever she is staying," said Loren. "I am sure of it."

"Her apartments will likely be here." Jo tapped the map with a thick fingertip. "Those are the chambers where guests of state reside."

"Then that is where we will go first," said Loren. "Sneak into Damaris' apartments and steal as many magestones as we can, and then bring them to the treasury."

"It seems a bold plan indeed," said Jo. "Audacious, as you said."

"But you have never seen us work before," said

Gem, grinning. "Or rather, you have never seen the Nightblade in action."

"Oh, leave *off,* Gem," said Loren.

But despite herself, she felt a growing excitement. When she had spoken against Wojin, she had seen Damaris' face. The merchant had been furious, yes. But she had also been surprised, and that surprise had been delicious to see. After weeks spent dodging Loren, predicting her every move, the merchant had finally been caught unawares. Loren's plan was too unpredictable, too unbelievable, for the merchant to have considered. This felt very much the same. Rather than try to draw Damaris out, Loren meant to go in. Why should Damaris expect them to come after her magestones? She knew Loren had no wizard by her side. And though she might know the treasury was one of their targets, she could not possibly guess that they would destroy its wealth rather than take it for themselves.

For the first time in a long time, Loren felt hope swell in her heart. This was going to work.

She was even able to ignore the voice in her mind. Duris' voice. *Never again will Jun sit the Dorsean throne.*

TWENTY-ONE

DAMARIS PACED HER APARTMENT. TWO PEWTER GOBLETS of wine sat on a table against the wall, untouched. Gregor sat in a massive chair—it had been brought in especially for him, since all of the room's normal furnishings were far too small.

The bodyguard studied his mistress with worry. Damaris' steps were calm and measured. She was not breathing heavily, and there was no flush in her cheeks. But anyone who knew her would know that she was seething, and no one knew Damaris better than Gregor did.

"This means nothing," he said softly. "The girl's theatrics only make her an easier target. Someone must have seen where she went. My agents will find her."

"Will they?" snapped Damaris. "You have said that for days now. Yet we have discovered nothing."

"These things take time," said Gregor.

Damaris stopped short. She sucked in a deep breath and let it out slowly, then lifted a hand to her forehead. "I know they do. I know it, Gregor. Yet we have no time. That was never true before. All these long years together, we have been able to take as long as we wanted. Or at least I thought we could. But now with the war, and with the Necromancer—"

The candle on the table guttered. Gregor looked at the room's door. A gust of wind? Most likely. But a thin sheen of sweat beaded on his forehead.

"They understand," he said. "They have told us they understand. After all, the brutes were no more help against Loren than we have been. The Nec—the *Necromancer* is more tolerant than we once feared they would be."

Damaris smiled at him, as though she could sense his heart skip as he said the word. "You have never named them before."

Gregor's jaw worked. "Forgive me. It is a foolish superstition."

"You are many things, my friend, but you have never been foolish. Indeed, in fearing them, you show your wisdom." Damaris sighed and leaned on the back of the chair opposite Gregor. "It will be all right. We *will* find Loren, and King Jun as well."

She looked up, across the room and right into Loren's eyes. "Duris will tell us everything."

Loren jerked, suddenly aware of her own presence.

When had the dream taken her? She had watched the conversation without even realizing she was there. Now she whirled about, looking around the room. Where was she? She had not seen this place before.

But the door was right beside her, and Damaris and Gregor were across the room. She threw the door open and ran through it, pounding down the hallway outside.

Behind her, Gregor's voice rang out. "You cannot run from me, girl."

Dark below take you if I cannot, she thought, and kept going.

A hand seized the back of her collar and hauled her around.

Loren screamed, drawing her dagger in an instant. She slashed. But the man who had grabbed her stepped back, easily dodging the blow.

It was not Gregor. It was the man in black. He gave her a sardonic smile from beneath oddly glowing eyes.

"Sky above girl, control yourself. I am not here to kill you, so do not give me a reason to. Come."

He took her arm and hurried her along. Now she recognized where they were: the palace of Danfon. Loren knew these halls well enough by now. But he did not take her where she feared to go: the hallway, and the dining room, and the secret passage leading back to Gregor. Instead he led her to the broad front hall, and then through the wide main doors to the courtyard outside.

The sun was high in the sky, and for a moment its light blinded Loren. When she could see again, she realized the man in black was leading her north. Soon she saw a small building ahead, and the man made right for it.

The treasury, she thought. *This is where the map showed it would be. But where are the guards?*

There were none at the front door, which opened easily under the man's hand. He led her inside. The torchlight struck her eyes, reflecting off gold, and for a moment it was as blinding as the sun had been. Senlin had not lied about the size of their hoard; before her, Loren saw more wealth than she had imagined could exist in all the world.

It struck her dumb for a moment, and she barely noticed as the man in black headed to the back of the room. But at last she followed him there. A large tapestry hung on the wall. Loren did not recognize the scene it depicted, but a man stood with hands raised to the sky. Storm clouds seemed to flow from his fingers, and they rained lightning and thunder down upon the foes who stood before him. With a start, she realized that it was the same man as the statue in the square, where she had spoken against Wojin before the crowd.

His pose in the tapestry was almost the same as the statue's.

The man in black pulled the tapestry aside. Behind it was a blank stone wall.

Loren froze. "What . . . ?" she said.

The man grinned at her. "My job is to know the secret ways no one else knows about."

He knelt and stuck a finger *into* the wall. For a moment Loren thought he must be an alchemist. But then she saw that there was a little nook there, cleverly hidden unless one looked for it carefully. The man's fingers disappeared inside, and then he pulled something. Loren heard a *click,* and two stones in the wall swung open. It revealed a passageway large enough to crawl through.

"In, girl," said the man. "They are coming."

"Who?" said Loren. But a sound answered her. She heard the door to the treasury burst open. Turning, she saw Kal rush in, Mystics at his heels. They saw her and screamed a battle cry as they charged.

Loren fell to hands and knees and crawled into the hole. But the man with the scars did not follow her. Instead, he swung the door shut behind her. Loren crawled on, listening. She expected to hear screams as the man died, the way Niya had inside the palace. But there was nothing—only the sound of men pounding uselessly on the stone outside.

The passageway went on for what seemed like forever. First it went down, and then it twisted left and right, and eventually it climbed again. Loren felt the walls as she went, but there was no way to turn left or right. And after a time, the passage ended.

She felt the wall with her hands. There was no knob, no lever. No way to get out. She began to panic. Loren did not fear tight spaces the way Annis did, but she was still trapped in the walls of the palace, and she had no idea how to get out.

Slowly, she drew three deep breaths. Then she remembered how the man had opened the passageway in the first place. Loren fumbled, trying and failing to keep her fingers steady.

At the top right corner of the wall before her, she found a chink in the stone. Her fingers sank inside, and she felt a lever. She pulled.

The wall swung open. Loren crawled through, and she was back in the palace again.

Quickly she rose to her feet and ran on. A moment before, she had known the layout of the palace, but now she was lost again, as though she had never been there before. So she kept running, guessing which way to turn every time she came to an intersection. Loren had grown up running through the forest, and her endurance had not lessened during all the long leagues she had traveled across Underrealm. But even still, eventually her legs and lungs began to burn. She was trapped here. She would never leave the palace. She—

Loren turned the corner and found herself before the dining hall. There it was, empty and clear. Beside her was the small iron door that led to the secret passageway.

"You know where you have to go, girl."

The voice made her spin. There was the man in black again. He leaned on the wall, his arms folded, his lips twisted in a smirk. But there, too, was Niya. She stood with hands at her sides, and her eyes were sad as they beheld Loren.

"It is the only way," said Niya, her voice soft.

"Darkness take you both," said Loren. "I am here for Damaris. Gregor is nothing, and he can stay in that room and rot for all I care."

Loren leaped into the dining hall. Niya cried out and reached for her. Even the man in black tried to seize her. But she slapped their hands away and ran. No one else moved to stop her. She reached the other end and flew through the open door. There, just a span away, was the open gate that led into the city. She was almost there. She was almost free.

An arrow pierced her chest.

Loren stumbled and fell. Her mind whirled back to Yewamba. She had been shot there, too. She remembered the shaft protruding from her chest, the fletching soft under her fingers.

No, not the fletching. Now the arrowhead was in front. It had slid straight through her ribs. A drop of her blood fell from its tip as she watched. She had been shot from behind.

Loren managed to roll on her back as she sank to

the ground. She looked up. There was the balcony. The one where Gregor always waited. In his hands was a massive longbow of yew, at least as long as Loren was tall. He wore an evil smile as he looked down at her.

All ways lead to Gregor.

She understood now. She understood. She could not escape Gregor. No matter what she did.

The dream released her.

Loren woke in the night, shivering and shaking. The terror of her dreams had begun to lessen, but this was different. This time the dream had not ended with Gregor moving towards her, looming in the darkness. This time he had killed her. She thought she had been clever to avoid him, but it all ended the same. She could not escape her fate.

Except that it was only a dream.

Annis lay peacefully on the other side of the bed. Loren shook her, and the girl's eyes snapped open. She sat up at once, drawing up the blanket. It was unnecessary—she and Loren both slept mostly clothed, for the girl was terribly modest.

"Loren?" she whispered. "What is it?"

"I have had a dream," she said. "Two, in fact, and I forgot to tell you of the other one. Let us fetch the others."

They went to the room that Chet and Gem shared. Uzo was on watch when they emerged, but if he thought it strange to see them awake, he made no remark. He only nodded as they passed, and then leaned back in his chair by the door of the common room. Together, Annis and Loren woke Chet and Gem, and they gave the boys a moment to collect themselves. Then the girls sat at the foot of the bed while the boys sat up against the headboard, and Loren told them all that she had seen.

When they had finished, Gem sat frowning. "I . . . I do not understand," he said lamely.

"Nor do I," said Loren. "It seems my visions are not *meant* to be understood."

"Except when they are," said Chet quietly. "Why, then, do we bother ourselves with them?"

Loren looked at him sharply. "Would you rather I did not tell you? If I had warned you of the dreams I had in Ammon, we might not have gone to Yewamba."

Chet shook his head. "I would rather we ignored them entirely—and that means you as well. You *cannot* still think there is nothing odd about this, Loren. Whatever brought these visions on—whether it is the Elves, as we first guessed, or something else entirely—it is using you, not helping you. For weeks you saw nothing, and now you have had three visions in only a few days."

"Even if I am a tool in the hand of some greater power, I am being used to achieve the ends I wish to accomplish," said Loren. "Whatever brought the dreams *is* helping me, whether or not that is the intention."

"Oh?" said Chet. "What exactly has it helped you accomplish?"

Loren spread her hands. "We seek Damaris. The dreams have helped us find her."

"You seek to capture Damaris, not pursue her. And the dreams only show you just enough to keep you always nipping at her heels."

"That is better than losing her entirely."

"You can say that now, because you do not know the end of this road."

"Nor do you," said Loren. "Nor does anyone. It is just as likely as anything else that the dreams are leading us to the end we seek."

Chet dropped his gaze. "I think you are being drawn along on that hope. For our road has led us to several ends already, and we sought none of them."

Loren fell silent, for of course she had no answer to that. Gem and Annis looked uncomfortably at each other.

"Yet . . . yet it all must mean *something,*" said Loren. "To ignore the dreams would be to give up. There must be a meaning within them. Or why would I continue to see the same thing, over and over again?"

"Mayhap the answer is not in what is the same, but what is different," said Gem slowly. "Things change from dream to dream. Might we look for clues there?"

"That still seems too plain," said Annis. "Never since we came to Danfon has Loren seen the mountains, as she did in Sidwan. Yet the mountains are not a very good clue."

"And I see Niya almost every time, no matter what I do," said Loren. "Yet she is dead. Or rather, Auntie is."

Chet's expression grew dark, and he turned away.

"One thing might be helpful, at least," said Annis. "You saw a secret entrance to the treasury. If it is there, that would help our plans immeasurably."

"If it is," said Loren. "But if it is not? We might be trapped, thinking there is a means of escape when none exists."

Annis sighed. "I suppose you are right. We cannot know what will help us until we are there, and then it may already be too late."

"I fear Duris will betray us," said Chet quietly. "What if she does? What if Damaris learns—or has already learned—about her meeting with us? What if Damaris knows about our way into and out of the city, as your dream suggests?"

"Then all our plans are for nothing," said Loren. She tugged at her hair. "But if that is the case, we should leave Danfon at once and never return. Our cause is hopeless."

Chet looked up eagerly, his eyes shining in the light of the room's lamp. "Would you do that?" he said.

Loren wondered the same thing. She had pledged herself to the High King. She had sworn to fulfill the duty assigned to her, and she had vowed to capture

Damaris. Yet if their plans were doomed . . . if *she* was doomed . . . could she knowingly walk into death? She could not help the High King as a corpse. Mayhap it was wiser to retreat now, to return to Kal with her tail between her legs and seek his instruction.

Her grip tightened on her dagger. If she did that, Kal might punish her. But then? He would use her again, just as he had aimed to from the beginning. He would devise a plan, and he would issue orders. What would Loren do, then, if her dreams showed her that *those* orders would lead to her death as well? Would she run from them? Was that to be the rest of her life, fleeing one dark premonition after another?

Before she could give voice to the thought, Gem spoke up. "I . . . I would not leave," he said. "Not if it were my choice. I will follow you to whatever end, Loren. But I do not want to live the rest of my life in fear. We know your dreams have shown you lies. I think we should use your dreams when we can—but I think we must ignore them when they tell us to do the wrong thing. And fleeing this city—leaving Damaris to work her evil in Dorsea—I think that that would be the wrong thing."

Loren nodded slowly. "I think you are right. I do not know why these visions have come to me, and I do not even understand them more than half the time. But I cannot—I *will* not let them turn my life to one of fear. I am a servant of the High King. I am not one of her soldiers, but I am like one. I follow her orders and carry out her will. Every soldier marches to battle knowing that they may die. We could die now, tonight, betrayed by one of Yushan's servants. That is not enough to make me flee from Danfon. Neither are my visions. I will stay."

"And I," said Gem.

"And I," said Annis.

"I will stay with you, then," said Chet softly. She met his gaze. Until he said the words, she had not realized how much she feared it—that *this* would be the moment. *This* would be when he chose to leave her. And in fact, she could see the sadness in his eyes, see his own fear. He had been hopeful, for a moment. He had let himself believe that Loren might actually abandon her duty, might leave Dorsea to its fate. She could see it in him now. He was disappointed, even crestfallen.

Yet he would stay.

Her dreams were no visions of the future. She did not know what they were, but they were not that.

"Very well," whispered Loren. "Thank you. And now we must all go back to sleep, for tomorrow we rob a king."

TWENTY-TWO

THEY ROSE EARLY THE NEXT MORNING, AND THEY LEFT Yushan's manor before the sun had come up. Loren brought all her party along, save for Annis. Kerri came with them as before, a guide through the streets. Loren had come to feel grateful for the girl's presence. Danfon was still a strange city to her, and it felt reassuring to have someone along to whom the place was so familiar. And though the words they had had together were relatively few, Loren had come to greatly value Kerri's counsel. She almost wished the girl were coming with them into the palace, but that was far beyond her area of expertise.

Soon the walls loomed above them. One six paces in height bordered the outer courtyards. It was a magnificent structure, and could likely hold well against even a determined attack by enemy forces. But the wall was built of rough white stone, and Loren knew she and her friends could scale it easily.

The problem was that the streets around them were too crowded. No guards were on patrol, but five warriors scaling the palace wall would surely draw attention from passersby. Loren already felt a bit conspicuous out in public. She wore her black cloak to hide her new, distinctive clothing, but the cloak itself was beautifully made, and she thought she caught one or two sidelong glances from people walking past.

Once they had walked the perimeter, they ducked into a nearby alley. "We should wait a bit," said Kerri. "Soon most people will have arrived at their destinations—the marketplaces and other shops. There will be fewer curious eyes around then, and we should be able to find a moment when no one is around to see us."

"I agree," said Loren. "Chet, would you fetch us some water and bread? We may be waiting here a while."

Chet took some silver pennies and headed for the nearest inn. The rest of them settled down to wait. Gem sat on the ground against the wall, silent with his own thoughts. Shiun and Uzo took up position at either end of the alley, watching for any signs of danger.

Two barrels sat side by side. Loren hopped up on one, and Kerri took the other.

For a moment, Kerri looked down the alley in the direction Chet had gone. "I have been meaning to ask—where did you all come from?"

Loren blinked at her. "I am from Selvan," she said. "Most of us are. Annis is . . . well, I suppose she is from the High King's Seat, though her family's home is in Feldemar."

Kerri shook her head at once. "No, I mean . . . how did you meet, is closer to the question. I know little enough about you all, but you are a forester, and Annis is a merchant child. Chet is . . . did I hear he was a hunter? And I do not know what to make of Gem. How did such a varied party come to join you?"

Loren chuckled. "That is a tale indeed. More than one, actually, and we do not have the time to tell them all now. Chet and I have known each other all our lives. I met Annis shortly after I left the woods where I was raised, and I met Gem a little while after that, in the city of Cabrus."

"Why did you and Chet leave the forest?"

"I . . ." Loren smiled and shook her head. "He did not leave with me. I left, and he left some months later. He went looking for me, in fact, and happened upon me in the city of Northwood." Her expression fell as she remembered it, and she went silent.

"Tales reached us of what happened at Northwood," said Kerri softly. "But I had not heard you played any part in that."

"Only by accident," said Loren. "The Shades—the ones who destroyed it—they were looking for me. And I lingered there too long, for I . . . I had lost someone, and I had also learned something . . . unpleasant. I spent too many days wandering the Birchwood, with Chet trying to lure me out of my sadness."

"You say he went there to look for you?" said Kerri. "Why?"

A small smile dusted Loren's lips. "Because he loved me. In truth, he had loved me for a long while before that. And after I left the forest, he was drawn out to find me again."

Kerri's eyes widened. "Oh, I . . . oh. I am sorry. I did not realize."

Loren's smile vanished. "You would have had little reason to. Things have not been well between us since . . . well, since before we came to Dorsea. Many things have happened to us in our travels together, and some were worse than others."

To Loren's surprise, Kerri looked down at her hands in a quiet fury. "That seems to be a common thread that wends its way through all of Underrealm in these days. It is why I grow frustrated that I cannot help."

Loren put a hand on her shoulder. "Yet you yourself said that we must accept the things we cannot change, the things we are blameless for. We can vow to ourselves that we will do better in the future, but that does not mean we must stew in the darkness now."

"How do you do that?" said Kerri. "How do you keep the sorrow away?"

Loren paused to think. She had wondered much the same thing, back in Northwood. She had sought comfort in Chet's company, but that had been little help. Only leaving the town had begun to lift her mood, even though that had been a dark enough day on its own. It seemed to her that taking action had been the best thing she could have done. That, and . . .

"Look at him," said Loren. She pointed at Gem. The boy was fiddling with a small knife from his boot. He flipped it back and forth across his fingers. It might have looked impressive that he did so without cutting himself, but Loren happened to know the blade was incredibly dull.

"Gem and Annis have been my solace through many dark times. Gem is always cheerfully arrogant—excessively so—and Annis always seeks to throw herself into whatever bit of work is before her, not to mention the fact that she has a brilliant mind. When I am unsure of what to do, or when I feel a dark mood coming over me, I only have to be around them, and they bring me out of it. And when they are frightened in turn, or mournful, I do my best to return the favor. Sometimes they want reassurance of safety or some plan of action. But most of the time it is enough simply to be with them, to tell a story and share a laugh.

Alone, any one of us would likely have fallen into sorrow. But we all look after each other."

"Friends," said Kerri. "I had few enough of those, even before the city was in turmoil."

Loren smiled at her. "Well, you have some now."

Kerri returned her smile, and Loren had to look away to keep herself from blushing.

Chet soon returned, and they ate the bread and drank the water. Then they waited, huddled in their cloaks against the cold, while the street beyond their alley gradually cleared. Before the sun had long cleared the tops of the mountains, Loren poked her head out. There was hardly anyone about, and the few stragglers would soon be out of sight. She looked up at the wall. There were no guards patrolling, but only some standing guard in the towers. If they climbed the wall right beside a tower, they should be able to avoid detection.

She turned to the party. "It is time. Ready yourselves."

They stood, shaking off the snow that had dusted them while they sat. Once the street was clear, Loren led them across it. She climbed first. The wall was as easy to scale as she had thought it would be, and soon she scrabbled over the top. She fell to her knees on the other side of the ramparts.

The courtyard beyond was empty. She could hear the soldiers above her moving about the tower, but their gazes were turned up and outward. Loren did not doubt that the army was on alert since her appearance a few days ago, but clearly no one expected her to infiltrate the palace directly, for the guard seemed to be lax.

Loren leaned back over the ramparts and motioned to the others. One by one they came up after her—all but Kerri. She would remain behind, for she would be of little help once they were in the palace.

Using Jo's map, they had very carefully chosen the place to climb up. Here, a smaller wall joined the palace to the main outer wall, forming a barrier between the front and back halves of the courtyard. This little blockade was less than a pace wide, and not designed to be walked on, but if they were careful they could use it to reach the palace itself. Loren glanced up one last time to ensure the guards were looking outwards, not towards the palace, and then she led her party across it. She had to control her speed—it would not do to slip on the snow and fall into the courtyard. But they reached the palace without incident. Just above them was a balcony. Loren leaped up and seized the handrail, pulling herself atop it before helping the others make the climb. Once they were all up, Loren tried the door. It was unlocked.

"Wojin is arrogant," said Shiun once they had slipped inside. "This was almost easy."

"It is to be expected," said Loren. "He only lets his most trusted guards watch the palace, and those are very few."

"They could at least check the locks," said Uzo.

"What if it is a trap?" said Chet. "What if Damaris guessed this is our aim?"

That gave Loren pause. It seemed unlikely that Damaris could anticipate such a plan as quickly as they had come up with it. Yet their entry did seem almost too easy.

She shook herself. "We will be cautious," she said. "If we see the jaws of a trap closing around us, we run. But we will carry out our mission. Let us go."

They had entered the palace very close to the apartments where they guessed Damaris would be. The hallway outside their room was empty, and Loren turned right, creeping down it. She feared that at any moment, she might recognize a location from her dreams. That could be disastrous, if the dreamsight struck her as it had when she met Duris. But nothing happened, and soon they had reached the last corner before the apartments. Loren peeked around it. There were two guards there, dark of skin and wearing green clothing. Yerrins.

Loren ducked back out of sight. "We have the right place," she murmured. "I see two guards."

"Easy enough," said Shiun.

"Gem, go back to the last turn in the hall and keep watch. I do not think we can take them silently. If more soldiers come, we will need your warning."

Gem looked up in shock. He had already begun to draw his sword. "I thought I was supposed to fight!" he whispered.

Loren gave him a hard look.

He gave an exasperated sigh. "Very well." Quickly he ran back the way they had come.

At Loren's signal, they charged around the corner. She, Uzo, and Chet ran wide, hugging the left wall to give Shiun a clear shot. Her arrow sank into the thigh of one guard, who grunted as she went down.

Before the nearer guard could draw his sword, Uzo was there. The butt of his spear cracked the man in his forehead. Finally, Chet pounced on the second guard. He struck her senseless with his staff—but not before a defiant yell burst from her lips.

"Well, someone will have heard that," said Uzo evenly.

"Then let us be quick," said Shiun, running up behind them.

Loren opened the door and leaped inside, one of her knives held before her. For a heart-stopping moment, she feared to find herself in the room from her dreams. But it was not the same room, and Gregor was nowhere to be seen. For just a moment, relief washed through her.

Then she saw the figure in the chair. It faced the window, and the sunlight cast it in silhouette. But Loren could see that its hands were bound behind the chair. It did not move.

Loren straightened, her throat going dry. Behind her, Chet and the Mystics hesitated.

She knew what she would find when she turned the chair around. She had seen it in her dream already. Loren shook her head, forcing her thoughts back to the present.

"Uzo and Shiun . . . search for a chest. A lockbox. Search the cupboards if you must. Find the magestones."

They went to do as she had bid. Slowly, Loren approached the chair. Chet went with her but remained a half-step behind.

"Loren?"

She waved him off. Step by step, she came around the chair, finding exactly what she knew she would.

It was Duris. She had been tortured to death. In the end, her throat had been cut, just as Loren had seen in her dream. But it was obvious that she had been dying for a long, long time before that. Bruises covered her face, and one of her severe-looking eyes was almost swollen shut. There were other wounds that looked far more painful, cuts all over her body that left blood running down her dress to soak into the carpet. Loren shuddered as she realized it must have been done overnight—they had met with the senator only yesterday.

"Nightblade," said Shiun. She had approached while Loren was distracted. "The room is empty. There are no magestones here."

Nothing but the corpse, thought Loren. *Duris, dead, just as I saw in my dream. What else among my visions is fated to pass?*

"Loren—" said Chet.

"Damaris outwitted us," said Loren. "She learned somehow that Duris had met with us, and she plied her for information. That means . . ." She looked up, working it out. "That means she could have traced us back to our hiding place. Somehow."

Uzo's eyes widened. "This was not a trap for us. The guard here is light because the soldiers are out scouring the city to find us."

"Or they have found the others already," said Shi-un.

Loren met Chet's gaze and saw the same fright in his eyes that must be in her own. "She could not have learned from Duris about Yushan's manor," he said. "Duris did not know. We took precautions."

"She knew about Duris before our meeting, and she followed us back from there," said Loren. "It is the only possible explanation—it is the only reason Damaris and Gregor would not be here. We need to leave, *now.*"

Footsteps pounded in the hallway outside. Uzo turned, hefting his spear, and Shiun drew an arrow. But they put up their weapons as Gem appeared in the doorway.

"Guards are coming," he said breathlessly.

"Time to go," said Loren. "Out of the palace, and then back to Yushan's home. We have to save the king."

They ran down the hall, back the way they had come. Loren heard the cries and bootsteps of soldiers in all directions. Just before they reached the room by which they had entered, they came upon four palace guards.

Loren's party launched themselves into the fray. She

herself downed one guard with a punishing blow from the hilt of her dagger. The rest fell before they could recover from their surprise. Gem got his chance to fight, fending one off with desperate swings until Uzo could pierce the man with his spear. Loren winced as she saw the spearhead sink into the man's chest.

The hallway was clear again, and their door was only a few paces away.

"Quickly!" said Loren.

They leaped from the balcony to the barricade and ran along it. Guards in the tower were looking inward now, but there were only two. Shiun paused, shooting one in the throat. His companion fell to the ground, taking cover. That gave them the time they needed to reach the wall, and they heaved themselves over it. As soon as they reached the ground, Kerri waved them over to the alleyway. On her face was a look of stark terror.

"I heard the alarm and feared the worst," she said. "Were you successful?"

"No," said Loren tersely. "And King Jun is in danger. Take us back to Yushan's manor, and do not stop for anything."

TWENTY-THREE

By the time they arrived, the manor had already been attacked.

They paused a street away, surveying the place. Soldiers wearing palace uniforms swarmed in and out. But they did not move with any great hurry. Whatever fight they had found within Yushan's home, it was already over.

"We could try to sneak in," said Shiun. "Mayhap the walls can be climbed."

"If we attack quickly, we could fight our way through," said Uzo.

"No," said Loren. "Until they abandon Yushan's home, we cannot safely approach. We . . . we must find another place to hide. An inn, or . . ."

A boot scuffed on a cobblestone behind them. As one they turned, weapons out. But Loren froze when she saw Jo.

"Come with me," said the bodyguard. He had a bandage around his forehead, and blood stained the left side of it—a new scar to go with the larger one across his scalp. "His Grace is alive. We got him out in time."

Without a word he turned and headed off down the street. Loren motioned the others forwards to follow him and quickly stepped up beside Jo. "What of the others? Annis? Is Annis all right?"

"The Yerrin girl is with us, and His Excellency escaped," said Jo gruffly. "But Yushan . . . she fell." He bowed his head for a moment.

Loren's steps faltered, and she had to force herself to resume Jo's rushing pace. Yushan had taken them all in at great risk to herself, but she had gone further: she had shown them kindness and hospitality like few people Loren had met in her travels. It was only by her bravery that Jun had survived this long.

Then Loren realized that the area they were in looked familiar. She peered around, trying to place it. At last it came to her: they were near the warehouse where they had met with Duris.

"The warehouse . . ." said Loren. "Jo, it is not safe here. That is how Damaris found us in the first place."

"We guessed that," said Jo. "There was a guard nearby, watching the place to warn her master if we returned." His scowl deepened. "But I found her. And now she will deliver no warning."

Soon they found the warehouse, and Jo led them around to the back door. He knocked, and a guard opened it. Loren entered to find them all there: King Jun, sitting on a crate like it was his new throne, and Senlin at his side like always. But there, too, was Annis. She leaped up from where she had been sitting on the floor against a barrel.

"Loren!" she cried.

Loren leaped forwards, wrapping her arms around the girl. She said nothing, only holding her close for a long moment.

"I was afraid . . . I was afraid you would not return." Annis' voice was thick with tears.

"I always will," said Loren. "Are you all right? Were you hurt?"

Annis pulled away, shaking her head and swiping at her eyes. "No. We were able to get out in time. Some of Yushan's guards held them off while we made our escape." She turned to Gem. He stood back for a moment, unsure. Annis waved her hands impatiently. "Oh come *here,* you idiot." She dragged him into a hug.

"I am alive as well, though it pains me that you did not care enough to ask." Wyle's voice surprised Loren, and she looked up to see him waving from one of the room's corners. He gave her a wide smile—but Loren thought it looked somewhat forced.

Loren went to him. He stood, and she extended a hand to grip his wrist. "I am glad to see you whole."

"I am glad to be so," said Wyle. "And I suppose it is good as well that you made it back safely. Good business partners are hard enough to find."

She smiled and then left him to go to Jun. The king inclined his head gravely at her approach.

"Nightblade," he said. "Were you successful?"

"No, Your Grace," said Loren. "Damaris predicted our plan. We could not find the magestones, and when we realized you were in danger, we left."

Jun frowned. "You should have remained and carried out your mission. My soldiers saw me to safety, but now we will have to make another attempt on the treasury. It will be harder next time."

Loren shook her head. "This warehouse is not safe, Your Grace. It is a half-measure, and we must get you out of the city at once."

The king's face grew stern. "I have told you I will not leave my capital."

But Jo stepped forwards to stand beside Loren. "You must, Your Grace. My duty is to keep you safe, and I can no longer do so in Danfon. Finding Yushan was a stroke of luck. But she is gone now, and we have nowhere else to hide. The Nightblade is right—though I slew one guard, it is only a matter of time before more come."

"Then let me reveal myself," said Jun, standing suddenly. Jo and the other bodyguards dropped to one knee, though Loren remained standing. "The people will join me."

"They will not, Your Grace." Loren spoke flatly, keeping all anger from her voice, no matter how great a fool she thought the king was acting. "Not before Wojin musters his army—which he is paying, not you—to have you cut down. Some loyal soldiers may rally to your side, but they will die."

Jun opened his mouth as if to reply. But before he could, Senlin shot to his feet. "Listen to her, Father. You have made your play, and it was brave. It might even have worked. But Wojin knows you. He knows you will—forgive me—but you will use more bravery than wits when you fight him. He is counting on it. You must survive, or there is no hope for the kingdom."

The king stopped short, turning to look at his son. Loren saw his expression soften, and his eyes looked almost mournful. After a long moment he turned back to them. "Take my son," he said. "You can remove him to safety, even if I fail."

"You *will* fail," said Loren. "Forgive me for speaking so plainly, Your Grace, but I serve the High King, not you. It is vital to her war effort that you are alive and on her side. You have no army, and now that Duris has been caught and murdered, none of the senators will join you."

Jun turned to look at Senlin once more—and Loren saw the fight leave him all at once. He sat back down, seeming to sag on top of the box. But the moment of weakness passed. He straightened his back, lifting his head to regard her. Slowly, Jo and the other guards got back to their feet.

"Very well, Nightblade," he said. "I will yield to your counsel. The High King is my liege lord, and I will do what is best for her. And I will see my son to safety as well."

Loren sighed with relief, though she tried to hide it. "I am glad to hear it, Your Grace." She turned and beckoned Wyle forwards. "We need to get out of the city at once. Can you lead us?"

"Sky above, yes," said Wyle. "I only wish you had asked me sooner."

Loren nodded and turned to Jo. "Ready yourselves to leave. We will be out of the city before the day's end."

TWENTY-FOUR

It was a sorrowful and bedraggled party that followed Wyle into the sewers. There were only two royal guards left, aside from Jo, and that put their number at thirteen. Loren had traveled many lands with only her friends beside her, and so it should have felt like a large group. But they walked beneath a city surrounded by enemies, one of whom had an entire army at his command. Against so many, thirteen felt useless.

At least thirteen is a number of fortune, thought Loren. *Mayhap that is a good omen.* But she could not quite make herself believe it.

Soon Loren was as lost in the sewers as she had been on their way in. Every tunnel and intersection looked the same. Occasionally there was a short slope taking them up or down, but that was the only difference in the midst of their long, trudging walk. But Wyle clearly knew where he was going. The smuggler never paused, turning at once every time they came to a branching in the tunnels.

Kerri dropped back to walk beside Loren. "How can he know where we are?" she whispered. "Everything looks the same to me."

Loren shrugged. "He knows the place well, the same way you know the streets of the city."

"Yet the city is made up of buildings. They look different. Down here, it is just the same dreary stone walls over and over again."

"You may see it that way," said Loren. "But Wyle sees it differently. I come from a forest. If you were to visit it, you would likely think that every tree looks the same. But I knew every tree in the woods surrounding my home. And even when I passed beyond the places I knew by heart, I knew the signs to look for. Where moss grew on trees, and the way certain plants leaned to catch the light. But when I came to a city for the first time, I was hopelessly lost, because every building looked like every other."

Kerri nodded slowly. "I suppose I can see the truth of that."

Wyle spoke suddenly from ahead of them. "We are

almost at the end. And forgive me for saying so, Your Grace, but not a moment too soon. I should like a very long rest after this is all over."

Jun did not deign to answer, but Loren smiled to herself. She could faintly hear a sound ahead of them. A murmuring, lapping noise. Running water. They were near the river.

Her dreamsight struck her, and her steps stumbled.

She had been near the river in her dream. When she had seen Damaris and Gregor, and Duris tied to the chair, dying. When she had heard Duris whisper the words: *Never again will Jun sit the Dorsean throne.*

Loren reached out, grasping, though she did not know what she was looking for. Her hand came down on Annis' arm, and she gripped it tight. The girl stopped and looked up at her in concern.

"What is it, Loren?"

"We are in danger," whispered Loren. "I . . . I think it is a trap."

Annis froze, looking down the tunnel. The others were a few paces ahead, and the gap was widening. Only Uzo was behind them, serving as a rearguard. He stopped short just behind Loren, brow furrowing.

"Nightblade?" he murmured. "Is everything all right?"

Loren looked back down the way they had come. "Have you . . . have you seen anything?"

Uzo's frown deepened. "Of course not. No one is behind us."

"I . . ."

Loren broke into a run, heading for the front of the group. Wyle was in the lead, with Jo beside him. The king and prince were just behind. They all stopped at the sound of her footsteps, turning in alarm.

"Nightblade?" said King Jun. "What is it?"

Before she could answer, Wojin's soldiers attacked.

Warriors in palace uniforms came charging from a side tunnel up ahead. They screamed a battle cry, and the sound echoed from the walls until it was deafening. It struck all the party into inaction, and they stood for a moment, dumbfounded as their foes approached.

All but Jo and Shiun. They leaped to the fore, weapons ready. Shiun caught Wyle by the collar and threw him backwards towards the others before she drew an arrow and fired. The shaft sped true, plunging into the chest of one of the soldiers. It pierced the chain, and the woman went down with a scream. Jo lifted his sword and met their enemies with a roar.

That broke the spell. Jun's other bodyguards mustered themselves and joined their commander with a shout. Thankfully the tunnel was narrow enough that the three of them could hold off the enemy fairly well, and even better once Uzo came forwards to aid them. The Mystic's spear was shorter than most, but it was longer than the swords of their enemies, and he used it to deadly effect, thrusting and withdrawing over and over again as his foes struggled to reach him.

But past the fighting, Loren could see a figure that

towered over the palace guards. There was a light farther down the tunnel, and it put him in silhouette. There was no mistaking the breadth of his shoulders, the power in his arms.

The way he always loomed over me from the doorway in his chambers, thought Loren.

And even shrouded in darkness, she could see the hateful glint in his eyes.

Gregor was here.

Loren's limbs shook. The dreamsight left her nearly unable to move. But somehow she stumbled forwards, seizing King Jun's arm. He jumped at her touch.

"Your Grace." She could barely force the words out. "We must get you away."

"The way out is through them," he said. For the first time, she heard true fear in his voice. Now he was in the midst of a battle, not planning one from afar. But Loren could not take pleasure in his sudden terror, not now. Not while her friends' lives were in danger.

"We cannot get out that way," said Loren. "We must go back to the city."

Without waiting for him to answer, she dragged him away from the fighting. Jo and the others were being forced back slowly. Loren had a feeling that would happen much more quickly once Gregor finally reached the fray. For now, the giant seemed content to press forwards at a measured pace, taking his time.

Why is he not attacking? thought Loren. *He must see that I am escaping with the king.*

More cries sounded out. Not towards the fighting, but from behind them. Loren froze. From the tunnels leading back towards the city, Loren saw more palace soldiers come charging at her.

No.

They were surrounded. There would be no escape. Her dreams had been wrong all along—or she had misunderstood them. She would not fight Gregor within the palace. He was here for her now. All her decisions had led to him in the end.

The soldiers were coming. They were only a few paces away. Shiun had fallen back, placing herself between Loren and the approaching Yerrins. Gem was by her side, his sword held forth, terror in his eyes. Annis clung to Loren's arm.

And yet . . .

Her dreams had shown her more than just Gregor.

She looked around, seeking . . . something. Did she know this place? Had she seen it?

The man in black had taken her here. And once he had her here . . .

Yes. There was a small opening. It did not even look like another tunnel, just an alcove. But she had seen it before.

"To me!" she cried, putting every bit of her strength into it. For a moment it seemed that the fighting paused, and her friends glanced back at her. "To me!" she cried again, and dived into the alcove.

It opened up into a small side tunnel, just as Loren had known it would. She followed it, dragging Jun behind her, and he pulling Senlin. Behind, the others followed one by one. Loren glanced back, squinting to see in the dim light. Jo and one guard were the last to enter the tunnel. The other guard shoved his commander on and turned, holding the alcove against pursuit.

Loren pressed on. Soon the side tunnel opened into a wider one. It was clear, but Loren could still hear soldiers shouting. They would wrap around soon and find Loren again.

"We have to keep moving," she cried. Taking her own advice, she pulled Jun further down the tunnel. She thought she remembered it now . . . she only had to keep going this way until—

Bent grate. Left. She saw it, sticking out of the wall just as it had in her dream. She turned left and pressed down the tunnel.

"How do you know where we are?" said Jun.

"It is enough that I do," said Loren. "Do not stop."

Suddenly, footsteps. Too close. Loren turned—but not fast enough.

Gregor came charging from a side tunnel. Loren did not see any other Yerrin soldiers with him, but he did not need them.

One ham-sized fist crashed into Prince Senlin. The boy flew across the sewer, striking the wall opposite. He slumped to the ground.

Most of them cried out, but King Jun was loudest.

Before Loren could react, he ripped his arm from her grip and attacked. He had no weapon, but then, Gregor had not drawn his own yet. Mayhap Jun thought he did not need one.

Gregor seized the king by the throat. His fingers wrapped all the way around the back of Jun's neck, and he squeezed.

Gem had fallen on his knees by Senlin's side, weeping. He lifted the boy up into his arms, trying to pull him out of the muck. But then Senlin coughed. Loren stared in amazement. The boy lived.

Jo cried out and attacked Gregor, who still held the king. Jo's sword came flashing down. But Gregor moved fast, faster than a blink, and drew his own weapon. It licked forth, parrying Jo's strike, and then Gregor's foot lashed out. It struck Jo in the chest, and Loren heard ribs crack. The bodyguard grunted as he fell on his back.

Shiun had moved to get a clear shot, and now she fired. The arrow pierced Gregor's arm through, but the giant did not even react.

"Stop!" cried Annis. "Gregor, stop! I command you!"

It was a desperate ploy, and it did not work. And now Gregor's sword was free.

He slammed Jun into the wall and plunged his blade into the king's chest. Such was the force of the blow that the sword pierced the stone wall behind him.

Jun jerked, and then his whole body went limp at

once. Kerri screamed, the piercing echo of it rebounding from the stone walls in a chorus.

Loren found herself by Gem's side, though she had not remembered moving there. She was helping him up, helping Prince Senlin as well. She was pulling them back, away from the giant.

"Come, come, we must flee," she said. "We must flee."

Where was Chet? She saw him now—standing in support of Uzo, but a step back, his limbs shaking. It seemed he might drop his staff at any moment. Uzo's spear was steady, however, as he advanced on Gregor. Shiun was behind him, nocking another arrow. She loosed it, but this time Gregor saw it coming. He dodged, and the shot went wide.

Gregor attacked again. Uzo expected him to use his sword to deflect the spear. Gregor caught the spear in one fist instead. His sword came from the other side, and it almost caught Uzo in the neck. But the spearman released his weapon and tumbled backwards. Shiun loosed another arrow. It hit Gregor's chest, but his armor repelled it.

Gregor flipped the spear around and threw it at her. Shiun dodged, but too slow. The spear struck her in the side. It did not run her through, but the sudden weight of it made her pitch forwards to the ground.

Sky above, no, thought Loren.

Her hand tightened on the handle of her dagger. Something coursed through her—not courage, not fear. Fury. She readied herself. Gregor was still distracted by Uzo and Chet. She could—

More battle cries sounded. The fury guttered in Loren's heart as she turned. More guards? Loren's could not even defeat Gregor on his own. If his soldiers had arrived to help him . . .

Dreamsight froze her in place as red cloaks flooded down the tunnel towards them.

Mystics.

Loren could hardly move. Her anger was gone, replaced by the terror of dreamsight. There was Kal, just as she had seen him, charging at the head of his soldiers. A rage was in their voices as well as their eyes, and they had drawn their swords.

But they were not charging at Loren, as they had in her dream. They scarcely seemed to notice her. They ran straight past her and attacked Gregor.

The giant was forced back step by step. In moments he had retreated down the same side tunnel from which he had appeared. Senlin was on his feet now, and Loren looked at him. She tried to ignore her own shaking hand.

"Your Excellency," she said. "Are you all right?"

"Yes," he said, shaking his head. "I was only stunned for a moment. I—"

His words choked off as he stared. Loren followed his gaze. There was his father, still slumped against the other side of the tunnel.

Loren stepped in front of him. "Your Excellency . . ."

"No," he whispered. "No. Father."

Loren tried to think what she could say, what words would convince him to move. But before she could, a rough hand seized her shoulder and hauled her around. She found herself face to face with Kal.

The grand chancellor's expression was a mask of carefully contained rage. Loren could sense it in the way his eyes flashed, the way his fingers squeezed down on her shoulder. His red cloak was wet in places, and Loren realized his fight had begun long before he found her little party here in the sewers.

"Girl," growled Kal. "Get your misfits out of here. Follow Jormund."

Jormund? thought Loren. And then the big man was there—tall and wide, though nowhere near so large as Gregor, the Mystic appeared from behind Kal as if by a spell. He gave her a brief smile, though there was a grimness to it that looked strange on his jovial face.

"Out of the sewers," said Kal. "Now." Then he turned and joined his Mystics in the fight. More screams told Loren that the rest of the palace guards had found them, and the sewers were now home to a pitched battle.

Senlin pressed forwards, trying to reach his father. But Loren and Gem held his arms, drawing him away. He fought them, but then Kerri swept in, and she took Senlin into her arms.

"Your Excellency," murmured Kerri. "He is dead.

I am sorry, but you must go on. We must get you out of here."

Uzo and Chet joined them—and they had Shiun slung over their shoulders. At first Loren thought someone had pulled Uzo's spear from her, but then she saw wood protruding from the wound. It must have broken when she fell. Chet's face was Elf-white, and his eyes were skittish.

"Jo?" said Loren.

Uzo glanced back. "I did not see him."

"Go to him," grunted Shiun. Her gaze drifted, going here and there. Loren thought she must be in shock. "I am useless anyway. Leave me here. One of the others can haul me out."

"Stop talking," said Loren, more sharply than she had intended. "We are not leaving you here. Jormund, go find the king's bodyguard. If he is alive, we need to bring him."

Jormund seemed a bit taken aback, but after a moment he went to do what she said. Shiun laughed, though her eyes still wandered. "Good. Good commander."

"Save your breath," said Loren.

Jormund soon reappeared. Jo was breathing, but unconscious, and Jormund had lifted the bodyguard over one shoulder. Now, he and a squadron of eight more Mystics escorted Loren and her friends through the sewers. They pressed on the way Loren had been leading them before the attack. Soon enough, she saw a bronze plate set in the ceiling.

Bronze plate. Right.

"Turn right," she said.

Wyle frowned. "That way does not lead to—"

"I said right," Loren said. She pressed on, ignoring the smuggler. The rest of them followed her after only a moment, with Gem and Annis giving her odd looks.

But Chet was not looking at anything at all. Loren was growing worried. He seemed on the verge of collapse.

"Let me take her," she said. She lifted Shiun's arm from Chet's shoulders and draped it across her own. Chet did not even try to argue, but only followed along, mute.

Soon they reached the door that Loren knew she would find. Jormund set Jo down and rammed his powerful shoulder against the door, but it did not budge.

"You will need my help," Loren said quietly. After all, the man in black had needed it, in her dream. "Gem."

The boy had been walking with Prince Senlin, consoling him. But he came to take Shiun's arm as Loren helped Jormund with the door. It opened, and Loren was struck by the smell of sweet, fresh air.

"It is a good thing you learned the sewers while you were here," grunted Jormund. "We would have had another fight if we had gone the way I planned."

"A good thing indeed," said Loren. She did not meet his eyes as she led the party back into Danfon.

TWENTY-FIVE

Loren's party hurried through the city, following Jormund's directions. Now that they were out of immediate danger, Loren found herself wondering at the man's presence. She had no idea how Kal had found them there beneath the city, but she was even more confused that he would bring Jormund with him. The large Mystic had been in Loren's party when she searched for Damaris in the kingdom of Feldemar, and she had sent him back to Kal with, in essence, a message that she was disobeying orders. She had half expected Kal to station Jormund in some remote outpost in an outland kingdom, certainly not to bring him along on a rescue mission.

But there was no time for a reunion now, and Loren doubted their meeting would have held much cheer in any case. King Jun was dead. They had managed to rescue Senlin, but this was still a disastrous blow. The renewed purpose she had found in Danfon seemed to have fled. What were they doing here? What *could* they do? The city seemed lost, and now they could not escape it. The terror of their situation wrapped around her like a shroud, threatening to choke her.

The others seemed to feel the same, but Chet was taking it harder than any of them. As they walked, he kept looking wildly in every direction. At any sudden sound, he jumped. The rest of them were trying to maintain at least some semblance of discretion—though that was hard with their wounds and the filth from the sewer that still covered them. But Chet was like a signal fire to any observer that something was wrong.

"Chet," said Loren quietly. "You must calm yourself. You will draw too much attention."

He did not answer. She was not certain he had heard her.

After what felt like an eternity, Jormund stopped outside a tavern. There was a door in the side, and he opened it to reveal a short staircase leading down to the cellar. Loren and Uzo hauled Shiun down the steps behind him. There were many more Mystics below, and several of them came forwards to help, pulling Shiun away from Loren and Uzo to help her.

"Chet!"

The panic in Annis' voice made Loren's heart skip, and she whirled as she heard a body hit the floorboards. Chet sat against the wall, hands balled to fists in front of his face. Loren fell to her knees beside him.

"Chet? What is it?" she said, her words fast with fear. "Were you wounded?"

She tried to pry his arms away so she could see if he was bleeding anywhere. But Chet shrieked and drew away.

"Do not touch me!"

Loren fell back on her rear, hands raised. Her eyes smarted as tears sprang into them. "I am sorry!" she said quickly. "I am sorry. I—are you hurt?"

It was as if he could not hear her. He took deep, heaving breaths, his chest rising and falling like ocean waves. Suddenly he turned and vomited on the floor.

"Here," said Gem. The boy knelt by Chet, pounding him on the back. Chet groaned and heaved again, but nothing came out. "Here, you are all right." Gem spoke softly, gently. It reminded Loren of the sewers of Cabrus, where he had used soothing words with Annis, trying to coax her out of her fear. He stroked Chet's back gently.

"Get up, girl."

Kal's growl drew Loren back to herself, and she shot to her feet. The grand chancellor stood before her, though she had not heard him enter. She was a few fingers taller than he, but she did not feel it now. His eyes blazed with fury, and their long flight since the sewers had not quenched his rage in the least. His nostrils flared in and out with each breath. She half expected him to spit in her eye.

"I have had it far past the bounds of patience with you," he said. "Darkness take the first day you came to Ammon. If I had known what a fool—what an incomprehensible *idiot* the High King had sent me, I would have sent you back to the Seat on the first available ship. You spurned my orders to hunt Rogan, you pursued Damaris—and then *lost* her—and now an entire kingdom has joined the rebellion because of you."

Shame had flooded Loren from the moment she saw Kal. She had been living with it since even before they came to Dorsea, when she chased Damaris across the kingdom of Feldemar. And during all their pursuit, she had shoved that shame away, thinking that she could assuage it if she could only complete her mission before Kal found her, as he must surely mean to do. But she had failed, and now he was here. Yet even in the depths of her embarrassment, anger rose in her breast at his words now.

"That was not my doing," she found herself saying, almost before she could think to form the words. "Damaris clearly set this in motion a long time—"

"Be! Silent!" he roared, loud enough to shake the walls.

And Loren obeyed. His was the voice of a battlefield commander, and it held incredible power when he was this close. Her legs grew so weak that she was surprised she could still stand.

"Do you think me a fool? I know the Dorsean rebellion was not undertaken overnight. Indeed, I heard rumors months ago that such an action might be afoot. Do you want to know why Damaris thought she could pull it off?"

Loren did not answer. She did not trust herself to.

"Because the Mystics left Danfon. The moment I learned you had come into Dorsea in pursuit of Damaris, I sent word to the grand chancellor of the Mystics in this kingdom. She pulled her soldiers out of the capital to find you and Damaris both. But that was just the opening the merchant needed." Now he *did* spit, a fat glob of phlegm that splashed on the floor next to her boot. "The High King made a mistake the day she let you enter her service, but no greater than mine in ever believing you were worthy of the honor."

Tears had already been in Loren's eyes. Now she could no longer restrain them. But she kept her face calm. Her lip did not tremble, and she did not sob. Thin drops merely leaked from the corners of her eyes, one at a time, racing to lay little tracks down her cheeks.

She still could not bring herself to speak, and so it was with great relief that she heard Annis answer instead. "I do not know that that is the case, Grand

Chancellor," she said slowly. "I know the Mystic force that was once in this city. They would not have been significant enough to deter—"

"*You* may shut your mouth as well," said Kal. He stepped past Loren, dismissing her as he went to Annis. Now he *did* loom, for he was taller than the girl, but Annis kept her back straight and did not cower. "I knew from the moment I met her that Loren was a naive thing, but I thought you had at least some glimmer of intelligence. Indeed, when I allowed you to go with her, I thought you might have some positive influence upon her. I suppose I should have known that it would be the other way around."

The room grew deadly quiet. Annis' eyes sharpened. Not for the first time in recent days, Loren thought she looked strikingly like her mother. "I told you this in Ammon," she said in an icy voice. "But you have never *let* me do anything, Kal. I have merely, on occasion, deigned to assist you in your efforts—but then, I thought you were an honorable man. I am less convinced of that, now."

"For all the good your help has done us," said Kal. "If we gained any advantage by your advice, it is lost. We managed one step forwards, but now we have taken two steps back."

"Some very pretty dances begin that way," said Gem.

The boy's mouth shut with a *click* of his teeth, his face going pale and his eyes widening. Quick as a landslide, Kal whirled on Gem and snatched him up by the tunic. Loren stepped forwards to pull him away.

"That is enough!" cried Prince Senlin.

Kal paused. The prince came from where he had stood in the corner. He wore a look of fury to match Kal's own, though his stance was a bit more composed.

"Unhand him at once, Grand Chancellor. You have made your point and more. But if it were not for the Nightblade, I would surely be dead, and Wojin's grip on Dorsea tighter than it is already. Whatever the Nightblade did before she and hers came to the capital is none of my business. But you are all in my kingdom now, and I am its rightful ruler. They serve me well—as they served my father—and they have my favor. If you care about restoring order and righting what wrongs have been done, you would do well to focus on that and stop this pointless ranting. You may think it does some good, but I am more inclined to believe it is only for your own pleasure."

Gem stared at the prince with wide and worshipful eyes. Everyone else in the room had gone still. Loren noticed Uzo looking at her, and the spearman arched an eyebrow. Loren wondered if Kal would dare to turn his ire upon the prince—the king now, she supposed.

After a long, scowling silence, Kal finally turned away. "Very well, Your Grace," he muttered. But his turn only made him face Loren again. She stiffened. Kal thrust a finger at her, and though his voice returned to some semblance of normalcy, she could hear the barely-contained fury lurking beneath it. "You are to take no action—not even the most insignificant—without telling me first. Anything more consequential than voiding your bowels requires my explicit approval. If you test me, I will pack you in a crate with straw and *ship* you back to the Seat to answer to the High King herself. You will do nothing but what I tell you, and you will do *that* the moment the order passes my lips."

Loren felt a twisting, evil feeling inside her. She recognized the tone of Kal's voice: one full of threats both explicit and implicit, promising greater harm than he would willingly speak of in front of so many witnesses. It was the same tone her father had taken with her for most of her life, and she felt a part of herself closing off, just as she had with him.

But Loren was not the same girl who had left the Birchwood nearly a year ago. She felt a sense of rebellion in her heart that she had never been able to muster with her father. So while her expression grew neutral and her hands went entirely still, her heartbeat thudded louder in her ears, and she felt a burning desire to get away from this man, to disobey him. To defy him.

She said only, "It will be my pleasure to do as you command, Grand Chancellor."

Kal studied her eyes for a moment. What he saw there must have satisfied him, if it did not entirely please him, for he nodded with a grunt. "Very well," he said. "Tell me everything you know—all that has taken place since you came to Dorsea, and especially what you have done here in the capital."

Loren glanced at Annis. The girl understood at once and stood beside her to help deliver the report. Together they gave a full account of all that had happened on their long road since Dahab.

For his part, Kal listened and did not interrupt, for which Loren was grateful. It made it easier to maintain the veneer of courtesy that had settled over her. She did not trust the anger in her heart. In one way she welcomed it, for it was a more powerful feeling than the weakness she had always felt in the presence of her parents. But she feared that if she unleashed it, it would come out in a storm that might irrevocably damage her already-tenuous relations with the Mystic and the precarious position of power she held.

When they caught him up to the present moment, Kal stood for a time, pulling his long beard in thought. Loren and Annis glanced briefly at each other.

"Our objective seems clear," said Kal at last. "We must restore Prince Senlin to the throne, and as quickly as possible."

"Very well," said Loren. They had intended to flee the city, but Kal's objective seemed far more reasonable now that they had the Mystics' strength of arms. "How shall we do it?"

Kal's scowl returned. "I shall determine that. And I shall call upon you if—*if*—I decide I require your help. In the meantime, you and your friends have quarters here. Go to them, and do not leave for any reason. And someone clean up her lover's sick before it stinks the whole place up beyond hope of cleansing."

Loren very nearly struck him. But she forced herself to remain civil, for a moment longer at least. "As you wish, Grand Chancellor."

She motioned to Gem, who helped Chet rise, and together with Annis, Kerri, and Wyle, they left the basement.

TWENTY-SIX

They had been given two rooms, with not quite enough beds between them. Loren led them all into one, but Wyle excused himself to the other, claiming he needed a moment to recover from their flight and their battle.

Chet took little note of Wyle's departure and collapsed on one of the beds. He rolled away from the others to face the wall, his arms wrapped around himself and his legs curled up. The rest of them sat, morose, in a circle in the room's opposite corner. None of them looked at each other, but only stared at the floor. Kerri was the least downcast among them, but even she seemed subdued, a far cry from her usual self. At last she seemed to muster some bit of humor, for she looked up with a little smirk.

"That Kal certainly seems a pleasant fellow."

Loren barely managed a snort. Gem picked at the threads of his trousers with a fingernail.

"Yes, mayhap that was an ill-timed quip," mumbled Kerri.

"I am stifled in this room," said Loren. "I need to get some air." She got to her feet.

Annis looked up at once. "I am not certain that that is a good idea," she said carefully.

"Because of Kal?" said Loren. "I could not care less what he thinks."

But she could not stop herself from thoughts of her father. Always she had been quiet and compliant when he was nearby, when he was within striking distance. Rebellious thoughts had only come when he left her alone. Her current mood was far too similar, and it left a bitter taste of self-loathing in the back of her throat.

I am not the same girl who left the Birchwood, she told herself. *Kal will discover that, and soon.*

"You . . . at least you should not go alone," said Annis.

Loren expected Gem to volunteer. But to her surprise, Kerri spoke up before the boy could. "I will accompany her," she said. "I could use a moment's fresh air as well, especially after those sewers."

She rose to her feet. Loren gave her a grateful nod,

which Kerri answered with a smile before following her out of the room.

They were on the ground floor of the inn. The hallway to their left led to the stairway down to the basement, and beyond that it bent around to reach the common room. But to the right, it ran to the inn's back door. Apparently the innkeeper, whom Loren had not yet met, was some contact of the Mystics. She turned left and led Kerri to the back door, and was pleasantly surprised to find Uzo there.

"Uzo?" said Loren. "I am surprised to find you on guard duty."

"Certainly you did not expect me to be resting," said Uzo, giving her a little smile.

"I half thought you might be imprisoned," said Loren. "Kal may not know exactly how to deal with me, but you are one of his soldiers. He can punish you how he sees fit."

"Yet I was only following orders," said Uzo. "Or at least, that is how the grand chancellor sees it. It does not do for a commander to punish his men for following the order of their officers."

"I suppose not," said Loren. She dropped her voice. "How is Shiun?"

"She is as well as can be expected," said Uzo. "Healers are tending to her, and she will survive."

"Good," said Loren, relief flooding through her. She could not have borne it if she had gotten the woman killed. "Now, if you please, let us out."

Uzo paused for a long moment, his mouth twisting. "Are you performing some errand for the grand chancellor? Because he told me that no one was to leave the tavern this way—particularly not you."

Loren's hands went to her hips. "I wonder: did Kal explicitly remove you from my command?"

"I—" Uzo froze, and then his lips split in a broad grin. "I suppose he never did, at that."

"Then you had better let me through. In fact, I *order* you to do so. After all, a commander wants his soldiers to follow the orders of their officers, does he not?"

Uzo looked towards the ceiling, hiding a smile. "So I have heard it said." He opened the door and stepped aside. Loren gave him a grateful nod and left, closely followed by Kerri.

Beyond the door was the inn's back alley. It held a large rack of barrels on their sides, several rows high. They likely contained ale, and there was a lowering mechanism to remove them when the innkeeper needed them. Loren began to climb the rack towards the roof. Kerri paused for a moment, looking up at her with arms folded.

"You are overly fond of rooftops, I feel," she groused.

"They are a wonderful place to get fresh air," said Loren. "And that is what we came for, is it not? Come on."

Kerri grumbled, but she followed Loren up. Soon

they sat on the edge of the inn's red tile roof, their feet hanging off into the empty air. It was nearly sundown, and the sky was a brilliant orange above them. Night's chill had not yet come, and the air was quite pleasant for winter. Loren tilted her head back, breathing deep of the crisp, fresh breeze. A part of her realized that the rooftop was exposed, but the far greater part of her did not care. She would not remain cooped up in an inn where, even when he was not present, Kal loomed over her shoulder.

Silence hung between the two of them as they watched the sun lower itself towards the mountains. In the end, Kerri broke the quiet, speaking carefully.

"I would guess that you do not feel particularly proud of yourself right now."

Loren snorted. She thought of Kal's accusations—that Damaris had escaped because of her, and that her actions had inadvertently led to Dorsea's capitulation. She was not entirely sure she believed it, but then again, she had long ago accepted that such politics were far beyond her scope.

"Not exactly," she said at last.

"You should," said Kerri. "Kal is wrong."

Slowly Loren shook her head. "I do not think so. He may have . . . overreacted. That has always been his way. But my actions were far from perfect."

Kerri turned to her, and she did not move until Loren at last turned to meet her gaze. "And do you think *he* is perfect? That he has never made an error, that he does not still make them even today? Everyone makes mistakes. Even if he *is* right—which I do not think he is—then he is at least complicit in your actions. If perfection is the goal, everyone is a failure."

Loren held Kerri's gaze for a moment, studying her dark brown eyes. It was Loren who turned away first. "Some failures are greater than others."

Kerri let those words hang for a moment. When she spoke, it was not to argue. "My parents were healers. When I was growing up, I saw them tend to others. They would not refuse care to anyone, and countless souls came to us for poultices, to have wounds sewn shut or bones set. I told you already that I was sick of the way Jun began so many wars. Part of the reason was that I would have to see my parents face his casualties. True, we were always far from the battlefront. But some soldiers returned with lingering wounds, and other injuries were related to the war effort—those who made weapons or constructs of war.

"After a time, I began to feel that my parents were somehow to blame, at least in part. They never did anything to prevent the wars, though I suppose it was mad to think that they could. But even in doing their duty, they would heal people who would only go back out to join the war again. But in the end I realized they had learned a lesson a long time ago, a lesson that I myself would not learn until later. It is the most important lesson of a healer, and it is something I have tried to keep in mind as I practice the art of the apothecary."

Kerri fell silent. The air was growing colder, and she rubbed her hands together to warm them. Loren knew it for a cheap talespinner's trick, but she could not help a smirk and a snort.

"Oh, go on," she said. "What is the lesson?"

Kerri smiled at her, but it was tinged with sadness. "Everyone makes mistakes, and sometimes grave ones. But the people who do the most good in life are the ones who keep trying—not in penance for what they have done wrong, but because they wanted to do the right thing in the first place. Penance is no worthy goal, not truly. Misdeeds are inevitable, but if we only try to correct them, we forget all the good we can do in life. I have only known you a short while, and I do not know what you did before you came to Danfon. But from what I have seen, you always do your best, and you fail less often than you succeed. Kal may try to pretend that he is better than you, but if he does, he is a liar."

She fell silent, and this time Loren did not prod her to continue. Kerri's words echoed in her mind, a gentle counterargument to the thoughts she had been plagued with ever since Yewamba.

She did not know if she agreed with the girl. After all, though Kerri might be the same age as Loren, she had not seen the things Loren had. It was hard to feel that she was doing the right thing when the nine kingdoms only seemed to slip further and further into chaos with every action.

Loren looked up at the mountains again, taking a deep breath and releasing it slowly. Then she pushed herself up from the roof.

"Come," she said. "We had better leave. Kal might come to fetch us from our room, and if he finds me gone, he may have a conniption."

Kerri snickered. "I know a medicine for that." But she followed Loren down to the ground.

TWENTY-SEVEN

They slept fitfully that night. The day's battle had passed, but it had left its mark on all of them. Though she did not dream, Loren shot awake more than once, thinking she heard the clash of steel in a sewer tunnel. Other times she woke at the sound of others stirring, coming suddenly awake with sharp cries. She heard the same thing through the wall in the next room, where Chet, Gem, and Wyle slept.

When morning finally came, Mystics brought them food to break their fast. Loren ate sparingly, not only because the food was much poorer than it had been in Yushan's manor, but also because her appetite had waned. She tried not to wonder if Kal would call upon her that day. If she had her way, she would have wasted no thought on the grand chancellor at all.

After choking down all the food she could, she got up and went to the next room. The others were all awake—even Gem, to her surprise. He and Wyle sat on the floor, eating their own meal, though they looked little more interested in it than Loren had been. But Chet was still on his bed, and Loren did not think he had touched his plate. He sat leaning against the wall, hands clasped between his knees. He looked up at Loren as she entered, his eyes like those of a corpse.

"Wyle, Gem," she said quietly. "Might you leave us alone for a moment?"

Gem glanced up at her, confused. But Wyle, bless him, did not hesitate. He rose, beckoning for Gem to follow. As they left, Wyle gave her a reassuring nod. But she scarcely saw it, for she never took her eyes from Chet's.

The door closed behind her. She stood in perfect stillness for a moment. Then she crossed the room to sit on the bed with Chet, carefully placing herself near the foot of the bed to give him plenty of room. Yesterday, in a moment of forgetfulness, she had seized his arms. Now she would give herself no chance to repeat the mistake.

Chet gave her a sad smile. "You know what I am thinking."

Loren shook her head slowly. "I do not take anything for granted. My dreams do not show me the future."

Chet dropped his gaze to his hands. "This time they are right. I have to go."

A long silence followed. Loren did not speak, could not answer. She had expected it for days now, ever since her dream in Sidwan. She had *known.* Yet the reality of Chet's words, the finality of them, left her breathless. The pain was not as sharp as when she had lost Jordel, but it was somehow deeper. After all, Jordel's parting had not been his choice.

"I do not want to go," Chet began. "Only I cannot—"

"Stop," said Loren. "I understand. I told you in Feldemar: you never have to explain yourself. Not to me. I have always understood you, Chet. How could I not?"

"Yet I must explain," said Chet, shaking his head. "I am breaking a vow. I made it to you, and I made it to myself, and it demands that at least some excuse be made."

"What excuse?" said Loren. "You have suffered more than—"

"Darkness take you, Loren, stop talking and let me speak!"

The words were neither harsh nor angry. They were desperate and pained, dragged from him as though each one agonized his throat. Loren's voice choked off, and her jaw worked to restrain a sob.

"I thought I was brave enough," said Chet. "Or, not brave. Resilient. If I could not fully give myself to your mission, I thought I could at least endure it. Last long enough, at least, for this quest to be over. I have known for some time that I would have to abandon the war. But I thought I could help you catch Damaris, and then I could leave with my conscience . . . not clear, but somewhat assuaged. Or I hoped you might tire of the chase in time, and then we could both go. But you seem tireless, and I can no longer keep the pace. Each day when I wake, I am breathless with the fear of death. Every night I fall asleep dreading that I shall never rise again. The terror creeps through me until I think it will stop my heart, and then until I wish it would. But this has been my plight since Dahab, and I kept on—but no longer. I see it now. I see that I endanger you all. I am weak. My courage will fail you at the worst time, and then your enemies . . . do you see? I am not only leaving for my sake, but for yours. I cannot follow you anymore."

I knew the dreams lied, Loren thought. *They always have. In them, he said the opposite. But I was right all along.*

"I will get you a horse," she said. "For supplies. You have a mount outside the city, of course, but you should have a pack animal as well."

"One horse is enough," said Chet. "Indeed, I never thought to own a horse in all my life. I do not know what I would do with two."

"Take the second one," said Loren. "It will make the journey easier. The Birchwood lies not far to the south. There may still be Shades in its western reaches. The High King has not yet driven them out. You should ride east for a while, but then you should be able to ride south and find home."

Chet shook his head. "Even now, you trouble yourself over me. I do not want to be any more burden than I have already—"

"Now it is your turn to be silent, Chet," said Loren. "You are not a burden, and you never will be. You have gone farther, done more, than anyone else in my life. I may have ridden longer beside Annis and Gem, but they did not leave home to find me. They did not travel for many leagues, all alone, only to seek me out. They did not . . ." She paused, forcing away the tightness in her throat. "They did not help me survive the Birchwood long enough to leave it in the first place. I pictured it often. Stealing my parents' dagger, but instead of making off with it, plunging it into my own heart. Sometimes the longing was so strong that I had to dig my nails into my own skin to prevent it. Only your friendship and, in time, your love, turned me from the path."

He was silent for a long moment before he whispered, "You never told me that."

"There was much I never told you. And I still keep some secrets. But this I will say plainly to you, and to anyone else: you speak of me as if I am some great hero, and you only a weight that I bear. I do not argue your right to leave, but I *will not* let you speak ill of yourself. I will not even let you *think* ill of yourself. Sky above, Chet, you saved the life of the Lord Prince. You are a hero of the highest renown, and Underrealm does not deserve you."

Loren forgot herself again for a moment. Her hand crept for him—just for his foot, just to feel his skin again. But Chet drew the foot back as if she were a striking snake, and Loren immediately withdrew.

"I am sorry," she whispered.

"No, it is not you," he said. "I still cannot . . . I still see . . . forgive me."

His tears broke at last, though Loren's would not come. She shook her head. "There is nothing to forgive."

Chet sat weeping for a short while, his face buried in his hands. At last he raised his head, but when he spoke, his words were still broken by sobs. "I wish that . . . I hope that after everything—if there is an anything after all of this—I hope you will come and find me."

"I promise that I will," she said. "I swear it."

"I do not know if we can . . . if it can ever be like it was before," said Chet. "But I want to know the answer."

"We will," said Loren. "But you must promise me something as well. Promise that you will try, at least, to find happiness. I was never able to give it to you, but now I charge you with that as your only mission: find happiness wherever it lies, and cling to it. Fight for it, and enjoy it as much as ever you are able. For my sake as well as your own."

"For your sake as well as my own," whispered Chet. "I cannot imagine it. But I will try."

Slowly he pushed himself up and off the bed. With cautious, tentative steps, he walked towards the door. Loren almost leaped up to embrace him—not because she had forgotten herself, but because who knew if she would ever have another chance?

Indeed, some dark voice at the back of her mind seemed to promise that she would not.

"Wait," she said.

His footsteps stopped.

Digging into the purse at her belt, she withdrew twenty gold weights. "For the horse, and for the rest of the journey home."

She held the coins in an outstretched hand, still gazing at her folded legs. She did not look up, for then she knew she would not be able to restrain herself from trying to hold him, from begging him to stay.

A long moment's silence stretched. He did not take the coins from her hand.

"Of course," she whispered. "I forgot."

She put the coins down on the edge of the bed and withdrew. From the corner of her eye, she saw his hands collect them up. Then came the sounds of him slipping on his boots, leaving, and closing the door behind him.

And then nothing.

TWENTY-EIGHT

Later that day, Kal summoned Loren and Annis to his chamber. In the small room, he had put an even smaller desk. Unlike the one in his council room in Ammon, this desk had no map atop it. There was only a single goblet of wine. Loren had no idea why he would have taken up so much of the room's limited space with the desk, except mayhap that it was a more impressive place for him to sit, subtly enhancing the impression he gave off as Loren and Annis stood before him.

Also in the room were Prince Senlin—*King* Senlin, Loren reminded herself—and Jo, who was now the boy's bodyguard. Jo wore no armor now, and bandages were wrapped thick around his torso. Loren vividly remembered the sound of the man's ribs cracking when Gregor had kicked him, but Jo seemed determined not to let such injuries deter him from his duties.

"I am glad to see you well," Loren told him as Annis closed the door.

"And you, Nightblade," said Jo.

"Enough of that," said Kal. He fixed Loren with a look. "I notice your lover left this morning."

Loren straightened, glaring down at him. She did not answer.

"Is it safe to have him running around out there?" said Kal. "Can we trust him?"

Loren kept any rancor from her tone, but it was a near thing. "I trust him a far sight better than I trust you."

Kal scowled at that, but when he answered, it was to change the subject. "I have been collecting information. Wojin did more than attack you in the sewer yesterday. At the same time, his soldiers rounded up those in the royal army who are loyal to Jun."

Annis gave a little gasp. Loren thought of Duris, the noblewoman who had offered to help them, and Morana, her daughter in the palace guard. "Were they executed?"

"No," said Kal. "There were too many of them, and even if Wojin is a treacherous snake, he is no fool. So many murders would only stoke the flames of anger that still burn in the people of this city. The loyalists have been imprisoned. We will free them when we can, but it shall have to wait. I have a plan. We know, of course, that we cannot let Dorsea remain part of a rebellion. It is a grave danger to all the nine kingdoms. Not only because of Dorsea's military might, which is considerable, but because it could sway the minds of other kings who have yet to join the war. Dorsea had already allied itself with the High King, and then it changed sides. Moreover, Dorsea borders five of the nine kingdoms. I know you never studied numbers, but that is more than half. Dulmun could not have chosen a stronger ally."

"Forgive me, Grand Chancellor, but we know this, and it has no effect on what we must do," said Annis. She had not lost all of her snippy tone from yesterday, being still angry at Kal for the way he had treated them. "You said you had a plan."

Kal's jaw worked. "We must depose Wojin and restore King Senlin to the throne. You lot had concocted a plan to raise the army against him. It was complex, and therefore doomed to fail. Much of that blame may be laid at your feet, I am sure, but I know, too, that King Jun was more honorable than he was practical. Meaning no disrespect to the dead, of course."

He inclined his head at Senlin. The boy's mouth had set in a grim line, but he nodded.

"In any case," said Kal, "I mean to remove Wojin the old-fashioned way: attack the palace with a small, determined group of soldiers, and kill him."

Loren balked, but she kept her mouth shut. Annis, however, did not restrain herself. "That seems a difficult task, to be sure."

"Difficult?" said Kal. "Yes. But we should be able to pull it off. The capital is in turmoil after the Nightblade's very foolish, very public display—the only good thing to come from your stupidity."

Loren's stomach did a turn. Not at Kal's words, but at his intentions. He meant to assassinate a king—a false king, but one sitting a throne nevertheless. She did not think cold-blooded assassination fit within the Mystics' purview. Yet she knew it would be little use arguing with Kal about it now. The grand chancellor's mind was set, and he would no doubt relish the opportunity to dress Loren down again. Off to the side, she could see that Senlin also looked deeply troubled. He had the same sense of honor as his father, and Loren imagined he did not look favorably upon assassination. But he held his peace. Why should he not? Kal's plan would put him upon the throne.

Kal noted Loren's hesitation. "Enalyn vowed that she would not force you to kill," he growled. "I am required to respect that vow. But if you think I will follow your foolish rules, you are very much mistaken. Though I will not order you to deliver the killing blow, you *will* aid my soldiers in this. You have ruined enough already, and a kingdom is in chaos because of it."

Loren lifted her chin. "Very well. I will help."

That made Kal subside, at least for the moment. "Good. And I have decided to grant you a boon as well. Once my men are inside the palace and have set about their work, you are to look for Damaris. You have chased her across two kingdoms. I doubt you will ever have a better chance to catch her. See if you can capture her. We will end Wojin tomorrow, certainly, but it would be better to kill two birds with one stone." He managed a grim smile. "Or rather, since you cannot be bothered to dirty your hands, to kill one bird and cage the other."

But Loren barely heard his jibe. She could think only of Gregor—and of her dreams, in which she saw him over and over again.

In the palace of Danfon.

"I will do my best," said Loren.

Kal fixed her with a hard look. "I expect you to do more than that. You will give every fiber of yourself to ensure this mission's success, as some small token of payment for your buffoonery so far. If you interfere in any way with my soldiers' mission to kill Wojin, I myself will ensure that the full weight of the King's law falls upon your head. Is that clear?"

Loren kept her face as still as a mask of stone. "It is clear."

Kal grunted. "Good. Now get out of my sight, and ready yourself. Tomorrow we topple a king. A false one, it is true, but nonetheless it will be no mean feat."

He waved them off, and together Loren and Annis left the room.

TWENTY-NINE

Loren returned to their chambers and informed Gem and Kerri of the plan. Gem sat silently in the corner of the room, not looking at her. He had taken Chet's departure hard, and had refused to even say good-bye. When Loren saw the look in his eyes, she could not help but be reminded of how he had been when Jordel died. But she forced herself to ignore it. If she spent too much time thinking of Chet's departure, she was not sure she would be able to go on.

When she had finished outlining the plan, Gem

finally spoke in a small voice. "I am ready to go whenever you are."

"And I will guide you, of course," said Kerri.

Annis smiled ruefully. "And I suppose I will remain here—again."

"Annis," said Loren, frowning. "You know that—"

The girl's smile only broadened, and she waved a dismissive hand. "Yes, I *do* know. I speak in jest, though I do so poorly. There is plenty to keep me occupied. I think I will meet with the new king. Likely he knows something of how to rebuild his court when he is in power, but I think I may be able to help him with some specifics."

Gem looked at her with sudden interest sparking in his eyes. "That is unfair! Why should you get to stay behind and have all the fun?"

Annis winked at him. "I doubt you would call the planning of finances and court appointments 'fun'—and if you did, I think you would only do so because of the company. You will do far better by Loren's side, but I can put in a good word for you with the new king, if you like."

Blushing furiously, Gem began to pick at his fingernails. "I do not know what you mean," he muttered darkly.

Loren smirked to see them jibing with each other again. It almost helped to remove the dark cloud of Chet's absence. But she noticed that Kerri did not join in the room's cheer. She sat completely still, and her gaze was far away.

"Kerri?" said Loren. "What is it?"

"Nothing," said Kerri quickly, looking up. "Nothing, I only . . ." She sighed and shook her head. "Oh, very well. I am worried. We had one good moment in the beginning, taking Wojin completely by surprise. But ever since then, he has outsmarted us at every turn. Even when we tried to escape. It has nearly gotten us all killed, and it *did* get King Jun killed."

Loren nodded slowly. "That is true. And sometimes I feel the same sense of foreboding. But this is a new situation. It was not Wojin who predicted our plans, but Damaris, who got her information by putting Duris to the question. But she has no one to turn to for information now. And Kal—whatever else he may be—is a cunning man. If he thinks this scheme will work, I am willing to try it."

Annis and Gem frowned but did not speak. And privately, Loren wrestled with her own doubts. Did she truly think Kal was capable of outwitting Damaris? She would rather have relied on Annis than the grand chancellor. The girl knew her mother better than anyone else. Loren had a suspicion—even a fear—that she was only submitting to Kal's will because she no longer wanted to be the one in charge. Her choices had led to many deaths already. For the moment, at least, she was content to let someone else make those decisions.

In the end, mayhap, she would find out at last whether or not all the killing could have been avoided—whether she was indeed the foolish girl Kal believed her to be, or if their foe was truly as devious as she feared.

Kal spent the rest of that night and all the next day in hurried counsel. Jo and Senlin gave him much advice on the layout of the palace and the probable distribution of guard patrols. Kal even summoned Kerri at one point. She went, despite some reservations, and came back a short while later. Kal had wanted to know details about the servants' quarters and passages, which Senlin and Jo had been unfamiliar with.

"That may be a good thing," said Annis. "I feared Kal might try a frontal assault. If he wants to know about the servants' passages, he may be trying for stealth—for as long as he can, at least."

"Mayhap," said Kerri, looking troubled. "Yet this all seems to be going so fast. He means to attack tonight. He has had scarcely more than a day to plan."

"He hopes to surprise Wojin—and Damaris," said Loren. "The more time we take to plan, the more time they have to guess our aim."

In the afternoon, Loren slipped away from the group to visit Shiun. The scout had been put up in a room of her own, and two healers tended to her wound—one a Mystic, the other not. Shiun was awake when Loren came, and she tried to push up on her elbows at once.

"Still yourself," said Loren, even as one of the healers leaped forwards to hold Shiun down. "I only wanted to see how you were doing."

"There is a hole in my gut," said Shiun. She tried to smirk but only managed a grimace. "Other than that, I could not be better." Her voice was tight with pain, and every other word came through gritted teeth.

Loren sat by her side, putting a hand over Shiun's. She glanced up at the healers. "Might we have a moment?"

They looked at each other apprehensively. The Mystic healer, a stout woman with dark skin and many bags of medicine on her belt, wagged a finger. "She is not to move for any reason."

"Of course," said Loren.

They nodded and withdrew. Shiun regarded Loren carefully for a moment. A thin veil of sweat covered her face, and Loren guessed that her wound pained her much more than she wished to show.

"Some rumors have reached me," said Shiun. "About words the grand chancellor had with you."

"Let us not speak of that," said Loren. "It is nothing you should worry yourself over. And I will not apologize for the events that led to your injury, for I know you would not want to hear it."

"Certainly not," said Shiun with a snort. "But then why have you come here?"

"I said I wanted to see if you were well," said Loren. Then she blew a long sigh out through her nose. "And I wanted to tell you that Chet left. We all rode many leagues together. I thought you ought to know."

Shiun's brows rose almost imperceptibly. "I am sorry to hear that. Though I suppose he was bound by no oath of duty. None of your friends are soldiers, not truly."

"No, they are not," said Loren. "I myself am not a soldier."

"Yet you are also not faithless."

Loren frowned and shook her head. "Chet was not faithless. He did more than almost anyone else I have met in my travels. In time—if our road had been somewhat less dark—I think he would have become a great man, and a great servant of the High King. A man somewhat like Jordel."

"You cannot be serious," said Shiun. "Do you think Jordel never walked any dark roads in all his journeys? That is what made him a great man—he never turned his course from the right one, no matter the pain it might bring him."

"Yet some pains are too deep," said Loren. "You know what happened at Yewamba."

"Actually, I do not *know,*" said Shiun. "You never told us. But I guessed. From the way things changed between you."

Loren gave her a hard look. "If you guessed right, then you know better than to call Chet faithless."

Shiun met her stare for a moment, but at last she turned her eyes away. "You are right. Forgive me. I suppose, in my own way, I am sad to see the lad go. And . . . may I speak frankly for a moment?"

"You may," said Loren, smirking. "Have you need to chastise me? Have I spoken too honestly with you, my underling, again?"

"Not that," said Shiun. "Sometimes honesty is necessary, as it is now. I worry for what Chet's departure might mean for your own peace of mind. He was good for you. I know he needed to look after himself, but now I worry about who will look after you."

"Why, you will, of course," said Loren. "The moment you are healed and back up on your feet, I expect you to return to duty."

Shiun gave a loud snort, then winced in pain. "I am hardly interested in providing the sort of comfort that Chet did, if you take my meaning."

Loren smiled and put her hand over Shiun's. "I am only joking. Do not worry about me, Shiun. Worry only about getting well."

A knock came at the door, and Loren turned just as it opened. Gem poked his head in the door. "It is time. Kal has ordered the attack to begin," he said. His gaze slid past her to Shiun. "How are you?"

"You have both asked me that, now," growled Shiun. "I have a hole in my stomach, master urchin. I am hardly well, though I will not die."

Gem grinned. "I am glad to hear it."

Loren gave Shiun's hand a final squeeze and then followed Gem from the room. In the main chamber in the basement, she found her party of Mystics ready to go. At their head, to her surprise, was Jormund. Loren drew up short before him, looking around, but Kal was nowhere to be seen.

"Are you to come with us for the attack?" said Loren.

"I am to lead it," said Jormund, giving her a grim nod. "I wish I had been with you in Yewamba. But I can make up for it now—at least in part."

Loren gave him a smile, but she knew it looked weak. What if he *had* been there in Yewamba? He might have died, as Weath had.

She heard footsteps coming down the stairs and turned to see Kal enter the room. Close behind him were Kerri and Annis. Kal stopped short and scowled at Loren.

"I have put Jormund in charge," he said. "He is not unfamiliar with this sort of mission. You are to obey his every command, just as you would my own. Understood?"

Loren nodded. "I will. You have my word."

Kal snorted. "The last time I thought I had your word, I—" He bit the words off. "But never mind that. I would rather not be at odds with you, girl. Do your job now, and I will consider that a good first step."

The hard wall Loren had built up around herself softened, at least somewhat. She gave him another nod, and this time it was more genuine. "Then I will endeavor not to let you down."

It was time to leave. Annis sprang forwards and gave Loren a hug, and then Gem. It was the first time in a long time that Loren had seen them share an open embrace without any awkwardness.

"Take care of yourself, you great fool," said Annis quietly.

"And you," said Gem.

Annis released him and motioned to Kerri, who started in surprise. "Come here," said Annis. "It is for good luck, I suppose."

Over Annis' head, Kerri looked at Loren with a little smile as the girl embraced her. Loren returned it. The muscles in Kal's jaw kept spasming, as though he longed to order an end to all this silliness, but he restrained himself.

Then, at last, it was time to go. They followed Jormund and his squadron of Mystics up the stairs leading to the street. A fine mist had come with the evening. Loren took that as a good portent: a dark and misty night for dark deeds. She followed the red cloaks into the greyness.

THIRTY

LOREN SIDLED UP BESIDE JORMUND AS THEY WALKED. "What is your first order, O my captain?" She tried to put an indifference in her tone that she did not feel.

Jormund chuckled. "I am no captain—though who knows? If tonight goes well, the grand chancellor might promote me. But my first instruction is that, once we are inside the palace, you should avoid the fighting at all cost."

"That is an order I can follow easily," said Loren. "How do you mean to sneak into the palace? We climbed the wall, last time."

"And that is still the best way in, but they will surely have redoubled the guard," said Jormund. "Therefore we mean to make a feint at the front gate. When they are distracted there, the larger part of our group will enter the same way you did last time. Once we are inside, Keridwen will lead us through the servants' passages to the king's quarters."

Loren frowned. "The main gate will be guarded. The mists will help, but surely they will still see us when we try to make the climb. We will be exposed."

"But we will not be climbing for very long," said Jormund, smiling. "Yond here is a mindmage."

He pointed to a man by his side. Yond did not look quite like Loren thought a wizard should—he was too short and wide for that. But he smiled at her and lifted a hand, and his eyes began to glow. A dagger flipped up out of Loren's belt to spin in midair.

"I shall get you on top of that wall quickly, girl." He had a voice like two stones grinding together. "I hope you can do your job after that."

Loren smiled at him before plucking her dagger out of the air and sheathing it once more.

Soon they reached the palace. A wide main road ran in front of the walls, and they stood in the shadows on the other side. Mayhap ten paces separated them from their target—ten paces they would have to cross in the open air. Guards stood in the windows of the gatehouse and the towers, but there were also two guards on the street in front of the gate. The mists would help cover their approach, but they would be seen before they could sneak in. A thrill coursed through Loren. It was the same feeling she had had just before they infiltrated and attacked Yewamba. She only hoped that the results would be somewhat better this time.

"Time to begin," said Jormund.

They attacked.

Ten of the Mystics stormed forwards, drawing their swords, with Loren and Gem close behind. They sounded no battle cries, and so the guards did not notice them until they were almost to the wall. Then a cry went up. Four guards from above loosed a volley of arrows, but Yond's eyes flashed. The arrows scattered in midair, clattering to the cobblestones. Then the redcloaks reached the soldiers on the street. With the benefit of surprise, the Mystics slew their foes quickly. Each fell pierced by many swords. Jormund turned to Loren and clasped his hands.

"Boot," he grunted.

Loren placed her foot in his hands and leaped when he heaved. That sent her almost halfway up the wall—and then she felt an unseen force seize her under the arms.

Yond's mindmagic, she realized.

The spell threw her the rest of the way, so that she did not even need to grip the top of the wall, but flew neatly over it to land on the other side of the ramparts.

One guard was on the wall just outside the tower, and she barely had time to look surprised before Loren attacked. The woman bore only a bow, and she could do nothing to block Loren's punch. Three times Loren struck, and the woman collapsed to the ground.

Jormund landed just behind her. At once he slammed his shoulder into the door of the gatehouse. It flew open, leading into the upper floor.

Five guards waited inside. One raised a sword, but Loren threw a dagger into his arm and then grappled with another. Jormund's sword flashed, felling two of them.

Loren's opponent tried to overpower her, but she threw a foot behind the woman's and pushed her back. The guard's head struck the wall, and she fell senseless to the floor. But her companion attacked, forcing Loren back with his sword.

Jormund came to help after the first few wild swipes. His sword battered the other man's away, knocking it from his grip. Jormund plunged the blade through the man's chest, and he dropped. The gatehouse was clear.

They ran to the wheels at either end. Jormund's meaty fists wrapped around the spokes, and he had the rear gate raised in only a few heartbeats. Loren was slower, but he ran over to help her finish it. Soon the gates were up, and they heard shouting as the guards inside the courtyard realized the palace was exposed. By that time, four more Mystics had made the climb, and they filed into the gatehouse.

"Hold this place as long as you can," said Jormund. "But once you are sure it will fall, get out alive." The warriors moved to obey. Two took up positions at the doors, while two others stood at arrow slits at the rear. They would be able to fire into the courtyard as the Danfon soldiers came to attack.

"Our job here is done," said Jormund. "Now comes the greater task."

He and Loren took the stairs down and into the courtyard, immediately ducking through the gate and back out to the street. With a quick gesture, he motioned the rest of the Mystics after him. There were fifteen of them now, in addition to Loren and her friends, and they made their way around to the same place where Loren had infiltrated the palace last time.

With the help of the mindmage, they made the climb far more quickly than they had before. No guards challenged them on the walls, for all had been summoned to fight at the front gate. They made their quick run across the side wall, and Loren led them in their climb up to the balcony that would let them in. But this time the door was locked.

"They have learned that much, at least," said Loren.

"Pah," said Jormund, grinning. "What good is a lock?"

He rammed his massive shoulder into the door twice, and the jamb splintered as it flew open. They stormed into the palace—but now they turned the opposite direction from last time, for they were making for the servant passages.

"Here," said Kerri. The girl's eyes were wide with fright, and her hands shook as she pointed out the right door, but her voice did not quiver. Loren was impressed. Kerri had said she was fearful when Wojin attacked the palace, but she seemed to be handling this battle fairly well.

Jormund threw open the door Kerri had pointed to. Inside was a servant, but before he could cry out, Jormund's meaty fist struck him senseless. Kerri directed them through the passageway, turning left and right as they made their way towards the kings' chambers.

The plan of attack was brilliant, Loren realized, for it would be almost impossible to find them here. They were in the walls of the palace itself, and all attention would be diverted to the front gate. If Wojin feared any attack, he would expect it to come from the palace's front hall. The servant's passages would put them only a few rooms away from the king's chambers, and while they would no doubt be guarded, they would have bypassed the greater strength of Wojin's forces. Indeed, even the servants' chambers were surprisingly empty. She supposed most of them must have gone to bed already, and the rest were likely hiding after hearing of the battle in the courtyard.

At last, Kerri held up a hand. They all came to a stop in front of a simple wooden door, and Kerri turned to them.

"This leads to the entrance to the keep," she said. "There is a small chamber, and then a door. Then stairs leading up into the keep itself, where the king's chambers will be found."

"Good," said Jormund. "And the Yerrins?"

"Once we climb the stairs, there is a passage leading away to the Yerrin apartments," said Kerri.

"We will break off from the rest of you once we make the climb," said Loren.

"Very well," said Jormund. "If you have not returned by the time our deed is done, we will seek you out in case you need our aid."

"I would appreciate that," said Loren, thinking of Gregor. She hoped that he would have been pulled away from Damaris' side by the fighting, but that seemed too fortunate to be true.

Jormund nodded and threw open the door. They rushed out of the hallway into a small chamber with doors on either side. Two guards stood before them, but they could barely draw their swords before the Mystics fell upon them.

In a moment the guards were slain, and Jormund opened the door to the stairwell. The stairs turned back and forth twice before emerging onto a landing before the king's chamber. Loren saw the door leading to the side hallway, and Damaris' chambers.

They all paused for half a moment, and Jormund turned to look at her.

"Good fortune, Nightblade," he said. "I will see you again soon."

"Good fortune," said Loren. She ran for the hallway door, Kerri and Gem on her heels, and threw it open.

An arrow flew at her from the hallway beyond. Loren dodged too late by reflex, but the arrow missed her anyway. She caught a glimpse of soldiers in Dorsean livery, and then she fell to the floor on her back. Desperately she kicked the door shut again.

"Jormund!" she cried. "Wait!"

She was too late. She heard the door to the king's chamber burst open, and the Mystics gave great cries as they stormed in.

"After them," said Loren, pulling Kerri and Gem with her. They reached the door to the king's chamber not a moment too soon. Behind them, the hallway door burst open, and Dorsean soldiers charged in, screaming. The opposite door flew open as well, and more soldiers came running from the other side. Loren leaped into the king's chambers, Gem and Kerri close behind her, and threw the doors shut.

The chambers were empty. There was a wide bed against the opposite wall, with great windows on either side of it, and many chairs and couches for the king to receive guests. But Wojin was not here, nor were any of his household guards. Jormund stood spinning in the center of the room, his sword drawn but impotent.

"It is empty," he said slowly.

"Jormund!" said Loren. "Guards outside!"

Jormund ran to her, and several Mystics followed. They put their shoulders against the door, leaning into the force of the soldiers beyond, who had begun to batter it.

"The bar!" said Jormund. His outthrust finger pointed at a bar for the door. Two of the Mystics heaved it up and placed it in its iron fittings, and then the rest of them fell back. The pounding and shouting from outside redoubled.

Yond eyed the door, his face grim. "That will not hold long," he said.

"When it falls, we fight," said Jormund. Loren could scarcely believe it, but a smile split his lips. "I do not think they will expect a mindmage."

"Jormund, there are far too many of them," said Loren. "And where is Wojin?"

"They knew," said Gem quietly. "They guessed."

"Yes," said Jormund. His smile did not falter as he looked down at Loren. "Yes, we have been thoroughly outwitted. Even if we could guess where Wojin has been moved to, we could never reach him, and certainly we could not surprise him."

Loren frowned up at him. "Then we must escape."

A huge blow crashed against the door. It rocked on its hinges. Jormund shook his head. "A few more strikes like that, and they will be inside. We will never have enough time to get out. But you will. Take your friends and go."

"This is *not* the time for some foolish last stand," said Loren. "Your death will not help the war with Dorsea. There are windows, we could—"

Jormund only laughed. "I told you, there is not enough time. You made your vow, Nightblade. You promised Kal you would obey me. Take Gem and Keridwen and get out." He looked down at her suddenly, and his smile went from fierce to wistful. "I may not have been in Yewamba, but this is not such a bad trade. I hope you will make sure they talk about me and my soldiers here, in whatever stories they might tell about all this."

Another blow crashed against the door. A large crack appeared in the bar holding it shut. Loren bit her cheek until she could taste blood, fighting the stinging in her eyes. "Darkness take you, Jormund. Of course I will."

"Then get out, you little twit. See to your friends."

Stooping, he lifted a chair that must have weighed at least as much as Loren, but which he hefted like a toy. He threw it through one of the chamber's wide windows. The explosion of splintering glass would have been deafening, if Loren had been able to focus on anything but the pounding at the door.

Jormund reached out and ruffled Gem's hair, and then he took Loren's shoulder and gave her a gentle push towards the window. She ran to them, pulling Kerri along behind her.

"They . . . they will die," said Kerri, sounding half-senseless.

"Many have," said Loren. "Many more will."

The Elves told you, came a whisper in her mind. A memory of her dream. *They told you. They called you Nightblade. The one who walks with death.*

Pieces. Pieces of the puzzle, and always assembling themselves too late.

There was no balcony outside the window, but there was a rooftop just a pace or two down. Loren kicked out some of the glass at the bottom so that they would not cut themselves, and then she looked at Gem and Kerri. Each of them nodded in turn.

She took one last look back. Jormund and his Mystics had their shoulders against the door now, and Yond looked to be bracing them with mindmagic. Jormund looked back at Loren, still wearing his mad grin.

A berserker's grin, she thought. *Like Niya. Is that why I saw her here in my dreams?*

Loren turned and leaped.

She came down hard on the tiles, Gem landing beside her a moment later. They both turned as Kerri made the leap, and Loren did her best to catch the girl and soften her landing. Kerri was crying, but she did not hesitate as Loren turned and led her running off down the rooftop.

Behind them, they heard a great crash of splintering timber, and then a chorus of battle cries rang out. Almost at once, Loren heard the sound of steel piercing flesh, like a butcher's cleaver sinking into a side of beef. Above it all she heard Jormund's mighty shout, laughing as he cut down his foes. But the laughter faltered. One last cry he gave, and then fell silent a final time.

They darted around the corner of the keep, and

Loren stuck her head back around it. No one had followed them out.

She ducked out of sight again and looked about. The roof of the palace had many peaks and slopes that they could use to hide from sight. They stood in a sort of valley between two of the peaks, and a third was between them and the walls, blocking them from view. But they could not remain here forever. Their first goal had to be finding a way out. There must be other walls, barricades like the one they had used to enter the palace in the first place, but Loren could not see any from where they stood.

"Kerri, do you have any idea where to go from here?" said Loren.

The girl stood against the wall, her gaze distant. When she did not answer, Loren put a hand on her shoulder. Kerri shook herself, then seemed to think for a moment, as though she was listening again to Loren's words in her mind.

"No," she said at last. "I . . . I know the palace, but not the rooftops."

"Gem?" Loren turned to the boy.

"I will search about," said Gem.

He crouched and crept forwards, making for the slope closest to the outer wall. Loren sat with Kerri, watching, heart in her throat. Gem poked his head up only far enough to peek with one eye, paused for a moment, and then slid back down towards them.

"Nothing easy that way," he said. "And more bad

news: the walls are now well guarded. I see many soldiers with bows."

Loren shook her head. There had been few guards when they infiltrated the palace. Wojin—or Damaris—must have commanded the guards to hide themselves until the Mystics were inside. Then they would emerge, leaving Loren and her friends trapped.

"Damaris outwitted us again," she said.

"No one is that clever," said Kerri, voice trembling.

"You do not know her very well," said Loren. "But then, you do not know me very well, either. We will escape this place alive. I swear it."

Kerri nodded, and despite her fear, Loren could see that the girl wanted to believe her. She vowed to herself that she would not let her down—or Gem, either. Even if it cost her everything.

Everything.

Loren froze where she sat. Realization came crashing down on her like a wave, robbing her of breath. For a moment it sapped her will, and she felt as if rising to her feet would be an impossible task. But she shook her head, clearing the feeling away.

She knew what she must do.

"Kerri," she said, her voice wooden. "Where is the treasury from where we are?"

Kerri opened her mouth to answer, but Gem spoke first. "I think I saw it just over that slope. It lies between us and the outer wall. We can reach its rooftop, but that ends a good ten paces before the outer wall. We cannot use it to escape."

"Not the roof," said Loren. "Follow me."

She crept up the slope and saw what Gem had described. From the peak, the roof ran down a short ways before ending. There was a small gap, easy to leap, and then the roof of the treasury. High in the treasury wall were windows—somewhat small, but large enough to slip through. A pale light shone from within. Lanterns or torches were lit inside, but not many. Mayhap even just one. That meant that if there were any guards below, they would be few.

"Follow me," said Loren. "Do not stop for anything."

Loren slid down the rooftop towards its lip. She kept a wary eye on the wall far beyond, but the guards there had no hope of seeing them in the darkness. They carried torches, yes, but the light could never reach this far, and would only keep the guards blind to the shadows.

At the rooftop's edge, she did not stop herself. Instead she jumped as hard as she could, curling and striking the window with her shoulder. The glass shattered easily under her weight, and she thrust out an arm to catch herself. It caught on the lip. She felt glass bite into her skin, but not deep. Most of it fell tinkling to the floor below.

She hung there, breath hissing through her teeth against the pain in her hand. There below them was the treasury: seemingly endless piles of gold and silver, both coin and otherwise. The riches stretched from one wall to the other. But there were no guards to watch them.

Only one figure waited for them down below.

Even in the grip of the dreamsight, Loren's heart quailed. The figure was tied to a chair, its head hanging down. Like Duris had been.

But it was not Duris.

She forced her thoughts back to the present and reached up, using the hilt of a dagger to knock away the rest of the glass from the bottom of the windowsill. Gem and Kerri would follow at any moment, and she did not want them to injure themselves. Then she fell, aiming for a shelf just below her. It rocked under her weight, but it did not fall. From there she clambered down. Above her, Gem reached the window, and then Kerri. Each of them began to climb down the same way Loren had.

Loren ignored them. She walked slowly across the floor to the figure in the chair. Blood soaked his clothing, running down the chair to pool on the floor. But his throat was not cut. He still lived—and at the sound of her approaching footsteps, he turned his face up to her.

Chet.

THIRTY-ONE

CHET GASPED AT THE SIGHT OF HER. LOREN FELL ON her knees beside his chair, slashing at his bonds with her dagger. His arms came free, but he could not support his own weight. He slumped forwards, falling hard out of the chair to hit the stone floor.

He had been cut. Tortured. Loren had seen a great deal of cruelty since leaving the Birchwood, but this was among the worst of it.

In her mind's eye, she saw Damaris here, a sharp knife in her hand. No dreamsight, but only a product of her own imagination—her knowledge. Damaris with Chet, kneeling beside him, behind him. Damaris, plying his skin, slicing the flesh beneath. Damaris, avoiding the veins so that he did not bleed to death too soon. Damaris, taking her time, making it last. Damaris, smiling all the while.

"Chet," said Loren. She rolled him over. "Chet, Chet." She threw off her cloak, balling it up and putting it beneath his head. Suddenly she realized she was touching him, her hands on his shoulder, his neck, his head. But he was almost senseless, and he could hardly withdraw from her even if he wanted to.

"No," gasped Gem. Loren looked up. The boy stood a pace away, looking down at Chet, his face a mask of horror.

But Kerri pushed past him, kneeling at Chet's side across from Loren. Without hesitation she tore Chet's shirt open to inspect his wounds. Where before the girl had been shaking with fear at their plight, now her hands were steady as she probed the cuts. Chet groaned at each touch of her fingers. But she only inspected him for a short moment before she looked up at Loren.

She shook her head.

Loren's mouth worked, looking for words. She found none, and looked back down at him.

"Loren," he gasped. His eyes opened, and they were clear. Loren withdrew her hands from him at once.

"I am here," she said. "I am here, Chet. I came."

"How did you . . ." He coughed. Blood bubbled

from between his lips. His face was bruised. She thought his nose must be broken. His red-matted hair stuck out in all directions. "How did you know where I was?"

"I did not," said Loren. "We were . . . we were running . . . I knew I had to come here."

It seemed as if he tried to nod, but the movement only made him grimace in pain. "The dreams."

"Yes," she whispered.

Chet began to weep. Hot tears slid down his cheeks, mingling with the blood, and silent sobs made his chest jerk. "It . . . it hurts . . . yet at the same time it is like I cannot feel it. Once . . . once she started, she would not stop. No matter what I said."

Loren did not have to ask who he meant. Damaris. "How did she find you?"

"I did not make it beyond sight of the city," said Chet. "They caught me. Gregor. Some others. The moment they appeared . . . I froze. Limp. Like a fawn when a wolf seizes its throat. And I . . . it was like I knew that it would happen. That it was inevitable. The Elves. They told you. I thought about it all the way back to the city . . . trussed up on Gregor's saddle."

Kerri looked at Loren in shock. Loren ignored her.

The Elves' words rang in her mind. *The one who walks with death.*

A wave of pain struck him, and he cried out. His hand gripped his shirt. Loren squeezed her fingers together until she thought they would break, keeping herself from taking his hand, holding him, touching his face. Not now. She would leave him alone for now, at least. Until . . . until after. She forced herself to be calm, forced away the despair that clawed at her mind, her soul. She must be strong. For him, not for herself.

"It hurts," he whispered again.

Loren's hand went to the hilt of her dagger. Not one of her throwing daggers. The dagger on the back of her belt. Finely crafted, with black designs made of magestone. The dagger Chet had used to kill Auntie.

"I could help," she whispered. "I can . . . I can end it. The pain would stop."

And deep within her heart, she knew she would. If he asked her to, she would. It would be the first life she had ever taken on purpose. But she would do it, to keep him from more pain.

"No," he gasped. "It is . . . I can feel that it is almost over. If . . . if I only have a few moments left . . . I would rather spend them with you."

Fresh tears sprang from his eyes. But they were different. His face contorted in grief, not pain.

"Do not worry," said Loren. "I will not leave."

"No, I . . ." He gasped against a fresh wave of pain before he could go on. "I told her. Damaris. I told her everything. Your dreams. The Elves. Your dagger . . . what it means to the Mystics."

Loren quailed. She had thought that nothing could overwhelm her grief, but now terror came flooding in to replace it. It was the secret she had held ever since Wellmont, when Jordel had first told her all the secrets of the dagger. That knowledge in the hands of Damaris . . .

But she forced such thoughts away. There would be time to deal with that. There would be no more time to spend with Chet. "It is all right," she said, determined not to let him see her fear. "You could have done nothing more."

"I did not tell her where Kal was," he whispered. "It was the only thing I could hold on to. And I had told her so much already . . . when I lied at last, she believed me."

"That was brave," she said. "That was brave, Chet. You saved many lives." She forced away thoughts of Jormund, of all the Mystics who had died in the palace just moments ago. Chet knew nothing of them. He did not need to.

"I am glad they will live," he whispered. "Glad I could do that much, at least."

"You have done so much more," said Loren.

A ragged gasp wracked his body. Suddenly his hand shot out to clutch hers. Loren looked down at her hand in shock. His fingers laced through hers. His blood still ran from wounds on his fingers, and it mixed with the blood of her sliced palm. She held him back, squeezing, giving him an anchor.

"It . . . it hurts . . ." he gasped. "I . . . you deserve better, but . . . please . . ."

"What, Chet?" she said. "I have water, I—"

"No," he whispered. "Please. Hold me?"

She lifted him up at once, lifted him to sitting, ignoring the grunt of pain. Kerri opened her mouth as if to speak, but she held herself back. Doubtless this would worsen the wound. But what did it matter? It would be over soon anyway.

It would all be over.

Chet's arms snaked around her back, but slowly, and she stroked his hair. He buried his face in her shoulder, and she squeezed, letting him feel her, letting him feel her arms around him. He turned his head, and she pulled back, thinking she was smothering him. But he kissed her, softly, briefly. She returned it. No passion, no lust. No time for that now. But she poured all of her love into it, into that brief moment of the meeting of her lips. And then they held each other again.

Chet shuddered. And then she felt it. Like a felled animal in the woods. The woods where Chet had taught her to hunt in the first place. She felt the life slip from him.

He was gone. Gone, to where she could not follow him anymore.

THIRTY-TWO

The treasury fell to silence. The only sounds were the muted voices of guards in the courtyard and on the walls outside, still no doubt searching for Loren and her friends, and the quiet, wracking sobs of Gem. But after a short while had passed, Kerri reached over and put her hand on Loren's shoulder.

"I am sorry," she said. "But we are still in danger."

"I know," said Loren. "I know."

Gently she laid Chet down, then took her cloak and stood to don it. She refused to look at him. They had to leave him here. Loren hated it, but she knew she must.

She went to Gem's side and put an arm around his shoulders. He turned to her and threw his arms around her, weeping, his tears soaking into her fine new shirt.

"The front door will be guarded," said Kerri quietly. "But . . . we might fight our way out. It is the only thing I can think of."

"There is no need," said Loren. She gingerly unwrapped Gem's arms from around her waist, and then she went to the corner of the room.

A tapestry hung there. Loren remembered it. The man in black had shown it to her. She pushed it aside, and there was only a blank stone wall. Kneeling, Loren felt for the chink in the stone. After a moment she found it, and her fingers pulled on the lever. Two stones swung open, revealing the passageway.

Kerri gawked at her. "How did—"

"I am the Nightblade," said Loren. Then she remembered what the man in black had said in her dream. "It is my job to know the secret ways no one else knows."

She led the way, crawling into the passage. Gem came behind her, still sniffling, and Kerri brought up the rear. Soon the passageway was completely black. Loren reached into her cloak and pulled out a magestone, breaking off a piece and eating it. Then she reached to the back of her belt and drew her dagger, holding it in one hand as she proceeded. With the magestone in her blood, and her hand on the dagger, the passageway was suddenly bright as day.

"I cannot see," said Kerri.

"You do not need to," said Loren. "There is only one way out."

Only one way out.

She crawled forwards, following the passageway as it turned left and right, warning her friends each time. Soon it sloped up, and she knew they were near the end. At last it came. She reached up, finding the chink in the stone and pulling the lever. The wall swung out soundlessly. Loren crawled into the open.

They were in the palace. The hallway was wide and tall, and there were many doors in it. To their left, Loren thought she saw the hallway reach the main front hall, while to the right it ended in a door. But in the middle there was a side hallway leading deeper into the palace.

"I know where we are. The front doors are that way." Kerri pointed to the left. "If the Mystics still hold the front gate—"

"They do not," said Loren. "They will have left, or they are already dead. This way." She started off for the side hallway.

"How do you know?" said Kerri. But she followed along, Gem by her side.

"It is enough that I do." How could she begin to explain?

Loren led them on the course she had been shown. They walked down hallways that felt familiar to Loren by now, though she had never seen them in the waking world. The dreamsight still had its hold on her, but it was not like before. Now, seeing the places from her dreams did not disorient her or send her mind spinning. Now it was like she was following a route marked on a map.

She turned the final corner, and there it was, as she had known it would be. Ahead, an open door leading to a dining hall, and beyond that, freedom. To the left, a small wooden door led to a serving room. Loren came to a halt.

"There!" said Kerri. "That gate is open! We can escape!"

"Take Gem with you," said Loren. "I must go another way."

They both stopped short. Kerri looked over her shoulder, towards the hallway that ran to the front of the palace. Voices drifted from that direction, far away but coming closer. "What do you mean?" she said. "What other way?"

"Loren—" Gem began.

"Shush," said Loren. "You and Kerri must go into the dining hall. Wait at the other end for a short while. Then run for the city. You will be able to escape. I swear it."

Gem set his jaw. "I will not leave. Not without you. Not after Chet."

That way is for others, but not for you.

"You are not leaving me," said Loren. "But there is one thing I must do first before I follow you."

He paused. "What thing?"

Loren gave him a sad smile and gently pushed his shoulder. "Never you worry, master urchin. But I swear this now: I will find you back at Kal's hideout. I would not leave you and Annis to fend for yourselves."

Gem looked up into her eyes, studying them. *Poor Gem,* thought Loren. *You cannot recognize a lie in my eyes. In Damaris and Auntie, I met two of the most cunning minds in the nine kingdoms, and they could not tell if I spoke the truth. What hope do you have?*

"Very well," said Gem slowly. "I believe you."

"Of course you do," she said. "Now go. Look after Kerri."

His chest puffed up a bit at that. Over his head, Loren caught Kerri's eye and winked. The girl gave a smile—little more than a small twist of the lips. Kerri had one advantage over Gem: she had not known Loren long enough to *think* she knew when Loren was telling the truth. Gem led the way into the dining hall, but Kerri paused for just a moment.

"You had better not have lied to that boy," she said quietly. "I *will* expect you back at the hideout."

Loren nodded solemnly. Then she turned and ducked into the serving room, pausing for just a moment to ensure that Kerri went to follow Gem.

Inside, she found the room laid out just as she had known it would be. Against the back wall was the shelf of dishes. Loren threw it away from the wall, not caring about the clatter it made. She was past that now.

The passageway beyond led to the ladder, and that led to the passageway above. That ended in the tapestry, and Loren pulled it aside.

She stepped into Gregor's room.

He stood at the other end, framed by the open doorway. In his hands was a massive longbow of yew, longer than Loren was tall. He faced away from her, scanning the courtyard below. The room was modest by Damaris' standards, but still held finery beyond anything Loren had ever seen growing up. The tapestry through which she had emerged was matched by one on the other side of the room, and all the furniture was carved of solid oak, inlaid with finely wrought gold. There were many lanterns around the room, but only three were lit, leaving the whole place dim. They were the only illumination, for outside the night was still misty and clouded. The moons and stars cast no glow upon the room, nor even upon Gregor himself.

Loren turned and closed the door to the passageway, making no effort to mask the sound.

Gregor's head snapped up, and he turned to her. For a long moment he stood there, studying her. Then, inexorable as a rockslide, he stepped into the room. One hand drifted behind him, closing the glass balcony door. He pulled a sash holding back a curtain, and it fell across the door, sealing the room against the last rays of torchlight from beyond.

This is the only way, thought Loren. *All roads lead to Gregor.*

"Hello, Nightblade," said Gregor. His voice rolled through the room like thunder. "Damaris promised me this. That together, we would make you suffer. And then, at last, I would get to kill you."

THIRTY-THREE

"I THOUGHT I MIGHT FIND YOU HERE," SAID LOREN lightly.

Gregor snorted. "Did you?" But he paused, and his eyes hardened to steel. "Ah. The boy told us things. Your dreams. Did they lead you here to die? Hardly a useful tool."

Loren shrugged, letting her gaze drift around the room. Across the room was the only other door. It led to the rest of the palace. To escape.

She turned away from it.

"They have proven more useful than you might realize. After all, they have told me where to find your mistress."

The bodyguard froze. Loren widened her eyes.

"Oh, did you not imagine I would know that? That I had not planned all this? While you waste your time here with me, Mystics are even now descending on Damaris' location and—"

Gregor charged.

Loren had expected it, but the giant's speed never failed to surprise her. She leaped away from the tapestry, making for the room's door. But Gregor anticipated the move, and his hand swiped out. Loren dropped and rolled—but her foot overextended, kicking a side table. One of the lamps fell to the floor, shattering its glass. The light went out, and the room grew dimmer still.

Quickly Loren scrambled for her feet. But Gregor was almost upon her, and she had to roll away from the door. He paused there, shoulders hunched, arms to his side. Loren thanked the sky that he did not have his sword on him.

"You did not plan this night," he growled. "If you had, you would never have left Chet for us to kill."

"You have no right to speak his name," hissed Loren. But she thought, *Even now, Gem and Kerri will be making their way across the courtyard. Almost there. Almost free.*

She circled, keeping her eyes fixed on Gregor. It almost made her forget his longbow, which he had dropped. Her foot hit it, and she nearly tripped. Gregor tensed, but when she righted herself, he subsided. In one fluid motion, Loren crouched and picked up the bow. It felt like a spear in her hands. If only she were Uzo.

"Do you think that will save you, girl?" said Gregor. "That little stick?"

"Cruel words," said Loren. "After all, it is *your* little stick."

Gregor growled and charged again. Loren leaped to the side, swinging the longbow at him. He raised an arm to block it, and it cracked over his forearm. Grunting in pain, he swung his other fist at her. Loren could not quite dodge it. It smashed into her shoulder, flinging her across the room. She rolled with the landing, fighting to her feet at once. In one hand she still held half of the longbow. The broken end was jagged and splintered. She thrust it at Gregor, forcing him back.

"I think I am at a disadvantage," she said. "If only I had learned to fight. I tried to get you to teach me, once. Do you remember? I begged you for swordplay lessons. But then, as now, you could not quite catch me. Will you not give me a sword again? It is the only way this fight will be fair."

"Who wants a fair fight?" said Gregor. "I have only one goal here tonight: to end your life, and to take as long as I can in doing so."

They had spun around each other again, and now

the balcony door was behind Loren. She reversed her grip on the longbow, throwing it at him like a spear. He batted it aside, but she had not truly meant to hit him. Loren turned, dashing for the balcony. She threw aside the curtain, her hand coming down on the latch—

It did not turn. Locked.

A fist bigger than her head closed on the hood of her cloak.

This is it.

Gregor flung her away from the door. She flew all the way across the room, crushing another lamp. Loren felt a sharp pain—broken glass, or a cracking rib?—and gasped.

Then she smiled.

Rolling over, she saw Gregor stalking towards her. He wanted to get his hands on her, pin her down, but he was moving slowly. He did not want to give her another chance to escape.

Loren's hand fell to her belt, closing around a knife. She drew it and threw.

Gregor halted, raising one mailed arm to stop the blade. But it flew straight past him—to strike the third and final lamp, sending it crashing to the floor.

The room went utterly black.

Loren drew the dagger from the back of her belt. In her vision, the room grew bright as daylight.

But Gregor was blind. And he would not know she could see.

Chet would not have told him, for Loren had never told Chet. She had not wanted him to know about the magestones.

Gregor took a cautious step back. His leg struck a footstool, and he stumbled, barely keeping his feet. Experimenting, Loren scuffed a foot on the floor. Gregor's head jerked towards the sound, but too far, so that he was looking to her left.

Loren's smile widened.

"You misunderstand the dreams," said Loren. He jerked again, following her voice. She let him hear where she was. "They tell me some things, but not everything. They did not tell me I would find Damaris alone in Yewamba. That you had abandoned her. And no, they did not tell me you would take Chet tonight. But if you think they did not tell me about you, here, now, you are wrong."

Gregor made his cautious way forwards, reaching for where he could hear her voice.

"I came here, Gregor, because I wanted to."

Softening her footfalls, she began to stalk around him. On the soft rugs of the room, she made less noise than the wind. Gregor swiped his arms through where she had been standing a moment before.

"This is pointless," he growled. "Do you think the darkness is your friend? It will not help when I get my hands on you."

From behind, Loren leaped. She plunged the dagger into his calf.

The blade parted cloth and flesh with equal ease. It felt . . .

Loren shuddered.

It felt so *good.* So *right.*

Had she really never used the dagger on another living person before? She knew, now. That had always been the dagger's purpose.

It was never meant for anything else.

She leaped back, even as Gregor groaned and stumbled to one knee. He reached behind himself, but she was already gone.

Loren darted in again. Her blade impaled his groping forearm.

Gregor gave a brief shout, quickly cut off. He tried to rise, but he had to favor his injured leg. It was useless, unable to support his weight. He swung a wild, angry blow that Loren ducked with ease. She struck again, plunging the dagger into the pit of his good arm. It fell useless to his side.

He placed her at last, and his fingers closed on the front of her shirt. But she had already stabbed that arm through. Now she sliced it again. She did not know where to cut, exactly, but the dagger seemed to. It parted muscle and tendon, and his grip slackened. His balance wavered, and he crashed to the floor on his back. Desperately he tried to push away from her with his one good leg.

Loren took one of the throwing daggers from her belt and flung it into his ankle. It flew hard enough to pin the limb to the floor beneath.

"And here I thought—" Gregor's words cut off in a groan of pain. "Here I thought you had no spine."

The words were defiant, his tone more so. But Loren could see it plain as day on his face, clear as if a lantern were right in his eyes. Fear.

Gregor feared her.

His chest heaved with every breath, and sweat ran from him in rivulets. She wondered how long it had been since the giant had been beaten in a fight—beaten so soundly that even his limbs were useless. If it had ever happened at all.

"You thought me weak for refusing to kill," said Loren. "You still do not recognize the truth. Murder is the coward's way out."

He grunted a laugh. "What do you call this, then?"

A fierce smile crossed Loren's lips. "I suppose I do not feel particularly brave at the moment."

That forced a laugh from him. "Then I go to my death with one consolation. This pain is nothing compared to the boy's. To *Chet's.*" He gave an evil grin into what was, to him, empty darkness. "I made sure he suffered. I relished every twist of pain on his face as I cut him up, one piece at a time. If I must go to the darkness below, I do so happy, knowing that nothing will ever bring back the boy you loved. The boy I took from you."

Loren crossed to kneel by his head. She leaned in close.

"I know you are lying."

He started at the sound of her voice so close. Only

one arm could still move, and he swung it at her, even though it could not grip.

She caught his hand on the blade of her knife

Gregor cried out—a scream of pain that she was ashamed of herself for enjoying.

"I know you are lying," she said again, easily, as though nothing had happened. "I saw Chet. He died slowly, yes. But not by your hand. When Annis and I first met, she told me. She told me how Damaris would torture information from her prisoners, taking her time with the pain, enjoying every cut. It was Damaris who killed him. And I promise you this. I will hunt her down. I will never stop until I find her. And when I do, I will not bring her before the King's justice. I *am* the King's justice. I will find Damaris and end her, just as I have ended you here, tonight."

It dawned on Gregor. Recognition. Loren watched it spread across his face like a tide creeping up a shore. He knew she spoke the truth, that she meant what she said. It was only a matter of time before Damaris was dead.

And just as that realization came upon him, Loren drew the dagger across his throat.

He sagged back to the floor, his lifeblood bubbling up. He coughed, choking, trying desperately to breathe. Blood spurted across his face and ran down the sides of his neck to pool, soaking into the carpet below, staining it. Like Duris.

Like Chet.

THIRTY-FOUR

Loren sank back on her heels, staring. The magestones and her dagger let her see every detail of Gregor's corpse. It sat there, silent, still. Confronting her. A sick, twisting feeling ripped through her gut.

She ignored it. Kal had given her a mission, and she was still in the palace.

First she went to the balcony and opened the door. The courtyard beyond was still empty, but guards stood on the wall beyond it. They did not notice her.

But they soon would.

Loren ducked back into the room and went to Gregor. She lifted his arm and pulled, but she could not move him. Clenching her jaw, she heaved. His body barely moved.

She went to the rug upon which he lay and seized the edge of it. Again she pulled. This time it worked. The rug slid on the wooden floor. It still seemed to her that he should be too heavy, but something—the thrill of the fight, some gift of the dagger—let her move him.

On the balcony, she lifted his head up until it hung over the railing. Then, straining and groaning, she managed to fling him over the balcony to land in the courtyard far below.

The body struck the smooth white stones with a sick *thud.*

That drew the attention of the guards on the wall. They cried out, and soon other guards came running from all directions. Soon there was a small crowd of them in the courtyard below, staring at Gregor's corpse. As one, they joined the guards on the wall in looking up at her.

Loren threw her shoulders back. Her black cloak and her new clothes were all stained in blood. She hoped they could see it.

"Gregor is dead!" she proclaimed. "Damaris of the family Yerrin is soon to follow. And the usurper, Wojin, will never escape the King's justice. Abandon him, or you, too, will face me before the end."

Then she vanished back inside the apartment.

She left by the front entrance, not the secret one.

Soon there was a staircase leading down, and she emerged into another hallway full of rooms. One of them had an open door, and she stole through it to the balcony beyond. This led her to the rooftops she had traveled with Gem and Kerri not long ago. She stalked around the palace's perimeter, stopping to look and listen at every window. Then, at last, she found the one she was looking for.

A balcony just above her head led to a wide glass door. Pulling herself up slightly, Loren saw Wojin. The false king was in urgent conference with an advisor, and Loren saw two guards inside the room as well. A single lamp lit the room. But none of them were looking at her, and in any case, the lamp inside the room would keep them from seeing outside.

She clambered up onto the balcony, sidling up to the doorway to listen. Wojin raised his head to speak to the guards.

"What of the attackers?"

"At least one still remains, Your Grace. You must stay here until we have confirmed the palace is secure."

Wojin gave an exasperated sigh. "This gambit was foolish. I told that Yerrin woman often enough. And she is not even here to face the same danger as the rest of us!"

Damaris, thought Loren. *She has left, then. Mayhap it is time for me to go, as well.*

Her gaze came to rest on Wojin.

Or mayhap not.

Loren burst through the door into the room. Wojin shot to his feet, and the guards went to draw their swords. But Loren struck before they could, kicking over the lamp. It was not complete darkness, for the window let some torch light in, but it was enough for her purposes.

One guard fell to a punishing blow from her dagger's hilt. The other only managed two swings before Loren brought him down. The advisor screamed and ran for the door, but Loren tackled him, then slammed his head into the floor to knock him senseless.

But no killing, she thought. *There has been enough of that tonight.*

Loren rose to her feet. "Wojin," she said. "What a pleasure to meet you face to face."

"Assassin," gasped Wojin.

"No," said Loren, shaking her head. "But I have killed Gregor tonight, and you are utterly at my mercy. Yet I was told, a long time ago, that not needlessly does the family Yerrin kill. And the Nightblade has at least that much honor."

Wojin swallowed hard. She watched the bulb in his throat bounce up and down. "What . . . what do you mean to do with me, then?"

"Silence you, for one thing."

She cut a gag out of the drapes and tied it around his mouth. Then she bound his hands before leading him out to the balcony. Once he was up against the railing, she shoved him in the shoulder blades. Wojin screamed into his gag as he fell, but she caught him by the ankles. Loren lowered him as far as she could, then dropped him to the rooftop below so that he fell on his shoulder. He grunted in pain. Loren jumped down beside him, then forced him up and back towards the palace. She bundled him in through a lower window.

"We are going to your dungeons," she said. "If you try to signal for help, I will make you regret it."

Wojin nodded in fear—but she saw a crafty shine in his eye. The dungeons would be guarded, and they would not be easy to escape from. That was the point, after all. No doubt he hoped he could trick her into trapping herself there.

Good. It would keep him thinking he had a way out of this.

The maps of the palace were still somewhat clear in her mind. She knew she was on the southwest end of the palace, and the dungeons were close by. She only needed to find a way leading down . . .

There. She shoved Wojin into a stairwell, barely catching him before he fell to the landing below. When they were near the bottom, she stopped and knelt, tying Wojin's feet as she had tied his hands.

"Do not move," she said. "I will return for you in a moment."

She ducked around the final turn in the stairs. Behind her, she heard Wojin start to struggle immediately. That was fine. He would not free himself before she was done.

There was a guard room before the door that led to the dungeons themselves. In the room sat a man in palace livery. He shot to his feet when Loren entered, giving a cry of alarm. Loren threw a dagger into the hand that reached for his sword, then subdued him with two quick strikes to the face. He slumped to the floor, groaning.

His belt held a ring of keys. She removed them and went back for Wojin. His bonds were not even loosened yet. He moaned in fear as she hauled him up and shoved him into the guard room. She unlocked the first door and walked him down the line of cells, peering inside.

There. A cell of healthy prisoners, clearly not here for very long. Their hair was cut short, and they were well-muscled and healthy.

"You there," said Loren. "Are you palace guards?"

One of the prisoners peered up at her, blinking. "What?"

"Palace guards. Did you serve in the palace?"

"I . . . did," said the man. "Who are you?" Then he noticed Wojin, bound and with Loren's arm around his neck. His eyes shot wide.

"Yes, it is him," said Loren. "I am looking for someone. Morana, of the family Fei. Where is she?"

"I am Morana," said a voice.

Loren turned. The cell across the hall held still more prisoners. One of them, a woman with her hair cut almost to her scalp, stood before the bars. She studied Loren with keen, severe eyes. Eyes Loren had seen before, in the face of Duris Fei.

Loren reached up and ripped out Wojin's gag. "Tell them what you did."

"I do not know what you speak of," said Wojin desperately.

Loren's dagger slid free, and she pressed the tip to his throat. "Not needlessly will I kill. But neither will I be gentle. Tell them what you did to King Jun."

Wojin gasped, trying to struggle away from the dagger. "I killed him," he whispered.

"Louder!"

"I killed him!" cried Wojin. "I took the palace by force, but he and his son escaped. But I found them after, and my soldiers killed Jun."

Loren pressed harder. The dagger pricked the skin of his throat, and Wojin squeaked. "And tell her what happened to Duris."

"We learned—Damaris learned that she was conspiring with King Jun," said Wojin, nearly weeping now. "We . . . we killed her."

Loren pressed just a bit harder. "Tell them everything. Tell her how Duris died."

"Damaris put her to the question!" cried Wojin. "She tortured her for information before cutting her throat."

Morana had gone very still, her fingers wrapped around the iron bars of her cell. She met Loren's gaze.

"Do you know who else in this dungeon is loyal to Jun?" said Loren.

"I do," said Morana, her tone clipped.

Loren removed her dagger and threw Wojin to the floor, where he crumpled in a heap. She opened Morana's cell and handed her the ring of keys. "Get them all out. Take care of this thing." She spat at Wojin's form on the floor. "I will send help as soon as I can. Senlin still lives. He will return to give you orders. Can you hold out until then?"

"We can," said Morana. But as Loren turned to go, she reached out and seized her wrist. "You did all this?"

Loren met her gaze for a moment. "Not on my own," she said softly. "Many people died to return the true king to the throne. See that their sacrifice was not in vain."

Morana nodded slowly. Loren turned and ran up the stairs, back into the palace.

THIRTY-FIVE

HER KIDNAP OF WOJIN HAD THROWN THE GUARDS into disarray. It was easy enough to find another rooftop to sneak away on, and when she found a side wall leading out, no guards were there to block her path. She climbed down the wall and made her way into the streets of the city.

Without Kerri to guide her, it took a great deal longer to find Kal's inn than it might have otherwise. But in the end, she found it all the same. When she approached the side door leading to the basement, the Mystic on guard moved to stop her at first. But when he caught sight of Loren's face, he gasped and stepped back. Loren ignored him, throwing open the door and descending into the room.

"Loren!"

Gem screamed as he flung himself into her arms. Annis was only a half-step behind him, and then came Kerri. They huddled around her, holding her close, the children crying.

None of them paid the least bit of attention to the blood soaking Loren's clothes. But in the end, Loren pulled back. It would be a while, she guessed, before she felt that these clothes were truly clean again, and she did not wish to sully her friends with them.

Someone had summoned Kal, and he came huffing into the room. He stopped dead when he saw Loren, staring at her for a moment in shock. Loren fixed him with a grim smile.

"Hello, Grand Chancellor. You seem surprised to see me."

"I . . ." he swallowed and forced the awe from his expression. "The boy and the girl returned, but from what they said . . . I did not know if you would."

"Yet here I am."

"Were they right?" said Kal. "Jormund?"

"Dead, with all his soldiers," said Loren. "But I captured Wojin. He is in the hands of Jun's loyalists in the prison. You must get all the warriors under your command and help them take the palace, as quickly as you can."

No doubt it grated Kal to hear her give such orders, but he had the good sense to hide it for the moment. She could see the amazement in his expression. He had likely never expected her to succeed. Loren did not think he had sent her to her death, not intentionally. But she had only been a tool to get his assassins within reach of their target. No doubt he was surprised at her success when all his Mystics had perished.

"Yes, well . . ." he said. "Good. Worse than I had hoped, but better than I feared. I shall . . . I shall act at once. Excuse me."

"Of course. I shall be waiting to give you a more complete report, when you are ready." Loren allowed herself the small pleasure of waving him away. He scowled at that, but he went, going back to his room to give the orders.

Loren had lied, of course. She would not be waiting for him.

She ushered Gem and Annis towards one of the rooms they shared. Inside, they found Wyle. He sprang to his feet the moment the door opened, his face going ashen when he saw Loren.

"Nightblade," he said. "You survived."

"I did," said Loren. "Though others did not. Close the door, Gem."

The boy hurried to do as she asked, and Loren went to sit on the bed. She was likely getting blood on the blanket, but she did not care. Annis and Gem stood before her, their eyes wide. But Kerri looked at Loren's face, studying her. Loren thought she saw something in the girl's eyes . . . recognition? Understanding?

"I killed Gregor," whispered Loren. "I killed him."

The room went still. Kerri's expression grew dour, and Wyle only blinked. But Annis and Gem looked at each other in fear. Only they could know what this moment truly meant.

"And I am leaving," continued Loren. "I must go off on my own again. Because I need to kill Damaris."

Annis sagged. She sank down on the bed, sitting on its edge. Her hands were shaking. Gem took them quickly, holding them between his own. "Loren—" said Annis.

"She killed Chet, Annis," said Loren. "And not quickly."

"No, I know," said Annis. "I . . . I understand. And I will come with you."

Loren shook her head slowly. "You should not. This is not like our journeys before. I am no longer running. I am looking to right a wrong."

"But none of our journeys have been like another," said Annis. "Yet we have always been together. I . . . I know what you must do. Gem and Kerri told me about Chet. I want to go with you."

Loren found it hard to speak past a sudden tightness in her throat, and her voice broke. "Then I welcome your company. It would be an emptier road if I did not ride it with you."

"I suppose it need not be said that I am coming as well," said Gem.

Somehow, Loren found the strength to smile. "Of course not. I was going to ask you to do so."

He smirked, but it died quickly. Loren looked past him to Wyle. At once the smuggler spread his hands, shaking his head.

"No. I have enjoyed your company, Nightblade, but I have ridden quite a bit farther than I had ever planned to. I believe I will remain here, reaping the gratitude of the new king."

"You can collect that gratitude easily enough by letter," said Loren. "I am certain Senlin will accommodate you. But we need to travel by secret ways that no one else knows. And we would pay you handsomely. Why not also earn yourself the gratitude of Underrealm's greatest . . . greatest thief?"

Her stomach turned. She had almost said *assassin.*

Wyle eyed the door to their room and pursed his lips. "I suppose it is true that I would rather not be in Danfon just now," he muttered. "I trust Senlin, but that Kal fellow . . ." He sighed and held up a finger. "Very well. But you will pay me full rates. I never give a discount, even to friends. It only cheapens the friendship."

"Fair enough," said Loren. "And thank you."

Wyle stood and bowed to her. "You are welcome, Nightblade. I am at your disposal—for a while, at least."

"Then let us not delay," said Loren, pushing herself up off the bed. "The road is long, and we should begin."

"Now?" said Gem, eyes widening in surprise.

"There is no better time," said Loren. "Damaris already has a head start."

"I think you are right," said Annis.

Loren nodded, then turned to Kerri. "Farewell, Keridwen. I am glad to have known you, even for a little while. Look after Senlin for us. He will need friends in the days to come."

Kerri's eyes flashed. Her hands balled into fists at her sides, and she tilted up her chin.

"No."

That gave Loren pause. She frowned at Kerri. "No?"

"No. I will not stay here to look after a boy. I mean, he may be king, but . . ." She took a deep breath and released it in a rush. "I want to come with you."

Loren's frown deepened, furrowing her brow. "With us? Why?"

"You know why. I want to do more. More than I can do here, even if I were to help Senlin."

Slowly Loren shook her head. "No, Kerri. You are a healer, a chemist. On the road we travel, I must . . . I must be a killer."

Kerri cocked her head. "I have never believed that killing was always wrong."

Loren opened her mouth to argue again—and then she closed it. "Very well," she said, shrugging. "You may come if you wish. But it must be now."

Kerri did not answer, but only fell in behind the children as they followed Loren out the door. Loren led them down the hallway, towards the back entrance to the inn. But as they passed one of the last doors, Gem came to a stop.

"A moment," he said, and opened the door.

"Gem—" said Loren. But then she froze. It was Prince Senlin's room. Jo had leaped to his feet as the door opened, but when he saw Gem, the bodyguard dropped his hand from his sword. Prince Senlin stood to greet Gem, dumbfounded.

"Master Noctis," he said. "Can I . . . can I help you?"

"I . . . I only wanted to say," said Gem. A flush crept up his cheeks, and he took another step into the room. "I cannot explain everything now, but I think—after tonight, I mean. I think you will be a very good king."

A small smile crossed Senlin's lips. "Thank you. That is reassuring to—"

His words died as Gem leaped forwards and kissed him. Senlin's eyes widened, and next to them both, Jo froze in shock. Then Senlin closed his eyes and gripped Gem's shoulders. For a moment, all of time seemed frozen, and Loren thought even her heart must have stopped beating.

Then at last, Gem drew away. Senlin took a small, sharp breath.

"That is all I wanted to say," said Gem. Then he fled from the room as fast as his feet would carry him. He seized Loren's arm and drew her along after him.

"Sky above, hurry, before he has a chance to say something."

Loren only caught one brief glance of Senlin, standing there with his fingers on his lips, before she passed from view of him.

They reached the back door. By some stroke of fortune, Uzo was on guard duty again. But then, Loren did not much believe in fortune any longer. No doubt this was some design of fate as well—the same fate that had brought her visions, curse and blessing that they were.

But time enough for those thoughts later.

Uzo glanced down at Loren in surprise as she approached, and then he eyed her companions. A grim look came into his eyes. Loren thought for a moment that he would try to stop them. Instead he merely reached over and opened the door for her.

"Thank you," said Loren quietly. "Fare well. Say good-bye to Shiun for us. She should understand."

"She will," said Uzo. "Fare well, Nightblade. It has been the greatest honor of my life—so far, anyway. Whatever you must do, make them pay."

"I will," said Loren. And she took her first step into the darkness—a darkness that she had fully embraced for the first time.

KEEP READING

The Nightblade Epic will continue. But it is not the only tale of Underrealm.

The Academy Journals series tells the story of the Academy for wizards upon the High King's Seat—and its new dean, Xain Forredar.

The first book *The Alchemist's Touch*. Get it here:

Underrealm.net/AJ1

AUTHOR'S NOTE

Raise your hand if you know what "fridging" is.

That's a trick question. You might not know the term, but you *definitely* know the trope if you've ever consumed books, movies, or comics.

This is the first book I've written since the end of what I've taken to calling the Restoration Project.

When I first started the books of Underrealm, I had no editor. None at all. That, of course, was a *huge* mistake. My books were published with typos and plot holes aplenty. I knew it, but I simply couldn't afford to pay an editor.

That all changed in 2015. But, unfortunately, at that time I ended up working with an editor who . . . well, let's just say I wish they'd never touched my books. Not only did they miss some of *my* typos and errors, but they ended up making thousands of "silent edits" to my work. Edits I never got to see, never got to approve or disapprove. And not only did that massively change my voice, but they actually *introduced* errors into the work. Real, factual typos and grammar mistakes, as well as errors in the world I'd built.

(As just one example, the editor changed one description of "ice in the south" to "ice in the north," because apparently they couldn't imagine a fantasy world that wasn't Eurocentric.)

So, from October of 2016 to May of 2017, I engaged in a huge project to re-edit and re-release all of my books. I eventually took to calling it the Restoration Project. Restoring the books to my own voice—but also getting them *actually* professionally edited by an *actual* professional editor.

I was so very happy when that project finally ended, just two months ago as I'm writing this. But then, all of a sudden, I found myself in an odd position: writing an entirely new book.

This is the first book that was conceived, outlined, written, and edited, *all* with my current workflow. And it's the workflow I plan to use from here on out. My editor, Karen Conlin, is fantastic, and I'd be a fool to release a book she hasn't worked on. My proofreaders are excellent; my beta readers are simply some of the best people.

The book you've just received is 100%, bona fide, pure Underrealm. Grade A. Just how I wanted it to be, and without any undesirables sticking their fingers into the mix.

(That means if you find a typo, I'm going to eat major crow—but at least it's a mistake I can own!)

Oh, really, Garrett? So it was entirely your *decision to kill Chet? Not sure you should be bragging about this.*

Yeah . . .

Okay, there's a bit to unpack here. Chet was . . . well, he was meant to be a few things.

You know by now that Underrealm is trying to be a bit different from a lot of fantasy universes out there. It draws from medieval times, yes—but it doesn't feel obligated to obey the usual perception of medieval culture when it comes to societal norms.

And why should it? It's not more 'unrealistic' to allow gay people to, you know, EXIST, than it is to have firemages and weremages. Or a Necromancer.

But with the exploration of gender, sexuality, and race in fantasy, there's some other things I kind of . . . needed to do.

You see, there's gender in *story*, and then there's gender in *storytelling*. The two are related, but also separate. You can have different rules for different genders in your *story*—but, subconsciously, most storytellers apply different rules for different genders in their *storytelling*.

One of the most egregious ways this has manifested itself is in the concept of "fridging." Like the word fridge, but a verb. In summary, it's when female characters are harmed or killed in order to further the storyline and character development of a male character.

This isn't *just* because they're women and women are treated worse in the story universe—a male companion of the male character would serve just as well—but because so many writers consider women characters to be little more than a prop that helps the male protagonist.

(If you're wondering, the word "fridging" comes from the surprisingly frequent number of times these women are killed and then literally stuffed into a fridge for the male character to find. Pleasant, right?)

So, from the beginning, The Nightblade Epic was meant to be an exploration of gender dynamics in fantasy and adventure stories, and what those dynamics would look like if they were flipped on their head. That's why Chet suffered what he did in the previous book, *Wer-*

emage. That's why he went through what he did in this book. And it's why his story ended the way it did.

Not only because I wanted to flip the trope on its head and see how straight white guys liked it when their sole representation in the story was used in this way—though I personally think that would have been a good enough reason, all on its own, to do so. But, I *hope,* I managed Chet's storyline in a way that's more respectful than "fridged" women usually get.

Because it isn't just fridging itself that's so annoying, or even its prevalence in storytelling. It's the way the women in these scenarios just . . . suck. As characters, I mean. They really *aren't* people to the storytellers. They're plot devices for the purpose of enhancing the person the writer *really* cares about—their protagonist, who's almost always a straight white dude.

But I cared about Chet. I *care* about Chet. No, he wasn't perfect. But he was mine, and I loved him. I tried my damndest to make him a real person—and to show what a *real person* would act like if they went through what he went through.

And holy shit, dear reader, when I wrote that scene, I cried. I stopped writing and I cried for . . . well, a good long while. And then when I was editing it? I cried again. Every time. There was no vindictive glee in what I did, the way it *really* feels like there is when some writers fridge women.

If you don't think Chet was well characterized, that's on me. But I assure you, it wasn't for lack of intent. And I hope it's just one example writers can use to understand their characters need to be *people*—even if they are victims who only exist to develop the hero into a better person.

So there you go. The first book I've written since the Restoration Project, and it culminates in a storyline I've been planning since *Darkfire*.

It's all over now, right? All downhill from here?

Hah. Not even close. The next three books? Also been planned for a *looong* time. They'll take a while to produce—but I promise I'll try to make them worth the wait.

And in the meantime, thank you so much for going on this journey with me. I hope I haven't hurt you too badly along the way.

Thank you for everything you do to make my life epic. Here's to lots more epicness in the days and years to come.

Garrett Robinson,
July 2017

P.S. This is also the first book I've published since my dad passed away, just a few weeks ago. He was a hell of a guy, and one of my biggest and earliest fans. I read him an early draft a few days before the end.

This book, and every one I write hereafter, is for him and my mom.

Garrett,
September 2017

CONNECT ONLINE

FACEBOOK

Want to hang out with other fans of the Underrealm books? There's a Facebook group where you can do just that. Join the Nine Lands group on Facebook and share your favorite moments and fan theories from the books. I also post regular behind-the-scenes content, including information about the world you can't find anywhere else. Visit the link to be taken to the Facebook group:

Underrealm.net/nine-lands

YOUTUBE

Catch up with me daily (when I'm not directing a film or having a baby). You can watch my daily YouTube channel where I talk about art, science, life, my books, and the world.
But not cats.
Never cats.

GarrettBRobinson.com/yt

THE BOOKS OF UNDERREALM

THE NIGHTBLADE EPIC

NIGHTBLADE
MYSTIC
DARKFIRE
SHADEBORN
WEREMAGE
YERRIN

THE ACADEMY JOURNALS

THE ALCHEMIST'S TOUCH
THE MINDMAGE'S WRATH
THE FIREMAGE'S VENGEANCE

CHRONOLOGICAL ORDER

NIGHTBLADE
MYSTIC
DARKFIRE
SHADEBORN
THE ALCHEMIST'S TOUCH
WEREMAGE
THE MINDMAGE'S WRATH
THE FIREMAGE'S VENGEANCE
YERRIN

ABOUT THE AUTHOR

Garrett Robinson was born and raised in Los Angeles. The son of an author/painter father and a violinist/singer mother, no one was surprised when he grew up to be an artist.

After blooding himself in the independent film industry, he self-published his first book in 2012 and swiftly followed it with a stream of others, publishing more than two million words by 2014. Within months he topped numerous Amazon bestseller lists. Now he spends his time writing books and directing films.

A passionate fantasy author, his most popular books are the novels of Underrealm, including The Nightblade Epic and The Academy Journals series.

However, he has delved into many other genres. Some works are for adult audiences only, such as *Non Zombie* and *Hit Girls,* but he has also published popular books for younger readers, including The Realm Keepers series and *The Ninjabread Man*, co-authored with Z.C. Bolger.

Garrett lives in Oregon with his wife Meghan, his children Dawn, Luke, and Desmond, and his dog Chewbacca.

Garrett can be found on:

BLOG: garrettbrobinson.com/blog
EMAIL: garrett@garrettbrobinson.com
TWITTER: twitter.com/garrettauthor
FACEBOOK: facebook.com/garrettbrobinson

EPILOGUE

DAMARIS SAT AT HER WRITING DESK, PENNING A LETTER bound for the Seat. Her room at the inn felt . . . empty somehow. It was strange. She had spent many years of her life without Gregor at her side. Why did this time feel different? Why did she feel his absence so keenly?

She shook off such thoughts. It would not be long before he came to join her. Indeed, it was only his paranoia that had made him send her out of the city in the first place. The dear man wanted to take every precaution, now that they knew this disturbing business about Loren's dreams.

Her quill paused on the parchment. Dreams of the future. It was a terrifying prospect—but also it seemed to her to be an incredible opportunity. What might she do if she could see what was to come? But the boy had told her the dreams came after Loren met with Elves, and Damaris was not so great a fool as to trifle with them in hopes they would give her the same gift.

A tremor of fear ran through her as she thought of Gregor back in Danfon. Alone.

She shook her head. Fear was ridiculous. Knowledge of the future could not help Loren. Eventually Gregor would figure out a way to draw her within reach. What good would foresight be then? At best it would show her just how Gregor would dismantle her piece by piece. Indeed, it seemed Loren had dreamed of it already, if the boy was to be believed.

And Damaris had used all her skill with a knife to ensure that, indeed, he *could* be believed.

Sighing, Damaris stood from the desk and crossed the room to refill her wine. Foresight was a power indeed. Loren was certainly misusing it. But it explained how she had always remained on Damaris' trail, always just one step behind her. What a myopic, uninspired use for such a gift.

Damaris rolled a knot from her neck as she sipped her wine. Some things, sadly, could never be changed. That was a fact of the world that she had had to accept long ago. Loren's great weakness was that she refused to accept it. Why, if Damaris acted the same way, her life would be spent in constant terror of the Necromancer and their—

The thought pained her. She shied away. Never mind the Necromancer. That thought must be stowed until she had devised a solution for it.

A knock came at her door.

Damaris paused. It was no attack, that much was certain. She had been fleeing across Dorsea fast enough that, even knowing where she was bound, Loren would never be able to catch her. Gregor? But no, the knock was not heavy enough for that.

"Enter."

The door opened. A messenger came into the room, stopping for a deep bow.

"Good eve, my lady."

"Good eve," said Damaris. "What is it?"

"I . . ." The messenger stopped. Her lips twitched, fighting for words.

A tremor passed through Damaris' breast. Her fingers tightened on the stem of her goblet.

"What have you come to say? Spit it out."

"It is Gregor, my lady. He . . . he is dead."

The goblet fell from Damaris' fingers and crashed to the floor, sending its wine to soak into the fine rug at her feet.

"My lady," said the messenger, leaping forwards to pick it up. "I will fetch a—"

"Silence," said Damaris. The messenger froze. "Was it the girl?"

The woman's skin went a shade paler. She nodded.

"Thank you," said Damaris. "That will be all."

The messenger opened her mouth as if to say something else. But she thought better of it, turned, and left the room.

Only then did Damaris let herself collapse into the chair by the writing desk.

Gregor. Her oldest friend. Her closest companion. Theirs was the greatest love she had ever seen or heard tale about—not the love of those who share a bed, but of those who share their lives together, their every innermost thought. Indeed, he was worth more than every man she had taken to bed all put together. He had saved her life, had been there as she raised Annis.

And now he was gone.

She did not weep openly, but she could not stop the tears from slowly leaking. Her grip tightened on the back of the chair until her knuckles had gone very nearly white.

And for the first time since she could remember, a feeling wrapped its deathly fingers around her heart. An emotion she was not at all familiar with. A pure, cold, unrelenting fear.

The dream took him.

The girl in the cloak knelt over Gregor. She leaned down to whisper something in the giant's ear, but she spoke too softly to hear. The man in black could only watch as the girl leaned farther over, drawing her dagger across Gregor's throat. The giant's blood splashed across the carpet. It gave the man in black a sense of grim satisfaction. The girl in the cloak had succeeded where he had failed.

The girl slowly stood and turned to him. Her eyes had that glow—akin to magelight, and yet different. He had never seen anything like it before—and that was not something he could say for most things under the sky.

The girl drew closer. The man tensed. He had not felt fear for a very long time, but he felt . . . awareness. Caution. His every sense strained, ready to react if she should attack him.

"I killed him," said the girl in the black cloak. "But I will need to kill many more."

"Then do it," he said. "No one can stop you."

"I am not ready," said the girl in the black cloak. "Not yet. Help me."

He chuckled and shook his head. "I am no nursemaid. Get someone else to draw the knife for you."

Her green eyes pierced him, holding him in place. She lifted the dagger and pressed its point against his heart.

The man did not like threats. The man liked to end threats. But he could not lift his hands to pull her away. The dream would not let him.

"Help me," she rasped.

The dream released him.

The man in black started awake in his bed.

The dreamsight passed almost at once. He took two deep breaths to calm himself, and it was gone. Gently he massaged his temples and then rolled his shoulders to relax them.

Moonslight through the window. Still night. That was odd. The dreams did not often wake him before morning. Not any longer.

He rose, drawing on his trousers and shirt and boots. He went to the door and opened it, stepping out onto the balcony beyond.

Talib was there, standing guard in the shadows. He glanced at her and frowned. "You should have gone. I do not need a caretaker."

She arched an eyebrow at him. "I did leave. I could not sleep. I came back."

He snorted a brief laugh at that. How very like her. She was his best soldier, and he would hate to lose her—though he already knew he must. "Has there been any news about what happened in Wellmont?"

"None," she said, shaking her head. "But then, you asked very general questions."

"They will mean the right things to the right people," he said. "Just keep your ear out. We must learn what happened there, before—"

He pinched the bridge of his nose. *Before what?* It was getting harder and harder to tell. Something was changing. Accelerating. Increasing the presence of the dreamsight in the waking world, leaving him more and more confused about what he had seen in true life and what in a dream. And it all had something to do with what had happened at Wellmont.

But he still did not know what that was.

Talib still watched him, waiting for him to finish speaking. She was one of the two whom he let see him this way. The boy had to see him as all-knowing, sardonic, and certain. But with Talib—and one other—he felt he could let down his guard.

In fact, he knew he must. Or he would never get what he truly wanted.

"There is something else," he said. "Someone else entering the equation."

"Oh?" said Talib. "Who?"

"You have heard of the Nightblade?"

Talib snorted. "A few whispered stories."

"Then that is an advantage, because she knows little enough of us. But she will. She is coming."

Talib shot up straight in her chair. "Here? To the Seat?"

"I . . . I do not know." He frowned as he realized it was true. He had never seen her in a location that he knew. Only in Dorsea. But he could not be certain that was where he would see her. "I only know she is looking for me."

"And what do we care?" said Talib. "She is little more than a campfire tale. She cannot have done half the things they have said about her."

"She has not. But she has done other things that no one speaks of at all. Not yet, at any rate."

Finally Talib stood, coming to stand before him. "Mako, I do not understand. What does she have to do with anything?"

Mako grinned, his teeth glinting in the moonslight. "In truth, I do not know. But I very much look forward to finding out."

www.ingramcontent.com/pod-product-compliance
Lightning Source LLC
Chambersburg PA
CBHW030809310726
48980CB00006B/440/J

* 9 7 8 1 9 4 1 0 7 6 4 6 0 *